About the Author

Jon Spiegler was born in New York City in 1986.

Abraxas 2000

Jon Spiegler

Abraxas 2000

Olympia Publishers
London

www.olympiapublishers.com
OLYMPIA PAPERBACK EDITION

Copyright © Jon Spiegler 2024

The right of Jon Spiegler to be identified as author of
this work has been asserted in accordance with sections 77 and 78 of the Copyright, Designs and Patents Act 1988.

All Rights Reserved

No reproduction, copy or transmission of this publication
may be made without written permission.
No paragraph of this publication may be reproduced,
copied or transmitted save with the written permission of the publisher, or in accordance with the provisions
of the Copyright Act 1956 (as amended).

Any person who commits any unauthorized act in relation to
this publication may be liable to criminal
prosecution and civil claims for damage.

A CIP catalogue record for this title is
available from the British Library.

ISBN: 978-1-80439-320-8

This is a work of fiction.
Names, characters, places and incidents originate from the writer's imagination.
Any resemblance to actual persons, living or dead, is purely coincidental.

First Published in 2024

Olympia Publishers
Tallis House
2 Tallis Street
London
EC4Y 0AB

Printed in Great Britain

Dedication

For Dorothy.

One magical movement from Kether to Malkuth

– **David Bowie, "Station to Station"**

Part 1

Hilaria

A rejection of TV is no use to me. TV is. We are. Imagine yourself. If you can see it in your mind's eye you can see it in the TV eye...

I believe the roots of this magical mystery lie in the masking of the real purpose of "art." It is not now, and has never been, mere entertainment.
— TOPY

***

ITEM: *Underground sensation Claire Labas has come to Chelsea.*
  "The energy is here. This is where the '90s will happen, these warehouses."
— The Maria Grim Gallery Catalog, 1992

Chapter 1

Chelsea, 31 December 1992

Amanda arrived in a taxi around ten with her boyfriend Saul, her philosophy professor for freshman year. He was an obnoxious, pedantic drug addict and none of her friends liked him. That being said, none of her NYU friends had invites to New Year's Eve at Hilaria. Saul kept his invitation in his jacket pocket, pride of place with his bumper of crushed Adderall.

"Getting on the list here means something. You know, Amanda? I really have been busting my ass. You're so lucky to be here right now, babe."

"Yeah... this is cool."

Amanda wore a leather jacket, two-tone scarf, Bikini Kill shirt, black jeans, Doc Martins. She was around 5'2", and since she met Saul, she'd never been smaller. They walked up the stairs, toward the music. Every three steps was marked with a symbol: three interlocking circles, arranged in a triangle, a Celtic Cross in the center. Amanda locked eyes with club kids and fashion types. She pushed through packs of men in Ray Bans, blazers and red pocket squares while they sized her up. Amanda sensed their eyes on her back. Saul climbed two stairs at a time, increased the distance between them. He got on line.

"Have your invitation ready when you're at the door," said the bouncer.

Saul tapped his foot until Amanda caught up. Amanda studied the symbol stenciled onto the floor. The crucifix, of all things, with the ring around its axis. Amanda watched strobe lights from the other side of the doorway flash over the design. At their turn, Saul handed the bouncer his invitation and they went inside. The loft was most of a full floor in a towering, long-abandoned factory off 11th Avenue. To their left, as they entered, was a full wall of giant industrial windows, views of the Highline, the river, and the piers. The windows were lined with couches with revelers piled on, passing bags of coke. The dance floor spanned from the couches by the windows all the way into the kitchen which the hosts repurposed into a cash bar. Models served drinks. The DJ booth was set up between the entrance and the windows. Around a hundred revelers danced.

Saul ordered champagnes. They cut through the dance floor and found seats by the windows. Amanda cut up lines of the Hilaria speedball, coke and ketamine.

A new DJ took over the booth. "NEW YORK CITY! HILARIA, WHAT'S HAPPENING? OH MY GOD!" Cheers from the crowd. "Happy new year! Happy 1993! This is our time! I'm DJ San Lo and it's on!" He spun upbeat, aggressive techno.

"Come on, let's dance." Amanda pulled Saul's coat. He was deep in conversation with a man around his age.

"Yeah, later." Saul pulled a bag out of his jacket pocket. "Here."

"You said we'd do ecstasy and dance!"

"Amanda, just do this, we'll dance later."

"Asshole," she muttered under her breath. She did a key bump and put the rest of the bag in her pocket for later. Between lines, she stretched her forehead on the glass and watched the wind shake weeds in the highline from her seat by the window. Saul ranted to a friend and a yuppie in a blazer, drunk on scotch. She wished he would just shut up. It aggravated her that she could still hear his voice over the music.

"I have to take a shit." No one heard or paid attention. She stood up.

Saul, without losing his thought turned his head and watched her get up. He went on. "Hey, hey." He tugged on her wrist. "Get me a whiskey, will ya."

Amanda rolled her eyes, lit a new cigarette, and walked around the loft. She went looking for epills. The scene disturbed her. A pack of men in thousand-dollar button downs high-fived while pairs of teenage girls made out in front of them. Models danced with investors, jerked them off on dance floor, blew them openly on couches. She gravitated toward a group of women passing a glass pipe. She asked for a hit. The coke made her feel better to be there. She touched the girl's shoulder and continued exploring. The pack watched her walk away and resumed their cipher. She was back from Saul's ketamine. She was balanced, she felt like she could hang out for a while.

Amanda felt a hand on her shoulder. She turned around but no one was standing behind her. She scanned the room; revelers danced or drank. They spoke at each other. No one looked in her direction. She studied three revelers, dancing and making out, rolling, sweating, veins pulsing. When she turned around again, the artist Joanne Pardes, one of the hosts, came up and snapped a Polaroid. Joanne wore a t-shirt with the Tree of Life in the background and a cannabis leaf imposed on top. Dark, beady eyes, bushy brows, thin lips, a narrow nose, a naturally stern look. She tied long black hair into a bandanna. She wore heart-shaped sunglasses and tight black jeans with new Air Jordan's. She chewed on a Camel. The grind of her jaw was audible over the music.

"Oh, hey. Can I see that?"

Joanne shook the photo. "It's not ready yet." She walked away, REVOLUTION FOR THE SAKE OF POETRY, hand written in block letters on the back of her shirt.

A man in his fifties sucked off a kid around sixteen in the hall between the kitchen and the back rooms, he seemed unfazed. He arched his head back toward the dance floor to make sure he wasn't missing anything. Amanda felt a hand on her elbow, her left hip, her ass. She swatted them away, couldn't connect limbs to faces. Revelers shook and swung. She made it to the wall, she bumped more of her speedball. She lit a new smoke, she looked for the bathroom. She pushed a sweaty, disembodied back and shoulders off of her chest and thigh. She walked sideways against the wall. The coke kept her airways open, the ketamine cool in the face of body heat. She blew past the line and pushed herself into the bathroom. Flashes went off, a crowd gathered around one of the hosts, superstar model Lexie G. Hinnon on the sink, smoking a parliament. A man and woman, both pale white, rail thin, sucked on her toes. They gagged, they sighed, they slurped their spit back.

A finance type in Oakley's and a Brooks Brothers blazer turned to Amanda. "Germans." He stuck his tongue out, turned back to the show. Amanda dug into her bag and took a big hit. She left the bathroom, pushed through more revelers as they forced their way inside.

She recognized faces from Limelight or Pyramid. She waved hello, stopped to hug a few acquaintances, wish them a happy new year, ask if they had any E left. Everyone already swallowed everything they had. They directed her across the room. She took another key bump. She drank half of a friend's vodka soda.

She checked out the installations. Sacred geometry and Lexie G. Hinnon catwalk footage projected on the walls. Maria Grim, the gallerist, taste maker, Hilaria's landlord, announced herself over the PA.

"Ladies, gentlemen! I present to you, your hostess! The one, the only, Claire Labas!"

The couches emptied out. Revelers rose to their feet, erupting in cheers, jumping into the air. Claire climbed the top of a table wrapped in a fur cape. DJ San Lo hit the strobe lights.

"Vote for me!" She threw off the fur; anorexic, naked, and hairless. The symbol Amanda saw everywhere throughout the building: the Celtic Cross inside a triangle was drawn on her stomach. She turned around. Joanne Pardes passed Claire a torch. She spit fire over the crowd. The revelers cheered. She turned around and spit another flame in the other direction. The Celtic Cross was painted on her back. San Lo dropped a loud, propulsive drum and bass track, Shotgun and Treasure's *Midnight Experience.*

The door from the stairwell swung open and a new dozen men in blazers and khakis walked in. Amanda blew past a pack of girls chatting in Russian, passing a bottle just outside the door. She climbed the stairwell. She felt a breeze from the rooftop. She followed the scent, fresh air. The door outside was cracked open. She stopped halfway to the ledge. She watched the Hudson River. The ambient noise from the Westside Highway was louder than the music downstairs. She closed her eyes and took in the moment, she let wind from the river run through her clothes, under her chin and through her hair. She let her sweat dry. She let it freeze. She looked up. The moon, like all other light, was an eight-pointed star.

"Hey, Amanda! Amanda! What are you?" Saul broke her concentration. His only tone was aggrieved. Maybe it was how much he snorted. The rest of his family had toned down the Yid affect. He sounded like he had a bad stomach. "Amanda what are you doing up here? Hey?"

"Did you get any E?"

"No... I was looking for you – what are you doing up here?"

"Can we just go now?"

"Yeah, sure. You already made up your mind we're leaving, I can tell. After everything I did to get us, you, this invite..."

The revelers counted down to midnight while they walked down the stairs. Six-five-four-three-two-one HAPPY NEW YEAR!

Excerpted from an interview with Morgan Gold, circa 1998

I had an ID that said I was twenty-two. It was really good, it worked, bouncers and liquor stores took it but I was still I guess, like seventeen, but I got in everywhere and some people who mattered started to recognize me. I wasn't going to school that often. I would take the train into the city on like Thursday and come home on Monday, maybe. But the spring before I turned eighteen, Lexie G. Hinnon found me in Washington Square Park. She had been discovered already and she already took those first photos at Hilaria, by the windows, with Jacques, Jacques Anzu. They were about to come out. When we had that party to celebrate the photos coming out in Vogue and Cosmo the same month… I had been there maybe a month, month and a half. But when she discovered me she hadn't broke yet. She knew she was about to, though, and she took me with her.

    She took me to meet Claire, Claire Labas at Coffee Shop off of Union Square. She asked me right off the bat why I wasn't modeling. What was wrong with me? The clock was ticking, *haha*. She was trying this whole *time is money* thing that week. Being very stern and businesslike, acting like she was Maria Grim. Claire wasn't really like that. She was actually kind of ditsy. She didn't need to be smart or well-read or even like, good at business. She just got whatever she wanted. Whenever anyone said no to her she would just attack them until they said yes. But this week she was acting like Maria Grim. *Snap, snap, snap.*

    She ordered bilinis and we did coke in the booth. Claire had amazing coke, it was never just white, which is what you think you want but you really want it to be yellow or pink, just like a tint but that's how you know it's really good. Claire never had just plain white coke. Then Lexie took out a vial of K and we started doing K. I kept up with them but I got really fucking high and needed more coke to stay awake. That's when we took a taxi to Hilaria. It was a loft inside this huge like, office tower with industrial warehouses and stuff right on the West Side Highway. It was the coolest place anyone had ever been. The windows wrapped around the corner so you got this amazing view of the river and the piers, you could see everything.

    I passed out on one of the couches by the windows and I woke up and it was night already. There was a small party happening, no one seemed to care that I had been asleep but I was really embarrassed. I went looking for Lexie or Claire but they weren't out there. They never hung out in the front of the loft, they were always in their bedrooms or that back room they had. That's where I would spend most of my time, in the back room.

I met Joanne Pardes in the back room when I went looking for Lexie. She was like *who are you?* Like she was a total bitch. I was like I'm Morgan I'm looking for Lexie. She rolled her eyes and asked how I got in. I said I took a cab with Lexie and Claire Labas and she changed her attitude. It was like I had been nothing and now, suddenly I was worth treating like a human being. Thanks so much! Oh my god she was such a bitch that day. Our relationship never got that much better, to be honest. But I always respected her for being so cool and such a great artist. Joanne was really fucking cool, OK? She was so ahead of her time. She like practically invented grunge in the eighties and her art is still really cool. I came to respect Joanne even if I thought she was a bitch. But when you're like seventeen and don't know any better and you meet Joanne Pardes you'll think she's the coolest person to ever live. Even Lexie thought that. Even Lexie knew Joanne was cooler than she was. Lexie couldn't actually do anything. That was part of her whole, like, thing. She was weak and stupid and that turns people on you know? And if you had money or drugs or connections she would make you feel really cool and smart and accomplished. That was her one skill. The guys who came to Hilaria, they loved hanging out with Lexie because she made them feel amazing. She had really good instincts. And Joanne would bring them back down to earth because she was so great, she just reminded them that they were pieces of shit. If you hung out with Joanne too long you felt really terrible about yourself. Either because she would just look into your eyes and figure out your secrets and just spit them back at you, or usually, she would just show off and what did you have to come back with? But everybody was so happy to be in the same room with her because they could go back to Wall Street and say, "I was hanging out with the biggest underground artist in the city at this exclusive Chelsea loft full of models." That was the specific appeal for Hilaria. Art and fashion, together. Claire didn't know anything about art, obviously Lexie didn't either. That's why Maria Grim put them together with Joanne. Maria represented Joanne before she found Claire. You can't say Hilaria was Maria's idea, but she was their patron.

Chapter 2

Claire Labas, Lexie G Hinnon, and Joanne Pardes

Claire Labas and her protege, Lexie G. Hinnon, moved into their Chelsea loft, Hilaria, in early 1992. Claire's friend Joanne Pardes moved in soon after. The three became a staple of the downtown scene, out nightly in Chelsea, Soho, East / West Villages.

Claire and Lexie were the muses for a movement's worth of fashion photographers. They walked red carpets with musicians and coke dealers. They left parties with Wall Street and real estate men. When the chattering classes asked "what comes after heroin chic?" Claire Labas stepped forward with a model and a mythology. They chewed benzos, blew ketamine and smoked base. They replaced most meals with Diet Coke and vodka sodas. The aesthetic: always bruised, unwashed. Scraped knees, cigarette burns and black circles under their eyes, but high fashion.

The southern edge of Hilaria was a twenty-four-hour operation. Five-foot windows made famous by Jacques Anzu's photos of Lexie G. Hinnon, views of the Hudson and the Highline. Day and night, someone was always in an armchair, snorting coke, drinking espresso, making moves. Smoking, reading magazines, scripts, shifting through head shots. Regulars included a short, intense Frenchman, a potbellied, pattern bald Russian in a turtleneck, a Jewish attorney from South Brooklyn always with his tie undone and a refractory grin. A fashion scout and a young model, a financier and a photographer would sit and talk, make deals. They traded stock tips, ground floor investments, Wall Street gossip. Talk of positions, coke and pills, drink orders, mortgages and rent rolls. Aspiring models, initiates into Lexie's collection of lookalikes, served drinks from a bar that separated the windows from the kitchen, the barrier between Hilaria's public face and the bedrooms and back room.

Claire, Joanne and Lexie didn't spend too much time by the windows.

They made appearances. Independently of each other they affected an aversion to light and wore shades everywhere. Lexie was mostly nocturnal, when Joanne did sleep it was usually during the day. The back room was private, as far as possible from the leering men by the windows.

Excerpt from an interview with Jacques Anzu, circa 1996

I met Claire Labas in 1987 or '88, independent of Joanne Pardes who I probably met around the same time. I absolutely couldn't tell you a date for either… I was immensely involved in graffiti culture at that time but I was making my name as a photographer too. I wanted to paint, really but everyone just kept asking me to take photos while they bombed some shit or did a mural, but I was also getting gigs shooting chicks and models, some softcore gigs.

Claire was an intern at the modeling agency she was at then. We met at a party and I took her picture. Back then I was always taking pictures at clubs or parties, portraits in the fucked-up lights on in the bathroom with that bright lighting you get… I was always packing film because all the graffiti writers would always ask me to go with them or I'd meet some chicks who wanted to me to take their picture. I was young and didn't know how to draw a line or set any real boundaries. Claire's photo was in a stairway, it came out really great, it was before she crafted the persona she was known for but really she took the way she looked in that photo and made it her entire aesthetic. When she discovered Lexie… Claire said at a rave somewhere, outside of the city. But when she discovered Lexie she brought her to me and said check this girl out she's a fucking star let's make her a supermodel. I took those photos that really launched her, and launched that style into the fashion world. But their whole style, that's where Joanne Pardes came in. What Claire was doing, knowingly, and Lexie at first unknowingly was bringing Joanne and her friend Helene Asher to the mass market. Those were Helene's looks, really, in the end. This was before the Perry Ellis show, this was before the whole industry embraced grunge and what Helene and Joanne were doing was more hardcore than grunge. Like if the riot grrrls formed a terrorist group.

Joanne Pardes' best known work, the video *I'm Not Here for Cuntish Questions (1988)* was played on loop at Maria Grim Gallery in the January

1992, 1993, and 1994 *Curiosity Culture* shows. The opening scene:

OPEN TO: *An abandoned building, lit with candle light. The walls have been demolished, only wooden framing, exposed brick, uneven flooring remains. Joanne, in a chair, wearing a white dress, prepping a crack pipe. She blows smoke, makes a fist, raises her arm above her head, crooked elbow. She shrieks, a primal scream, eyes bulging then shut closed.*

Voiceover: Life's got to hurt! There aren't enough cruelties. Get at me, motherfucker.

She mutilates her body with the crack pipe, lit cigarettes, a five-inch knife and a razor blade, eyes fixed into the camera.

Cut to black.

Chapter 3

The Lower East Side, April 1989

Every night, Helene Asher sang in her sleep. She hummed, mumbled, harmonized. Joanne Pardes listened through the walls. She loved Helene's voice. When they were awake Joanne pushed her to sing. She bought her beers and peach schnapps, rolled up spliffs, all toward putting Helene in the mood for a song right there on the sidewalk, on their roof top, or under a tree in Tompkins. She was easy to coax into song, but Helene hated her voice. She was embarrassed that she couldn't hold a note. The secret was to listen in before she realized what she was doing and clammed up. Joanne swooned every time Helene hummed a jingle off TV. Helene could reduce Joanne to tears with *Making Plans for Nigel*. Helene had no idea Joanne recorded her while she slept. Joanne kept the tapes under her bed, they were their only secret. Joanne told Helene everything otherwise, she just knew Helene would hate that her singing voice was on tape.

April 1989, she chanted a siren's call for her whole hour of REM sleep. When she woke up, poured a coffee and lit a smoke, she felt off. She felt like getting out of the house. She locked up, hit the street. Helene and Joanne lived on Bleecker St. off of Lafayette from 88–91. She walked a block east to Neil Irving's loft, ZIKES HQ, or Thirteen, as the heads called it. She knocked on the door, someone poked their head out and came down to let her in.

"Helene, all right!"

"Is Neil home?"

"Yeah, yeah, we're um, finishing a meeting, why don't you hang out down here?"

The ground level at Thirteen, intense smells of cat piss, smoke, mold, dust and sweat. Old furniture, broken coffee tables, school desks, counter space for Neil's pamphlets and fliers:

MELATONIN – THE SECRET TO BETTER MARIJUANA HIGHS? THE ZIKES! MANIFESTO, BOB DYLAN GEMATRIA BY JAY WATERMAN, LIBERATE WOODSTOCK NATION! HOW THE YOUTH CAN GET BACK INVOLVED BY N. IRVING AND J. WATERMAN.

Helene took a seat on a beat-up old couch floating in the middle of the room. She admired a mural, the Yippie Flag, the red star, black background, a dark green cannabis leaf in the foreground. The image hit her; she pulled out her notebook. She sketched out the tree of life and drew a cannabis leaf over it. She bought an ounce of 3's ($3 a gram) and took the sketch home, got stoned, and got to work. She drew the tree of life with a ruler. She pulled the leaf's contours from memory.

She sold a quarter ounce to a contact in the Village and took the proceeds to Pearl for supplies. She bought Gesso; black, red, and green paint and a tube of gold for highlights. She painted her masterpiece. A black background, the ten Sefirot in gold, outlined in red, like the lines connecting each sphere. The sugar leaf was a lush forest green, floating over the diagram. She painted the caption in silver: THE CYBER GRIMOIRE.

She finished the canvass and fell asleep. She sang a carefree, whimsical *la-la-la-la-la*. She woke up rested, picture-perfect memory of the strangest dream. She opened her notebook. Still half asleep, she followed the dictation, wrote what she heard verbatim.

She asked Joanne in the morning, "What do you think this means?" Joanne read through Helene's notes. Helene tapped the paper. "This is our spell. It has to be."

"Do you really think so?"

"We have to try to know…"

"Three nights, starting now, will you?"

"Fuck… Is this? It?"

That night they dressed like ninjas and wheat pasted posters.

FUCK CHRIST – ONLY HXLXNX CAN SAVE THE WORLD
    READ THE CYBER GRIMOIRE
    INVEST IN THE CYBER GRIMOIRE – GUARANTEED RETURNS IN PERPETUITY

They covered Bleecker from Bowery to 6th. They hit MacDougal and Sullivan before they covered West Broadway, Spring, Prince, Wooster until they ran out of paper.

20 April 1989

Helene Asher drew a circle on their kitchen floor.
"What time is it?" she asked.
Joanne Pardes checked her watch. "It's after midnight."
"Then it's time."
"I'll get 'em!" Joanne pulled a jar out from under the sink, tampons soaked in a tincture of grain alcohol, acacia, datura and henbane. Joanne pulled one out and passed the jar to Helene, took off her clothes, put in the tampon. Helene followed. They removed their jewelry beforehand, went to St. Marks and had whatever they couldn't get out themselves removed by Carlos, their piercer. They washed out their hair dyes and stopped using deodorant. They dabbed mint and rosemary oil on their fingertips. They ringed the circle with eight candles.

Now for the moment of flight. The sacred meal was a White Owl cigar, green tea soaked with PCP. Helene lit the flame; Joanne held the blunt in her lips and took the first hits. She exhaled and passed the dust to Helene. They developed a rhythm, one, two, one, two, three, one, two, one, two, three, one, two, one, two, three. They passed the blunt back and forth until it died. Colors changed. Blues were green, purple was suddenly closer to orange. Check out the breeze from the kitchen window, it's silver!

Helene asked, "What is the word?"
Joanne answered, "Hermes."
"What is the password?"
"Mercury."
"What is the word?"
"Lemuria."
"What is the password?"
"Atlantis."

They volleyed back and forth until they floated to the ceiling. They gripped each other's arms tight. They intoned: *What the raven bringeth, ye shall drink. What the raven bringeth, ye shall drink. What the raven bringeth, ye shall drink.*

Joanne's eyes opened. She left her body. She spoke. Helene listened. It was just like when she dreamed up the incantation, every word she received etched itself into Helene's memory. When the entity left Joanne's body, it left out the open window. Helene saw the transformation in Joanne's eyes. Joanne felt herself come back. She was the first to realize that they were no longer floating. They regained their sense of the floor. Helene stood up and rushed to her bedroom and began to write out what Joanne told her.

Joanne blew out half of the candles. Her mouth was too dry for more. She ran the tap, gulped down glasses of water until she quenched her thirst. She considered her aromas, sweat, rosemary, and a scent she didn't recognize. She reached for Helene's Camels. She lit up, the rush took her back to childhood. The bottoms of her feet against the floor still felt novel. She heard Helene's pen against paper, the turn of her pages. Joanne did her best to stay silent and maintain Helene's concentration.

She wondered how much time she lost. She tried to estimate how long she'd been back. She referred to her cigarette, she tried to figure out how long it was burning. She pulled and looked again, measured the growth of the ash. She tapped it into her hand, gently, she kept the cylinder intact. She turned to the clock. A few minutes before one am. She watched the seconds tick, the long hand turn, and she relearned time. She felt jet lagged. She finished the cigarette. She blew out the rest of the candles, turned on the kitchen light. She drew a bath.

Excerpted from an interview with Jacques Anzu, circa 1996–7

Helene grew up this hippie chick, like she grew up in Woodstock on a commune. But the thing about hippies after the '70s, especially in the eighties, is there was way more of the Manson Secret operating out there than the media tells you. Now you see all this sixties shit on TV. Every time I watch TV you hear *Turn, Turn, Turn* and shit like that. It's all about remembering the sixties. I was a small child in the sixties but I have this image in my mind that was constructed for me, without my input, of what the sixties looks like. But that's fake. Hippies are tough motherfuckers. They're rednecks. A lot of them are fascists, which is interesting because that media construction of the sixties is a bunch of idiots calling everyone a fascist. But that was actually something that I found interesting about the hippies Helene introduced me to, these guys were probably better armed than Manson. They had guns, fucking pipe bombs. We went shooting rifles on their land, target practice all day with the men while the women cooked a big dinner. Helene got out of there because it was like growing up Amish. It was very fascist. We were in upstate New York where everyone is supposed to be growing weed and listening to Dylan and it was like the mountains of Idaho. She was doing that punk thing that she made into her style, that look that you saw filter into the mainstream with the Hilaria chicks. There was no space to develop that upstate. But she took us up there to hang out. It was strange, it really felt like Spahn Ranch. I've read everything on Manson. I know. But they fed us wild venison. That was fucking great, haha.

Helene and Joanne had very hippie tastes a lot of the time. The hippie / punk thing. That was what they were doing. Merging punk and hardcore with the hippie thing, but the hippie thing Helene grew up in, which had a hard edge. Chaos magick was something that appealed to them in that regard, that overlap between punk rock culture and the more mystical world that Helene came out of. It kept her horizons larger than the neighborhood and whatever small bore bullshit that you're up to in the Lower East Side. That's why I'm out of there. Everything is small stakes but then at the same time some junkie asshole, some crackhead is about to kill you and there's cops *everywhere!* What bullshit, man. And it's all over stupid, uncomplicated, just boring shit. Drug shit, sure, but now it's just... I doubt Helene Asher, should she have lived through all that and none of this shit happened, I seriously doubt she'd be in the city. Maybe not that hippie commune but she'd be onto something else.

Chapter 4

The Lower East Side, 1989

Helene Asher locked herself in her room and refined the notes she took the night of the ritual into a screenplay. She made a point not change any of the received language. Anything the entity Joanne channeled said that night was written into the script, as was anything Helene received in the precipitating dream.

Joanne dropped sandwiches, coffee, pills and cigarettes at her door. She recognized something significant was happening on the other side of the door. She heard the typewriter almost constantly, day and night. Helene left her desk to use the bathroom once or twice a day. She showered twice a month. Joanne tried to keep Helene's diet varied and made sure that on top of the speed she took daily, she took a multivitamin.

In the time Helene wrote her script, her stomach was in near constant revolt. Helene had headaches nearly every morning and afternoon. Her period came three times in the six weeks she spent writing. She emerged from her bedroom in the last days of Spring, late May / early June, sunken in, pail and thin. "Check it out." She gave Joanne a stack of paper. *"Whore of Babalon – Consort of Chaos."*

Excerpted from an interview with Jacques Anzu, circa 1996–7

Helene worshiped Patti Smith… The legend behind Patti Smith, Mapplethorpe, Jim Carroll, the Saint Marks Poetry Project. Patti influenced Helene's wardrobe. She dressed in the outfits from all the album covers and the Mapplethorpe photos. Usually she wore a black beanie, t-shirt or wife beater and torn up jeans like *Radio Ethiopia*.

Excerpt of an interview with Morgan Gold, circa 1998

The photos of Helene Asher I saw, they were the photos by Joanne Pardes that looked like the cover of *Horses*. Helene, she was really cool looking. In her black cap with the men's dress shirt and black tie around her neck, blazer over her shoulder. Then she threw off the blazer and the shirt and was dressed like Stanley Kowalski. She shook her hair out. That photo was so cool. Her fist was in the air, she's yelling something. It was in their hallway in the East Village so the paint is peeling and there's this hideous tile on the floor, so cool.

Saugerties / Woodstock New York, 1989

Helene Asher, Joanne Pardes, and Jacques Anzu were cast, crew, production and direction for *Scarlet Woman 89*. The primary set was an old barn halfway between Saugerties and Woodstock, deep in the forest. It was the property of an old couple who didn't mind the local kids using the barn to have a little fun, as long as there's no damage or fires. Helene was from outside Woodstock, she thought of this place immediately.

Since Helene channeled the ritual to begin with, she wrote herself as the Red Woman. Joanne would play The Initiate. She suggested Jacques for the Man In Black. Helene just said to make sure he didn't have AIDS and was serious about magick. Joanne brought Jacques the screenplay and he agreed to sign on.

They spent the weeks leading up to their trip upstate shooting b-roll on Super 8 in the Lower East Side and Chinatown. Joanne painted Helene red, head to toe. Jacques and Joanne shot Helene walking naked through an abandoned building on 12th St. first illuminated by daylight and again at night, lit with candles.

Helene shot Joanne, wearing a ski mask and a black funeral dress, her hands wrapped in prayer beads, gripping a massive hunting knife. Jacques shot them lighting up a trashcan, then a dumpster. They shot coverage of Helene in red, passing through Tompkins by the fountain. She walked in the street on 9th between B and C then under the Manhattan bridge, wrapped in shadows.

Excerpted from an interview with Jacques Anzu, circa 1996–7

Joanne did great work. When I met her she was doing performance art, spoken word, but it was really raw, really compelling. She made a zine, maybe two, can't remember anymore... She made videos. My favorite was called *I'm Not Here to Answer Cuntish Questions*. She made that almost entirely by herself. It was excellent. It was her take on Kern and Lydia Lunch. Like if you've seen *Right Side of My Brain*, but she was cutting her arms up. She burnt her thigh with a crack pipe...

She was into lying in bed and talking into her tape recorder. She would lock herself in her room for days on end, bumping dope or K and doing notes into a tape recorder. This is where she got her voice overs... She liked her voice best when she was all dehydrated and miserable. The voice-overs were her poetry or just fragments. Lots of ambient sound from downtown, Tompkins and Delancey St. and *uhh*, 13th St.

Did that show anywhere?

Maria Grim. There are copies but they're hard to find. I don't think there are many copies. I'd pay for that tape now. She sold zines, one of them was a kind of print version of the movie. She took photos of the video playing off a TV set, and she transcribed the voice-overs onto paper. I have a piece Joanne did, mixed media piece, ninety-one or ninety-two. It was from the shoot we did in '89. Helene with the bowl cut, painted red... Standing straight, arms stretched up, wrists bent backwards. She drew a triangle inside a pentagram inside the Tree of Life over Helene's armpits and pubes. Thick sharpie above her hands it says CONSORT OF CHAOS... On the bottom there's a poem she wrote. Someone should try using it as a prayer, you know? When she gave it to me, she said it was charged, that's why it's in my altar.

Chapter 5

The Maria Grim Gallery, 1993

The Maria Grim Gallery, around the corner from Hilaria. A 10,000 sq.ft. space with 30-foot ceilings, stacked with the city's luminaries. Atonal modern classical plays on the PA. Two open bars serve wine, beer and champagne. The caterers are dancers and male models with chiseled features, tight white shirts and bulging black pants. They pass out canapes of smoked salmon, creme fraiche and micro greens, sushi or flutes of bubbly.

The Spring group show, the season kick off. Maria and her people selected fifty works; they're selling like mad to a high-powered guest list. Art buyers, investors, and critics – friends and contacts alike from Maria's thirty years in the business. Maria wears a white dress and a fur coat, smoking from a cigarette holder, tonight's prop. It matches the fur. Big oval frames, magenta and gold with tinted lenses. Straight black hair cut off ahead of her shoulders. She does the rounds.

"You look fantastic. Darling! Two kisses! We don't see each other like we used to, so sad… What do you like here? What do you want?"

The owner of a building management company buys a photo collage of atomic tests. Goldman employees accounted for twelve of the night's sales, Lehman employees for eight, Travelers for four. A hedge fund manager buys the most expensive painting in the room for a cool million and leaves with an entourage behind him.

Lexie G. Hinnon and her rising star Morgan Gold enter the gallery. Lexie lookalikes, Marina Jay and Britney Rose, immediately get behind them. They mimic Lexie, anorexic, malnourished, their slips fall off their shoulders. The pack is menacing. They feel dangerous, they darken the mood. The revelers fucking love it. They march into the bathroom, the room exhales all at once.

Joanne Pardes pretends to follow the collector who just bought her

Psychogeography 2000 for twenty-five grand. He rants about Paris '68, how he could he finished the thing once and for all. "Now that we have the internet – we can do the whole thing over again and win this time. We'll be free. Free from government, the regulators, political correctness..."

Joanne puts her arm around her date for the evening, Linda Solomon. She appeared at Hilaria as a hanger on, commuting on weekends from the Five Towns. She studied Hilaria and Claire's entourage. She forced herself into Claire Labas' and more importantly for her, Joanne Pardes' lines of sight. She did what she could to be noticed. She mastered the gang's aesthetic. She dressed in fishnets, torn shirts and tanks. She gave herself cigarette burns and amateur piercings. Most wannabe adepts dressed like Lexie G. Hinnon but Linda followed Joanne Pardes. Her work was paying off. The clique let her follow them from gallery opening to after-party.

Linda was at every event at Hilaria, every opening at Maria Grim. She proved she could hang. She dropped ecstasy and bumped ketamine with Morgan, Marina and Britney. Linda discovered they wanted to be models, to follow in Claire and Lexie's footsteps. It meant remaking themselves in Lexie G Hinnon's image: emaciated, blond with visible roots, razor cuts, tracks, accentuated black circles under their eyes. It meant picking through raver clothes, baby T's, tube tops and baggy pants.

Joanne gave Linda a pink epill stamped with a helvetica e. They washed their stacks down with champagne. They stopped every few feet to greet someone and Joanne introduced Linda. Crowds broke off into their natural cliques. Groups organized around affinities, gender or drug of choice. Bankers and real estate agents traded cards. Art assistants got drunk. Revelers drank wine and exchanged notes. Models paired off with talent scouts, talent agents, lawyers, and accountants. A clique of porn producers kibbutzed with a commercial broker. A French art buyer and a hedge fund manager exchanged information. For every whale, there were two or three revelers. The galleries had their own following: a class of high end moocher the industry depended on as shills for their productions. The galleries needed bodies to make every opening feel like a spectacle. The gallery scene chatted amongst themselves. They double fisted their drinks, smoked herbal cigarettes and Lucky Strikes. Women with big framed glasses and pencils stuck in their buns circled men dressed in berets and tweed jackets with shoulder pads, rail thin with big curly hair. Columnists and critics chatted with artists. Maria's assistants hustled through the crowd.

"Maria would like to see you."

The open bar closed when the show sold out. Revelers filtered out as they finished their drinks. Coke dealers gave their cards out to financiers and real estate agents. Art buyers and gallery employees cracked open bottles of red and passed them back and forth. Maria took a dozen or so VIPs upstairs for drinks. Painters and photographers passed spliffs back and forth. The bathrooms emptied out, wired revelers rubbed freeze on their gums. They figured out amongst themselves how to split which taxi to the Tunnel or Limelight. More hit the bars along 8th Avenue or 23rd St. A select few drunkenly climbed the Highline and dug the view. The rest, the elite, rounded the corner to Hilaria.

He was between forty-five and fifty, short, compact, a unit. He wore a King's Row tailored three-piece suit with a red silk ascot, tinted rectangular glasses. Shoulder length salt and pepper hair styled back with gel, a handmade cologne. Linda sat on his lap, arms around his neck.

"Here, take this," he said, nasal Port Jefferson accent. He gave her a pill, she swallowed.

"What is it?"

"Beta blocker, I'm going for a certain vibe."

"Oh." She pretended to know what that meant. She looked at Joanne and Lexie. Joanne nodded her head. Lexie smiled, catlike. Port Jefferson Man drank clear liquor and club soda from a straw in a Collins glass. Linda looked over at Morgan Gold, positioned on a man in a gray suit with a skinny black tie. He was swarthy, Mediterranean, early to mid-forties. Probably Israeli. Morgan petted his face, he gyrated. He wore a chain, rings, cuff links. He pulled her in by the waist. He breathed in her hair and grunted.

Linda felt the old man's hands pet her leg. "Let's raise a glass, huh? It's good to be in New York City. Everyone, cheers." His friend lifted an Old Fashioned. The two men touched glasses, they stomped their feet in unison, one, two, one, two, three. "96!"

Linda looked back at Joanne again. Joanne nodded her head upwards. Linda leaned into the old man. She petted his chest. He carried on a conversation with his friend about the view. They liked Chelsea. "I could invest here." He ran his hands up and down Linda's thigh.

Joanne watched the tableau. The men, the girls, the Persian rug on the floor, the couches, the windows. Lights reflected off the black, oily surface of the river and back into the loft.

"Baby, what are you drinking? Rum and coke, right? Let's get this sweetheart a rum and coke, huh?" Lexie snapped her fingers and Marina got up to make the drink.

Marina wore a size 2 silver dress and Lexie's blowout. Linda took quick sips that bounced off the roof of her mouth and down her throat. She didn't like the taste of alcohol. She kissed the man on his neck.

"All right, all right, cool, cool," he said. He lit a Nat Sherman.

Lexie took a bump of K off Joanne's fist. Joanne smoked a Marlboro. She drew shapes in the air. The man holding onto Morgan whispered in her ear and she smiled at him. He released his grip. She got up. He wiped off his lap and straightened his jacket. He cut up lines of coke. He gave Morgan a rolled up $100 bill.

"Ladies first."

She did her lines and handed back the bill. He did the rest and picked up the freeze with his finger and rubbed his gums. "Let's go." He stood up and they walked out together.

Linda felt a sweaty hand inside her shirt. "Let's get some more drinks over here, what's happening? Aren't we having a party? Let's get some music, you like techno, sweetheart? Of course, you do." He snapped his fingers at Britney. "Let's get some techno music going."

Linda looked at Joanne. Lexie, splayed on the couch, arched an eyebrow behind sunglasses. Marina replenished Linda's rum and coke and the old man's Collins glass.

"Mm, these are good, good job." The old man undid his fly. "Drink up, sweetheart."

Joanne nodded her head. Linda sucked down the drink. She ran her hand down his stomach.

Excerpt of an interview with Morgan Gold, circa 1998

Joanne picked up this girl Linda who was hanging out at Hilaria, and always following us around. She was just like, there one day and then just never went away. Well, wait, she would disappear sometimes before she was there permanently but it was always like a weekend or something. But otherwise, she was just there... Linda was crazy naive, like more than usual, really sheltered, but she had run away from home and really didn't want to go back. She was seventeen so the cops would be looking for her until her eighteenth birthday and then her family couldn't do shit, but I think if they caught up with her, they'd lock her up in a hospital until her eighteenth birthday. She'd been locked up a few times before and didn't want to go back. She was actually lucky to end up at Hilaria and not somewhere else. Someone could have eaten her alive, you know? So, what Joanne did to her was nothing. It was mostly sex shit between them. I heard Joanne yelling at Linda and Linda would cry until she'd slap her in the face. They did it to each other. She busted Joanne's lip doing that, it definitely made her cum when Linda busted her lip. But Linda would cry first. In public, though, you never saw her complain, you just saw her nod her head. Joanne, like gave her a scarification on her arm. Lexie was there for it. She took pictures but they got lost. Lexie was really bad at keeping track of things. She didn't care about anything except a few things that she kept very close and a picture of Joanne and Linda wasn't one of them.

Chapter 6

April 1993

Linda Solomon's seventeenth birthday. A basement rave in Chinatown. San Lo spun fast, intense house and jungle records. The temperatures were in the high nineties all night. They rolled on epills stamped with dolphins. Joanne tucked her turquoise leotard into torn up jeans with an unbuttoned Hawaiian shirt, sleeves cut off over her shoulders. Her signature heart shaped sunglasses. Her arms were sleeved with scars, cuts, punctures, and burns. She turned to Linda, sucking down a bottle of water. She grabbed Linda's arm. "Are you as bored as I am? Come on."

Linda couldn't hear her. Joanne tugged her away and pulled her toward the exit. They emerged sweaty, gasping in the fresh air. Joanne shimmered. She shot a snot rocket. "Let's do something new."

"OK!"

"Come on." Joanne waved to Linda, extended her hand. They headed North. The streets were empty. Joanne lit a full book of matches and dropped them in a trash can. Linda caught up as the flames danced. "I could shoot a gun right now, oh my god!" Joanne ran her hands up her scalp. "Fuck!"

Linda felt a breeze on her skin. She shuddered. She swooned. She sucked on a Camel. She cooed. Each new sensation was pure joy. She exhaled out of her nose, savored the experience. She pissed behind a car. She grabbed onto Joanne and pressed her face into her skin. Their sweat mixed together. Linda breathed her in. Joanne held her, ran her nails through her hair, and swayed until she felt like she could overheat. She fanned herself and her eyes rolled back. "Let's go watch the sun rise."

The next morning, Linda woke up in Joanne's bed for the first time. She watched Joanne sleep. She resolved to follow her, wherever it took her. She moved into Hilaria. She claimed a corner of the back room as her own when she couldn't sleep in Joanne's bed or on her floor. She ate her meals at gallery openings. She lived off fruit and cheese, canapes, chips and dip, sushi. There wasn't any food at Hilaria. Lexie said nothing tasted as good as it felt to be thin. Lexie and her adepts replaced most meals with blow or Adderall.

Lexie said, "When you're hungry, you're really thirsty. All you need to do is drink something, smoke a cigarette and you're back."

Excerpt of an interview with Morgan Gold, circa 1998

Claire Labas, Lexie G Hinnon, Marina Jay, Britney Rose, these girls Stacey, and Katie, and Linda Solomon. That's everybody, I think. We were all on Orange Stars, with the eight-pointed star prints. Joanne was the DJ she only listened to Psychic TV and um Coil? So that was playing… This crazy techno…

Claire locked the door to her bedroom and didn't come back out for the rest of the night. Marina and Britney and Stacey went to dance with the guests. I was dancing with Katie. Lexie took Polaroids of Joanne and Linda hugging, making out, all sweaty and red… She was screaming, over the music, "This girl is the best! I could just – uhh! I love her! I love her!" *Hahaha.* Linda was sitting there; she couldn't talk she was smiling so wide.

Lexie said, "You're the two happiest girls in New York!"

Chapter 7

Hilaria, 1993

Lexie marched into the backroom and put a vial in Linda's hand. "Go out by the windows and hang out."

"Oh, uhh, thanks, Lexie." Linda dug out a bump.

Lexie glared. "That's pure shit, don't waste it."

Marina Jay and Britney Rose tended bar. A muscular man in a tight three-piece suit, early fifties with a military fade smoked a cigar and walked the models through how he wanted his Old Fashions made.

Lexie came out. "Gavin? Oh. My. God!"

Gavin Lee turned away from Marina. He smiled ear to ear, gnawing on his cigar. "Why don't you come over her and let me look at you, Lexie."

Lexie ran to Gavin. He picked her up, all eighty-eight pounds, and swung her in a circle. They breezed past Linda on their way to the back room, Lexie over his shoulder. She laughed maniacally. He shut her bedroom door behind him with the bottom of his shoe.

The front door swung and a pack of men in suits spilled out. A preppie, blue-blooded type in his early forties approached Linda's seat by the window. Blond hair, blue eyes, a blazer and a cravat. "Arthur." He put his hand out. A firm, deal maker's shake. He took a seat next to her.

"Linda."

"So…" He put his arm around her, casual. Minty breath. He scanned her body. He pulled two Dunhills from his jacket and lit them with a Zippo, passed one to Linda. "What are we getting into tonight?"

Linda took a mirror from the nearest side table and emptied out an eighth of a vial Lexie gave her. She chopped it up and offered him the mirror.

"You first."

Linda took a line in either nostril, she passed it over and he snorted the rest. Marina Jay put a house CD on the stereo. The preppie blond pulled an eight ball from his pocket and spooned a pile onto the mirror, cut up new lines. "You first..." Linda blew as much coke as she could until Arthur was satisfied. "Let's dance."

Excerpted from an interview with Jacques Anzu, circa 1996–7

The magick that Helene Asher and Joanne Pardes were interested in was about making contact, breaking through whatever barriers are standing between them and us. It was about opening a line of communication and using those processes in their art. Great work those two produced, bouncing ideas off each other, modeling for each other. Joanne, if you believed her, said that she doesn't remember anything from when Helene made contact. She lost that time. She came to and Helene had just had this amazing experience... This was always occurring purely inside Helene's mind until Joanne blacked out. That was the confirmation that what they were doing was working. It was change in nature dependent on their will. Pisses me off that they never recorded this. We'll never know what Joanne channeled, what was said. But there was a two-way conversation going on. Helene saw results. That she had Joanne, right there, acting like a lightning rod, acting like a telephone line direct to the Mauve Zone...

Watch *Scarlet Woman 89*. You can find it, go to... Kim's. Go watch it. That ritual we do, that incantation that we're doing, Joanne, myself, all of that came to Helene through ecstatic transmission. There was a process, something working itself out between Joanne and Helene when they had an apartment down on Bleecker St. and Lafayette. Helene said, and I don't think she made this up, that she woke up from a dream with step-by-step instructions completely memorized and when she followed the instructions, with Joanne's help that she *received* the script for the movie. When we shot the film she made it clear that we needed to follow the script and that there was no room for improvisation or choice. Fine by me. It was her vision.

Chapter 8

Hilaria, 1993

Joanne Pardes took Linda to the back room. Walls lined with couches, the floor covered with soft rugs. A TV, a stereo and crates of CDs and tapes, a round table, some chairs. It was dim, no windows, no natural light, just Christmas lights and small lamps.

Joanne gave Linda two bumps of ketamine and they sat back on the couch. Linda studied the contours of Joanne's face. The drug reveals new contrasts, new ways of seeing shadow and light. Joanne stared at the Christmas lights and the point where the wall intersected with the ceiling, fascinated. "The world, the universe, reality, it's a collection of infinite loops."

Linda watched Joanne levitate from her seat. She swooned. She moved closer to her, leaned her head on Joanne's shoulder.

"I'm going to stack twenty-three TVs here, against the wall. With strobe lights, and the TVs will give you the opportunity to merge with the signal, and the strobe lights will bring you there. I've been working with this one set and through my work I've realized I need more. That's how this all operates, you start walking the path and as you go, you discover what to do next."

She spilled more K onto the table. "I have these videos I took of the room in negative reversal and I'm gonna screen them on some of the TVs. What you have to do is just take in the entire wall in at once, passively, you know. You need to just sit there and stop moving... If you need to do something, which is inadvisable, make sure it's rhythmic... You just merge with the TV. You have to let it consume you. This is the dangerous part of this work. You're giving the systems of control a way in. You're going to see everything, fascism, war, degradation, sexism and it's going to penetrate you. Turn on the news. Watch as much as you can. Let the propaganda influence you. Make yourself believe the lies. That's key. You need to fall into the hole. The idea is to walk out of the mouth of the beast intact, immortal, completely invincible…"

"How?"

"Magick, you need to use magick to protect yourself. You're experiencing an attack on your soul. You have to take that energy and use it to your own ends. It's powerful. The whole force of the eternal empire is in that energy. Yeah, you know, like take that energy and you direct it to where you want it to go… In magick, you never know what the finished work will look like the same way in art, even if you have that image in your head, the third mind hasn't had its say yet."

"The third mind?"

"I made a piece, once with someone and we created this third stream of creativity, independent of ourselves but intrinsically linked, you know? And she's gone but I don't know, the third mind, it's with me. And we work together."

"But how?"

"Magick, beb!"

"Like witchcraft?"

"Sure… I'm an artist, a witch…"

"So, you're an actual witch?"

"I do magick… You've like never, before?"

"No, never."

"Why not?"

"I don't know?"

"Your first stop is Hermes."

"Where are you going? What are you doing?"

"You're… breaking through, somewhere else, so you can communicate…"

"Where do you go to communicate?"

"The Mauve Zone."

"Where's that?"

"It's a… position. A, like dimension – it's… imagine like pure nothingness, pure potential… I'm seeing it now."

"Me too." Linda's jaw went slack and her mouth fixed itself open.

"Hermes is your first stop. When Hermes finds you, when you're chosen, when you, like, stumble upon him, you'll be ready and… You'll enter your transformation."

Joanne squeezed Linda's hand. "Do you know about Set?"

"Set?"

"Set is the god of the gateways… This New Millennium is his time. This whole Aeon will belong to Set and Hermes and Pan and Baphomet, Ahriman, and Lucifer… Now we can actually like, we've never had the tools before now… Cybernetics explain everything we've tried to understand for like, millennia. The loop, right, is the eventual organizing pattern for any natural form. Matter, time, energy the results of constant positive feedback. Infinite self-compounding, self-regenerating processes. We didn't have, like, the technology we have today a thousand years ago. Even if magicians in 993 wanted to welcome the new millennium with the true practices, the ancient ones they didn't have like, computers to perfect the ritual, to get the right symbology, the right energy – the actual position of the stars! We have technology, systems, methods, maps… Because, like, our calendar is so fucking fake. They just made it up, it's not a real calendar, you need to pay attention to so many moving parts, all at once. That's where astronomy comes in. Satellites, telescopes, we can chart the cosmos now… Now we can, like, access tantra and Thelema, En-Sof, and do you know about the Process?"

"No."

"Oh my god they're brilliant… But you know what? I have this book I need to show you, this incredible woman, Alice Walsh. Now we can just like, create our own realities and then live in them. No matter what happened before, you can ascend and like create a whole new universe all around you. Now we can like, decode the entire fabric of reality with computers, the web! We can create the ultimate ritual."

Chapter 9

The Lower East Side, June 1993

Saul Davis took a walk to Chinatown. He wore a tweed jacket, a big mop of curly hair, round shades. He went to a spa he liked off East Broadway, smoked a bag of heroin in the bathroom and booked a ninety-minute massage. He recreated the opium den of his imagination. He stripped and laid face down. The masseuse washed his back with a hot towel, slathered him in oils. She went to work on the knots in his back and shoulders. He let his mind focus on his hunt for Amanda.

Saul amazed himself, his own depravity. The things he imagined once he tracked her down. *I need you to understand that I'll put up with basically anything aside from humiliation.*

Do whatever you want, pursue your desires, but this needs to be answered for. I didn't know you to be hateful… I really thought you knew me well enough to know the sacred place my identity as a man… Its centrality to who I am… Your drive to attack me, my identity, that can't simply hang between us indefinitely. We needed to close this circuit, move forward…

He thought about purifying her with fear, buying a ski mask, finding her address and climbing in through the window. He wanted to make a hand print on her wall in her shit. Then he considered a slower, more protracted campaign of psychic warfare. Instead of or ahead of any home invasion…

"So muscular, so handsome."

"Don't talk. I'm thinking. Keep going, strong hands." The masseuse channeled her hatred into Saul's back. He loved it. "Yeah good. Try and hurt me."

He saw, too, how anything so unpleasant could just as well be avoided. *You could welcome me back into your life. You could hold yourself accountable. You could demonstrate your growth. I understand now that you were young and immature when we met, that I could have overestimated your emotional adulthood. But enough time has passed that you should have worked on yourself by now... If not, wasn't this intervention even more urgently needed? Come on.*

The time flew by, the clock went off. She wiped him down with a towel and left the room. Saul was relaxed, blissed out. He hadn't felt so loose in years but he could have sworn this was the kind of place they finished you off. He wondered why she didn't offer. It would be reflected in the tip.

Saul Davis was a columnist at Overthrow Magazine and three nights a week he hosted *Truth Tonight* on W-ACL. The studios were in the western side of Midtown, bleeding into Hell's Kitchen, a depressing place to walk at night. Saul walked with his shoulders at his ears, clutching a cigarette with his teeth, hands in his pockets, tuned in to the misery, anxiety, the smell of blood.

"Seekers, friends, good evening. This is Truth Tonight. I'm Saul Davis. I'm a writer, a journalist. Maybe you've seen my work in Overthrow Magazine... Here we are, broadcasting out of a Temporary Autonomous Zone. Midtown, Manhattan, Space Ship Earth. Check it out, dig it. We're talking about desire, here. We're talking about freedom, real freedom. Not the freedom you're hearing about in government schools. Not that PC party line. Tonight, on the show, we're going to... we're talking about the animal instinct, inside every man. Our closest primate relative is the Bonobo chimp. They're lovers, not fighters. They're doing it, friends, they're doing it all day. Gentlemen, they're getting it on. That's nature, that's our instinct, man. Your desire, that power source, fueling your machine, that's the Bonobo chimp, my friends. The freedom of – you know what? Before I take your calls, I need to tell you all, and this will probably be in my column in Overthrow Magazine next month – hmm. Folks do we have...

"We have breaking news. Breaking news, bulletin, you heard it here first: YOU ARE AN AUTOMATON. YOU'RE A COG IN THE GOVERNMENT MACHINE. YOU'RE NOT FREE. YOU'RE NOT LIBERATED. YOU'RE AS BRAINWASHED AS ANYBODY... You heard that here first, a little, breaking news, for you. The news never sleeps, and friends, neither do we.

"Now I'm going to take your calls. What's happening, what are we talking about? I want to talk about desire, man. I want to talk about what's happening inside the individual. How do we accelerate out of our current position toward a truly authentic self? What's happening? 201 number, calling from a 201 number what's happening?"

"Hey, hey, am I on?"

"201 number you are on."

"I'm calling to say the truth is out there, man… I'm on the path, I'm going to find it."

"Let me know when you do."

"I wanted to know your opinion. They're saying conservatism is the new punk rock."

"Oh?"

"Do you agree?"

"I think libertarianism is the new punk rock. The individual. That's what it's all about. It's about what happens inside the individual. It's about desire."

"Do you—"

"It's about following your inner voice. You know what's real for yourself the way I know what's real for me… Keeping it moving, calling from a 212 number."

"It's Stirko and I need the whites and Persians listening tonight to pay attention. If you kiss a feline's anus with proper intention, Sheitan himself will appear before you."

"Moving on! Next caller! 212 number, 212 number."

"Hey! Hey! I've got a radio behind my ear, don't need that. Don't want it. Get it out of here. You're messing with the cycle! Hey I'm talking to you! Hey!"

Saul hung up. "I wonder if this caller has read his Deleuze and Guattari? His RD Laing? All right a 718 number! 718 number you're on Truth Tonight on W-ACL."

"In the beginning God held the west and the demonic hordes held the east!"

"Who's this?"

"This is The Sergeant."

"Where are you calling from?"

"The Bronx, America, The United States. Your listeners are fortunate this early morning. They can learn a lesson. In the Beginning, God held the West. Satan and his demons held the East. We grew side by side, parallel to each other."

"Where'd you pick this up, Sarge?"

"It's The Sergeant, my name. My teacher gave me this lesson. In the Beginning. God created the West. Satan created the East."

"Who was this teacher? The Lieutenant? The Colonel?"

"He was the greatest man I'll ever know. You are unfortunate to never have met him."

"But who was he?"

"Do you believe in angels, Sir?"

"Have you listened to this show before? I believe in the individual."

"My Teacher spoke to angels…"

"Caller?"

"After each lesson he spit in my mouth. I'd swallow the spit and that's how I memorized each word, learned the right way to do these things. You do them wrong they don't work or they summon demons, angry dead, not the good spirits who want to help you and me. The good spirits, like God and the angels, they want us fed and happy and prosperous, making babies, making money, planting the seeds."

"Thanks for passing along the lesson. Calling from a 212 number, 212 number…"

"There's a phone number. You see it places, all right. There's people handing out leaflets with the number on it, with stickers everywhere, the graffiti has the number. It's on the radio in the commercials it's in the alternate signals, the thirty-three signals, the emergency signals, the x10 signals, everywhere. The phone number is a portal. They pay people $10 an hour for their eight-hour shift. They sit at the phone, when the phone rings they hit two buttons, the first recorded anything said over the line, the other played the tape: a drum beat and black noise. The phone rings off the hook. These operators are busy people. The end of the night they remove the tape of the recorded calls, label it with the date and put it in an envelope. This envelope goes in a room somewhere. There's proof for all of this somewhere, some office tower, some basement. They'll load a new tape into the recorder and let their replacement into the office at the end of their shifts. It's twenty-four hours a day. The calls keep coming. The black noise keeps coming. It all just keeps building on itself in a big spiral. It all gets worse every day!"

"Who needs a job it pays $10 bucks an hour?"

Chapter 10

The Lower East Side, 1993–94

Amanda lived in a studio in a medium sized apartment building between 1st and A. Never mind how Saul got the address. He leaned into the buzzer. Amanda answered her intercom. "Who is it?"

"Special delivery." She hit the buzzer. She opened the door. She looked like she could cry when Saul Davis appeared before her. "What are you? Fucking? Doing here?"

"I have some gifts for you…" She stared at him, anxious. "Burning a hole through my pocket…"

Amanda went for her cigarettes. "What? What did you bring?"

He looked around. He pulled a couple bags of heroin out of his pocket. Amanda bit her lip. She shifted her eyes around. She exhaled. "This doesn't change anything… between us or, you know… You get that, right?" She sucked on her teeth. She knew what she was doing.

"Just a friend bringing a gift over."

"You're—" She breathed in and out. She ground her molars. Saul walked in. Her shoulders tensed. Her stomach cramped. She sat down. She studied Saul.

"Do you have tin foil?"

"Yeah, it's in the kitchen…" She thought for a moment. "Stay there, I'll get it." She went to the kitchen, opened drawers, slammed them shut. She muttered to herself, moved trash around. "God dammit!"

She came back with foil, a straw, and a pair of scissors. "All right… give it to me." Saul dug back into his pocket, gave her a bag. He watched her prepare her hit. She snipped the straw in half, tore a piece of foil. "Give me your lighter."

Saul pulled out his cigarettes, lit up then gave Amanda the lighter. She lit the flame under the foil, sucked the vapor. Saul watched; his jeans tightened. He chewed on his filter. Amanda exhaled.

He was her professor in 1992, his third year as an adjunct. They hooked up Spring Break that semester. The relationship turned dark quickly. Amanda got away when she overdosed on Valium a month after classes resumed. She dropped out of school then disappeared. The incident, while never investigated, probably led to the philosophy department's decision to no longer offer him classes.

Saul made the decision to fall back on the family trust and write his novel. He produced a three-thousand-page manuscript about a college student named Samantha. She seduces her professor, a singular genius in the field of analytic philosophy. The bulk of the text was a series of monologues by the professor: his critiques, theories, desires. The text, like many at the time, made precious innovations in type setting and use of punctuation. Voluminous footnotes were a novel in themselves, ruminations on Hakim Bey, Georges Bataille, Deleuze and Guattari and Nietzsche. The end of the book, Samantha condenses the professor's ideology into a final monologue before she firebombs a mall. In the final scene, she's cut down by federal agents. The professor watches her die. He realizes he might be the first to live forever.

After a round of revisions and rewrites where he mostly cut out expository biographical information about Samantha, *Untitled – A Novel by Saul Davis* was two thousand pages' long.

Amanda exhaled, relaxed from the dope. "Give me one of your cigarettes." She looked at Saul again. "I've hated you for like, a while now."

"That's not necessary," Saul quipped.

"You—" She laughed. "You ruined my life, you realize that, right? Look at me!"

Saul took a key bump of dope. He held a child's capacity to ignore other people's emotions, a singular shamelessness. "Well, moving on…"

Chapter 11

August 1993

Morgan Gold and Linda Solomon sat together in the back room. Giuliani was speaking on the color TV. "Lexie says I get to do head shots later. Then like a whole shoot. Fuck, could you imagine? It's so cool."

"Yeah, wow. Like, good luck."

"Why don't you want to take head shots?"

"Huh? I don't know… I'm busy? Joanne takes my picture all the time. What's the difference?"

"Linda come on."

"What?"

"It's so different!"

"I don't think I'm a model, you know?"

"What about an actress?"

"Yeah, no, I don't know."

"So why are you here?"

"For Joanne."

"The rest of us want to be models. It's fucked up that you don't."

"Hey! Fuck you." Linda flinched, tensed up, and turned away.

"Fuck you! All you do around here is fucking breathe the air and fucking get high all the time. I'm working my fucking ass off! I hate work, it's fucking bullshit! God I hate you, Linda!"

Linda turned red and balled her fists. She stormed out the back room, up the hallway to bang on Joanne's door.

Chapter 12

Chelsea, 30 December 1993

Ahead of New Year's, Maria Grim had Joanne and Linda over for dinner. Joanne interpreted the invite as a request for pitches. Linda was excited to eat a meal. Maria's loft was around the corner from Hilaria, upstairs from Maria Grim Gallery. A private staircase took her to the gallery floor from the back of the loft. Choice pieces from her collection hung on the walls. Paintings, silkscreens, photographs, sculpture, one-of-a-kind furniture. Her rugs were handmade from Morocco, Afghanistan and Iran. Artifacts from North Africa, India, the Andes and the Amazon. One wall was dedicated to a 12' x 8' black and white photo of Nan St. John and Sarah Bremure.

Francisco Grim's ashes were displayed on the mantle. He died in 1986, making her a multimillionaire. His will divided his assets in two, equally, and distributed them in lump sums. $2.6 million to Maria and $2.6 million to the Church of En Sof. Maria got 80% of his real estate holdings, the other 20% reverted to The Hemlock Circle Trust.

Dinner was spaghetti with garlic and olive oil, a salad with olive oil and vinegar, bottles of Kava. Maria finished her portion, smirked when Linda reached for seconds. Joanne did her best to keep Maria's attention. "I want to do a wall of TVs, like, ten by ten, you know, a huge wall of feedback and snow. I want to record the sound and play it back, create a space where you have this wall of TVs and this amazing sound and you can feel the feedback, you know?"

Maria drank Frenet and Coke, smoked a spliff with clove tobacco. She sat back in a Versace jacket, a slim black skirt, a black and white checkered shirt. "Linda, how do you like Hilaria?"

"Oh, it's um, it's great. I love it here."

"Do you plan on a career in fashion? Art?"

"No… I haven't really thought about it?"

"What do you want to do?"

"I guess, hang out with Joanne?"

"Good answer," said Joanne. "Maria, what do you think of the idea?"

"It's fine, we can talk, but Linda, your ambition? It's to tag along? Don't get me wrong, I like Joanne, you have a good taste in company. You found Hilaria. But what about your desire? What do you want?"

"I... want to go out, see people, hang out. I want to be in the scene."

New Year's Eve, 1993–4

When Joanne Pardes moved into Hilaria and set out designing the back room she collected old black and white TVs, found a few mid '80s color sets in the trash, and bought another six from the Salvation Army with Claire's money. Now Joanne was up to fourteen TVs, stacked in the wall of the backroom. Two strobe lights and all the sets were live. Some were hooked into antennae, some were bars of color or the holy snow. Local news, the ball in Times Square. The back room was just as crowded as up front.

Linda and Joanne pushed through throngs of revelers to get into Joanne's room. Linda leaned into Joanne's lap. Joanne weaved her fingers into Linda's hair, twisted her wrist. She wore a white face mask ala Phantom of the Opera, a Sonic Youth shirt and black leggings.

"Do you feel the like, power in here?" asked Joanne.

"I guess?"

"The fucking place is charged, beb." She snorted a bag, hummed a fanfare. "*Charge!*"

Hilaria's 1994 New Year's party featured DJ's Treasure and San Lo, spinning all night in shifts. Claire LaBas offered up her bedroom as a green room. It gave her a chance to hang out with the performers, for photo ops. Maria Grim and Claire LaBas hired a coven of witches out of the Bronx on Jacques Anzu's recommendation for midnight.

Maxine Mauve and Carlos lived off the Grand Concourse. Carlos worked days as a piercer on 8th St. and Maxine practiced magic full time. A patronage network supported her pursuits. VHS tapes of her rituals circulated around the world and the money kept pouring in. She had hundreds on any given night performing rituals for her. The spirits loved her. They kept her fed, prosperous, and stoned.

Claire filled her room with every candle in Hilaria. Maxine and Carlos made their way through their requested ounce of haze. Claire kept the room as empty of revelers as possible. San Lo was at work outside spinning techno. Treasure from Christlandia leaned back, feet up on two chairs, eyes closed, headphones on. Maxine burnt calea, rosemary, sage and lavender with raspberry bush. She and Carlos sat quietly, smoking a blunt of Pepper Haze, preparing for their performance.

Claire got a thrill out of the excessive crowds, pushing the limits of what Hilaria could hold before windows started breaking. She wondered if the ceilings could handle the volume. Transgression, the boundaries of excess, her only thrill these days. "Have you ever thought about, I dunno, sacrificing a like chicken or like lamb or goat on stage?"

"Not really, no?"

"It would look so cool, you hang the thing by its legs..." She made a guttural noise in her throat. "The blood drains into the stage... Oh! You can burn the guts right there. Cut the stomach open and just like, go for it."

"I mean, I guess?" Carlos hit the blunt, stayed polite. "This party is crazy, it's cool!"

"Thanks... You know, I'm thinking after you're done I'm going to take some needles out and put on a show too."

"Oh yeah?"

"Everyone's so scared of blood, I love it."

Lexie opened the door and pushed it closed with her back. "I can't fucking deal with this outside. They're everywhere!"

"Here." Claire offered Lexie a mirror and a vial.

Lexie cut up some lines, occupied herself. "Is there fucking—" Lexie rubbed her sinus.

"It's heroin, love, chill out." Lexie went for more. Maxine watched the display. Lexie G. Hinnon was an animal.

The revelers counted down to midnight. San Lo dropped a DEATH HURT track and cranked up the volume. When the air was ready to catch on fire, San Lo announced Maxine over the PA. "Hilaria! Ladies and gentlemen, we have something you ain't seen before. We're welcoming the new year. Check it out! It's my brother and sister! Give it up Hilaria! Oh my god!" Maxine and Carlos took the stage. Maxine carrier a torch and a bottle of Devil's Springs. San Lo dropped *I Put A Spell On You.* Maxine spat fire. The revelers lost it. Carlos peeled his shirt off, spun it over his head and threw it into the crowd. Maxine secured the torch, put the bottle down. She slipped fish hooks into Carlos' back. She whispered an incantation. Carlos meditated through the pain. Maxine fixed the hooks to a harness. She fixed the harness to a pulley system rigged above the stage. Maxine pulled Carlos up to the ceiling. He swung over the crowd. Treasure backed Maxine, gave her the slack to step away. She circled the stage, spat fire in each direction. She secured the torch, dropped the bottle. They eased Carlos down. The revelers cheered. San Lo dropped a jungle track and the room shook.

Excerpt of an interview with Morgan Gold, circa 1998

New Year 1994 was legendary. People still talk about it. They still tell me they were there that night. Everyone was there. You couldn't move. They opened up everything except the bedrooms. Joanne Pardes took over the whole back room. She was doing this art project with TV sets and strobe lights. Maria Grim backed it. "Joanne Pardes, artist in residence."

I couldn't even look at it or go in there. It made me so nervous, it gave me a headache, but people were just like stampeding in the back room to see it. Usually when we threw parties the back room was off limits or maybe sometimes like a VIP section but instead Joanne just let everyone inside. I spent the whole night in Lexie's bedroom with Marina and Britney. Because Joanne opened up the back room, the hallway was just as crowded as anywhere else.

Chapter 13

The Lower East Side, 1989

Helene Asher and Joanne Pardes sat at their kitchen table and watched Eddie Mad Dog draw out their designs. "I always like to redraw one more time before I do the stencil. It gives me a feel for the image... You know I did the WEREWOLFs on Steve Sinclair and Mario Millions? We did those Venice Beach, 82... Marathon session. No one else was doing that Vato-Cholo calligraphy like I was..."

Joanne was up first with Solomon's Key: an eight-pointed star wrapped a circle on her wrist. "Don't hate me 'cuz I'm beautiful." Mad Dog hit the foot pedal and his machine purred. The tattoo took around twenty minutes. Joanne looked away. She wore her sunglasses so Helene couldn't see if she cried. Helene, fascinated, watched Mad Dog work. She got a kick out of watching Joanne squirm.

"Stay still, darling." Mad Dog finished the piece, sprayed her down, wrapped her up. He put the needles in a bottle.

He directed his attention to Helene. "All right, Babe, let's do the stencil." Helene got up, took off her t-shirt. "Shoulders relaxed, arms hung naturally... All right now, don't even breathe." He sprayed her lower back down with green soap and applied the stencil. Another heavy spray. He lifted an eyebrow, checked out different viewpoints. "Another perfect placement. You can breathe again, sweetheart."

Mad Dog set up a machine with a 1-liner and a machine with an 8 round. "All right, get comfortable... *don't hate me 'cause I'm beautiful.*" He hit the pedal and started outlining the seven-pointed seal, thick sturdy black lines. Using the 1-liner, the single needle, he wrote BABALON 77-77-77-7 throughout and around the seal. He sprayed the finished piece with alcohol, then green soap. Mad Dog dropped the needles in a bottle, cleaned up the station. He packed everything into a backpack. He opened a beer and lit a smoke.

Joanne and Helene ran to the bathroom to look in the mirror. "So cool!"

"I'm the mother of abominations, baby..." Helene bent to see her reflection from the back. "Fuck! Love!"

Mad Dog put on new gloves, dabbed the tattoo with a paper towel, wiped off the alcohol. He sprayed her lower back with cold water. Her eyes rolled back. Mad Dog directed the photo. Joanne, left, faced the camera in her black tank top and torn jeans, Helene with her back to the camera. Their tattoos aligned in the center of the shot.

He taped on their bandages. He hung out in the living room with Joanne while Helene got ready. The Steve Sinclair and The Werewolves Ten-Year Anniversary Show at the Continental started in an hour. Mad Dog was on the list and he was taking them both as his plus one.

Hilaria, 1994

Sunlight flooded through the windows from the East. The kitchen was empty. The couches by the windows were cleared of lurkers. Lexie's adepts slept in the backroom. Claire was out until three or four. Eddie Mad Dog was in from LA, at Hilaria to tattoo Joanne. They collaborated on the design, Kali on her hill of skulls while the Twin Towers burned in the background. They worked for eight hours straight, with around ten coke breaks. Joanne smoked a bag of heroin the last third of the tattoo, the end of the color and the highlights. Linda sat close by. She wore her headphones, read zines and *The Voice*. She played DJ, flipped tapes over every now and again, chose new music. She played Psychic TV *Take the Jab*. She put on a mixtape Mad Dog gave her with Officer Down, Civil Diss, and The Werewolves.

Mad Dog admired his work and his reflection in the mirror. Joanne was overjoyed. He wrapped up her arm.

Spring Equinox, 1994

Joanne carved the Tree of Life into Linda's arm with an Exact-o-blade. Aside a few stray tears, Linda held steady. Lexie watched from the other side of the room, a couch against the wall, fascinated. She shot Polaroids. Hilaria was never this quiet. No music, no one spoke. They breathed, smoked, panted, sucked their teeth, snorted a blend of coke and dope. Lexie listened to the sound of the blade cut Linda's skin open. Lexie watched

Linda transcend.

Linda kissed Joanne's lips when they finished. Linda's face was wet with tears. Joanne wiped the blood and sanitized the scar. It spanned from the bottom of the ditch halfway down the forearm. Each of the ten Sefirot were marked with a star. Lexie stood up and wandered into her room. She wanted to feel something. Joanne bandaged Linda's arm. She hugged Linda with all of her force. Linda cried into Joanne's shirt and clawed into her back. Joanne took Linda to her bedroom and held her. They fell asleep. Joanne dreamed of Helene.

Excerpt of an interview with Morgan Gold, circa 1998

I was there for some of Joanne's magic stuff. We did a seance once. Me, Joanne Pardes, Linda Solomon, and Claire Labas. It didn't end well. It was the first time I saw Joanne cry. Up until that point I thought she was invincible, and always cool. But that's always an act. No one is actually that cool. But she totally just embarrassed herself and she knew it and she just didn't care anymore. She just burst into tears.

That was when she started to lose it. When she was doing magic, and pulling us all into it. I know that's what she was doing before she moved into Hilaria but she put it aside for a while, she was doing other things. Then, yeah, she got back into magic, and I was like, OK wow, this is scary.

Chapter 14

Hilaria, 1993–1994

Joanne Pardes and Linda Solomon sat together cross legged on the floor in the backroom. Everything was dark but the TV sets. "It's no longer a weapon against you, when it's snow or feedback even. You can fall into the matrix and get right back out again whenever you want. Watching snow on the screen, you plug into the patterns, the frequency, the waves of light. After hours of meditation on the web of black, white, and gray flashes, the feedback, white sound, we'll elevate."

On different days, they used different psychedelics in front of the snowy TV. Mushrooms: the snow pulses, the light from the TV trails, the sound of the feedback soothes them. Acid: fond memories play out on screen, under the snow. Ketamine: their third mind recognizes the underlying patterns in the snow.

When Joanne first moved to Hilaria, she locked herself in the back room and began working with the TV set. Spare said a desire needs to be forgotten before it can be fulfilled, so she wiped her mind. She plugged it in and let the feedback wash over her. Joanne watched the snow for days long stretches, pinching herself, digging a knuckle into her leg every time she blinked or nodded off. Eventually, after days of focus on the TV set, she merged with the signal.

During a particularly long, grueling session with the feedback, one of Lexie's adepts burst into the room, making noise, humming *Fire*. Morgan Gold chased after her and pulled her from the back of her tank top. "Are you retarded?"

Joanne passed the cosmic test. She didn't break her focus on the snow.

She read through her notes and Helene's surviving notebooks. She approximated Helene's recipe, acacia, henbane, and datura. She trained Linda on the ritual, taught her each step, every motion, every word. They drew a pentagram in the back room, locked and barricaded the door. They put in the tampons, soaked in the flowers and grain alcohol.

"What is the word?"

"Hermes."

"What is the password?"

"Mercury."

"What is the word?"

"Lemuria."

"What is the password?"

"Atlantis."

The holy meal was two fat lines of ketamine. They floated to the ceiling. "What the Raven bringeth, ye shall drink," said Joanne.

"What the Raven bringeth, ye shall drink," Linda repeated back. They took each other's hands, they intoned together. "What the Raven bringeth, ye shall drink." As Joanne kept chanting, Linda was suddenly catatonic. Her eyes fluttered; her grip went limp. Her blood ran cold, her pulse slowed down.

She opened her mouth. "Listen to me."

"Helene?"

"Listen to me."

"Helene, is that you? It's me, beb. It's Joanne. Joanne Pardes. Helene?"

"Listen to me, listen to me, listen to me… Listen to, me listen to. Me Listen, to me listen…"

"Helene, if it's you, can you tell me?"

"Listen to, me listen to, me listen, to me listen!"

Joanne felt herself descending, she felt the ground against her body. She was planted on her back, knees up, feet on the ground. She stood up and left the circle. Linda came to. "Did anything happen?"

"No, something went wrong." She shook while she tried to light a camel, she fought off a throb in her throat.

"I'm sorry, was it me?" Linda pulled her knees to her chest. She felt naked.

Joanne got dressed. "We couldn't break through, I couldn't… receive anything."

"What did she say?"

"I said she wasn't there. It didn't work… It doesn't matter, fuck it."

The next full moon, Joanne led a seance in the kitchen. She bounced the creeps out for the night so they had the front of Hilaria to themselves. Claire Labas, Lexie G Hinnon, Morgan Gold and Linda Solomon sat with Joanne at the table. They stayed quiet, they kept their grips steady, taking care not to break the circle.

"I'm trying to reach Helene Asher. This is Joanne..." Silence. "We're talking to Helene Asher." Linda watched Joanne through her eyelashes. She looked desperate. She kept her face shut tight, she waved Claire and Lexie's hands. They limply followed Joanne's gestures. "I'm trying to reach Helene."

Claire gathered the others and brought them into her bedroom to get high and listen to CDs. Joanne cried alone at the table.

Excerpt from an interview with Jacques Anzu, circa 1996

In 1989, I acted in *Scarlet Woman 89* with Helene Asher and Joanne Pardes. Helene was the writer / director / star, it was her movie. The subject was a magickal system Helene was developing called The Cyber Grimoire. We performed rituals which the chicks, Helene and Joanne developed. Helene had a macho streak, but I was there for the masculine energy. We rehearsed in their apartment on Bleecker and Lafayette. We shot the film upstate outside Woodstock...

It was a wild few days...

I already knew Joanne. We had always gotten along it's why she suggested me out of all the studs downtown. There's a scene in the climax of the movie where we fuck, me and Helene. She's covered head to toe in red paint, which is supposed to be blood. Joanne was the DP for that scene. We shot that scene for hours, different angles...

What were you on?

Helene ate a bunch of these very powerful mushrooms and then pissed into a bottle once she was tripping. We drank that, all weekend... And we were doing speed all weekend. We had hash and we had some K. But what we did that day, it worked. I made it work for me. I came back here and had never been busier. I started huge collaborations, a lot of painting, I met Lexie G Hinnon maybe a month after this working, come to think of it, she hadn't changed her name yet. That was Claire Labas, they met around then, 1989, 1990. This all began to unfold right after we made this film. Helene's luck though... She was probably already headed in that direction but she just fell apart. I think by the last time I saw Helene, Joanne was already hanging out with Claire Labas and Lexie G Hinnon and well, you know how that all ended.

Did you introduce Joanne Pardes to Claire Labas?

It's possible I introduced them, but Joanne was a magnetic personality and Claire really was attracted to Joanne and pursued her independent of me. And obviously they became way closer to each other than I was to either of them, really. Joanne needed a place to stay, she wasn't going to stay in that apartment with Helene's ghost torturing her every fucking night and I think they were evicting her anyway. But even if I did, either way I can't be held responsible for what Joanne did or what happened there. And I was already out of the picture. I'd left that scene already...

Chapter 15

Hilaria, 1994

Lexie G. Hinnon made Linda up in lip gloss and pastel eye shadow. She sprayed her in cheap scents tween girls liked. "Car's coming." Lexie sniffed Linda, up and down. "OK. You're good. Get going. The car will pick you up."

A Suburban was idling outside. Linda got in the back. Gavin Lee, the military haircut Lexie was so enthusiastic about, sat in the passenger seat. "You're… Linda." He read from a post-it note.

"Yeah, Linda."

"Buckle up. Want anything?"

"What do you have?"

"Do you need to relax?"

"Sure, OK?" Gavin gave Linda half a Xanax. They drove up the Westside Highway to 42nd and turned into the city, into Times Square. They turned on Sixth Avenue. Gavin and the driver were silent. Gavin scanned foot traffic. They turned somewhere in the fifties and drove into an underground garage.

"Do you need anything else to relax?"

"Should I?"

"You tell me."

"OK?"

"Here's one more. The Ram doesn't like druggies. He doesn't want you stoned out. I know that's your whole image but, tonight, be yourself, OK?" Gavin had the squarest head Linda had ever seen. She couldn't place his accent, somewhere Southwestern? "We're going to exit the vehicle and take the elevator upstairs now. Get ready to exit."

Gavin and the driver got out first. The back seat didn't open from the inside. Gavin opened the door for her. She followed the driver, Gavin at her six to the elevator.

Welcome to the Hemlock Hotel.

Linda stood with her back against the elevator wall. The driver got out, checked the hallway and they led Linda to the Circle Suite.

"We'll get the call when it's time to take you home. Have a fun night." Gavin reached over Linda's shoulder with a key card and opened the door. He knocked on the door, one, two, one, two, three.

"Hello, Linda, come in." Bishop Thom 'The Ram' Walsh sat in a leather-bound chair with a glass of scotch in his hand.

"Hi…"

"Come in, come, do it, let me look at you." He smiled with his whole face, a wide grin, white teeth. "Please, take a minute to read the room service menu. Enjoy the mini bar. Make yourself comfortable." The Ram sat back in a leather-bound chair. He pulled out a cigar. "Do you really think the best tobacco on earth comes from Cuba? The Cuban *art of cigar rolling* well that's undeniable, but we have the best of Cuba here, in the US of A. Miami, home of millions of free Cubans. The *art of cigar rolling*, that lives on in a free Miami, my goodness, hmm. You know? Linda, make yourself a Rum and Coke, Cuba Libre!"

Linda pulled out dark and light rum and diet coke from the mini bar.

"Go ahead and mix yourself a cocktail, go ahead. Have you decided on anything to eat?"

"I'm OK with this."

"There should be some chocolate bars in the mini bar. Eat those. To go with the alcohol. I insist."

"OK…"

"I'm going to take a shower, if you're not having dinner."

"OK…"

"The remote control is on the coffee table. Put on whatever you want. HBO, MTV…"

"OK, cool."

"Put on MTV. Eat a chocolate bar." He smiled again. He finished his drink. He took the cigar into the bathroom and closed the door. Linda looked around the suite. The room was furnished with antiques, Antebellum originals from the Hudson School hung on the walls. She turned on the TV and flipped channels, landed on MTV and stayed there, per The Ram's instructions. Ace of Bass, R Kelly, a block of commercials. The Ram took about twenty minutes to get ready. Linda inspected the mini bar. He opened the door. "Come on in."

She entered the bedroom. A massage table was set up by the bathroom door, a bottle of oil and towels were laid out on the dresser. Linda climbed on The Ram's back. "Start with the shoulders... Mm, work on the arms... mm, very good." She put her body weight into it. He purred. She massaged his hands and arms, he sighed. The ram turned around. Linda massaged his pectorals, neck and face.

She pulled down the towel, he went erect immediately. The ram closed his eyes and put his hands under his head. When he busted he turned around onto his back. "Come here, drool it back, slowly... very good." He went to take a shower and Linda returned to the living room. She had a cigarette and a bottle of SoCo.

The Ram emerged from the bathroom dressed in slacks and a monogrammed Polo. He pulled a roll from his pocket, counted bills. "This... *two hundred* right here, is just between you and me. The rest you take home and give to Lexie."

"OK." Linda swayed off the benzos.

"Let's get you home." The Ram went to a phone and called Gavin to the door. "Have a good night, Linda." The Ram was already in his bedroom. He closed the door behind him.

Gavin knocked on the door, one, two, one, two, three. Linda opened the door and he walked her to the elevator, the Suburban was idling at the elevator door in the garage. "We can stop at Wendy's on the way back. McDonald's?"

"I'm OK." Linda lit a new cigarette.

Chapter 16

Hilaria, 1994

Claire Labas called a meeting with Joanne and Lexie. She was ready to kick half the girls out. She blew an eight ball and ranted at them. "The place sucks now, it's always so dirty in here. Lexie, why aren't your fucking people cleaning up after themselves?"

"I dunno?"

"Because they're little fucking kids. Tell them to get it together. I saw a roach yesterday."

"It's too crowded," Joanne added.

"Yeah, it's too crowded." Lexie glared at Joanne.

It was resolved everyone had to leave except Morgan, Marina, Britney and Linda.

Chapter 17

Downtown, 1994

Saul Davis made for an easy ADHD diagnosis, especially on speed. He maintained a network of shrinks up and downtown, east side, west side, Nassau by his parents. Each assigned Adderall. He evangelized the drug to anyone who'd listen. "Best speed I've ever had, clean, pure, corporate. It's tremendous. Here."

He wore black jeans, black Nikes, a black T. The only hint of his wealth, a Brooks Brothers blazer. He had curly black hair, olive accented skin, a big nose. Saul kept the open bars in Soho and Chelsea written in his calendar. He liked to describe himself as a *social animal*. During the day he hung out in Washington Square Park to let the public see him read and write in his notebook. He lived a few blocks west, off Christopher where Waverly intersected with itself.

Saul went to park and copped from a contact named Rios. From what Saul could gather he lived in the park. He said he was from Puerto Rico and couldn't go back. "We fought the cops. I fucked them up, they were scared of me." He seemed young, maybe twenty. He could have been fifteen or thirty.

Saul gave Rios forty and waited twenty minutes. He sat back on a bench, smoked cigarettes and read Bataille. Rios came back, eyes like pinballs. "I had to smoke it to show them. Let's go somewhere over there." They hit McDougal, Rios handed off the dope and he disappeared onto Minnetta, back to 6th Avenue.

Saul shoved the product into the bottom of his inside breast pocket. He bought a new pack of cigarettes. Then he went through his haul. A bag of heroin and two vials of crack. For $40? That motherfucker. Now he had to do this all over again.

He went looking for Rios. Thieving asshole probably shot Saul's dope and was nodding off somewhere. He locked himself in the Waverly diner bathroom to snort the bag of heroin off the Bataille book. He went through his money while someone knocked on the door. "In here!" he whined.

***

He found himself on the East Side. He bought $100 in what he was promised was superlative dope from a guy named Tank. He stopped in a deli for a cup of coffee, more smokes. He almost walked out without his change. He went to Amanda's. He rang her bell.

"Who is it?"

"Me."

"Why, what's up?" she said into the intercom.

"So, can I come up? I'm... you know."

One of Amanda's neighbors walked out of the building and Saul went upstairs. He knocked on the door. Amanda stood in her threshold, face balled up, hands fisted. She wore an Officer Down shirt and sweat shorts.

"What happened to your leg?"

"Oh yeah, I think I kicked something." There was a gash, healing slowly, ringed with bruises on her right shin.

Saul let himself in. He took a seat on the couch, a convertible futon. He lit a cigarette with her lighter.

"So?"

"So what?" asked Saul.

"You can't just, like—"

"What? I was in the neighborhood."

"I was watching TV."

"Oh man! The TV? That's a mind control device, Amanda," he croaked at her. "Conformity machine!"

"Oh my god, shut up!" She fought back tears, bit her lip, took one of his cigarettes and lit up. "You said you were holding... right? You said that?"

"Bring me some foil." He took out a bag of dope and Amanda came back with foil and a straw. They stared at the TV. The apartment was austere. The futon was one of two pieces of furniture, she also had the coffee table. It was cluttered with trash. Ashtrays, soda cans and bottles choked with cigarette butts, blunt guts, sink water and spit. The only art on the walls were a poster for Nights of Cabiria and a painting of Anita Berber, they came with the place.

Her eyes fluttered, she hinted toward a nod.

"Do another," said Saul.

"Yeah, yeah, yeah..." Amanda flicked the lighter and sucked up more vapor.

"Yeah, do it." She slumped into him. He pulled the crack out of his pocket. "Hey, Amanda, look."

Amanda's eyes widened. She pushed her way up, using Saul's shoulder, reached under the futon. She came back with a stem. "Give it to me."

She beamed up, he groped at her. He put his hand in her shorts and fumbled around. He put his head inside her shirt. He breathed her smell. She went weeks at a time without bathing. She coughed and he snatched the stem from her. He sucked in the remaining smoke. He exhaled and kissed her neck, bit her collar bone and licked behind her ear. She tried to watch TV. "Hold on a second." She took another hit.

He took off his blazer, his belt, undid his jeans. He thought back to when she was matriculated, clean, almost bubbly. He pulled off her shorts. He first saw her in Washington Square in a purple NYU sweatshirt, a plaid shirt underneath, torn jeans, long frizzy hair. She was alone, reading his syllabus: *Desire and the Individual.*

***

"Friends, listeners, this is *Truth Tonight* on W-ACL. I'm Saul Davis. We're broadcasting, as we do three nights a week, from a temporary autonomous zone in New York City. Mao, say what you will about Mao but he said revolution isn't a dinner party. You need to fight a protracted war for what you believe in, that's, that's important some times. I don't know if I'll be taking your calls tonight, because I have some things to say... I think what we should do is start a new movement. Why not, right? What do we have to lose but our chains? But this time, we're going to be a movement of individuals, and instead of governments we have desire. How about that? We're not PC, we're pragmatic radicals. We're thinkers. This is a knowledge revolution. The real revolution is inside every man's heart...

"I go for what I want, when I don't get it, I apply the lessons of history to fixing it, OK? When I was in academia, that was important to my success in the field. You don't take no for an answer. You blind yourself to no, you learn not to understand the word, you move forward. This is *Truth Tonight* on W-ACL. It's 2.32 in the morning here in our Temporary Autonomous Zone in New York City."

Saul left the Thursday gallery open bars and went looking for a taxi. He staggered around dramatically when he drank. He carried his blazer over his shoulder, he was spinning, browning out. Most drivers passed him up because he looked liable to puke or piss himself. A yellow cab picked him up on 8th Ave. "Where we going?"

He gave the driver Amanda's address. "1st and... A." They pushed east. Saul smoked out the window, the driver told him to watch his head. They arrived and Saul threw a twenty into the front seat and practically fell out of the cab. Saul hit Amanda's buzzer in long, five or ten second bursts until she answered. "What the fuck?"

"It's me, let me up."

"Who?"

"It's me, Amanda! Don't be like that."

"Who's there?"

"It's Saul, let me up."

"No!"

"Let me up, Amanda!"

"Go away."

He hit her button again. He held it down, he put his entire weight into it, he faced the sidewalk. Two minutes of sound and Amanda relented. The door opened and Saul let himself in. He climbed the stairs. Amanda was red. "You fucking asshole! I was sleeping." Saul blew past her, through the door and beelined to the couch. He took out a bag of dope, a credit card, a twenty. He cut lines. "You can't just fucking show up here in the middle of the night, you fucking asshole, oh my god. I fucking hate you so much, you never leave me alone. You're so fucking annoying!"

Saul snorted the heroin and extended the straw to Amanda. She sat down and took it from him. She snorted the lines he cut up. "Give me a smoke."

Saul took his pack out of his pocket, dropped a lighter behind him and went to the bathroom to puke out the wine.

"You're gross. Close the door, fuck!" She turned the on TV, an infomercial. She did another bump. Saul flushed the toilet and rinsed his mouth out with water. Black mold around tub, in the grout. He took a moment to steady himself. He prepped his cock to semi hard.

"Here, I've got more."

Amanda took the foil out of Saul's pack of cigarettes and smoked the remaining dope on the table with the snotty $20. Saul dropped another bag on the table and dropped to his knees. He took Amanda's underwear off and buried his face. Less licking than fucking her with his nose. He jerked off while he ate her out. She smoked the rest of the heroin and fell back asleep.

Saul fell behind on the Overthrow column and they went to press without him. He grew a beard. He ate once a day. Sandwiches, pizza, ice cream bars. He fell behind on his Adderall intake as the heroin overtook the speed. A month went by, he hit the galleries again. He smelled bad. The rest of the gallery scene froze him out as a moocher and an asshole. When he was holed up inside he concocted new lies, he edited the lies, worked out the kinks. The premise was sound. When someone recognized him, asked him where he'd been, he repeated the story he'd concocted for his return to the public, that he'd been beaten within an inch of his life.

"Now we have a caller, 212 number. 212, you're on Truth Tonight on WACL."

"Hello? Hello?"

"You're on the air."

"I am. OK! Fantastic. OK. You have a lot of kooks on here. A bunch of crazies. But that's what I like. I listen to your show and I just have the best thoughts. I can't stop thinking but it's good thinking. I just wanted to call in and raise everyone's consciousness for a moment. The Inquisition started in the 1233. What else started in 1933?"

"The Nazi rise to power?"

"But also Roosevelt is elected! Seven hundred years, exactly, since the inquisition."

"A 718 number, always an interesting perspective. You're on the air on Truth Tonight."

"I have a quick message and I'll yield the rest of my time. When we restore the natural order of things it'll be so destructive, so traumatic that anyone who lives through it will be permanently changed. It's your righteousness – or lack thereof, that determines your place in the Tikkun state. The United States of Tikkun."

"A quick message, a full sentence. A premise and a conclusion. What more could we ask for? Now we have a 201 number."

"I'll show you how to cleanse your pneuma."

"I bet you will, and look at that, another 201 number, two in a row!"

"Truth Tonight! It's Frank, Frank here."

"Frank what's going on, what's your subjective view?"

"My wife, my wife of twenty-six years is reading Managing Modern Life Part Due, all right? She won't do anything else but read this book. She finishes the book, I think to myself, all right, all right back to normal and she starts the book all over again. Truth Tonight audience, if someone in your life tries to bring that book into your house put the, listen you can't have this. It's not just my wife, listen there's something off here. This is my message, get that book out of your house before someone reads it, all right?"

"Frank, we have the board lit up like Times Square, we're going to move on but you got the word out. We have a 718 number. Something different."

"The freaking ghetto kids. They're committing crimes at eight years old. I heard the most dangerous place you can go is right outside a school in the ghetto. The gangs are waiting out there ready to do an initiation. They say there's a whole points system. Now this is the blacks doing this. When they victimize a black, they'll get one point. A Puerto Rican they'll get two points, do you follow? When they victimize a white person it's the most points. Now here's what I want to know. Where is the mayor and our cops?"

"What do you want them to do, caller? Are you suggesting a politician is going to change something? We have a 212 caller, 212 number."

"Mr. Davis, since the first time we spoke, I have it here, it was February 1991, since that first time we've spoken I have completely, and I mean completely turned my life around."

"Oh, hey yeah, all right, man."

"I'm living proof that anyone can do it because among the things I know now is I was wasting my life, my vitality. Get on the World Wide Web. Follow the Lemurian calendar. Locate the frequencies and you make that the basis of your success plan. Buy securities daily. Sell at the right time. Make the right decisions. How do you know you've made the right decision? Are you following the Lemurian calendar? Have you located your frequencies? You'll know you're making the right decision. Instead of sitting on your *butt* watching channel 35, you could be doing your own research. Mr. Davis, get on the World Wide Web. Follow the Lemurian Calendar. Locate, your, frequencies! You can't lose. Change your life. This is how you do it. It's not through welfare, it's not through working your way up. You need the third way. You're going to get on the internet, follow the Lemurian calendar, locate the frequencies. Do you have fillings in your teeth? Well, my friend, you're out of excuses then."

"You heard it here. Get on the computer... 212 number, this is Truth Tonight."

"This is The Avenger. The collapse of Sirius B and the rise of Islam are curiously close, huh? Three monotheistic systems, a complete circle of sun worship and what do we get? No more red star in the sky! Ever since the birth of the current paradigm, of the three monotheistic systems dominating sun ritual, we've had a blue dog star."

"Fascinating, another 212 number, 212 number."

"Hello? Am I on?"

"212, number you are on."

"Hello, Saul. Hello, everybody. It's Timothy, how do you do."

"What's on your mind tonight?"

"Feminists are sterilizing hyper-intelligent men. What say you?"

Chapter 18

Excerpted from an interview with Jacques Anzu, circa 1996–7

Yeah... around when I was shooting Shotgun 95, I was filming at an apartment some punk musicians had taken over. You know the Werewolves? Yeah. The owner of the place had cancer or AIDS and was a big Werewolves fan. One day, there were a hundred guys hanging out, getting high. Guys from big hardcore bands and old timers, mostly. That footage is under lock and key. There are some great shots of Joanne Pardes over there, that was our last time hanging out, really. I took her there. It was a very male place and her presence was cool, as a juxtaposition. And she was never, you know, that effeminate. Around that time, I was working with some skateboarders, doing video with them. We were hanging out in Canarsie, at this skate spot. That and my photography, the Oannes paintings showed around then too, early '95. I didn't have time, and the Hilaria scene was really seedy by then.

October 1993 – April 1994

When you walk down the street, and you think of downtown, New York City, when you think of Tompkins Square and Rikers Island – you think of Steve Sinclair. Katz's Deli, Paul's Cheeseburgers, The Methadone McDonald's where you can buy benzos – you think about Steve Sinclair.
    The Werewolves, Cold War

The Werewolves were formed in Canarsie in 1979 by Steve Sinclair and Mario Millions. Bassist Eric O'Reilly and drummer Al Killer completed the original lineup. Their 1980 debut album, *Punk Rock Genocide*, fused punk, hardcore and metal. Their 1981 follow-up, the classic *Punk Rock Killing Fields* expanded their reach. The *Killing Fields* Tour, 81–82 brought them through the South, Midwest and West Coast and resulted in *Sinclair and The Werewolves – Live in San Diego*.

Al Killer was arrested for aggravated assault and sentenced to five years in prison in 1983. He was replaced by Chuck Puke for *Hardcore Serial Murder* (1984). Eric O'Reilly died of AIDS in 1985. He was replaced by Frankie Zero, who stayed with the band through 1990.

Mario Millions' favorite players were James Williamson, Harley Flanagan, Johnny Thunders, and Earl Slick. He watched Giallo movies and shot heroin on his spare time. He maintained a svelte 120lbs since the late '70s. He wore a leather jacket, his Nihilistics shirt, leather pants and belt buckles. A skull, 4P, and iron cross rings, a leather cowboy hat. Millions kept Sinclair high for twenty years. Theirs was the most lasting relationship either man ever had.

Their musical collaborations brought the best out in each other. Millions wrote *Punk Rock Genocide, Methadone Mayhem, Me and Spacely Out By The River, Robbed/Cut by City–As Chicks, Mad Dog: Violent Fuck...* tracks that fans considered among the best in the entire Steve Sinclair *oeuvre*. The Werewolves released *Punk Rock Holocaust* in 1988, their final studio album. It was considered a lesser work by fans, but notable for the opener, *Serial Killers That Fuck*. Chuck Puke was murdered in the North Bronx in 1988. The killing was never solved. Frankie Zero took over on bass, Al Killer, free from prison rejoined for the studio sessions and a short tour in support. They announced their breakup in 1990.

Ed was a dying Steve Sinclair super fan. A representative, a nurse employed by the family, approached Millions via the record label. Ed lived in the whole top floor of a six-unit corner building on 23rd St. on the far West Side. His family owned the building. He wanted the last days of his life to be a Werewolves song. He wanted to fucking party.

"Come hang out with Ed, it would mean the world to him. He doesn't have long. He was there at CBGB 1980! Webster Hall '86, does that ring a bell?"

Millions and Sinclair moved into the apartment. They watched videos of legendary shows from around the world, Italy 87, Japan 89, LA 1992. The luminaries of early '80s hardcore and punk passed through: Jerry Murder, Steve Piss, Mike Massive, Mike Jones, and the Tattooer Eddie Mad Dog. Guys who'd jammed with Dee Dee Ramone, Walter Lure's band, The Cro-Mags at CBGB in the '80s. Anyone Sinclair or Millions would call a friend was invited over to party and listen to bootlegs of Right Sector, Race Rock, Satan 83.

Lower East Side dealers Bad Mike and Diamond stopped by three times a day. The punks in Tompkins, Washington Sq, Union Sq, and Astor Place all made trips to 23rd St. to hang out with Sinclair and Millions, buy them heroin or beg free hits off of Ed.

Joanne Pardes and Jacques Anzu climbed the stairs to Ed's apartment. A Murder Junkies track played through the wall. Jacques knocked on the door. A punk in his late thirties with a tallboy in his hand opened the door. Sinclair and Millions came out to greet them. Sinclair was in a bathrobe, tighty whities stained with piss and cum. WEREWOLF across his chest, the 4Ps on his stomach. Millions wore his signature leather pants and vest, a photorealistic Manson on his chest, WEREWOLF across his collar bone. Punk Rock Laurel and Hardy, obese and rail thin. Millions tipped his leather cowboy hat to Joanne. She nodded back.

Steve Sinclair rested a tallboy on his gut between his pierced tits. "Hey fellers, this is my friend Jacques! This motherfucker's a world-famous photographer, he's taking my picture today."

Anyone awake waved hello, grumbled what's up.

"You're some kind of cop, man?" 730 came out of the kitchen. "Who you know, man?"

"Sinclair invited me here, who are you, man?"

Sinclair got between the two. "730, chill out, don't make me warn you again. I just introduced the guy myself and now you're questioning who my friends are? It's time you start pulling your weight around here, pal."

"Steve, you brought a scorpion into the spot."

"Give me a reason, 730! There's a lot of bench sitters around here."

730 relented. He had light brown skin, peroxide bleached hair, buzzed a half inch long, scars on his lip and neck. "I didn't mean anything disrespectful, man. This is my family, anyone goes to jail in the next week, anyone I don't know has a problem, feel me?"

"Whatever, man."

"Why don't you take my picture then? All good, right?"

"Find me when I'm all set up. I just got here."

"I can get you something?" asked Sinclair.

"What's everybody up to?"

"We're partying, man. We've got dope, we've got coke, we've got base and wet…"

"Let's do some coke."

Sinclair took Jacques into Ed's room to meet his host. "Jacques Anzu, meet Ed, the realest motherfucker I've met in years."

"Cool place, man." Jacques took Ed's picture, sitting up in bed, sunken in and faded, next to Sinclair, bloated and worn out. He dedicated a roll of film to Ed's bedroom. To his pills and IV drip, his sharps container, his laundry basket.

Jacques followed Sinclair around the house, stealing candid shots. He stepped over garbage and house guests. He avoided corners, walls, furniture, didn't touch anything.

Joanne stayed and listened to Ed rant. "The eighties was supposed to be another sixties. I wanted to see the year 2000. Now I'll be dead within the year, half my friends are already gone…" He asked Joanne to leave him alone, he went to sleep. She pulled out a marker and found an empty spot on the wall, HXLNX. She wandered into the living room and found Jacques. He blocked out a series of photos where Sinclair, Millions and Joanne passed a crack pipe and blew smoke into the glare from the West Side.

Jacques shot portraits from whoever was willing to be photographed, stole more shots of guys on the nod or fixing behind a corner. He documented the graffiti, the broken furniture, holes in the walls, bottles overflowing with hypos. He shot tags: ENGLISH – PEZ – 667 CRU – PUKE – POLAK – EVIL STEVE – STRAPS – SPAZ – NCV – 8EN/MAKH/A10.

Jacques felt the crash come on from the lines Sinclair gave him. The scene grew overwhelmingly depressing.

"Hey, Joanne, it's time to split."

Ed's body was a time bomb. The whole conceit, the only reason Ed would give his home over to the drug culture was that he was about to die, and the sooner the better really. He made his death into a spectacle, something interesting when most of the death he saw around him was rote, interchangeable, devoid of personality.

The party lasted six months. When the coroner arrived, they were horrified at the conditions Ed died under: syringes carpeted the floors. Every surface was covered in spent 40s and beer cans, two liters of coke, almost everything overflowing with piss. Cigarette butts, wrappers, blunt guts, abandoned shit stained clothes. DEMONIKKK'S NOMADS WUZ HERE, HYPO CREW $$, GG ALLIN SCUMFUC, 88 RIOT CRU, SiNCERiOUS, HATRED – SEATTLE WA… The Missing Foundation Martini Glass, the Circle A, Swastikas, hand prints.

Removing the body was an occupational health issue. Thousands of needles everywhere, the cum, shit and piss… There was a splash of blood across the wall of one of the hallways from when Mitch from Demonikkk's stabbed 7.30 in the arm. Furniture had been broken apart, lit on fire then pissed on. Knives and ninja stars dotted the walls. Nothing of value was left. The kitchen appliances were sold off, as was most of the furniture. The paramedics refused to enter. A gang of punks carried Ed's body into the hallway.

Chapter 19

Hilaria, September 1994

George Moynihan, reporter for *HYPE MACHINE*, sat at the corner windows, across from Claire and Lexie. He recorded their conversation and took notes in his pad. "Clarie Labas, Lexie G. Hinnon, thank you for taking the time."

"Oh, it's not a problem," said Claire. "Today was good for me."

"You just got back from LA?"

"Palm Springs. I went to Joshua Tree, experienced Death Valley."

"Business or pleasure?"

"I walk the line of business and pleasure every day," said Claire, pleased with herself. "Vacation."

"It's been a busy year, if anyone deserves a break…"

"It's so important to take care of yourself, to get out of the daily grind. New York can be a tough place, so much competition, so much aggressive behavior. Even if you're not looking for trouble, if you're a successful person, negativity will pursue you. Everyone you meet, they almost always want something from you. It's so hard to make new meaningful relationships when you're a public figure. You have a lot of people who feel as though I haven't actually earned your success and whatever you've made for yourself is really theirs. So much entitlement. You can't let them in. Once they're in, there's no way to get them out. They're in the walls."

"What do you mean?"

"Sometimes, you need to burn sage when a person leaves your house, OK?" Lexie cut in.

"This is something I've always noticed in the fashion world. The parasites who hang around models…" said Moynihan.

"It's why no one in Hilaria has a boyfriend," said Lexie. "They'll start dating a guy because he's in a play off Broadway or like on a billboard but then the play is over and he's just sort of there, hanging out on the couch.

They'll just be there until some other girl shows up, thinks he's hot, takes him off your hands. Take your lovers and move on. It's, like, the '90s, come on."

"George, have you read *Managing Modern Life* by Alice Walsh?" asked Claire.

"Can't say I have."

"It's genius!"

"George, you really should read it," Lexie added.

"There's a whole chapter in there about making sure you're never limited by the company you keep. This is something that's very important to me. We're curating an entire way of life here and it only takes one person's negativity to throw everything into question."

Moynihan made a note. "Claire you've said Hilaria is the New Factory and you're the New Warhol. Does that make Lexie your Edie Sedgwick?"

"Absolutely." Lexie cut back in. "I would die to stay hot."

Claire's eyes rolled back behind her sunglasses. Moynihan bit his lip, crossed his legs. What a fucking quote. He stumbled for something witty. "You'd? Jump out a window?"

"Yeah, sure." She dragged a parliament and looked at the smoke, stayed aloof, on brand.

"Lexie, this fall has been big for you."

"Right, we had Fashion Week, Lexie G. Hinnon, Morgan Gold, Marina Jay, all over the place. You couldn't miss us. I walked half the shows that week because no one defines the times like Hilaria, OK? They're, out there, like catching up with us. "

Moynihan nodded his head. "You're setting the tempo."

"Absolutely."

"Tell us about your plans, Claire."

"Sky's the limit. We have our Halloween parties coming up. It'll be Friday through Monday. We'll have DJ's, performances, fashion, installation art. We'll have magic…"

"What about long-term?"

"By next year, Hilaria will be world-famous. We'll be the word. We'll be, like, the symbol. We'll be the face of this scene."

"I was at your 1994 New Year's Eve party. What an incredible event!"

"Thank you," said Claire.

"When I was on the dance floor, bumping up against who knows how many people, dancing to incredible music, the energy it was through the roof. I've never experienced anything like it. And I suppose my question is what's going on there?"

"Here, at Hilaria?" asked Lexie.

"How do you create that feeling? I've spoken to dozens of people who were there that night and they've all said something similar, there was an energy none of us had ever experienced."

"You were experiencing Hilaria. That's what we strive to create, an experience you can never forget," said Claire. "It's true. We created a burst of energy that could have taken down an airplane. That's what we set out to do and we did it."

"But how?"

"You pack the house, you give your people spectacle, something they've never heard before, seen before, every sense is enriched. That sense of discovery, that's what our new year's events are all about."

"It was almost... magical?"

"Not almost."

"There was magic involved?"

"Of course. That's what the party scene is, it's an energy source. All those people, full of desire and adrenaline and excitement. It's erotic! You can take that energy and bottle it, temporarily, but you can bottle it. We invited a witch to come to my bedroom and at the stroke of midnight performed a ritual, channeling that energy and letting it run through us, myself, Lexie, Joanne and her friend. This was private, before they performed for all of our guests. We communed with the third mind that event created."

"*Third mind?* For our readers who don't know?"

"Right now, as you and I speak, the third mind is shaping our conversation just as much as you or I am, your questions, my answers, they're both... informed by our third mind, which is independent of either of us, but once we've created something together, it's real. It's as real as anything else, this table, your pen."

"Fascinating, and you're saying on new year's at Hilaria that entity was, born?"

"Not born, but manifested, I'd say."

"What does it do, or want?"

"What do you want? What do I want? Think of our motivations, either of us, swirl them together, now imagine your interests are no longer yours but someone else, are you following?"

"I think so."

"This is such an important idea. This is why raves, these mass events, with dance music, they're one of the most potent tools we have for creating new consciousnesses."

"What are you doing with this energy?"

"We're using it, believe me," said Lexie.

Chapter 20

January 1994

From '87–'94, Joanne Pardes worked irregular shifts at an S&M dungeon called Buckles on 30th St., the sixth floor of an old office building off 5th Avenue. The owner, Joel Wolfgang claimed status as a warlock. He'd conceived of dozens of magical rituals. Whenever the stars aligned, he carried them out in his living room. He claimed to channel the rituals from a voice that came to him in his dreams. "A matronly Southern gentle lady."

He lived on West Broadway, just south of Houston in an old factory conversion which he owned alongside the building next door. He rented out the lofts next door and the storefront below to the long list of designers setting up in Soho. At night he had the building to himself.

Wolfgang's hands were decked with rings. He wore a brown leather vest with a black and red pinstripe shirt and black and red embroidered leather pants. His cape, a newsie cap and a bowler hung on the coat rack. A walking stick with a scorpion trapped in amber as a handle leaned on his thigh. Jacques Anzu's *Dance for Moloch* hung over his mantle.

Joanne Pardes brought Linda over to meet Wolfgang. He dropped down with a sigh onto his couch. "You know what this calls for?" he asked rhetorically. Linda sensed Joanne's excitement. Wolfgang took out a box, selected two bags out of several and began cutting up two separate white powders on dedicated mirrors. "Coke on the left, K on the right. Here… start with this coke." He took his lines first, gave Joanne the mirror.

He went in for the ketamine as Joanne went in for the blow. Wolfgang hit a button on a remote control. He played Death in June's *The World That Summer* on powerful speakers. Wolfgang relaxed on the couch, lit a Black and directed his gaze at Linda. She snorted the ketamine. She looked back at him. Joanne elevated.

"Bright future, Mistress Linda." He took his rings off one by one, lining them up, facing him on the table. A skull, a 4P, an iron cross, a pentagram.

He was short, 5'5", a big mustache, angular jaw, tight muscles. He pressed his weight. Dumbbells and barbells had a corner of the apartment. Thick salt and pepper chest hair poked out of his shirt. "You know what I like about you? You get with the program. You're not a complainer, you have a good attitude. If you keep that up sky's the limit. You could have a career. You could have a..." He stopped to think. "... you could have a career. Attitude is everything. Positivity is key. Thoughts, you understand, are made of matter just like this table. Thoughts have angel wings, Linda." Wolfgang nodded his head and she began to nod along with him.

"Magickal things happen when people cross paths with me. I can be a guide. Now that we know each other, you'll notice synchronicities, incredible things will start to happen. You wouldn't be the first who has had the opportunity to call me a mentor, or a guru. I've been known to help break down barriers inside a student's mind, freeing them forever from their hang-ups, for instance, so they can attain greatness. It all starts with the right attitude. What you need to do is picture what you want in your mind, you need to concentrate on it, visualize it, manifest it. Every great power, since the dawn of civilization has understood that power derives from the mind. Your power, the energy that – I can tell you Linda there are *intense* powers emanating off you. That energy, your energy, can be directed to do literally anything, Linda. Your thoughts are only different from this table, the brick and steel this building is made of, by degree. What do they all have in common? They can all be shaped, worked into new things. This mirror, Linda, is vibrating. The wood under our feet, it's vibrating. Everything is vibrating. It's only a matter of degree. Do you want to learn how to solve these mysteries, Linda?"

"I think so." The K relaxed her jaw.

"Think harder."

"I do."

"Linda, you see, I'm what we call ascended. We're chosen at birth, we arrive evolved. Do you understand?"

"I... think so."

"As we approach the epoch, more of us are ascending. We, the ascended are the *axis mundi* between earth, the cosmos, the material and the angelic. And I'm offering you the opportunity to consort with angels... Have some more coke, I see you want to. *Do what thou wilt*, Linda. It shall be the whole of the law." He smiled, nodded, licked his lips. "Linda, I want you to come and take a seat on this chair, over here."

Wolfgang stood up. He turned the music off. The silence brought Joanne back to the room. "Hey what's up?"

"I'm sharing technology with our Linda, she's about to learn the power of auditing... Linda, I want you to take a seat." Wolfgang sat down in a chair spaced two feet apart from an identical piece. Le Corboursier chairs, black cubes, leather with deep seats and high backs. "Get comfortable, put your arms up, very good. Linda, I want you to start breathing, not an automatic breath. I want you to think about how you breathe. I want you to start by breathing in and then holding your breath and then exhaling. These are each separate motions. They each are part of the whole. They each matter and without one, the other two would not suffice to keep us alive. So, breathe, one... two... three... Excellent, now do it again." He stopped talking to inhale, pause, and exhale. "One, two, three... All right, excellent, don't stop, focus on what you're doing, hear my voice, listen to what I say, but focus on your breathing... Breathe in, hold, exhale. That's right."

Joanne watched Wolfgang at work, fascinated, one leg up on the couch, back against the armrest.

"Say something, Linda."

"Hi."

"Hi. Yes. Hello. Now Linda, I want you to call up your first happy memory. The first time you remember smiling."

"I was on the beach."

"Good. Now go back and retrieve more information me, bring it back here. Tell me more."

"I was on the beach. Kids from the neighborhood, we played in the waves."

"Good, now tell me again, more details."

"It was a summer day, at the beach. With my neighbors from next door. We went to the beach off our street. Beach 10th Street. We played in the water. We ran into the ocean when the water receded and we ran away from the waves."

"Again, tell me more."

"I was three years old. We went to the beach with our neighbors, the Moskos. We went to Beach Ten. We set up a blanket on the sand. We ate sandwiches from home. The children, we played in the water. We ran into the ocean when the waves receded and we ran away when the waves came in. I was laughing, smiling. I would laugh hardest when the waves hit the backs of my legs, my feet." Linda smiled, recounting each detail.

Wolfgang stroked his chin, legs splayed against the leather of his chair. "Now you understand the process, how to retrieve details, bring them together, how to begin ordering your mind. Now, Linda, I want you to recall a memory that brings you pain."

"I nearly drowned, when I was younger."

"Tell me from the beginning."

"I went to the ocean and I walked in and a wave swallowed me up. I blacked out under the water, I thought I was going to die or that I was dying. I barely knew what it meant, I didn't know that I could die, I thought just animals, birds or fish died. I woke up on the sand. I was OK, just terrified and all alone…"

"Tell me, from the beginning, retrieving more data, go deep, into the cabinet and pull it out."

"I was asleep, I got out of bed. I left the house, and I walked to the ocean. I walked across the sand and then I walked into the water. I had never been deeper than my knees, that's when we turned around, but I kept going. I felt the water at my waist, I walked until the water sometimes it splashed and it hit my chin. That's when the wave came. I was under, I didn't know what to do. I didn't know how to swim. The salt hurt my eyes, I shut them. I thought I was going to die. I didn't know that I could die, I thought just animals, birds or fish or cats died. But I realized that I was going to die. It hurt, the shells at the bottom of the ocean floor they were sharp they scraped my skin. At first I just heard the sound of the water, and the waves but then all I could hear was laughter. They were laughing at me. I felt so ashamed and I was so afraid to die and they were laughing!"

Tears fell down Linda's face, her eyes stayed shut. "They wouldn't stop. There were so many of them, it was so loud… They didn't stop laughing. It didn't stop until I was out of the water, I just, just as suddenly as I was under water I was back on the beach, on the sand. And I began to breathe again. I vomited salt water onto the sand I buried it so no one could see. I ran back home. It was only two blocks but it seemed so much longer. I was running away from the sound, the laughter, whatever it was. I went back to bed. I threw out the clothes I was wearing when I was under the water. I didn't want them to recognize me."

Joel Wolfgang watched the contortions of Linda's face. He savored his entree into her mind, crossed his legs, lit a new Black. He grinned ear to ear, a gold tooth shimmering. "Great job, Linda. Now go back to the beginning and tell me everything, all over again…"

***

That night Joel Wolfgang woke up from a nightmare. He remembered every detail. He could recall it like a movie, play it back, over and over. He dreamed he was splayed across a wooden table, strapped down with leather, cut open and disemboweled. His organs were dropped into a fire, one by one, sacrifices to Inana. He screamed himself awake. He hyperventilated his way to the kitchen where he drank water until he calmed his breathing. He poured a scotch and down the hatch. He lit a black. "Oh fuck." He poured another finger of whiskey. "Oh fuck, *whew.*" He massaged his cock, poured another shot.

He returned to bed; the booze calmed him. The tobacco grounded him. *Who am I? Who am I?* "I'm Joel fucking Wolfgang, I'm in my goddamned bedroom and I'm jerking off, motherfucker!"

Wolfgang went back to sleep with a pillow between his knees. He snored when he went near alcohol. He dreamed he was swimming through cool water, fast, keeping pace with the dolphins. *Tremendous.* Deep underwater, he heard the voices in the distance. Gasps, astonished laughter. He understood, in the context of the dreams, that he'd won the favor of the mermaids. He'd never been calmer, more serene. He could breathe underwater. He was flying! Just as suddenly he was awake, late morning. He noticed wet sheets. He pulled them off the mattress on his way out of bed. He turned his rolodex to G, made a call. He put on a pair of leather pants, black vest and long black jacket, his cape and his Derby hat. He put on his six rings. He hailed a taxi to the Maria Grim Gallery.

Chapter 21

Fall 1994

Amanda woke up in Bad Mike's bed, paralyzed. She dreamed of a dismemberment. Amanda watched demons, indifferent to pain and suffering, torture innocents for their entertainment at the foot of her bed. They disemboweled a body. The screams pierced her eardrums. They laughed, they licked their lips, they drooled. Frenzy in their eyes. They looked at her. "Amanda! Amanda! Watch! Look at us! LISTEN TO ME!"

Her shaking woke Bad Mike up and he pulled her out. "It was a nightmare. It's all right babe. Just a dream. You're all right, you're all right." He went to get her a drink of water.

"Don't go!"

"I'm not going anywhere." He took a hair tie off his wrist and pulled his dreads back. He gave her a glass of water and a fresh cigarette. He sat silently while she calmed herself down. They fixed and went back to bed. She clung to him, cried in her sleep. He stared at the ceiling until he dozed off.

Amanda and Bad Mike developed the plan together. She'd let Saul find her again. They'd meet near The River. She'd make him take her to cop. The trap worked, just as planned. Saul and Amanda met on Avenue C. He kissed her forehead. She let him do it. "I knew you'd come to your senses."

"I can't imagine like, hiding forever…"

"Finally!" He kissed her on the lips. She tried to relax. He moved his hands under her shirt and across her back.

"Let's get well first, hold on."

Saul pulled back. "All right, all right. I get you." He lit a smoke. "So, you're getting well now?"

"Is that a problem?"

"No. No, I think it's hot."

"Come on." Amanda bit her lip. They pushed South on C to 6th St. and then they turned toward The River. They walked the footbridge over the FDR. Amanda stayed ahead of Saul. She hid her face with knockoff Ray Bans. She kept her hood up and her hands in her pockets.

"You know Amanda I'm working on a new piece. Have you heard of Daniel Rakowitz? Sure, you have, he fed his girlfriend's head to the bums in Tompkins Square. You remember that, right? I'm going to do a screenplay. So much potential there…"

"This is where they said to wait. Do you have the money?"

"Yeah, yeah, here." He pulled a roll of twenties out of his pocket and gave it over.

"Just wait here, behind the wall." That was the signal. She heard Bad Mike come out from behind the bathrooms. He rushed Saul from behind. He drove him into the wall of the footbridge, smashed his nose and forehead into the concrete. Amanda turned around to watch, equally repelled and fascinated. Bad Mike stabbed Saul one punch after the other, lungs first to keep him from screaming. He cut intestine, the liver and kidneys, under and through the ribs. Saul bled, choked on blood and shit. He looked over at Amanda, recognized she wanted this finished so she could run away, so she could get away with this. Her fear signaled to Saul there was no way he would survive. She needed Saul to stop breathing before the cops came. Bad Mike wrapped his arm around Saul's neck, kept him steady while he searched for the one hit that shut his lights out. He felt Saul's body go limp, let him fall against the wall. They ran off. Amanda bit her lip again, tasted blood.

Bad Mike lived at 10th St. Squat, between C and D. They crossed the FDR and *walked* home. No running, nothing suspicious. Amanda was immediately paranoid. She felt exposed on the street, anyone looking out the hundreds of windows she'd passed since they crossed the highway would know who she was. They'd remember her face. Everyone knew. Amanda imagined a world without TV, radio, newspapers, magazines, porn. People just looked out their windows, waiting for murder suspects to flee the scene. What about security cameras? What about dog walkers, joggers? They were the ones who found the bodies, right?

For Bad Mike, the adrenaline was like a shot of coke. No one would ever know shit. No one saw shit, no one heard shit. The River was a dangerous place for a guy like Saul. Bad Mike wore gloves, a ski mask and a leather jacket. He was going to burn their clothes in a trash can in the back of the squat. He'd get rid of the knife, but outside the neighborhood. Bad Mike put his hand inside Amanda's clothes, felt up her skin. He directed her left hand to the bulge in his jeans. She looked up and he nodded to her. "When we get back its Scotty for a while, keep this going, then I'm gonna fuck the shit out of you, babe."

"Yeah, cool." Amanda was barely listening. She liked the idea of getting high. She was ready to feel something new.

"I've got a big-ass rock back at the spot. We've got dope and fresh works for when we come down."

The thought made the paranoia bearable. They made it back to 10th Street. Bad Mike took his keys out. They got inside the building. Bad Mike locked the deadbolt behind him. They went upstairs and into the apartment. They got away with it.

Chapter 22

September 1994

Joanne Pardes hailed a taxi on 10th Avenue straight to Joel Wolfgang's apartment. He rang her up, opened the door in a bandanna and a silk robe. The loft smelled like weed. Wolfgang smoked Hashplant by the QP. "Joanne. I haven't seen you in months. What are you up to? How's that little number you brought over, your protege?"

"Linda, she's, she's trying, I guess?"

"Oh, she's not giving you what you need?"

"I'm trying to reach someone, they're trying to reach me and I'm trying to use... Linda is trying to – I'm trying to use her to reach this..."

"You almost lied, there. A plot hole..."

"I'm trying to use her to reach Helene. We're not doing it."

"I can sense a lie before it's out of someone's mouth. What are you hiding?"

"Nothing."

"What do you want?"

"I want to break through."

The hairs on the back of Wolfgang's neck stood up. "Is that so?"

"I know you've done it before. I want you to do it with me."

"Your desire is central, but your *willingness* to submit. There's always something stopping you. It's natural. But it's in the way. It needs to be destroyed."

"What is it?"

"You have to tell me. Why are you ashamed? Why are you afraid? Why won't you do what you have to do?" Wolfgang tapped a vial of coke and made a pile on the table. He licked his index finger. He picked a razor blade off the glass. He cut up thick lines. He inhaled and resumed his stare. "I'm going to wash and anoint myself. Stay here, think about what you want. What you really want."

"OK." She snorted what Wolfgang left her, lit a Camel. She thought about Helene. Her eyelashes, her nose, her teeth, her burn scars, her shoulders, her knees.

Wolfgang returned with a safety pin run through the bridge of his nose. His robe was open. He shaved his pubes. His prick, around four inches, was doused with essential oils. He pulled a bag of pure MDMA from his robe. "We're going to draw a circle; we're going to break barriers. Go to the kitchen and get me some salt."

Joanne followed Wolfgang's command. She drew a pentagram on the floor in salt. She took off her clothes. "Do what it takes," she said.

Joel Wolfgang prayed from between Joanne's legs. "I DEMAND YOU SHARE YOUR SECRETS FOR I AM WORTHY! I DEMAND YOU SHOW ME THE VIEW FROM THE LAND OF THE DEAD! I AM AVAILABLE TO YOU, LISTEN TO ME. IN THE NAME OF LUCIFER, ACCEPT MY GIFTS, ACCEPT MY OFFERING. LISTEN TO ME. IN THE NAME OF LUCIFER ACCEPT MY OFFERING, SHOW YOURSELF TO ME. LISTEN TO ME. DECLARE YOURSELF, SHOW ME, SHOW ME. LISTEN TO ME."

Joanne looked down. Wolfgang's hands gripped her knees, he held himself upright. "I HAVE ALREADY WALKED THE PATH OF THE LORD OF ILLUMINATION, THE LORD OF ENRICHMENT. I HAVE ALREADY SWORN MYSELF TO LUCIFER. I HAVE DECLARED MY LOVE!" Joanne felt his screams vibrate in her asshole. She grabbed the back of his head, she dug her nails into his neck and scalp, she pulled him in.

Joanne raised her first. "HAIL LUCIFER!" She humped his face. He spread her ass open. "SHOW YOURSELF TO ME!" She wrapped her legs around Wolfgang's head. She summoned Helene to the front of her mind. Helene's dreadlocks like Medusa's snakes. Helene's tattoos on her sternum, her arms, and lower back. Her piercings in her ears, her septum, her tongue, her nipples. Her body hair, her scars, freckles, moles, birth marks. How she liked to paint her toenails, the hair ties she kept around her wrist. "HAIL LUCIFER! HAIL LUCIFER!"

Wolfgang felt the vibrations gather at the base of Joanne's spine. He sucked harder, he increased his tempo, he slipped his other fingers inside, pushed deeper. He stood up to watch her cum. He forced her knees apart. He put his arm around Joanne's neck. He barked at her. "Piss on me, piss on my cock." Joanne arched her back. She forced the stream forward it bounced off his chest and his gut. "Say it."

"HAIL LUCIFER!" Joanne dug her nails into Wolfgang's back. He reached back and smacked her across the face.

"Louder!"

"HAIL LUCIFER!" She gyrated, wrapped her legs around him. "HAIL THE LORD OF ENRICHMENT! HAIL LUCIFER! HAIL THE LORD OF REVELATION!" He pulled on her hair. He turned her around. He fucked her from behind.

"LISTEN TO ME! I AM WORTHY OF THE SECRETS OF THE DEAD! I AM THE MASTER OF THIS DOMAIN!" Wolfgang felt the rumbling in the soles of his feet. He pulled his prick out and spread Joanne's ass open. "I AM THE MASTER OF THIS DOMAIN!"

Joanne screamed, "HAIL LUCIFER!"

Wolfgang pulled out and exploded. "HAIL LUCIFER! I AM THE MASTER OF THIS DOMAIN! HAIL LUCIFER!"

Joanne intoned; she felt his load hit her back. "HAIL LUCIFER! HAIL LUCIFER!" She concentrated. She shut her eyes. She let her incantation take her to Helene. She recalled her features. She felt a stream of piss hit her shoulder. He pulled her hair back.

"I'm the master of this domain," he said, looking down, nodding.

She sucked, she gagged, she slammed her soft palate into him until she wretched and vomited on his stomach. Diet coke, Oxy Contin, Atavan, ecstasy, her ulcer.

Chapter 23

October 1994

Joanne Pardes devoted Autumn to channeling Helene. She told Linda to stop shaving and to change her brand of cigarettes from Reds to Camels. Joanne tied one of Helene's dreadlocks into Linda's hair. She pierced the cartilage in Linda's right ears and put in one of Helene's studs. Lexie pierced Linda's nipples and put in Helene's U rings.

Helene Asher was always stoned so they drank Green Dragon, a tincture made of Devil's Springs and Bleecker Street 8's. They carried out Helene's channeling ritual, another seance in the kitchen with Lexie and Morgan. Claire didn't participate. In the morning, Joanne, Lexie, and Linda walked from Hilaria to Port Authority. They took a bus to Kingston and a taxi to Woodstock the next day. They brought the green dragon, a half ounce of weed, a bottle of Oxy Contin, some freebase, and the witches' broomstick – the acacia, henbane and datura infusion.

They checked into a motel outside of Woodstock. Lexie locked herself in the bathroom with a bottle of laxatives and smoked all the crack she brought with her. It was a separate stash from what Joanne and Linda brought. Joanne took Polaroids of Linda. The room was varying shades of brown and tan, all the same by degree. Linda was thin, pale, dehydrated, tired from travel, long nights of ritual magick, and daily drug binges. She was on her period; the ritual was timed to it. Joanne put the camera down, they piled into one of the twin beds. Lexie had her own for whenever she left the bathroom.

The next morning, they took a taxi to a burnt-out barn house on the edge of some woods. "This is the place," said Joanne. She hustled into the structure. No ceiling, three walls, and an unstable loft. Linda trailed behind. Her bag was heavy. She made it inside, put her load down and collapsed against her pack. Joanne walked the perimeter. Someone kept the place relatively tame; the weed growth was only months old. The remains of the barn, save for the loft, were steady. "This is where we did it. *Scarlet Woman 89*."

They waited for the sun to set. Joanne ran Linda and Lexie through their roles in the ritual. She recalled the steps they took five years back. Linda would take Helene's role. Lexie would perform as Jacques Anzu. Joanne resumed her role. She spoke her lines exactly as she had before.

Joanne spray painted a pentagram ringed with eight eight-pointed stars. The three women entered the circle. Joanne led the invocation. "We invoke Helene Asher. LISTEN TO ME. We invoke you, Helene. LISTEN TO ME."

Linda felt herself float above the circle, into the ether, the air under her body. Lexie worked her fist into Linda. Joanne, in her pose at the base of the pentagram, continued her incantation. "We invoke Helene Asher. LISTEN TO ME. We invoke you, Helene. LISTEN TO ME."

Lexie's intensity never wavered. Linda writhed, gasping. Lexie's arm was painted in blood up to her elbow. Linda hissed, gnashed her teeth. Joanne locked eyes with Lexie, nodded her head, exhaled from her nose. Lexie masturbated with her free hand, the energy spiraled upwards, into a mist of copper and salt, piss, spit, days of sweat. Each motion generated new frictions, more energy, more force. Lexie and Linda came. Joanne screamed at the moon, tears and spit, sweat from the heat underneath her body. "We invoke Helene Asher. LISTEN TO ME. We invoke you, Helene. LISTEN TO ME."

Lexie and Linda collapsed on the grass. Joanne waited for an answer.

The bus ride back from Kingston was tense and mostly silent. Linda slept, curled up against the window. Lexie and Joanne glared at each other for two hour long stretches, punctuated with some light reading, *Vogue* and *The Voice* respectively. The bus stopped at a rest area and most of the passengers got off to smoke. Joanne and Lexie entered their second hour of sneering. Linda ran off the bus and quickly sucked down most of a Camel before it was time to hit the road again.

"Why didn't you wake me up? It's fucked up you can't smoke on the bus anymore." Linda was thirteen when Greyhound banned smoking. "Jo, can I listen to your Nick Cave tape?"

"Whatever you want Linda."

All aboard! Back on the highway, Lexie turned from indifferent toward Linda to vaguely affectionate. She offered Linda a Xanax and her magazine. She watched Joanne read the Voice. Linda and Lexie had both showered in the motel before they headed back to the city. Joanne was smeared with dirt, she stunk of BO and Linda's blood.

They took a cab back to Hilaria and began planning for Halloween.

Chapter 24

The Lower East Side, 1989–1994

DJ San Lo was an underground staple since the late eighties when he showed up in the Lower East Side with a trunk full of broadcasting equipment. He moved into 10th St. Squat and set out to launch a pirate radio station. A series of dance parties in SOHO and the Lower East Side called *The Nine Elixirs* bolstered the station. An impressive list of DJ's and promoters coalesced around the signal, 537 RADIO and did what they could to hold him up. The project was run on a shoestring budget with mostly stolen equipment. The guerrilla structures and illegal nature of the station didn't make for less work. An FCC license would have let them set up a permanent location, broadcast live 24/7. Just as much of San Lo's creative energies had to go into evading the feds, corporate radio, CON-ED, and the cops. The signal covered most of Manhattan, South Bronx, Staten Island, parts of Brooklyn, a corner of Hoboken. San Lo broadcasted three or four nights a week.

"Yo, it's the neo-beatnick Anarcho magickal revolutionary. Abject, seedy, liberated, self-sufficient – enlightened, self-interested. Yo, you were taught you were an animal. You're really a machine... It's DJ San Lo this is 537 Radio, what's up, people? What are we getting into? What are we doing tonight? We're rising up, we're rising... to the occasion? What's up? Yo, I was walking the streets last night, had my headphones on, I was one with the streets, you know? I was listening to this tape that my fam made for me, and each time I turned a street corner, you know, every time I hit a new block, the music it made sense for that moment. Magick, yo. Like every time I took a step, the music just corresponded to the movement, it just, felt so right. So, this goes out to fam, you know who you are. This tape, this mix is so inspired, so brilliantly arranged that I just have to play it in full. I'm just hoping that whatever you all are getting into, whatever you're getting into right this minute has this level of inspiration, the thoughtfulness.

Mixtapes are art, man. This tape is high art. And that's what I'm opening the show with tonight. A'ight, a'ight. Let's do this. This tape opens with a track by Shotgun and Treasure, and how could it not right? If you're in touch with the underground right now, 1994, you're listening to Shotgun and Treasure. Let's get tonight's action started. Viva the revolution!"

Excerpted from an interview with Jacques Anzu, 1996–7

The organizer of the Nine Elixirs parties, DJ San Lo died of an overdose in 1995 leaving a just massive hole in the scene. I think San Lo was just as significant a loss as anything that went down at Hilaria. I thought the best events going on from maybe 1991 until they ended was the Nine Elixirs Parties. It was the final days of new material. Soon after, everything was a pastiche. You found novelty in the use of the material or the biography of the artist instead. *Hey this producer is a schizo, this DJ killed three hitchhikers!* The community kept Nine Elixirs going but without San Lo at the center, the community that he had cultivated almost immediately fractured. The Garden of the Immortals Parties were an attempt to give the Nine Elixirs community somewhere to go. DJ Shakti Sun spun music she thought San Lo would play. She should have just been herself. The parties felt artificial, like self-consciously reverse engineered Nine Elixirs. The Garden of Immortals Parties faded out after six months, it was only years later where everybody decided the events were important, historic even. Mercury and Sulfur took over the promotion when the garden imploded. Just to be bitchy, they called the party Shiva Moon, the opposite of Shakti Sun.

Chapter 25

Halloween 1994

Joanne Pardes was excited. "Claire wants to see you!"

"What happened?"

"Come on, Beb." Linda got up. She gathered her Walkman and her cigarettes. They left Joanne's room and knocked Claire Labas' door.

Joanne walked away. Linda went inside, Joanne went back to her room. "Come on in. Close the door." Claire sat at her vanity in a silk robe, smoking a Marlboro Light. Her bedroom was bigger than any other section of the loft. Massive windows, blocked off from the street with screens. One of Maria Grim's Afghan tapestries hung behind her king-sized bed. She handed Linda a mirror with yellow coke cut into lines. Linda took two and put the mirror down nervous she'd drop it.

"You're so hot," said Claire. She took a couple drags while Linda beamed. She did a line. "Joanne *loves* you, I like you... we should talk."

"Claire, thank you."

"Yeah. So, what do you want, Linda?"

"I dunno. To, like, be like all of you."

Claire smiled, a broken k-9. "To be like Joanne?"

"Oh my god she's incredible."

"You can keep staying here..." She took another line and gave Linda the mirror. "Someone is coming over tonight. I want you to stick with him, stay by his side."

Joanne gave Linda a vial. She nodded her head and slipped it in her pocket. "Don't do any of it, all right? Find DJ San Lo. Get him alone, get him back at his place. Give him *this*." Joanne ran a hand through Linda's hair. Linda's eyes fluttered. "Ah, Linda." Joanne's speech was slowed down to a drawl. "Here's two rolls." She put them in Linda's hand, closed Linda's fist and kissed it. "I'll be here if you need me, Beb." She lowered her sunglasses, lit a cigarette, and lay back across her bed.

Linda left Joanne's bedroom, she peaked into Claire's. The door was open and a pack of Claire's friends blew coke and pawed at each other, screeching nasal laughter. Linda floated past the dance floor. Lexie, Morgan, Marina and Britney danced with the creeps who hung out by the windows. Jungle music blasted over the PA. Revelers held onto water bottles and sucked pacifiers. Sweat and cologne hung in the air.

Linda found San Lo waiting for the bathroom. She stopped and watched him talk with his hands. He pontificated in the direction of an art critic who listened with one ear. San Lo pulled a bag out of his jacket pocket, dug a key inside and took a heavy bump. He offered hits to the art critic. The line moved. San Lo continued, demeanors changed. The art critic sucked down a cigarette, listening, interjecting. He asked for more.

Linda caught San Lo leaving the bathroom. She grabbed him by the wrist. She took out the epills Joanne gave her. She put one in San Lo's mouth. He looked at her. She excited him.

"I need something to drink!" he yelled over the music. He pantomimed a drink and she read his lips. They went over to the bar. Linda cut the line and San Lo ordered waters. Linda took her pill. They danced to jungle, drum and bass. They sucked down their water. Linda felt the body heat from everyone around her. Her heartbeat synced with the music. She made sure not to let go of San Lo's waist.

He took her to the stairwell and whipped it out. Linda climbed up to him and sucked his cock. San Lo pulled a glass stem and a torch from his pocket. He packed the pipe, lit up, exhaled. "Yo, baby doll..."

She looked up, saw the pipe, grabbed his dick with both hands and sucked on the pipe, the coke was still burning. "Don't let it go to waste, baby." She exhaled, resumed the blowjob.

He pulled her hair, dug his nails into the base of her skull. He fucked her soft palate. He exploded, Linda pulled her head back and spit cum on the wall.

"Let's go back to your place," she said. "I want you to fuck me. Do it there."

Linda staggered around San Lo's apartment. "I'm so—fucked up."

"Yeah? Want some water?"

"Sure. Yeah..."

San Lo found a glass and opened the tap. He came back, Linda took the drink. "Hold on, I feel like having a line of something."

"Oh cool, here." Linda took Joanne's vial out of her jacket pocket and gave it to San Lo. "It's really good shit."

"Oh, thanks! Yo, you saved me a trip. I like you, girlie." He emptied it out and cut the powder into four lines. He did three. He suddenly looked up. Something was wrong. Linda saw panic in San Lo's face. His eyes read POISON.

She exploded upwards, she knocked over the CD case over and kicked it away, toward the wall, under the radiator. She watched him claw at his chest and neck, he tore his shirt open. His hand turned blue. He collapsed onto the table.

Linda put her hand on her mouth, she ran for the door. San Lo had locked everything. She turned knobs. She gasped, sobbed, her vision turned blurry. She managed the chain, unlocked the deadbolt and ran out the door. She ran down the stairs, into the street and three blocks to a community garden. The sun was beginning to rise. She cleared the fence, hid behind a tree and wept.

Chapter 26

ABC NO RIO, 1991

Helene Asher had lost so much weight she may have shrunk in height. She wore a turtleneck and tight jeans, big sunglasses. She cut her dreads off. She wore a beanie over her buzz cut. She wrapped herself in a black shawl to keep warm. "Good afternoon, thank you all for coming." She leaned on the podium, an unlit spliff in her hand. "Today I'm proud to introduce *Scarlet Woman 89.*"

The standing room only crowd burst into whoops and cheers. Instant quiet when the lights shut off. She took her seat between Jacques and Joanne against the wall. She leaned on Joanne's shoulder and lit the joint.

BECOME BABALON
OPEN TO: The old barn at the edge of the woods, decrepit and overgrown. Old gnarled trees, thick canopies, heavy shadows. Bright, mid-afternoon sun.
CUT TO: Helene stands over the camera and looks down. Blond dreadlocks that fall past her shoulders, lip and septum rings. Stainless steel half-moons in her nipples, ILDABOATH written across her sternum in a straight line. The camera lingers on the Tree of Life tattooed on her forearm. She gathers menstrual blood, running down her thigh to a ceremonial cup on the floor.
CUT TO: Over a black velvet blanket, inside a circle of salt. Joanne holds Helene's arm's, kneeling in hero pose. Helene writhes on the floor, mid orgasm, legs wrapped around Jacques Anzu who leans on Joanne's shoulders.
CUT TO: CLOSE UP: Jacques Anzu busts on Helene's stomach, Joanne collects the cum and mixes it with blood in their ceremonial cup.
CUT TO: THE RED WOMAN walks through an empty street at night.
CUT TO: Lit by their car's high beams, Helene sculpts an eight pointed

star out of salt. A figure wearing a black cape enters the frame. They take off their hood. Jacques has a shaved head, a black stripe painted across his face, over his eyes. Helene and Joanne carry a lamb, hog tied, into the middle of the circle. Joanne wears a black stripe painted across her eyes. Helene's stripe is in red. Helene holds the lamb in place. Jacques mouths an incantation. All three drop their robes simultaneously. Joanne has an eight pointed star painted on her back. She pulls a butcher's knife from out of the frame. Jacques joins Helene in restraining the lamb while Joanne slits its throat. Joanne and Jacques put their hands in the lamb's blood and smears it onto the Helene's body until she's painted red.

CUT TO: A trashcan fire rages.

CUT TO: Joanne and Jacques, backs to the cameras, on their knees before the Red Woman. She dips her finger into the cup and draws the seal of Babalon on each of their foreheads. She mouths a prayer.

CUT TO BLACK

CUT TO: *THE CYBER GRIMOIRE – SCARLET WOMAN 89*

Chapter 27

Excerpted from an interview with Morgan Gold, circa 1998

I watched Joanne snap. It was really scary, OK? Like days before everything happened, she was already terrifying. She was on the worst crack binge of her life and she wouldn't let me leave and remember, Joanne, she's like famous for doing shit with crack pipes. That was like one of her signatures, so that was like front of my mind the whole time…

She told me her whole life story. She was from Brooklyn, a really bad area. Really bad. That's why she did so well in the Lower East Side, even downtown, Brooklyn was tougher. But she didn't really know anything about art or the scene or anything until she met Helene Asher who taught her everything, helped her find herself. She gave her the look, the punk thing, that was Helene's look. Helene was a punk. She was obsessed with Patti Smith and Lydia Lunch; those were her two idols. She taught Joanne how to make video, how to paint. She said that she hated her body before she met Helene and after she didn't care. It's why she didn't shave or wear makeup, because Helene didn't. She could do whatever she wanted to her body because it was hers so whether she hated it or not didn't matter. All that mattered was that she could do what she wanted to it. That's why she did all that shit with razors and burns, because she could. No one was stopping her.

So, when Helene died, it really fucked her up. She found Helene's body. She says that she just held her and cried over her body all night and she didn't call the cops until the morning. She was already long dead when Joanne found her. She said that she wanted to kill herself that night. She just ended up not doing it, but it was basically an accident she was still alive. Imagine if she died that night? But she couldn't live in their place any longer. It was Helene's place and the landlord wouldn't let her stay. That was how she moved into Hilaria. Maria Grim suggested it to Claire Labas. Claire knew Joanne would bring star power to Hilaria. Joanne was actually better known until Lexie really broke and Claire became world famous. So, they really, like never needed her to begin with. Joanne needed Claire.

1–2 November 1994

Joanne Pardes holed up in the backroom. All of the TVs played back at once, three strobe lights fixed to the top of the center box. Black and white sets hissed, a constant wall of snow. Color sets malfunctioned; psychedelia affected feedback. TVs hooked up to antennae played local news and sitcoms. Joanne played two boomboxes on the floor. One was tuned to FMU and the other played tapes of Helene Asher singing in her sleep.

When spirits were high, Claire and Lexie were in the back room with Joanne. There were new rocks to chop up, maybe a line of heroin to even things out. They needed their fill. They dutifully checked in, made sure Joanne had everything she needed. Binge #1 had worked out fine. A muscle pop of ketamine helped Joanne crash at the end of the party. It was after they got back from Woodstock. It was a bad week, grimy but nothing particularly dark. Crack, heroin, TV. Nothing out of the ordinary for Hilaria, really, and none of the self-mutilation that characterized binge #2.

Binge #2 was more sinister from the outset. The first time she cut herself that week was after she hectored Lexie into shooting a few rolls of film. Joanne smoking crack, tearing her clothing and eventually cutting herself on the back of the wrist with a butterfly knife. Nothing deep. Lexie suggested they smoke some heroin. Joanne smoked more coke. "You have like six fucking child prostitutes to go boss around, Lexie. I do what I fucking want."

Lexie stormed out, went to her room and locked the door.

Joanne blew a thick cloud of smoke, turned on a TV, snow. "My favorite channel! Check it out." She took another hit, tuned into the feedback. She stayed in her seat until she eventually fell asleep. She woke up with a sore neck. Half a bag of heroin and then she got to work on a big rock. She ran to Lexie's door. She knocked. "Beb, I'm sorry. I didn't mean whatever I said last night. I know you were mad, but check out what I've got." She knocked again. "Come on, check it out…"

When Lexie opened the door, Joanne was sobbing. Lexie hugged her, petted her back. Morgan came to the door from Lexie's bed to watch Joanne bawl. Lexie leaned into the threshold for support. Joanne was dead weight; Lexie felt her shins split. Morgan propped Joanne up. They carried her to the back room. Morgan fixed an antennae and they got channel 13. They watched a nature documentary, smoked more crack. "I just don't know what to fucking do anymore. Lexie, I can't explain why but I feel like I don't have much time, it's already too late for me you know?" She started to cry again, snatched the pipe from Morgan's hand, something was still burning.

"It's never too late." Lexie petted Joanne's back. "What would Alice Walsh say? *It's never too late.*" She took the pipe, the torch and lit up whatever was left inside. "Morgan push this."

"Hey Morgan," went Joanne. "Did Jacques Anzu ever take your picture?"

"Yeah, he did."

"Did you suck his dick after?"

"Yeah, we fucked after, whatever, you know?"

"Back at his place, the loft in Brooklyn? Did you fuck inside a pentagram on the floor?"

"How did you know?"

"I taught him how to do that, all right? That fucking dilettante. That motherfucker, that lucky fucking asshole. You're so fucking stupid, Morgan. He's richer than everyone in this room combined and you fucked him inside a circle and you didn't get shit for it. Head shots, Lexie should have just given you some fucking head shots by now..."

"Jo, what's wrong with you?" Lexie said out of the side of her mouth.

"...you know what he's doing in there? He's using you like a fucking... instrument. Did he fuck you in the ass, Morgan? Morgan?"

"Yeah..." Morgan lit a cigarette, bunched her face up.

"He's taking payment for head shots by using your fucking asshole to protect himself from whatever it is that's fucking tearing me apart inside!"

"We showed the photos at MGG..." Morgan protested.

"Lexie where's my dope?"

"Fuck off, Joanne."

"What? Because I insinuated that you're exploiting this fucking crack whore who had to come with you to witness one of the worst days of my life?" She cried into her hands.

"Fuck off, Joanne!" Lexie got up.

"Don't you dare fucking go anywhere." Joanne put her finger in Morgan's face. "Stay where you are, smoke some of my base, go ahead, come on. You know you want to. Do what thou wilt, Morgan. Let it be the whole of the law." Morgan picked up a stem and the torch. She beamed up, she held in the smoke, choked, exhaled. "It's nothing personal, really. I mean, you're a cunt to Linda, and she was good for me. I could blame you for a lot of shit, you're not like innocent by any means, god no…"

"I'm sorry, Joanne."

"No, shut up. It's OK. I'm not like even blaming you for it. You just like, clashed, personality wise. I don't think you get a chance to bully many people, you know? I think that most of the time someone else is taking a shit on you. You just saw an opportunity to bully her, you know? Like this is fucking high school. My fucking house is high school…" She started to cry again. "Have you ever been in love, Morgan? Have you ever loved someone?"

"Like Lexie?"

"You *love* Lexie G. Hinnon?"

"Sure." Morgan lit a new cigarette, gave one to Joanne.

She tore the filter. "I actually loved someone, who loved me. She was my best fucking friend. One day she just started to like, atrophy. She like started to rot, I guess?"

"Helene?"

"Yeah." Joanne began to cry.

"I found her dead in our bathroom. She OD'd. There was nothing I could do by the time I got back. I'm why she died, because I wasn't there. If I was home, she'd be alive, maybe, you know… Hey, let's do a little dope, all right? Cool out a little?" She held her face in her hands, shook, sobbed.

Chapter 28

Excerpted from an interview with Morgan Gold, circa 1998

I knew these French kids. They were a couple years younger, still in high school. They were really well connected for their age. They got excellent coke. It wasn't Claire's coke but it was great and I had been in that spread in *HYPE MACHINE* and in the shows at fashion week. They knew my face so they invited me to the upper East Side to hang out. Classic teenagers with the house to themselves for the weekend but it was a townhouse off Park Avenue! In the '60s, yeah, and their parents were in France or whatever for weeks at a time.

It was really fun, like so much champagne and French wine and coke, everyone had so much coke... but everybody was like "Can you introduce me to Claire LaBas? Can you introduce me to Lexie G. Hinnon? I've never, like, you're the first celebrity I've ever met." What? But like, I started to realize that I could make my own name. Maybe I could be even more famous than Lexie because the big difference between me and Lexie is I was smarter than her...

These teenagers, the French kids, they had a lot of older friends, people my age, people older. Like adults, like industry people. They're like, hanging out at a high school party. Of course, it's in the town house and everything but still! But I brought Marina and Britney once and I finally got Lexie to show up but it was a couple of days before the party ended.

But Philip Salo was there one night and he discovered me. It was just like meeting Lexie all over again. He was just back from Israel; he had gotten married and his in-laws were financing the film. I was a big fan of his work. He made *Killer Detective* and *I Can't Just Die in My Room*. And he was at this party. He wanted to make a movie called *The Daniel Rakowitz Story* but it ended up being different because he would have been sued. We were introduced and that's when I got cast in my first role. I played this teenage runaway hooker junkie girl and can I be completely honest? I based the part on Linda Solomon. All of the choices I made, I thought really hard about like, what Linda would do. I know that's horrible but it was a really great performance and great art comes from a lot of places and it's important to be completely, radically honest... But it was a horror movie kind of based on that horrible case in the '80s when that man fed the homeless people in Tompkins Square Park a stew made of his girlfriend's head. Like really violent, really terrifying slasher movies had just come in style and the difference between the other directors, no offense, but Philip has the darkness within him and he has such control of it. He's such a genius... I get murdered and fed to the homeless in Washington Square because he wanted that beautiful shot against the fountain with all the bums lined up. Those were real bums. So authentic... But *Lexie* was so mad that I did anything independent of her and Claire. I was like Oh My God. Like, they weren't out talking to film producers or anything. They were focusing on Lexie's modeling career, which of course was important but it's not as if I ever agreed not to take, for instance, an acting job in an independent film with an important director. They almost didn't let me do it. At first they didn't want to but I went to Maria Grim and she was like "Are they crazy?" So, I was in the film. Everything I've done since started there and I did that on my own. But Lexie was so mad. She like stopped talking to me. It's why probably that we weren't together when it happened.

Excerpted from an interview with Jacques Anzu, circa 1996–7

Do you have any theories on the killings?

The cops say she did it, everything public makes it look like she did it, but the cops are full of shit. Joanne had also completely transformed as a person by then, so it wouldn't be... It'd be a huge waste if she did because Lexie wanted to die and was headed, just hurtling into the fucking void. They were doing thousands in coke every, shit, every day. Lexie was defined by her death wish. Remember when she told *HYPE MACHINE* she would kill herself to stay beautiful—

I'd die to stay hot.

Yeah, that was it. She took a bunch of girls down with her too.

Two suicides following the murders, Marina Jay and Britney Rose.

So, Joanne is tied into it, regardless of the details, you know?

Well, from my reporting it seems that almost everyone she came in contact with from 1991 to 1994, excluding well, you, has had it pretty rough.

I could give you a list as long as my fucking arm, aside from Helene, of people Joanne and I who have in common who have died since '91. Between 1989 and 1991, I went to twenty fucking funerals, man. It's savage out there. There's a lotta ways to go. ODs, murder. That's what defines our times. Something, for my entire life has hung over us, it's defined the world we live in.

What is it?

Hard to say, but it's all around us. I've been in its presence but it wouldn't reveal itself to me. Maybe that's why I'm here today. I have a feeling you don't survive that revelation. Once you see its face, maybe you're already dead.

Does this explain your interest in magic...

Interest? My involvement with magick is because once you've done certain things, seen certain things in the context of magick, or alchemy or anything in that realm, it's very dangerous to drop your practice. You don't just walk away... discard whatever energies or phenomena that you were interacting with. These things don't like disrespectful behavior and they react to betrayal. Think of Yahweh, jealous motherfucker, cruel motherfucker... I have a connection with the dead... I didn't consciously ask for this, but something inside of me was already deeply connected with the realms of the dead, ever since I could remember. Throughout my life it's only gotten more intense. So as much as magick is about your will as an individual, there are forces that understand far more about us and our psychic limitations than we do about their whole fucking... ontology. When you're an artist you're more connected with these forces than someone who isn't relying on their creativity to get on in the world. And creativity is not the capacity to create something new, out of whole cloth. Creativity is the capacity to tap into the chaos, take that energy and mold it into language. When you're tapping into those energies, you're inevitably going to encounter the realms of the dead. Because that's the only dimension where the future is already determined...

Two Dead in Chelsea Loft

Two models connected to the case found dead in apparent suicide

HYPE MACHINE, 2 November 1995, by George Moynihan

Two luminaries of the Chelsea fashion world were found dead Monday in a loft known locally for raucous parties and A-list guests. Police are exploring a potential murder suicide scenario. "We have what appears to be the same cause of death," said a police source who spoke to the News on the condition of anonymity, "but it's too early to say who killed who and whether the perpetrator is among the dead. We haven't ruled anyone, dead or alive out as a suspect."

Marina Oxana (18) and Britney Smith (16) were found dead of an apparent group suicide in a nearby hotel the next day.

Claire Labas, the controversial heiress and fashion scout was taken to St. Vincent's Hospital and pronounced dead on arrival. Also found slain is the 1993 model of the year Lexie G. Hinnon, who lived with Ms. Labas and was considered her protege.

"Lexie had a lot of young women who looked up to her because there was no one else quite like her, that's why you had the devotion," said gallery owner and neighbor Maria Grim. "If that's what this is, devotion, well I just don't know how to say. They were all like sisters."

Artist Sought for Questioning in Chelsea Murder Suicide
HYPE MACHINE, 16 November 1995 By George Moynihan

The roommate of slain models Lexie G. Hinnon and Claire Labas, Joanne Pardes has not been seen or heard from since Monday's discovery of two bodies in the loft the three women shared and the subsequent suicides of two models who frequented the apartment.

"Currently she's a person of interest. We want to know if she's OK, if she's in any danger we urge her to get in contact any time, day or night. At this juncture she's only wanted for questioning." Ms. Pardes moved into the loft, commonly referred to as 'Hilaria' in 1992 and has lived there continuously since. Her disappearance is concerning to investigators. A search of her bedroom did not suggest she packed any of her belongings with her, said persons with a familiarity with the case.

"There was a suitcase in the bedroom that could be understood as a 'go bag' that was left there. That might point to a situation where she left against her will. We are also considering her a potential missing person."

Chapter 29

Excerpted from an interview with Morgan Gold, circa 1998

If Joanne went into the back room I might be dead. We were fortunate in that way, she didn't even come in. Marina barricaded the door shut. I wasn't sure that was a good idea because Lexie might need our help, we might need to let her in. But she was already dead in the other room and Claire, I heard Claire died slower than Lexie. Lexie died pretty quick, they said. But Claire bled out, alone in her room, which is really fucked up, OK?

But Marina and Britney, who both died that weekend after... they killed themselves. It was such a terrible time... It was probably good for me, to get out. And moving away from fashion was a blessing for me. I started getting offered more parts when I was in the hospital. I really needed that – pause. It was life-saving. Phil Salo wrote a part for me in *Blackmail* and I was nominated best supporting actress in the Independent Spirit Awards. I mean, look at Marina, look at Britney. I think it was what they saw, they couldn't process it. They couldn't see a way forward without Lexie. They lost who they were. I never let that happen. There's this book by Alice Walsh, *Managing Modern Life*. I read it again when I was in the hospital. She says it over and over, "it's never too late."

Artist Connected to Chelsea Murder Suicide Found Dead

HYPE MACHINE 22 April 1995 By George Moynihan

Joanne Pardes, artist and roommate of slain model Lexie G. Hinnon and heiress Claire LaBas was found dead of an apparent suicide. The medical examiner estimates Ms. Pardes took her own life around midnight of the 20th.

Ms. Pardes was a graduate of SUNY Purchase and a member of the Lower East Side, Soho and then Chelsea art scenes. She appeared in the well-received independent short film *Scarlet Woman 89* with artist Jacques

Anzu, released in 1991. She showed artwork at galleries as notable as Maria Grim Gallery among others.

Investigators and the Manhattan DA's office have closed the cases in Chelsea. "We've never seen a single piece of evidence anyone outside of the women police found in the apartment and the now deceased was involved in these deaths. We have come to the conclusion [Joanne Pardes] did murder [Claire LaBas and Lexie G. Hinnon]. The COD for the two young women found connected to the case have been ruled drug related, though we do believe this was a mass suicide event."

Chapter 30

November 1994 – April 1995

Joanne raided Claire's bedroom. She pulled out 6k in cash, about an ounce of coke, several bundles of heroin, pills of every variety, vials of liquid ketamine. She pushed everything into her pack. She kicked Lexie's door open and did the same. More coke, heroin and pills. Three thousand in cash. Enough cash to run. She didn't need to worry about getting high for a while. She had what she needed to keep her head straight long enough to make a clean getaway.

She stepped over Lexie's body in the hallway. She fit as much of her fist as she could in her mouth. She needed to get out of Hilaria, immediately. She stopped in the bathroom to wash her hands. She left the loft for the last time. She locked the door behind her. She wore her brown leather jacket, sunglasses, black beanie. She had the clothes on her back the contents of her pack. She could buy whatever she needed to replace. She ran down the stairs.

She pushed north, up 10th Avenue, toward the bus station. Don't run, keep a normal pace, blend in with your surroundings. When Helene died, she felt the same fear, but then it was tempered by grief, horror, disbelief. Now she experienced the real thing, real fear, a physical sensation, pure animal fear. She wiped tears off her face, lit a new smoke. A cop car drove by, she wondered how her body would react. Would she shit or piss, would her knees buckle? They passed her. She sucked in smoke and exhaled some of the fear. She felt the stress in her joints. She stopped to catch her breath under scaffolding. The Lincoln Tunnel was somewhere to her left, the high 30s. She gathered the energy and charged to the bus station, into the bathroom. She washed her face. She locked herself in a stall, she fixed on Xanax and a couple bumps of heroin. She could die in the stall or she could keep going. She left the bathroom when she calmed down. She found the right kiosk. "One way to Kingston."

The night she died, Joanne returned to the barn outside Woodstock, where she recited Helene's words outside the circle in 1989, where she tried to break through with Linda and Lexie just months before. Joanne swallowed handfuls of pills, sucked down coke from a two-liter bottle. She wrote a note before she cooked up the shot of heroin that she hoped would kill her before the cocktail she swallowed took effect.

The note was three sentences long, and to most, meaningless:

BECOME BABALON COLLIDE W GOD. THIS IS HELENE. LISTEN TO ME.

Chapter 31

Excerpted from an interview with Jacques Anzu, circa 1996–7

Did you introduce Joanne Pardes to Claire Labas?

It's possible I introduced them, but Joanne was a magnetic personality and Claire really was attracted to Joanne and pursued her as a friend independent of me. And obviously they became way closer to each other than I was to either of them, really. Joanne needed a place to stay, she wasn't going to stay in that apartment with Helene's ghost torturing her and I think they were evicting her anyway. But even if I did, either way I can't be held responsible for what Joanne did or what happened there. And I was already out of the picture in those last days. I'd left the scene and was working on *Shotgun 95*.

So, the piece on your altar, that was made before Helene died.

Definitely. Joanne didn't make art about Helene's death.

Why do you think that was?

She found Helene's body and it did something to her psyche. Do you know about the mechanics of traumatic events, the transformations they kick off? I wouldn't place myself in her mind if I could. That's never been an interest of mine, empathy, but in Joanne's case that's what kept me safe and intact through our friendship, but I think what happened... I think, whether she intended to do so or not, she channeled something. She was open to this phenomenon, perhaps. If she knew it and was indifferent to what was happening, what it would mean... Joanne walked into a space where strange things were happening day and night and four fucking people died... Helene and then Joanne, in her own way but the same way, you know, fell for the trap. Happens to magickians or witches or whatever who have one foot in and one foot out. Alchemists without the correct training, impure motives, they ended up mixing chemicals that killed them in seconds... They fucked with forces they didn't understand because they liked the aesthetics and it killed them.

So, you do think Joanne was somehow—

Don't put fucking words in my mouth. This is a theory. If she did knowingly bring some kind of force or energy into that place with her that's... That's a good explanation for why she went upstate to OD. You've seen the movie. You know what that spot looks like. We don't know what kind of magick she was doing up there before she did it. To me it all points to something truly sinister happening in that loft. Those rituals were cutting edge, she was developing her own system, and Claire gave Joanne a place to perform all these rituals and a charged environment to do them in. I'm never going inside that building again.

What do you even do in that situation?

Really you tear the building down. Firebomb that shit.

Well, I guess that's as good a place to leave it, right?

Part 2

Chaosmosis

"...Anzu's eye for the abject, addled, outlaw, auto-didactic Shotgun – of influential underground duo Shotgun and Treasure, the brilliant techno outfit that released 2 records – STAB NYC *and the genius post-*Jungle Anarcho Europa Art Concept *– is the key to this video: a gritty by choice, fuck you motherfucker to the system, that says not only do I paint on your walls but I piss on them too, I will take the streets back for myself, I will pursue my desires be they to create or consume – and for Anzu and Shotgun, perhaps what makes them such a perfect collaboration, the line between the 2, creation and consumption are fuzzy concepts, perhaps what Anzu has called the "mauve zone"?*

– **A review of SHGN 95, *HYPE MACHINE*, January 1996**

Jacques Anzu is one of the most brilliant artists to ever venture into the gutter. Have you seen Shotgun 95? This is the end of the 20th century, right here, the art of Jacques Anzu. The art of Jacques Anzu is the experience of hurling yourself into the void of the 21st century. Look at this video and tell me that Y2K isn't already here...

– **Maria Grim to *HYPE MACHINE*, 1996**

What is The Syncretistic Church of En Sof?

En Sof is a set of Technologies anyone can use to live a better life. The more you are willing to put in, the more you will get out! But we see every day that En Sof has something for everyone.

The Syncretistic Church (SC) is a group of like-minded human beings who have made a commitment to the study and thus further understanding of En Sof.

What is En Sof?
What is En Sof?
En Sof is the moment prior to the event of creation.
What is En Sof?
En Sof is the potentiality preceding the emergence of time.
What is En Sof?
En Sof is the elements, the forces, the phenomena.
What is En Sof?
En Sof is all things, all people, all times, all dimensions.
What is En Sof?
En Sof is the sum of all creation, it is the impossible that must be so.
What is En Sof?
En Sof is the time before time. The time before the beginning.
What is En Sof?
En Sof is inside and outside, above and below.

Chapter 32

The Hemlock Hotel, 1994

"Brothers of The Hemlock Circle..."

"Excelsior!"

"96. Welcome, thank you for coming tonight. Welcome again to this meeting of the Hemlock Circle Speaker's Club. I am Gavin Lee, the organizer emeritus of the Speaker's Club. Tonight is sure to be a highlight because I know that there may be Navy men, inventors, tinkerers, but the one thing the brothers of the Hemlock Circle have in common of course, is we're landlords, investors in the oldest security there is. We're not necessarily technologically savvy. I know some of you are still getting a handle on your TV remotes. But we have a luminary in the brave new world of technology. Virginia Parker attended Stanford University, where she graduated with distinction in 1977. She has been a powerhouse in the financial and tech industries, a key player in the intersection of the two. Today she is the co-founder and CEO of Network Solutions, one of the top IT consulting firms in the world. Brothers of The Hemlock Circle, I present Virginia Parker." Gavin stood back, stomped his feet, clapped his hands. The brothers stood up, clapped one, two, one, two, three. They chanted *96! 96!*

Virginia took the podium. She wore a gray pantsuit, a diamond and platinum broach, pearl earrings. Her hair fell just below her ears. Perfect posture. She was completely relaxed. She exuded confidence. "Hello, good evening, everyone. Thank you for that introduction, such an honor to speak to a room just packed with talent and intellect. As Mr. Lee so eloquently said before, I am Virginia Parker, co-founder and CEO of Network Solutions. We are an integrated IT, analysis and security firm. We have a mission we take incredibly seriously. Our mission is that on midnight, 1 January 2000, no one on earth will notice a thing. They'll raise their glasses, they'll kiss their loved ones, they'll dance the night away. The next morning, maybe a little hung over, right? Maybe just tired, but when they go to take out cash at the ATM, nothing will be any different than when they took out cash for a taxi on New Year's eve. When they open up America Online, check their order on Amazon.com that nothing but the date will have changed. A seamless transition from one century to another. They'll look back and say *Y2K, what a bunch of hype, nothing happened!*

"I want you to stop for a second and think about how many times a day you interface with a computer screen or use a service you know is powered by a computer or connected to the internet. Your bank, your doctor's office, your home PC... Think for a second, go through your day. For those of you already familiar with tech, please bear with me while I bring the rest of you up to speed. There is a potential scenario we have always understood, since the earliest days of computer science, that the switch from 1999 to 2000 could lead to system failures. Over time we've hypothesized catastrophic consequences. Perhaps they will be as benign as some websites go down, some inessential functions misfire, but that's not a risk we can afford to take. Systems that were built without an accounting for numbers past ninety-nine are part of nearly every choke point in your life. This could be the most expensive disaster in history. Our energy systems, our financial systems, our defense systems all contain potentially explosive resets in the face of double zero. In the mind of the network, we have not entered the twenty-first century, but we have returned to 1900. This would mean that the information our systems are built on, the history that we have digitized, the codes we have written could be erased because that history won't have yet occurred. Rolling network failures, hardware meltdowns, power outages, supply line disruptions, water shortages.

"We created a calendar which is far from arbitrary. Through our developing command of the flows of matter, our calendar's correspondence with any solar or lunar patterns are immaterial. What matters instead is that the structures we have built to supplant nature are timed to this calendar. That is the potential risk in front of us. That is why we at Network Solutions aren't going to work each morning we're going to war."

The room burst into applause. Virginia nodded her head. They broke into formation, one, two, one, two, three. one, two, one, two, three. They chanted *96! 96! 96!* They sat back down, Virginia continued.

"I believe that Networking and Information Technology is the sum of all previous knowledge, from the most basic truism to the most occult mysteries and just like the mysteries there are perils, there are pitfalls. We have reached the first existential risk of the information age. The Y2K problem, gentlemen is a potential apocalypse. But that is where we come in. Network Solutions is growing in response to the demand for our consulting services. We are helping Fortune 500 companies, major law firms, financial houses and a myriad of specialty clients – like the Hemlock Circle, identify where they're exposed and we show them how to fix their networks in preparation for the new millennium. In that process we help these organizations modernize their systems, replace outdated hardware and components, update their security protocols, and fix other issues. Bringing Network Solutions into your office could help keep the rest of us safe. Y2K is just as much of a collective action problem as a technological problem. We need to rely on each other to address where, within our organizations we have potential pitfalls. We can't allow chain reactions. We can't allow preventable failures in our systems. We're still building out the internet, we're still seeing exponential growth in computing power. Innovation in every sector is so rapid that it's practically impossible to keep up. Why should we let Y2K stop us? Network Solutions is ensuring that the year 2000 will be the most successful in history. Network Solutions is dedicated to a seamless transition into the new millennium. Thank you."

The brothers of the Hemlock Circle stood up, clapped and stomped. one, two, one, two, three. They chanted *96! 96! 96!*

Chapter 33

The Hemlock Hotel, 27 December 1999

The final Hemlock Circle event of the second millennium combined the annual St. John's Day party and the ten year anniversary of The Circle's New York City real estate holding company, HCT Capital Management. Tonight 120 guests, brothers of the Circle in good standing, gather in the basement party room of The Hemlock Hotel, a wide-open space surrounded by columns and archways. Twenty tables, room for a dance floor. A stage is set up against the left wall with a podium and the PA system. A sign printed on poster-board at the door says it all:

"Tonight, We Are Going To Party Like It Is 1999!"

The basement is stocked with liquor and ice. Two servers, a busser and a runner take care of the room. Brothers mingle, eat hors d'oeuvres, drink and be merry. They backslap, kibbutz, crack jokes and spin tales. Banners hang at the entrance and on the back wall, WELCOME, HEMLOCK CIRCLE.

Gavin Lee, CEO of 360 Global Assessment takes the stage. He barks into the microphone. "Brothers of the Hemlock Circle!"

"Excelsior!" they reply in unison.

"96!" Gavin wears a beret with a red pompom on top. Gavin has his suits tailored tight so he bursts out of his vest, his muscles and martial spirit impossible to contain. His red cravat bares the seal of the Navy. "Honorable mentions. Let us recognize the top investor of 1998–1999! Tonight, we honor Brother in Good Standing Donald Toberoff!" The crowd howled, they stomped and clapped, one, two, one, two, three.

Toberoff stood up and spun his fist. He cupped a hand and his mouth and yelled out, "96! 96! 96!"

The crowd went wild. They cheered, they howled, they wooed. "Excelsior!"

Gavin bites into a cigar and lights up with a Zippo. He exhales upwards and the brothers take their seats. "Brothers, I'm so proud to introduce this man to you. He has been a mentor, a role model. He is among the most impressive men I have ever known. We only need to look to this man if we want an example for how a Brother should act. We call him The Ram, I believe, because no one uses their head as a weapon quite like this man." Gavin nods his head, looks upwards and to the right, lets the spotlight hit his face. Most of the time when he speaks, this is when someone snaps a photo. He knows how to outline his jaw. The crowd gets on their feet, stomping, clapping, one, two, one, two, three. "It is my pleasure to be the last brother in this cycle to introduce your 1993–1999 President, Bishop Thomas, THE RAM, Walsh!" Gavin's eyes opened wide, he made his war face. He stomped the stage. He clapped his hands into the microphone.

Bishop Thom 'The Ram' Walsh, in his collar, steel Celtic Cross and thousand-dollar suit, jumps on stage. "Brothers of the Hemlock Circle."

"Excelsior!" they boom back.

"96! Friends, thank you for coming. Gavin, thank you for seeing me off. Brothers! Gavin Lee!" One, two, one, two, three, one, two, one, two, three. "What a joy. I feel it. Do you? The wind is at our backs. That's right! Everyone let's thank our wonderful executive committee, let's give them a hand!" The Ram leads the Circle in a new round of applause, one, two, one, two, three. He's a youthful, even boyish fifty-nine-year-old with straw blond hair, an angular jaw, defined chin, high cheekbones. Piercing, intense blue eyes behind wire rimmed glasses. He's built like a quarterback, like a Navy Man. He and his brother Bob have been dedicated members of The Circle in good standing since the sixties, just like their father and grandfather before them.

"This Saint John's Day, we can celebrate assured that we are still very much in an upward trajectory. We can celebrate this Saint John's Day knowing that for the past decade, for every step of this city's recovery, The Hemlock Circle has been there, with our sleeves rolled up, doing our part. Incredible work. Was it easy? Of course not! We're not the kind of men who take on easy tasks. And that's why our best days are still ahead! But now we can celebrate a tremendous achievement. Ten years of success for Hemlock Circle Trust's property management arm! The EXIT Plan worked!

"At our 1989 St John's Day Party, the Executive Committee presented you all the EXIT Plan and we launched Hemlock Capital Management. We resolved to succeed here, in the Greatest City on Earth. We were taking a venture only the boldest men in this industry were prepared to take. That venture has been a proven success. The growth we've seen over the past decade has been historic, it's been miraculous!" The crowd began to cheer, to stomp and clap, one, two, one, two, three. He shouted over them. "We're still growing, we've outpaced our goals 38%. That's right! 38% past our goals from the 1989 EXIT Plan. We've seen our portfolio grow a whopping 156% Give yourselves a hand, right there… We have acquired ninety-two properties over the past ten years, ninety-two. We have constructed one hundred and fifty-three buildings, brothers, 153 buildings, fantastic!" The room filled with applause, hoots, *96! 96! 96!*

"There were arguments at the time that our goals, 200% growth over ten years was impossible. Friends HCT Capital Management has exceeded every marker. We have made history! Give yourself a hand, you did this!" The room rose to their feet for a standing ovation. The Ram shook his fist. "Onward to victory!"

The brothers began to clap in unison. One, two, one, two, three. Two claps, three claps and stomps. The sound echoed. The rhythm boomed. The basement's acoustics were designed around the Five Note Call. Thom put the microphone back on the stand and joined in. He clapped, he stomped, he waved his arms. "Upwards!" One, two, one, two, three. "Onward! Upwards!" One, two, one, two, three. The room shook, the cheers, the stomps, the rhythms echoed through the basement. *Eye of the Tiger* played over the PA. The crowd whooped and cheered. The Ram pumped his fist in time with the music. He raised and clapped his hands, he led the crowd, clapping and stomping in unison. "Do you feel it? Do you feel this energy?" The crowd roared. "Onward! Upwards! To the twenty-first century! Onward to the New American Century!"

Chapter 34

Maria Grim Gallery, 1994

The Maria Grim Gallery 1994 *Breakthroughs +/- Brilliance* Show. Virginia Parker, CEO of Network Solutions and her assistant Madison Toberoff studied two Jacques Anzu silkscreens, *Black Iron* pts four and five. Maria and Virginia were wrapped in each other. Maria flagged down someone from her staff. She put red stickers on the wall next to each painting.

"Is he here?" Virginia nodded to the paintings.

Maria sighed and shook her head. "My love, he just refuses to come here when we have our shows." She turned to Madison and gave her a card. "My new private line."

Back to Virginia. "We can get you something? You want to relax upstairs? I've moved up there. It's wonderful–marvelous. All the building is mine."

Virginia held up her flute of champagne. "This is delicious, Maria. What else could I need?" They laughed. "Let's go." She turned to Madison. "There's an open bar, go have some fun. We'll be here for a while." Virginia went off with Maria.

Madison smiled, nodded. She wandered the gallery. She looked at paintings. She accepted Kava and a canape. The room was packed, revelers got loaded. She gravitated toward the bathroom. A dozen young girls, dressed alike railed coke off a corner of the sinks. A dozen gigantic blonde blowouts, mini-skirts, baby T's. When she left her stall she approached them.

"You're hot," one of them said to her.

"Can I?"

Another girl cut her a line. The coke looked pink in the light. She took a twenty out of her wallet, rolled it up and took the hit. Clarity, energy, confidence. "Fuck, fuck... Thank you." The girl nodded and gave her another.

"I'm Madison."

"Morgan, Morgan Gold."

"I'm here with my boss. She went off with the owner of this place and told me to go have a good time. And now I'm here, and I just met you. I don't get out much it feels so good to like meet someone you know?"

"Yeah!"

"Are you from Connecticut?"

"Westchester."

"Oh my god!" They hugged.

Lexie G. Hinnon made her entrance. The girls made room for her. A hundred pounds, a small black dress, long oily, knotted blond hair. D&G sunglasses.

"Lexie, check out Madison," said Morgan.

"What's up."

"What's up. Yes. Hey, hi!"

Marina Jay dumped a bag of coke onto the edge of the sink and cut up Lexie's lines. Britney Rose cut her a new straw. Lexie got to work. Everybody was silent.

"We're out in like twenty," said Lexie. She left the bathroom. The girls resumed chattering.

"Are you as thirsty as I am?" asked Madison.

"Oh my god!" said Morgan.

Chapter 35

Wall St., 1995

Virginia Parker leaned back at her desk, reading through summaries from the analysts. She put the papers down and massaged her forehead. Into the intercom: "Madison, it's time for a latte."

"Right away," Madison said back.

The direct line rang. Virginia picked up.

"Hello."

"Virginia Parker?"

"Speaking."

"The next voice you'll hear is Mr. Walsh. Standby…" A click. "…Virginia."

"Bobby!" Virginia smiled, sat up.

"I'll be in New York tomorrow, landing in the afternoon. I'll let you choose the restaurant, but let's plan for six thirty."

"Madison will figure it out."

"That's good, good. Something hip. Until then." He hung up.

Virginia hit the intercom. "Dinner tomorrow, six thirty, for two, somewhere *hip*. Is Blue Ribbon still *hip*?"

Madison thought for a beat. "Go with Nobu. I'll book the table."

Virginia and Bob Walsh, CEO of 360 Global Assessment sat for a long dinner of sashimi, sushi, sake and champagne. "So, how's Alice?" asked Virginia.

"Our Alice… Keeping busy. She finished a new book, Part 3, out next year. You'll get your galley soon, I'm sure. When's the last time you spoke?"

"We had a call on her birthday and then on Thanksgiving, then New Year's Eve."

"Did she clue you in on any plans?"

"No, just that she was juggling projects. You know how she plays it… How's Katie?"

"Never more perfect. She'll graduate two years after Kip!"

"And Kip?"

"He wants to follow his school friends to Harvard. I put my foot down there. I said you can choose but it's Yale or Stanford. That or spend your trust fund on tuition."

"Madison will write my letter to Stanford Monday, just to gild the lily."

"I'm afraid he'll go to Yale, peer pressure."

"Nothing *wrong* with it."

"I said to him, look, you'll have a fine life if you go to Yale but Stanford you'll be on the cutting edge. Things don't stay the way they are forever, be a revolutionary!" He shook his head and laughed. "You know what he said? *Plenty of revolutionaries went to Harvard, Dad!*" He took a big gulp of sake. "When Kip was born Nan said we'll know we're parenting him correctly when he doesn't see the work we put in. That we should raise an entitled, spoiled brat because his destiny demanded it. Well, I guess I ought to give myself a hand."

"He'll fit in brilliantly at Yale." They both laughed. "When Kip was born, Nan and Sarah were happier than I had ever seen either of them." Virginia smiled, closed her eyes and played the memory back. "Sarah cried, and cried into Nan's arm. Nan just smiled, ear to ear, could barely speak. Imagine that! She held Sarah's hand, tapped on it, while Sarah just… They loved Kip so much. It was beautiful to see, you know? Transform into grandmothers. They just snapped right to it."

When they finished dinner, the bodyguards drove them uptown and saw them upstairs. When Walsh came to New York, he stayed at the 360 Suite, the corner of the 10th floor of the Hemlock Hotel. The suite adjacent was for bodyguards. He maintained a six-man team, all ex special forces, US, Brazilian, Israeli. Two on, four off. He had the Brazilian with him and a New Jersey native SEAL to drive. The hotel was routine, he was part owner, priority on the suites. "They swept while we ate. We're clear."

Virginia freshened up. Walsh put Al Jerreau on the CD player and mixed himself a Negroni. He opened a pack of Nat Shermans. Virginia came out of the bathroom, poured herself a glass of white.

"Want one?" Walsh gave Virginia a cigarette and a light. Walsh wore gray slacks and a charcoal polo. Salt and pepper hair and mustache. He crossed his legs and leaned back in his chair. He studied his drink.

"So, what had to wait until we had a secure location?"

"I'm retiring." He raised his glass and drank the remainder. "They're disbanding the team, wrapping up the program, moving the resources elsewhere. The protocols are so well developed they don't need us anymore. You know what we are? Victims of our own success."

"That's—wow."

"Just saying it out loud, to a friend, it's – it sounds right."

"The program, Bobby."

"Their reasoning is we've produced enough subjects... You know how boring this all has become? The foundation asked me for a proposal, a new project, and I just don't want to do this full time anymore. If I feel like working, I pick up the phone and I can give a talk, consult... I'll stay on the board at 360 but I'm stepping down as CEO. Gavin Lee can take my position. He's earned it. He's been there since day one, by my side. There's a reason he's my brother's man."

"Bobby..."

"If I'm going to travel, I'm going to travel to places I want to see. Virginia, they couldn't pay me enough to stay in San Diego. What an awful fucking city."

"Where are you going to go?"

"I have some ideas. There's the ashram outside Varanasi, I have a condo in Haifa, might just go there for a while. I might just go sailing."

Virginia was at a loss. She smiled, downed her wine. "And Alice?"

"She wants to go trekking in the Himalayas. I told her there's a Maoist insurgency in Nepal. She should go to Chile, Patagonia... But Virginia, with the program winding down, I'm taking one of the subjects with me. The prototype. We can deploy him for Y2K. There's a protocol, you'll get the file, learn it, and you'll get the most out of him."

"Thanks Bobby."

"Say, how far along are you ladies in planning this all out?"

"We have the contours mostly, err, figured out."

"I'm impressed by how you've handled this process. You have our confidence, Virginia."

"Thanks. It's an... undertaking, but we're committed."

"But you have a..." He motioned.

"We do."

"Ah good. What's her name?"

"Amanda."

Chapter 36

Early Spring 1996

Linda Solomon turned twenty on the psych floor at Bellevue. She got out two weeks later, a Tuesday, last day of the month. She was down to the clothes on her back and a big paper bag filled with a bottle of Klonopin, her Discman, Walkman, CDs and tapes. She bummed a cigarette from a hospital worker. She adjusted to the sun; it burned her eyes. She breathed in the fresh air. The hospital let out into Yuppie Manhattan, Turtle Bay. Blue skies, the last winter chills. When they locked her up there was still snow from on the ground, now trees were blooming.

Linda spent a few hours in the stores surrounding 34th St. boosting. She stole AA batteries for the Walkman. She took some extras, some for backup, some to sell. She walked out without incident. Next door, she stole a few leather wallets, a few pairs of sunglasses. She put on a pair of aviators, switched to a Fall tape and hit another store. A security guard gave her the look and she turned around.

A pair of boosters caught her eye from across the street. She watched them walk out of JC Penny with 100s in clothes, artists. She followed them to a CVS, entered a minute later. She watched them get busted at the door on the way out. One guard came for him, one for her. "Hey, asshole, get off of me." She shook the guard off, pulled away and ran. Her boyfriend sighed when he saw she got away. Could have been him if he'd just bolted. Linda snatched some shampoo and blew past the guards. They had their man. They let her pass. Linda felt for his girlfriend, standing outside Macy's crying.

Linda bummed cigarettes off tourists shuffling across 34th. She went to JC Penny and stole some jeans and blank shirts. She needed underwear but her instincts told her to get out. She chewed another Klonopin. She took the extra batteries, wallets and sunglasses downtown to a bodega on Avenue D, a clearing house for junkies. She left with $20 and a pack of smokes.

Linda crossed the 10th Street Footbridge over the FDR drive into East River Park. She stopped to watch the water, put a mixtape on her Walkman. She took the path along the river down toward the Fish Market. She wore Joanne Pardes' Nova Mob shirt, jeans and a light plaid short-sleeve button down. She took off the top layer and stuffed it in her paper bag. She walked to the Sea Port. She bought a coffee and smoked by the sailboats. She thought about where to go and who to talk to, where to stay. She made a few dollars in quarters, made her calls. No one had a free couch. She went to Tompkins and asked around. No one had a place to stay. The park was the wrong place to ask, anyway. She sunk her last quarter into the phone.
"Yeah?" Neil Irving picked up on the second ring.
"Hey! It's Linda."
"Where have you been man?"
"Oh, I was in the hospital. I just got out."
"Are you, *uhh*, better?"
"Yeah, thanks for asking. Is it cool to come over?"
"Yeah, yeah. Just ring the bell."

Neil Irving was co-founder of ZIKES (69–75) with the Garbageman Jay Waterman, the Pieman Larry Hay, and Tom Forcade, the deceased founder of High Times. After ZIKES fell apart they founded Woodstock Nation Liberation Organization (WNLO, 75–90). ZIKES' most notable moment, the 1972 Republican Convention in Miami Beach they picketed the Yippies for renting a motel room. The WNLO never lived up to its coming-out party, their picket of Richard Nixon's first post-presidential appearance in New York. Now they organized the yearly pot march.
Neil ran his operation out of a three-story loft building on Bleecker and Bowery where he'd lived since 1968. Previously, the building was the headquarters of the Pablo Light Show until they left for San Francisco. Neil and his people took over immediately afterwards and had been there ever since. The ground level, a large open storefront with couches against most of the wall space and chairs scattered. Milk crates and tables broken in every way you could imagine. The back wall was a mosaic of concrete and glass bottles. The front wall showcased the Yippie Flag mural. It was a meeting place, part social club, part organizing hub, open to the scene by

invitation.

Neil lived in the loft on the second floor. Ten-foot industrial windows faced Bleecker St. The area up front was office space, four Macs and two printers, a few metal filing cabinets. The Western wall was lined with bookshelves, spanning almost the entire loft front to back. Science fiction novels and almost thirty years' worth of pamphlets and movement literature. Stacks of newspapers lined the bookshelves. The entrance to the loft was on the East side wall lined with rows of tables running from the office area all the way to Neil's meeting place in the back.

Neil held court in a worn-out armchair against the back wall. He slept in a loft bed that hung over the middle of the room. The drop cut the loft into its distinct areas. Thirteen buzzed with the *appearance* of activity. People did their best to look serious. If they looked busy enough, Neil might give them some weed to take home, at least he'd get them stoned, pass a joint and they'd be there to smoke it. A good way to look busy at Thirteen was to make plans to submit to Neil. He'd think them over. Maybe he'd hand you a few hundred dollars, you'd have a reason to hang out upstairs all the time. Process, activity, constructive action toward a goal, these things were done for the sake of their own virtue. Working on a project at the loft meant Neil's largess: weed, meals, French Roast coffee.

The computer guys up front smoked their own joints and talked about IT. Eight cats moved freely around the room. Their boxes were scattered throughout the loft and always needed changing. Most of them hid on Irving's loft bed during the day. They pissed where they wanted.

In the back, a tearful Pieman told some crust punks about his health issues. He was four hundred pounds, walked with a cane. He wore a felt beret, a big star of David around his neck. In the '70s he pied Phyllis Schlaffley. He drank a ginger ale and smoked his own Irving joint. The crust punks drank beer and spliffed roaches they collected around the room with Top tobacco.

Linda rang the bell. A techie, aviator frames and a pony tail stuck his head out of the window.

"Hey it's Linda. I called before."

"One second, I'll check." He pulled his head back into the window. She chewed a new Klonopin, they were frowned upon upstairs. She waited about a minute for one of the punks to come down the stairs and let her in. She recognized about half the room from Tompkins and St. Mark's.

"Linda, yeah, come on in." He turned to Pieman. "She just got out of the hospital."

"Oh wow. Well, I hope you're better." Pieman looked up at Linda, watery eyes.

"Yeah, I guess. Thanks."

"Sit down, here, this is the eights." Neil gave Linda an inch wide joint. After a month of benzos and Thorazine the weed went right to her forehead. She passed it left, a kid she didn't recognize.

"How are the fours?" Linda asked, uptight to be around so many people.

"Fours are good. Good, yeah."

"When things are less busy I'll get um, four fours."

"Yeah, man! Hold on." He went into the middle of the room. "Hey, man, hey! Hey!" Everyone stopped what they were doing. "Who really needs to be up here, right now, man? Really has work to do?" He dug into his pocket and produced two of his signatures. "Here, man. Jai? Jai, can you take everybody who doesn't really need to be here downstairs, man?"

Jai wrangled anyone gawking, sitting at computers with screensavers going. "Come on, we're going downstairs."

Oh, shit man, is that a joint? I was just heading down there. Hey, Jai, can I come? The floor emptied out, save for Pieman and the IT guys. Neil climbed his ladder to his loft bed. He climbed back down with a black garbage bag under his arm. He lifted a cardboard box off a table behind the armchair, revealing a three-beam balancing scale. He measured out four grams of the 4's. *Get Up Stand Up* played through the floor. Pieman got up and made his way to the exit, leaning on his cane.

"Linda, can you lock the door behind him?" Neil measured out five grams. When she was back upstairs the weed was ready.

"Hey thanks…" She exhaled. The benzos gave her confidence. "I was wondering if I could crash downstairs tonight."

"How long?"

"Tonight, maybe tomorrow?"

"Tonight and tomorrow is OK, but not into the weekend."

"Wow Neil, thanks!"

"Yeah, you're welcome… Say, how about a shoulder massage? I have a knot in my right shoulder, over here."

Linda stood up and walked behind Neil's chair. He rolled his neck. He passed her his joint. She took a hit and stubbed it out. She worked on his neck and shoulders with both thumbs. "Yeah, man, all right. Right there, oof… Far out." He sighed. She dug downwards, into Neil's back. He was built for a man his age, mid-fifties. He still bench-pressed three times a week, lifted dumbbells in his armchair most days and hit a heavy bag he kept in the basement. One day he wanted to launch a boxing gym down there. "Yeah, man, yeah, go lower... oof right oh – man! Right there!"

***

Linda slept in the storefront, an old couch that smelled like cat piss, under a hemp blanket with a couple throw pillows. Cats slept behind her knees and over her head. She didn't remember her dreams when she woke up. It was early, still dark. She lit a cigarette, there were snipes all over the place. There was a toilet behind a piece of drywall in the back corner. She got herself together. She left the building, turned onto Bowery and walked north toward St. Mark's. She went to a bodega and got a coffee and a bag of Drum. The sun was on its way up. She pulled a half-smoked Camel off a bar window ledge. She put on her sunglasses. She pulled a copy of the *Voice* from a box. She picked up empty packs off the sidewalk.

Between leaving Hilaria and her stay in Bellevue, Linda sold spliffs on St. Marks. Parked on the steps of the old Electric Circus where ten steps could hold up to fifty, fifty-five punks, Linda sold $5 joints spliffed with rolling tobacco. She sold out daily, usually by six. Most of the time she was forced to accept change, dirty singles but sometimes she'd come in contact with a higher roller, sell five joints at once or the opportunity to gouge a tourist with a $10 spliff presented itself. Mostly, though, it was three punks or skateboarders putting their pocket change together, haggling her down to $4.50. The steps were hard stone and it hurt to sit there. Across the street was more comfortable but they ran her off within minutes.

Linda would come into something more lucrative every now and again too. One hundred ecstasy tablets, a sheet of acid... She had a contacts that hit her up whenever they came into a surplus. She took whatever to the cube and found customers immediately. Circles of ravers, goths, punks, nondenominational freaks... Self-identified werewolves and vampires, the occasional ninja. Circles of teenagers, twenty-somethings, leering adults, a constellation cliques, subsets of subcultures orbiting the Black Box. When she sold out she'd be back in an hour with more for that last batch of customers' friends. She thought all the time, if she could just do that every day she'd be all right.

Chapter 37

Seattle, 1970

Nan St. John learned to read at two, knew her Bible at four. Nan was the first woman on either side of her family to go to college. She received her MA in theology at Harvard in 1957. Her father, a one-time bootlegger and self-made millionaire, died that same year, prompting a decision to take her inheritance and first travel to Mexico then Panama, Brazil, Argentina, Uruguay and Chile. From Patagonia she traveled to South Africa then India, where she stayed from 1960–65 before two years in Nepal and a year in Tibet, studying Buddhism. In 1969 she returned to India and met Sarah Bremure in an ashram outside Varanasi.

Sarah Bremure came from a large upstate New York family, heir to a cartel of Northern Hudson Valley dairy farms and orchards, a savings and loans in Kingston. They stretched from Westchester to the Berkshires, with a branch of the family farm in Suffolk County. Sarah was born small, grew up sickly. She nearly died several times as a child and remained short and frail throughout her life. Sarah and her older sister Meredith joined The Church Scientology in 1958. Meredith remained until her death in 1988. Sarah was declared an SP in 1965. In response, she fled to India.

Now, 23 July 1970, Nan, Sarah and their new friend Bob Walsh climbed off a private jet in Seattle. American soil, Sarah began to cry. Nan held her shoulder. Nan licked her lips and closed her eyes. A light, misty rain. She let the drops hit her forehead.

Walsh rushed over to his brother, Sgt Thomas Walsh and their friend Andy Kipling Anderson, and Anderson's flunky in sunglasses and wingtips, waiting on the tarmac holding umbrellas. The Walsh brothers hugged. "96."

"96!" Walsh grabbed Anderson's hand and elbow. Anderson grabbed Walsh's shoulder. "Welcome home, Bobby."

"Thom, Andy, meet Nan St. John and Sarah Bremure. My two new best friends."

"Ladies." The Ram and Anderson shook their hands. Anderson's man carried their bags into a limo, everyone piled in and spread out in the back. Sarah had never been out West before. Nan had been gone just shy of thirteen years.

Anderson was Mormon, blond hair blue eyes, six one with a straight posture, the Walsh's man in The Bureau. Anderson was a talker. "Seattle rain, lush forest, smell that wet asphalt…" Walsh opened his window to let his smoke out.

They took a suite with a view of the Space Needle. The Walsh's hit the hotel bar. Nan watched TV and Sarah quizzed Anderson about his time as a missionary. Hours flew by, Anderson's man reminded him of the time and he got up. He left a briefcase on the coffee table.

"Andy, you left your case!"

"No, that's yours. Let's all meet again soon, I'd love you to meet the Anderson's!"

"Nan, lookie here!" said Sarah.

"And on this rock…" Nan counted 100k in cash in thousand-dollar bundles.

Chapter 38

San Francisco, 1971

Managing Negativity sold out well ahead of 20 April. The venue set a second date on 21 April and sold out the next day. Walsh and Sarah sat in the front row for the 20th, backstage for the 21st. Loud applause greeted Nan as she took the stage.

"Imagine how horrifying it must have been not to have known if the sun would ever rise again! Imagine what you would do if winter never ended? What if one night the sun set and then it never came back again? It just abandoned you? Imagine that, think about what that would do to you. Show a little empathy, put yourself in your ancestors' position. They weren't wearing shoes."

The crowd laughed. Nan paused, smiled. "But seriously, now, take a tic, think about it. Imagine you didn't know you were on the planet earth, spinning in orbit, with the two planets between us and the sun and you know the rest... imagine now that you didn't know these things. Imagine you'd never been taught astronomy, astrology, physics, germ theory, Kabbalah, The Reg Vedas, The Book of Mormon, or LRH's technology. Imagine you lived with your family in a cave. What would you be willing to do so the sun never abandoned you, that when it went away at night and you had to light a fire to survive until the sun came back and the predators of the night hid away? Now I don't know, I don't think we can know, whether the burial rituals or the sacrificial ritual came first. What if they were one and the same? Only later some group of us people separated the two? But I'll tell you what we know they were doing. They were making every sacrifice they could to make sure that the sun returned to them, gave them warmth. They gave sacrifices to the moon, thankful for the glow. Their grandchildren down the line would map the cosmos, but this hadn't happened yet. They hadn't gotten there. They still had to hash these things out, sitting around the fires, crafting their systems. They'd speak on the next cave over, how they lost the favor of the sun and froze to death or, or caught a disease! Imagine knowing nothing about germs and encountering disease! You see a man in his prime cut down in a series of days from disease, what do you do? You're awestruck, you're terrified. You know that nature is indifferent to your suffering. We don't know that today but your ancestor who we're talking about, they knew that better than they knew anything at all. You don't have Jehovah, Lucifer, Jesus Christ or Ishtar to turn to. You don't have the Pantheon or The Dharmas or the Vedas. You don't have a Zodiac! You have the Sun and the Moon. You don't know their relationship to each other. Do they work together, are they in combat with one another? Which is actually there to protect us, which could abandon us at any moment? What is the sun doing to the moon, cutting it into that crescent melon shape and then letting it live again, filling up the whole sky… lighting up, letting your ancestors know that it's returned and they've lived to see it…"

Chapter 39

Tompkins Square Park, 1996

Linda found Bad Mike in Tompkins. She gave him $20 for a bag of coke, $10 for benzos. Mike said to meet up with his girl Amanda. She served Linda by the bathrooms. Amanda had managed to shrink even smaller, even thinner. She was growing dreads. She had a dot tattooed next to right eye. She wore a dirty thermal and a black pair of overalls. Linda liked Amanda, thought that they should be friends.

"I've gotta go, see ya," said Amanda. She turned away.

Two crusties accosted her from the benches by Avenue B. "Hey! Amanda, where's Bad Mike?"

"I don't know who you are, leave me alone!"

Linda put her headphones back on went to Ray's for a coffee to wash down one of the bars. She paid in change. She chewed the pill and washed her teeth with coffee. She put on her sunglasses, one of Joanne's mix tapes. Side B of *Queen of Siam.*

She cut back through the park and waved back at some punks, stopped to sell them weed. They passed 40s and rollies, strummed on guitars. A runaway slapped a bench for percussion. Linda hung out for renditions of *I Turned Into a Martian* and *Bite it You Scum.* The punks played The Werewolves' *Punk Rock Genocide.* GENOCIDE, GENOCIDE, THIS IS PUNK ROCK GENOCIDE! She made back some of the money she'd spent. She left the park, put on a new tape, Joanne's Sonic Youth mix. She headed to The River through 6th St., she climbed the bridge over the FDR. The sky was turning purple. She sat down on a bench and watched the sunset.

Chapter 40

The Bay Area, 1975

Alice Simpson and her best friend Virginia Parker attended their first talk on Alice's birthday, January 1975. Alice was at Stanford as a legacy. She held on with a C average. Virginia, her freshman roommate, on the other hand, was the smartest person she'd ever met. Alice was in awe of Virginia Parker. She counted Virginia's successes as her own. She was on course to graduate with a 4.0, a major in computer science and a minor in business administration. She had a job offer lined up at Xerox upon graduation, possibilities seemed infinite.

Nan St. John covered every inch of the stage. She held the microphone like a pro. The room was packed and she fed on the energy. "Reality, what's happening in this room, what we see in front of us, what a sight, right? We're all sitting in our chairs, we have our coffee, our donuts. We're all wearing appropriate clothes, no one is in a bikini or a winter jacket, right we're in dresses and blazers, pants or stockings perhaps. No one is stinking up the place, everyone here bathed before they came…"

She got a laugh and she smiled. "What's all that? Hmm? That's consensus. We're all in agreement that in this plane of reality, we sit in our chairs, we wear clothes, we groom ourselves. We drink coffee from cups, eat donuts from napkins. We're not lined up at a stream, lapping up water, no we're sipping our coffee. Our consensus is so rich and complex that those coffees, one of y'all is drinking your coffee with creamer and sugar, one black, one of y'all I'm sure has cream and nothing else, that's how I like my coffee. Someone's drinking Sanka? Huh? Huh, right? Right?

"We have multilayered choice right there – whether you want your coffee sweet or bitter, whether you're adding milk or cream or the powdered stuff. Whether you're having a Boston Cream doughnut or a French Cruller doughnut or an old-fashioned doughnut… Each choice sets you off on a different direction but you're still in the room, you're still in your chair, you're still in this audience. Those are the boundaries of your reality. What am I getting at, in case we're getting lost, is that our consensus reality – which is so infinite in its possibilities is made up of materials that could have assembled themselves in just as many ways as the choices that y'all could have made just milling about the refreshments but they assembled into the confines of this room!

"Reality predates our consensus. What's always been here, in microcosm and macrocosm simply assembled itself the way it did because of choices or accidents or catastrophic events – the deaths of stars, for instance, that's a good one, nice and dramatic." She smiled and the crowd laughed. "The force that predates Jehovah or maybe the universe that predated ours, I've thought for years on this... We're, together, everyone in this room right now coming up with a new way to decipher that reality. What we have right now in front of us is our different systems, what do I mean? I mean the Abrahamic Faiths. I mean Wotan or the different pantheons, these languages! If you take that language and you apply it to reality, you'll unlock new truths and new pathways and new lights, new potentials! New potentials! What's the last time you were greeted with a new potential? I hear the word all the time but never a *new* potential. It's about your inherent potential, what you inherited from mommy and daddy, the son and the daughter are born with potential, sure but what about when they're grown? They can make their own choices and they learn to pull back a minute and through the application of the technologies we're developing in this room – right, this moment they'll be unlocking *new* potentials!"

Gasps, a slow clap that built, then crescendoed. The room shook. "That's right! That's right! Let's create something! Right now! Let's make something new!" Roaring cheers. She nodded her head and the room quieted. "The goal here, not the promise, nothing is promised, the goal here is extended cognition. What does that mean? It means going past the established, understood limits!"

Chapter 41

Shotgun and Treasure

Shotgun and Treasure was an electronic and multi-instrumental duo from New York City. Founded in 1988 by street artist Shotgun (ShGn) and Copenhagen born Ghanaian musician and producer Treasure. They were considered one of the Lower East Side underground's most important acts of the early 1990s, known for spectacular psychedelic live events where new compositions were constructed on the spot.

Jacques Anzu shot the cover and jacket photography for their seminal tape, STAB-NYC. The front cover photo was taken under an aqueduct in Queens. The back cover photo depicted Shotgun and Treasure wielding chef's knives on Avenue B and 8th St. The photos were shot in winter of '91. Tompkins Square was still closed and fenced behind them.

Their second album, recorded in Copenhagen in 1993–94 – *Anarcho Europa Art Concept* was far more influenced by the European Jungle and rave scenes than the American Techno, Downtown NYC noise, and East Coast Hip Hop rhythms of STAB-NYC. Ecstasy replaced PCP. The album sold well in Europe and the track *Christlandia to Rotterdam* was a club hit for years to come. Treasure was denied re-entry to the US in December of 1994 and wouldn't be able to return until 1996.

Shotgun 95 came out of Super 8 footage Jacques Anzu took of Shotgun from 1994–95. They bombed rooftops throughout the city, broke into abandoned industrial buildings to tag the concrete floors. Anzu recorded Shotgun painting the roof 10th St., a menacing, grotesque SHGN. The letters knotted into each other, white, purple and gold highlights over a black background. Anzu's photos of Shotgun crouching over the piece, wearing Ray Bans and a black beanie, the sunrise in the background sold at Maria Grim Gallery and served as poster art for the film. Shotgun used whatever footage he wanted as part of his projection collage. *HYPE MACHINE* called it the best short of the year and "probably the best film ever made about graffiti."

***

Linda was on the list for a party in the basement of 10th Street. Treasure spun all night. A hundred revelers shook. Linda danced with Shotgun. They stuck together, pressed and grinded into each other. Treasure blended jungle records no one in the room ever heard before with drum loops he recorded himself. Treasure took a break and one of the *Crazy Baldhead Soundsystem* selectors spun early '80s dancehall. The basement filled up with chocolate and haze. Shotgun pulled out a dust blunt. Linda grabbed Shotgun by the shirt and kissed him. They left the dance floor, they went upstairs.

Shotgun pulled out a razor and cut a Dutch Master open. He rolled a blunt, lit up, took two drags and passed it to Linda. "Shit with that for a minute, itch all good." Shotgun went into his bathroom and closed the door. The apartment was stacked with crates of records and art supplies. The only furniture was a mattress on a loft, a table with three chairs, and the filing cabinet. Light from a bulb swinging above the kitchen and Christmas lights on the wall. The blunt made Linda thirsty. She reached for the flat bottle of Coke in her bag. She went through Shotgun's crates of tapes. She fought the urge to steal. She picked a tape labeled *Halloween 92* and loaded the boombox.

Shotgun came out of the bathroom and smiled. "Thish was Halloween one year. Amazing experience, good shpectacle." He sat down at the table and razor-bladed another dutch and rolled a new blunt. "Electronic funk, drum and bass explosive – hip hop elements."

Linda sat back down at the table. Shotgun lit his own Dutch. "How do you feel?"

"Yeah... thanks. Shit, I'm..."

"Haha, thatch good though."

Linda smiled and closed her eyes and listened to the music. She got up and danced. Shotgun joined her. They blew dust in each other's mouths and pressed against each other, collided and bounced off each other, time and space synced up the music. The tape ended. Linda pulled off Shotgun's shirt. She grabbed him and pulled him toward her. She bit his chest. They moved on each other; the signature aggression of the dust blunt. They fucked on the table.

When they finished Shotgun pulled out a large pad of good paper and a marker. He finished a work in progress, a SHGN in red and black. Gold, blue, green zigs and zags. "Gallery commission. Street artists: in demand now. They like their art authentic suddenly..." Linda put on a new tape, a hip-hop demo. She didn't recognize the rapper. *537 LES, KICK MY OWN SLANG LET MY BALLS HANG.** The tape played through, she put on a techno and jungle mix. They found their rhythm. Shotgun drew, Linda closed her eyes and danced in her seat. He finished his piece. He turned it around to show her. "I think itch dope?"

"This is amazing!"

"Thought sho."

"Looks finished." Linda gave it a critical eye.

"Yeah, I think sho." He picked up the piece by the top corners and hung it up on a string he ran from the bathroom to the front door, about fourteen feet. He returned to the table with a bag of tea leaves soaked in PCP. He razored a white owl and rolled up. He smoked.

"I want choo play yar something." He produced a tape. "Thish is myself with Treasure. New demo." He put it on the boombox and turned up the volume. "Thish is hardcore dusthead shit. Thish is the vanguard." Dozens of loops, layered on top of each other, cut ups, samples from myriad sources. Everything clicked.

***

Linda and Shotgun got dressed and left the squat with a backpack full of paint. They roamed outside. Linda was lookout. Shotgun did a few quick tags on the way. They walked to the Williamsburg Bridge.

SHGN LES 2DAY 2 YR 2000. SHGN – NYC – COPENHAGEN. SHGN – 4ALL. (c) 1996.

Linda gave a heads up whenever anyone or anything was coming in either direction. They made it to the bridge. Linda smelled herself, she felt feral. Shotgun lit a blunt and got to work on his piece on the footpath, a bomb about twelve-feet wide. SHGN in the same colors he'd used back at home: red, black, gold, blue, with green highlights. Linda watched the water. She relaxed. A breeze ran under her clothes and cooled her skin, dried the sweat.

Chapter 42

San Francisco, April 1976

Sarah Bremure arranged two comfortable chairs, face to face. Nan St. John and Bob Walsh took seats in the corner of the room, out of sight. Virginia Parker and Sarah sat down. "Just pretend they're not here. Their presence doesn't matter. This is about us, what happens between us, the dynamics between our chairs... Are you ready?"

"I think so," said Virginia.

"Everything that happens here, you already know."

"OK."

"Now close your eyes."

"OK."

"Sit back, relax. Tell me about a happy memory from when you were a girl."

"OK... Rye Play Land, the bumper cars, with Dad."

"Tell me more."

"We're in the amusement park, Rye Play Land. It's summer, we went to the beach in the morning... we have sunburn but we don't care. We're in a bumper car together, I'm behind the wheel. We're laughing. We speed into the wall..." Virginia smiled.

"Do you smell that night?"

"Yes."

"Do you hear that night?"

"Yes." Virginia relived the experience.

"Good, good. Now tell me about a memory that haunts your dreams."

"When I went to live with my grandma, to watch her die."

"How often do you dream about that time?"

"Most nights."

"Tell me about it."

"I was eight. My family, Dad, Mom, and I, we moved to Grandma's house in Riverdale, in the Bronx. It was terrifying, always. My parents changed into different people; we stopped being a family. Until Grandma died, then we just went home, like it never happened."

"Tell me about this again, with more detail, more data."

"I was eight years old, eight and a half. Father and Mom told me we had to leave Yonkers to go to Riverdale, to stay with Grandma. I didn't know I had a grandma."

"How did you adjust?"

"I hated the house. I hated my bedroom, in the attic. Grandma terrified me."

"Why?"

"I watched her disintegrate. She was terrified by everyone, and she didn't know who I was… The fear on her face, it told me to be afraid. I didn't understand what was going on, only that I needed to be protected from it, and no one was protecting me. But what scared me most was the house. It moaned at night. My bed shook while I slept, things fell off shelves. I was terrorized, every night."

"What did you see?"

"I watched my father sit in the back yard, drinking his Manhattans and crying. Mother read magazines in the living room. She'd stopped speaking and ate one meal a day, breakfast, alone, once Dad and I were gone. Dad drove me to school and was off to work until seven or eight. She kept getting thinner. Dad kept me close. We were best friends. But when we'd go home, I had to go to my room to do my homework and Dad would go in the backyard and get drunk and cry."

"What happened next?"

"Grandma died in her sleep. Dad burst out laughing. I asked him why, it frightened me. Death was so terrifying and he was laughing. He just said 'she was in pain. What she went through wasn't right. This part of our lives is over now. We can go home now.' Dad sold the house, we went home. We tried to forget we ever left."

"Now tell me, from the beginning, with more detail, about this memory again."

Chapter 43

Berkeley, CA, 1976

"There was a Rabbi of antiquity who said, I love this, if God gave the Jews the Torah in the correct order, they'd all be waking up the dead left and right. All of creation, all of reality was preceded by the Torah. They taught the Torah, ordered correctly, is Jehovah's true name...

Nan St. John circled the stage. "We have our fun sure but I think we've all gotten to know each other enough that it's time to address some problems and start looking for solutions. Does this world we live in, was it made by a creator god? What if creator god is a misnomer? What if it's only part of the truth? What if that god took part of herself and – think of a parent who throws her son out of the house. She's taking part of herself and banishing it from herself. Each time, the first time when she birthed the son, this time when she punishes him, it's another birthing, this exile. Well, the god that did that is the same god who made the wilderness we cleared and the bay we bridged over and we made Berkeley California out of wilderness...

"This is the hard edges of civilization, the war, the crime... negativity. This is where our identities derive. I'm sorry to break it to y'all but your identity is the product of millions of years of suffering, alienation, subjugation. The tears of slaves and exiles wandering the wilderness. Their communities said go to where your surroundings will kill you. Die alone. Die as the days entertainment for the spirit of the desert or the tundra." She held her head, distressed. "Oh my!" The crowd laughed uncomfortably.

"That's where identity comes from. It's a form of madness that we've turned into the cornerstone of civilization. Identity is a form of psychosis. It divides humanity into sons and daughters, monarchs and slaves. You think there's identity in the kingdom of Heaven? You think once you've transcended you still have your CV, your race, your sex? Gender that's been – well since we started farming that's been a dividing line. We can bicker over who really runs what...

"Jehovah's madness, Jehovah's self mortification, that's our own. That's our drive toward identity instead of transcendence. We've been choosing identity over transcendence and it's driving us away from ourselves it's splitting us into smaller, more volatile parts. We're coming apart. We're facing down identity, we're facing down madness! That burning question: WHO AM I? That's your self-destructive urges in place. That's you running away from the transcendence, from En Sof! You heard me. Your life is you running away from the thing that you really want! You want to turn around and embrace En Sof, to be reabsorbed by time, space, to be one with the cosmos, life as a force! But you're self-hating and suicidal by design. You're scarring your skin, you're eating bad food made of junk, you're turning your children – your own making, lose out on the street. You're letting sons pimp out daughters, daddies pimp out sons! You're letting war and famine and mass rape occur. For what? So, you don't have to consider the infinite, so you can just look slack jawed into your own identity! Identity is that crumbling bridge, that road, more potholes than asphalt, the old sock that's coming apart at the seams. It's not suited to hold the totality of the human being, our inherent connection with the rest of En Sof, our special position regarding the divine… Identity is the wrong context in which to study the human experience. It's, I would say, where our ideas on hell come from, trying to do it all from the bottom of an overflowing cup. I won't let you be hopeless any more."

The crowd rose to a standing ovation. Virginia Parker, from the seventh row, the reserved section, looked at Alice Simpson. Tears streamed down her face. Alice turned and fell into Virginia's chest. The crowd cried, wailed, cheered. They stood on their seats. "Nan, we love you!" The air was thick. Virginia felt the potency. She held Alice harder. She let go, she wept.

***

"We came upon someone who is so clearly possessed by other dimensional greatness that our system is in itself vindicated that she came to us. She's a leader! The foundations, action, thought and spirit—" Nan knit her fingers together. "They're in perfect harmony. 33.3."

"The numbers, Bobby!" Sarah took over. "DOB 1955. Huh, hmm?"

"When in '55?"

"December." Nan beamed.

"This is her here, that's our Alice to the right." Sarah gave Walsh the photograph. He studied Alice.

"Bobby, we're in the presence of greatness. This is the new generation!"

"It's occurred to me, here, that I'd like to meet Alice…"

Chapter 44

Bleecker St., 1996

Back at Thirteen, Linda Solomon's run into the Thursday Meeting. Cranks introduce points of order, hangers on take a minute to acknowledge what Neil's doing here, man. Neil calls the proceedings to a close. "All right. Meeting over. Adjourned, man."

The room brakes out into smaller conversations. Cliques form, beers crack open and new joints circulate. Volunteers gather folding chairs and carry them downstairs to the first floor, to the back of the storefront. Neil chats with Jay Waterman, The Garbageman, author of the *Dylan Kabbalah* and *Dylan Gematria*.

Zenya explains to the group why pot's really legal. "The UN declaration on human rights says so. I have the papers, look." Aging hippies and anarchists chat it up. Friends from the AIDS fight maintain their own cipher.

Linda Solomon's stoned and feeling paranoid. She wonders if she might piss herself. She's sunk too much time listening to these people rant to leave empty handed. Two, nearly three hours now. She flags down Rick, who runs the buyer's club when Neil's not around. He wears big brass frames and a Giants cap. "Hey, can I get that shit now or?"

"There's too many people here now to take out the scale. You'll have to wait until after dinner."

"When is that?"

"Shouldn't be too long. Why don't you hang out and then come with us. We're getting Chinese food."

"I don't have all night, you know?"

"Different hours on Thursdays. You can see how important these meetings are… It's cool, we're having Chinese food…" The rest of the retailers are hanging out in their own clique, comparing notes, and might even also get to go for dinner. Neil buying dinner confers status.

They leave Thirteen, single file down the stairs onto Bleecker St. and march together down the Bowery until they find an open restaurant. Neil orders for 14. They pack into two round tables with Lazy Susan's in the middle. They inhale shrimp with broccoli, roast pork and Peking duck, mu shoo tofu, ribs, chicken wings, white and brown rice.

Linda fills up, dumps packets of sugar in her teacup. In the Bleecker St. pecking order, she's sitting at the lesser table. She doesn't care. Linda's not political. The discussion at Neil's table is about names she doesn't recognize and causes she has no opinions on. Her table, on the other hand, discusses music, art, and dope. She listens while Steve Sinclair from the Werewolves talks about the Golden Era, 1982. "We did *the Punk Rock Holocaust World Tour* that year. Heavy music. Heavy times." Sinclair's missing the teeth in the left side of his face. It gave him a Bell's Palsy look. He gnaws on his food with the right side of his mouth.

Nico Quick from the Burners and Riot 84 digs sugar out of his tea cup with his nails. He piles rice and lo mein on his plate. He claims three ribs. "Where's the fantail shrimp? Come on!"

Mort Fort Knox, an old time drag performer with stories of the St. Marks speed scene. "Pass me a rib, baby."

Pearl and Richie sell Xanax bars at the McDonald's on Delancey St. They have a section eight apartment on 13th and C. They sublet the couch for $5 a night. Richie's blind in his right eye. They're known city wide for riding the subway and only arguing when the train is in the station, silent in the tunnel.

Uncle Bob, either a pathological liar or a paranoid delusional Navy vet with his own Section 8 apartment lined with aluminum foil. He claims to know how to build a nuclear weapon. "They're probably horrified that you and I are hanging out, huh?" he says to Mary Chambers, who had country records in the '70s and probably hasn't experienced joy since 1986. Linda's the youngest person at the table. A couple teenagers sit with Neil, stoned, hanging onto the conversation. *Yeah, fuck Abbie Hoffman!*

Commotion, table one. Jay Waterman goes off on the necessity to purge rock and roll of its fascist and Maoist elements. He jumps to his feet, puts his finger in Mayer Vishner's face. "You're negative, man! All the time with your negativity! Say something positive about the movement, man. I dare you!"

Linda's transported to Far Rockaway, the High Holy Days, limp Jews playing tough, acting like they might come to blows. Two men in their forties or fifties with tits, FUPAs, pattern bald, shoulder length hair.

"Jay? Why would I do that in this day and age? Come on man, you know?" He half-laughed, half-cried.

"Jay, come on." Neil cringed. Making Mayer of all people look reasonable! "Mayer, don't make this uncomfortable, OK, man?"

"All right, OK!" Mayer put his hands up.

"If I hear an unkind word that came out of your mouth, Mayer…"

"Jay!" Neil turned red, pounded the table, shook the dishes.

"What, you're going to throw a brick through my window, Jay?"

"He's been saying we're illegitimate! What's going on?" Waterman fumed.

"You guys invited me out for this?" Jay's rejection of nonviolence made Mayer anxious, but the world outside of his apartment made him anxious. "Was this some kind of ambush? Neil?"

"Mayer, come on, man!"

"I'm going home. Neil, thanks for dinner. Bye everybody. *Bye!*"

Back at Thirteen, Linda bought ten grams of 4s and finally got out at ten or eleven. She started walking to 10th and D, to Shotgun's. She'd smoke him up. She didn't know where else to go.

Chapter 45

August 1977, Shelter Island, New York

Virginia Parker graduated with honors, Alice Simpson by the skin of her teeth. They moved to the Upper West Side. Alice's parents rented them an apartment off Central Park. Alice went to work an office job for her uncle's law office. Virginia went to IBM.

Alice kept correspondences with Nan and Sarah weekly, sometimes twice a week and spoke on the phone twice a month. She listened to Nan's talks on tape every day, she memorized every word. What eventually became *Managing Modern Life* grew out of her journals on how she applied Nan and Sarah's teachings to her work and relationships.

The phone rang. "Alice, it's Sarah. Big news, sitting down? Bobby Walsh just signed the paperwork on a beach side home on Shelter Island! We're coming, sweetheart! We're coming to New York starting the last week on July and staying indefinitely."

"This, is! Sarah! I'm so happy!"

"Remember this moment, my love. Oh, Nan wants to talk to you…"

"Alice."

"Nan!"

"You heard we're coming to Long Island?"

"Sarah just told me."

"I want you to do something important. I want you to start meditating on your cycle, keeping track of things, all right?"

"Sure, Nan."

"When your moon comes you call me from now on, very important."

"Of course, Nan."

Alice's period came. She phoned Nan on the 603 number. "Oh good, right on time. I'll have a car come this evening. Say seven. Why not take a long weekend too?"

The Town Car arrived at seven sharp and picked up Alice outside her building. They took the FDR. Even as the sun set the temperature was still in the nineties. The driver pumped AC, wove through traffic. When they achieved a steady speed, she opened the windows and felt the hot air blow through her hair and her clothes. They arrived at a ferry dock and drove onboard.

Alice got out, had a cigarette meditated on the ocean air, the motion of the tides. It was cooler than the city, low seventies.

Nan St. John opened up immediately. "We heard you pull up. Come on in and cool off. Hot one, huh?" Nan wore a silk blouse and linen trousers. She worked an ivory and paper fan under her chin. "We're drinking gin. Come on in."

Nan led the way. They traveled through a hallway lined with seascapes, antique tables, fresh flowers every four feet. They reached the living room, forty-foot ceilings, a glass panorama of the patio, a lawn, the beach in the distance. A large stone fireplace, more nineteenth-century American landscapes, antique pottery and sculpture. Clay and bronze on pedestals. Atonal modern classical played loud on good speakers. Bob Walsh wore a white linen shirt and tan chinos, a fresh haircut, newly trimmed mustache. He reflected on his Negroni. "Bob, you remember Alice."

"Alice!" He uncrossed his legs, spread his knees out and put his glass down. "I'm mixing the drinks. Alice, what are we having?"

"Oh, um, what Nan is having."

"That's a gin and tonic, coming right up." Walsh went to the bar and mixed Alice's cocktail.

"Well, I have preparations to tend to." Nan stood up, finished her drink. "Mm, you two should get acquainted." She left the air conditioning and went out to the backyard. She walked through the grass, looking up into the sky, counting her steps. Walsh watched Alice watch Nan. He sat back on the leather sofa, ashed a cigar in a crystal tray.

"What's your sign, Alice?"

"Capricorn."

"Very good."

"What's your birthday."

"The 7th."

Walsh smiled, laid a white powder Alice assumed was cocaine out on a mirror. "Is it eleven yet, Alice?"

"10.59, wow!"

Walsh raised an eyebrow, cut up lines. "This is called MDA. Here." He took a line with a rolled up a 100. He passed her the mirror and her own bill. "Go ahead."

The drug burned her sinuses. She looked up, stretched her palm back against her forehead. She caught Walsh experience his first wave of heat. The pain dissipated; the sensation gathered in the soles of her feet. Walsh stood up, walked up to Alice. He touched her shoulder. She felt waves of energy pulse through them. "We should get ready," said Walsh. He left the room.

Alice stood up. She floated toward her room. Intuition guided her. She found her door. A bed and a desk, a local wicker rocker, a full length mirror on cast iron feet. A pitcher of water and a glass was waiting on the desk. She drank. She experienced a cigarette. She shuddered. She drank more water. She ran her fingertips down her scalp. She gasped then sighed. She massaged her forehead in a circular motion. She took off her silk blouse and linen trousers. Her robe hung on the mirror. She wrapped herself inside of it. Nan knocked on the door and let herself in.

"All set, love?"

"What should I do with the tampon?"

"The water cup, love. Bring it with you."

Nan painted a 10×10 square on the grass. She painted a circle inside the square. She situated the sigils at each point, N,S,E,W. Nan stood at the southern-most point inside the circle. "Come, both of you."

Walsh put out his hand. "Alice." They walked inside the square, toes at the border of the circle.

"Under Sirius, LISTEN TO ME, I am open. LISTEN TO ME, I am prepared to see and hear you. LISTEN TO ME. Show yourself..." She looked to Walsh. "He will enter from the East." Walsh stepped inside the circle. He took off his robe, folded it and placed it on the floor outside the circle. "She will enter from the West." Alice entered the circle, dropped her robe on the ground.

Walsh was slick with sweat. Military build, salt and pepper chest hair. Alice stepped into the circle, dropped and took his cock in her mouth.

"LISTEN TO ME. I wait at the gates for your message. LISTEN TO ME. You will announce yourself to me!"

Alice felt each of her arteries pulse. She felt her heart beat in her lower back. She gripped Walsh's torso with one hand, she smeared blood across her stomach and the fronts of her thighs with the other. She laid back in the circle. Walsh climbed on top of her. She covered his face and chest in blood. Lightning gathered in the sky. Thunder roared. Storm clouds, rain fall. "PRESENT YOURSELF! GIVE ME YOUR REVELATION! WE INVOKE YOU – GIVE US YOUR REVELATION! LISTEN TO ME!"

Chapter 46

Great Neck, Long Island, January 1978

Nan St. John admired the packed house, took a sip of water. She took it in. The silence of a thousand people was something to behold. She leaned into the lectern.

"So, what are we talking about here? We're talking about an entity who through a prophet said you'll only obey me, worship me, consider me, sacrifice to me, pray to me, me alone. You will not worship the other gods, give them my sacrifices, ask them for what I could give you. Even if they come to you and offer you what you really do desire, especially if they come to you offering, you better not take it. No, no, no! You better come crying to me instead. And guess what, unlike the others I don't reward the righteous, I only punish sin. Why has this power conquered the globe?

"The book of prophets has been on my mind, this week. I've been thinking about these people, these *strange people,* let me tell you something." Hundreds giggled. Nan smiled.

"It's a humbling experience to consider the prophets. They were imperfect people, weirdos, right? In the book of Jonah, he's given a message and he runs away from his responsibilities. He's swallowed up by a sea monster and he's eventually released, a changed man, who goes forth and fulfills prophecy. He is dead inside the creature and reborn when released. Death and rebirth separate Jonah the deadbeat and Jonah the prophet. Jonah and the wale, is one of scriptural passages that digs deepest into our shared heritage.

"To live inside the belly of a great beast, a great *sea monster*, specifically is a form of death in anticipation of rebirth, and that my friends, is why we're all here today. We are interested in immortality. In the archaic religions, the primitive peoples around the world, when they're uhh, segregating an initiate child in a hut, that child is experiencing death in the belly of the beast. They emerge, sometimes a ghost – the intermediate between life and death, painted white… Sometimes, they emerge fully formed as an adult and just go wild ripping through town, depending on the tradition. But they're emerging from death, alive, a new form. This is an imperative of life. Our need to regenerate, to heal wounds and such, is our need to stay alive. When we inhale and exhale we are simulating, ritualistically, death and rebirth.

"The sun's rhythms, from our earliest beginnings were understood as a cycle of death and rebirth. When the moon drags the tides in and out, that's right. It's ritualistically simulating death and rebirth. So how do we master this cycle? How do we harness this cycle so that we will never cease to be reborn? That's the real question. You will not stave off death. You will never outrun this, my loves. It will occur. But how are we reborn? What keeps this cycle running?" Nan paused, took a sip of water. She felt her audience hunger for the answer.

"Have you tried this? When we impart wisdom to the student, we are the Mama. The Mama creates life, births the building blocks of the sum of totality, the Son and the Daughter. This is the path to immortality. Birth and rebirth! And this path is defined by the student teacher relationship. We think we're getting the better of death itself every morning, right? When we rise with the sun, greet the new day. We say our morning prayers, greet the sun… We're going about our sequence of rebirth. Now we need to do just that but, more intensely. We need to wake up by a degree we've never tried before.

"Rebirth! That's the key in the cycle of death and life. The goal, you see, is to make sure that when we die we'll be reborn and when we're reborn, we'll die again. I used to live in San Francisco. I was walking around there and I hear a little girl with a guitar singing *those who aren't busy being born are busy dying*. I think that's true, tautological, maybe, also, but it's getting at the problem. Hmm? Half of it, I'd say. Those who aren't busy dying aren't busy being reborn. Where are you in that cycle? Can I pick one of y'all from the crowd, ask you where you are in that cycle? No? Didn't think so. You're not thinking about life that way. You're thinking about death as the absence of life the way black is the absence of color. You're not considering rebirth.

"The belly of the beast can be hell, absolutely. Look at a painting from, say, the 1400s, the tortures of hell. It's all down in the guts of some grotesque creature, it's a microcosm, it's not even its own domain, it's just part of a bigger whole. Living in a giant creature's belly and living in hell underneath the crust of the earth are identical experiences, folks. The geographical detail doesn't matter a hoot to the dead inside, they're subject to any kind of torture! They just want deliverance. This is an intolerable existence and there needs to be a way out. That way out is rebirth. Our need to regenerate, to heal wounds and such, is our need to stay alive. When we inhale and exhale we are simulating, ritualistically, death and rebirth. Everywhere you go, you are looking at approximations of the only process that matters, the process of life begetting death begetting life. You emerge from your mamma alive. That means that your gestation was your first experience with death, the first ordeal. It will not be your last! Will you be prepared to be reborn when you die this time?"

Chapter 47

Williamsburg, Spring 1996

Color bounced the off clouds. Black turned to purple. Jacques Anzu faced east, toward the sunrise. He took Polaroids and color shots with his Canon, references for later. Jacques didn't rush, he hustled. He put the cameras down, took in the sky. He lit a clove, hummed *Gnossienes*. The sun arrived; the light was electric, radiant blue. Jacques put on his sunglasses. He gathered his cameras and went downstairs, unlocked the studio door and dropped the gear on the kitchen table. He pinned the Polaroids on a 12×13 canvass. He mixed pinks and purples. He painted stripes and compared them to the photos, matched colors. He painted chaotic layers of color, swirls, and dashes.

He stopped to meditate. He sat at his altar for an hour, eyes closed, he recited his mantra and let his thoughts go. He burned votives, black Muerte candles from the Botanica on Havemeyer. A bottle of wine, opened, untouched. Photos of Helene Asher, Joanne Pardes, Jack Parsons, the Beast 666, Grant, Hitler, Manson, GG Allin, Madam Blavatsky and Alice Bailey. He ground his teeth. He let his mind race, meditated on the Kali Yuga, Y2K, oblivion. A pastiche of images, Jerry Bruckheimer and Michael Bay, Aleister Crowley, Anton Levey, L Ron Hubbard, Robert Anton Wilson, Evola, Von-List, Lovecraft's Old Ones reset the cycle, wipe the slate clean.

***

Jacques cut a tab off his sheet of double dipped Celtic Cross. He dragged a primed 10×12 canvass to the wall with the best light. He divided the canvas into quadrants with black spray paint. He sketched out where he wanted the painting to go, four symbols and the Tree of Life in the center point. On the lower left-hand, he sketched out an inverted pentagram, the Leviathan

Cross to its right. He chose the eight-pointed chaos symbol for the upper left, the 4P's of the Process for top right. When the acid hit he'd add color, shapes, dimension and dynamism.

Carlos rang up. Jacques was glad to have company. Carlos broke up most of an eighth, rolled an enormous blunt. He made a pile of seeds on the windowsill. He wrapped the Dutch's outer leaf around a cold can of beer to keep it wet. "There's this hippie across from CBGB who sells weight for a dub."

"Is it any good?"

"It's three bucks a gram!" Carlos lit up. "You smoke this blunt you'll be fucked up."

"Over here I get haze."

"It's not haze if it's not from Washington Heights."

"It might be, I don't care, man." Jacques exhaled out his nose, passed it back to Carlos and went for his Leica. He captured Carlos exhaling smoke into the sunlight. He tied back shoulder length dreads with a black bandanna. He worked on MacDougal St. for an asshole from Lebanon, fourteen-hour days, selling glass pipes behind a counter between piercings.

"I'm fucking bored, man," said Jacques.

"*Haha,* asshole." Jacques got a shot of Carlos laughing.

Chapter 48

19 April 1978, Shelter Island, New York

The community gathered on Bob Walsh's private beach. Alice wore a handmade silk dress, a bouquet of roses and lilies. Walsh wore a newly handmade three piece black suit with a red ascot. Virginia Parker and Maria Grim stood by Alice's side. The Ram, Bishop Thom Walsh was best man, flanked by Francisco Grim, all in matching three piece-suits and red ascots.

Nan St. John wore a flowing, pale blue and white dress with a green shawl over her shoulders. She stood with her feet in the water. She addressed around thirty guests. "What we're witnessing today is a key to unlocking the universe's mysteries. The rite of marriage! One of the most potent days in a person's life is their wedding day. It's everything. I mean it, it's everything. It's totality in one ritual! With wedlock, the collision of the darkness of the Son and the light of the Daughter, the joining of complimentary opposites, consumes the subjects, the Son and the Daughter, they have joined the totality, they have been initiated into the infinite. You've gone from baby to child, from boy to man, man to woman. Now you'll transition from student to adept."

She put her hands on Alice and Bob's shoulders. "You are now adepts of the totality! By joining together, you have made the world more whole! Love is so powerful because it's a force of the universe. It's flowing like a river! When our desires, our so human need for connection triangulate with that force, y'all have an energy that powers nature itself. It's gravity, the tides, the wind, fire and lightning. What is the difference between the elements and love? What is the difference between electricity, lightning, and love? What's the difference, y'all? Form! The only difference between love and water and electrical current is the form that they take. Otherwise, they are the same: flows. Flows that can only be temporarily channeled, temporarily diverted. Those flows only stop until that dam just crumbles against the mighty weight of Jehovah!

"Our creative drive to make music or sculpt clay into pottery, or to use our erotic drive to make a family! This bond that we're forging right here, today, is a product of that creative drive! It's energy flows in action! What an awesome thing! Our connection to En Sof is expressed in our interactions with love. Love is in many ways a third force, here. We have two people, Bob and Alice and then we have the force of love, Eros, the drive to create a union. A family. Love is the force that drives the generations forward!" Applause swelled, crescendoed.

"Some occasions, they make me quote the bible." The crowd laughed. Nan smiled. "Matthew 19:6. Right? Right? *Wherefore they are no more twain, but one flesh. What therefore God hath joined together, let not man put asunder!* It was the cosmos that put these two together. Jehovah chose this union. You know what, y'all? These two, well they're about to be one flesh and I don't see the point in waiting any longer to make that so. Bobby, Robert Walsh do you take Alice to be your lawfully wedded wife. To have and to hold, in sickness and in health, however long you two shall live? Do you love my Alice?"

"I do."

"Alice Simpson, do you take Robert to be your lawfully wedded husband, to have and to hold, in sickness and in health, however long you two shall live?"

"I do!"

"In front of our families, at the edge of this glorious ocean, I do pronounce you man and wife. You may kiss the bride!"

Nan fanned her eyes. They hugged each other, looked into each other's eyes and kissed. Alice turned and hugged Virginia, then Nan then Maria. Walsh shook his brother's hand and bowed to Francisco. Alice and Walsh turned to the guests; they joined their fists in the air. The crowd rose to their feet.

Chapter 49

Williamsburg, 1996

Jacques Anzu was far and away Maria Grim's favorite painter and she considered him among the best photographers alive. Maria attributed Jacques' photos of Lexie G Hinnon for Hilaria's explosion and Claire LaBas' status as the queen of transgressive fashion. Ever since, a constant stream of up and comers passed through Jacques' loft, models, musicians and artists.

The phone rang. "Yeah."

"Jacques, Jacques."

"Yes, Maria."

"Jacques, it's Maria Grim."

"Yes, Maria…"

"I'm coming over today."

"Oh really."

"Something is wrong?"

"No, not at all."

"Good. They are here for the weekend to buy art and then they will leave, you're my first stop in Brooklyn. Three o'clock."

"Three o'clock." When Maria Grim called it meant he should put out his best work. A visit from Maria paid for a year's food, rent, drugs and pocket money in one day. Her commissions were usurious but all he needed to do was open the door. Jacques didn't go to his shows, he left them to Maria Grim Gallery. If buyers wanted to come to the studio, they were welcome to do so. He didn't need to debase himself further. When Maria was over with a buyer, she did the talking. If she wanted Jacques' input, she'd she signaled otherwise, "let's hear from the artist."

Jacques painted Kali, Buzuzu, Aiwass, Sheitan, Baphoment, Typhon, Set, Cthulhu, Manson, Jim Jones. He depicted magickal ritual, demonology, old and new gods, fictional and mythological beasts, sacred geometry, killers from Giles De Rais to David Berkowitz. Set was probably his favorite subject, the rapacious, violent psychopath, the god who flung his cum around, who topped then murdered Horus. Jacques' Set paintings put him on the map. His gallery show in '88, a series of canvasses that mixed spray paint, acrylic, blood, cum and screen print sold out immediately. His Aiwass series made him his first million. A fifteen-foot canvass of Cthulhu sold to a private collector for twenty-five grand. One canvass of Set-Typhon went for thirty. One show at Maria Grim in 1991, sixteen abstract canvasses he called *The Mauve Zone Paintings* grossed four million. Almost everything went through Maria.

She rang the bell. Jacques came down in leather pants, an open white silk shirt and aviators. "Maria." They kissed both cheeks.

"Jacques, these are my friends."

"Jacques Anzu." He shook their hands, turned around. He led Maria and the buyers up the stairs.

"He gets better light up top of the building." The buyers dealt with the climb up. Jacques unlocked the studio door, lit a clove. He sat at an armchair by the window. One of the buyers looked agitated. The walk, the loft, the art itself all bothered him. The other buyer, a short European man, aging rough, appreciated Jacques' Oanes paintings. Maria gave him her attention. "So? What do you think here?"

The buyer pointed to three canvasses, he nodded. Maria took out a leather planner and noted the sales.

"Jacques, call tomorrow."

"Yes, Maria."

She closed the door behind her. He'd find out tomorrow about the exact sums. He rolled a blunt, put a tape on the boombox. He pumped Cypress Hill out the window.

Chapter 50

Long Island, 1980

Nan St. John died in her sleep on 30 April 1980. Kipling Simpson Walsh was born on 2 March 1980 in San Diego. Nan and Sarah were in San Diego for the birth, they had only returned to Shelter Island three days earlier.

Sarah Bremure found Nan's body when she didn't wake up that morning. Sarah prayed by the bedside. She climbed in Nan's bed and held her. She wept until the sun set. She called an ambulance. Virginia Parker and Sarah's nephew Pierre arranged the funeral. Virginia and Walsh split the costs. Her funeral was held on 4 May 1980. Bishop Thom Walsh, with his steel Celtic Cross around his neck, led the ceremony. Sarah gave the eulogy.

"Since we lost Nan, I've been so hurt." She stopped and dabbed her eyes. She shook her head. "We weren't ready. We needed her. The work that Nan St. John devoted her life to was the end of suffering for the human race. We must continue. We must..." She fought through the tears. She pulled the microphone closer. "I will not let my grief stand in the way of our work. We will continue Nan's life work. We will end war, poverty, crime and deviancy in our time. We have children! We will not leave them to the wolves because we lost our dearest friend, who has been by our side every minute since we..." The Ram put his arm around Sarah. She gathered herself.

"We are going to continue our work because Nan St. John did not die. Nan Saint John ascended to heaven, alive! Nan St. John remains a prophet! Her work, our work, is to spread her message. Our work is to hear her call! Our work is to teach our children what Nan St. John would have taught them herself. Our work is to understand the pain we're all—" She broke down again. The Ram patted her back, he whispered in her ear.

"Jehovah's word comes to those ready to hear it. You don't hear the word unless you are chosen! If you're capable of hearing the word, understanding the word, communicate it to your family, your community! Nan heard Jehovah's message for the new millennium, interpreted it and related to us, her family and community. Our work is to understand what Nan taught us, that death is the precursor to rebirth. Nan St. John is already reborn! Nan St. John will never stay dead! And it's our work to say to Jehovah, THANK YOU. Thank you for letting us know this pain. Thank you for showing us what it feels like to lose what matters most. We are passing through an ordeal today. We need to say it. THANK YOU, JEHOVAH!"

The mourners stood up, they cried back, in tears, "Thank you, Jehovah!"

Chapter 51

Lower East Side, May 1996

Linda slept in the storefront at Bleecker for a few weeks until Obsidian took her spot. "Look gorgeous," she told Linda over coffee and pork buns, "you had that good real estate almost a month. I'm bouncing you out before you have squatter's rights."

Linda moved from couch to couch, two or three nights at a time before she moved on. Her best nights were on a sectional with some nice girls from NYU and Parsons who lived on Third Avenue. On nights she couldn't figure out where to go, she fell back on a fucked-up hostel in Chinatown, windowless rooms with bunk beds, a bathroom where someone dragged their works on the sides of all the toilet paper rolls to clean the blood off. The hostel was better than the street, not much else. A shelter that charged cash. Everything about the place was punitive. They used the same cleaning products as The Tombs.

Lorie lived in the hostel full time. Section 8 paid for her room. She thought Linda was stuck up. "You take too many showers when you're here. They know you're in there so they can go in and go through your shit. Stupid. You want that? They'll go in with their keys and they'll snoop around while you're washing your ass."

Checkout was at nine. Linda slept until eight thirty, checked out at 8.59. A right turn off the Bowery on Houston or 1st St., North East to the park. She got coffee, sucked in the fresh air. She shot out snot rockets, the cloying plastic smell of the hostel.

Some days she went south to Delancey and copped pills on Christie St. in the park or Essex St. at the McDonald's. Methadone patients mixed benzos with their doses and got rocked. She went looking for Pearl to trade spliffs for Xanax. She found her listening to the radio on a bench off Broome St, drinking a beer wrapped in brown paper, swinging her legs. She wore knock off Nikes, acid washed jeans and a leather jacket. She wore big sunglasses, her hair was tied back tight, her hairline was receding. They swapped ten dollar worth of product in either direction.

"You like Madonna?"

"She's all right."

"I taught her how to move!" Pearl put her hands up and danced in her seat.

Chapter 52

Columbus Circle, 1 November 1982

Leading up to *A Night With Sarah*, Sarah Bremure gave several sermons and each was better than the last. With each talk she felt like she brought more of Nan to the pulpit. She resolved enough time had passed that she owed it to the congregation to come into her own. This was her signal to the flock that she was ready to lead.

The front row was reserved for Bob and Alice Walsh, Virginia Parker, Maria and Francisco Grim, and real estate millionaires Don and Minnie Toberoff. Sarah couldn't find an empty seat in the entire theater. Pierre and Bishop Walsh stood right off stage.

"Good evening everyone! Look at all of you. I love every one of you! Thank you!" They gave her the first standing ovation of the night. "Tonight, we're going to get to the heart of the matter. Tonight is the night future historians will say she laid it out there. Tonight is the night we talk about En Sof."

The congregation erupted in applause. "What are we talking about when we talk about En Sof? The potential, the moment before creation. When we say En Sof, we're saying potential. This is both power in theory and power as inevitability, unrealized but very much primed to burst forward into the fore, front and center! There was a moment before time exploded forth and became time. The big bang, right? What preceded the big bang? That was En Sof. En Sof is inside and outside, above and below, the elements, the forces, the phenomena, all things, all people, all times, all dimensions! The moment before Jehovah created heaven and earth, said it was good, this was a power which had not been used so it would drive the edges of the universe forward. En Sof preceded all things, nothing we can measure or even conceive of preceded this moment because it was *only this moment that preceded anything...*

"This seems impossible, but it must be so. The last moment before the emergence of Time. The time before time. The time before the beginning. If you pray on this, I can't tell you what will come of your prayer but it will be wonderful. Prayer on this liminal, unmeasurable thing. When I pray on this, these questions, I feel so vital, so energetic, so healthy. When I pray on En Sof, the time before time I'm exercising the part of my mind that connects me with Jehovah. It's a muscle like all the rest. You need to work it out. If you've already prayed you know what to do. But this time, you ask Jehovah about En Sof. Ask Jehovah about this infinite nothingness colliding with all of existence. Ask Jehovah what it means when the light of the daughter collides with the darkness of the son. When I pray on En Sof I know that I'm on the way to Jehovah!"

"Thank you, Jehovah!" they yelled back. They cried; they held each other. They cheered. "Thank you, Jehovah!" The room chanted in unison, whipped themselves into a frenzy. Sarah closed her eyes and took in the energy, bathed in the sound. She leaned into the microphone. "Let us pray." The room immediately fell silent.

"Jehovah, we assemble here today in your glory, in awe of you, your power, your laws, and your messengers. We thank you for your good graces, Jehovah. We thank you for your protection. We thank you for your assistance in our battles, our struggles, our ordeals. Thank you, Jehovah, for your love. Thank you for your support in this time of trial. Thank you for guiding us while we found our way. It's in your name that we formed your church. We know only your love can defeat evil. Thank you, Jehovah. Amen."

Chapter 53

1984 Aspen, CO

1983–84 was a time of significant growth. Sarah Bremure spoke in the homes of members in The Hamptons, Martha's Vineyard, Chesapeake Bay, Sedona, Palm Springs, Monterey and Napa. An invite only retreat with Sarah at Maria and Francisco's compound in Belize collected one hundred of the church's most influential members for a long weekend of meditation, lectures and fellowship.

Now it was the first days of spring. Virginia Parker took a Friday night red eye to Aspen, deep in her memory palace, replaying beach days with her father, a drive to Stanford with Alice, a weekend in Monterrey before senior year. She felt the plane land. *Welcome to Aspen, please wait until we have come to a complete stop before standing up. And gee, it's a perfect sixty degrees tonight, take a look at that.*

Pierre waited at the gate. He took her bag. "I love you, Virginia!" He gave her a long hug. He wore a suede jacket with fringes on the breast, an old pair of Levi's and cowboy boots. He combed his hair to the right. He wore a mustache and red tinted aviators.

"I love you, Pierre."

"The flight was all right?"

"It was wonderful, thank you."

They left the airport, got in the truck. "Nice right? Dodge, American made." The sun began to rise in the mountains. Virginia studied the colors. She felt the elevation.

"Here. Drink some mountain water." He gave her a canteen. "You'll need to just keep drinking the stuff until you adjust to the elevation. We're miles high now and only going up." They wove through mountain roads, keeping a top speed around thirty-five most of the way. The trip took about an hour. They arrived at Toberoff's ski lodge around six thirty. The pine, oak and stone house was built on the side of a mountain. Modernist furnishings, a sunken living room. Picture windows in the back framed the mountainside view. Virginia stopped to smell the blue sage. "Pierre, it's remarkable here!" She walked the pebble driveway with flower gardens on either side of the path to the front door. Sarah Bremure sat on the other side of the house, drinking coffee on the patio, smoking a joint, watching the sun rise. Pierre brought Virginia's bags into her room. Virginia headed straight for Sarah.

"I love you, Sarah!"

"I love you, Virginia! So much, come here."

"Don't get up." Virginia rushed to Sarah's seat. She lowered to her knees and put her head in Sarah's lap, her hands around Sarah's waist. Sarah ran her hands through Virginia's hair.

"What a glorious sunrise."

"I had a view on the way up here."

"My nephew gave you the canteen, right?"

"Right away, for the elevation. Delicious, the most delicious water!"

"We'll show you later, snow melt from the peaks of the Rockies. We can take a walk over to the old well. It's gold rush era, very pretty tableau. We can go when Pierre leaves to pick up the Don and Minnie, they'll be here, I believe tonight. Pierre will know, he has the flight information." She took a long drag on her joint, spliffed with raspberry bush and rose petals. "Why don't you have yourself a little nap to recover from your journey before the Toberoff's arrive. Pierre will wake you with coffee when it's time to get ready."

Don, Minnie and Madison Toberoff arrived in their vacation clothes around five thirty. Don wore a denim shirt and slacks. Minnie wore a khaki romper and a silk shawl. Their sixteen year old daughter Madison wore dayglo nylon shorts and a sweatshirt. Don announced the family. "I love you, Sarah!"

Pierre mixed cocktails. They gathered on the patio. Sarah had a champagne cocktail, Virginia had white wine. Don had a Toronto. Minnie drank gin martinis. Madison drank cokes. After two rounds, Sarah, Minnie and Madison went for a walk to the well to see the view. Virginia sat with Don while he smoked a cigar. Pierre came outside, spent. He took up a lawn chair, put on his headphones and had a beer and a cigarette.

"How are you adjusting, the elevation?"

"Oh, just fine. Pierre had water ready when he picked me up, from the well, and I took a little power nap before you arrived, so you can call me acclimated... Pierre said we have a good draw in the morning?"

"I have caterers coming at eight tomorrow. Guests should arrive between nine and ten. I have fourteen commitments. So, catering for twenty. We'll have coffee and breakfast between nine thirty and eleven. Then I'll introduce Sarah at eleven. She'll speak until cocktails..."

"Thank you for your generosity, Don. This is a truly incredible place. What a joy!"

"You should consider it yours. We'll make a key. Come whenever you want."

"I accept, Don. Thank you."

"Our Madison will be attending Columbia next year upon graduation. She's in Dalton. We're very proud."

"She's a brilliant girl."

"She's a math whiz and an athlete, a thinker and a doer. You know she already has her major figured out, Virginia you'll like this: a major in business with a minor in *computer science*."

Virginia's eyes widened. "Well, I'll need an intern this summer..."

"You know I really did hope you'd say that."

***

In the morning, guests filed in. Don Toberoff gave the first toast. He thanked The Brothers of The Hemlock Circle in attendance, nine of his fourteen guests were members in good standing. He gave the room over to Sarah.

She stood up and delivered pure Nan St. John: "Something I find remarkable about Jehovah is that he works toward perfection. His creations are imperfect... Well, come on, we're among friends. They're grotesque! Adam was a massive, monstrous pile of clay and primordial shit. A hermaphrodite! This was before Eve, the first mother in the Abrahamic paths, was pulled from this deep well of potency and, and erotic, feral energy, Adam. Eve was Jehovah's working toward perfection. Eve was extracted from this abominable hybrid of angel and beast – but she was more refined. The advent of the feminine was the revision of the first creation, right? This was the process of taking the stuff of an Angel and making a new being, a new potentiality out of it. An Angel with a nuclear connection with the erotic, a giant with an infinite well of vitality! Jehovah's word comes to those ready to hear it. You don't hear the word unless you're attuned to it. And if you have Jehovah's blessing and THE WILL to carry his message forward you must stand up and speak!"

Chapter 54

Williamsburg, June 1996

Jacques Anzu came out of meditation, lit a clove and got to painting. A canvass was stretched and ready. He opened a large can of black, covered it wall to wall. He let the paint dry, went over to the stove and made espresso, smoked another clove. He put on black jeans and a black turtleneck. He made another pot of coffee. The paint was still wet. He found a piece of black construction paper and a fine brush. He tested gold paints, pentagrams in either value. He tested whites. He tore the paper down the middle and took them to his kitchen table. He concentrated. Black and white was striking. Black and gold was more subtle, better for the background.

He burned a pentagram, an ankh, and an inverted crucifix pattern onto a silkscreen. He pressed the screen, face down onto the canvass and used a plastic pallet to spread the paint. He took his time. Precise motions, left to right, corner to corner. The finished product looked perfect.

He went to the window and rolled a cone. He watched the shadows from the ally. He sat back in his recliner, rocked back on the spring. He stretched out his back and scratched his knee through a hole in his jeans.

He heard torch lighters and tubercular coughs outside. He hit the button. Jacques rigged a microphone outside his window. Choice audio, made good samples. Jacques listened to four crack smokers. Grunts, vinyl jackets against the brick wall. They passed around two pipes, hisses, stage whispers. *"Do the push, push it before you give it to me. Push that shit."*

Jacques turned up the volume on a pair of headphone. He'd recorded freestyle ciphers, fist and knife fights. Hasidic men and boys, truck drivers and coke dealers fucking the gig workers from under the bridge.

A neighbor stuck his head out the window. "Fucking Crackheads, get the fuck out of here! Now!"

"We're moving man! Fuck you!"

"Fuck me? I'll call the cops. I see who you are, let me catch you in the streets. I call the police you junkies!"

Two of the smokers stayed to argue. *"Bitch you're always are starting fucking problems."*

"You're a fucking pussy. You're a fucking faggot. I hope the fucking cops come, because you're a fucking bitch! My cousin's in Rikers he'll fucking cut your face!"

Jacques returned to the canvass. The pattern was perfect, could have been printed by a machine. Jacques picked a tape at random from a pile of cassettes, Side B of Officer Down's *Tompkins Square Everywhere.* He opened a white can of paint and taped out geometric patterns on the canvass. He stenciled the white lines over the black and gold background.

He put on a mix tape, Steve Sinclair and The Werewolves, more Officer Down. He lit a clove. He flipped the tape over. Side B was all Missing Foundations. He peeled off the tape. Precise, sacred geometry over the print. The painting was finished.

The buzzer rang. Maxine Mauve and Carlos came upstairs. "This is the ritual," said Maxine. She gave Jacques a VHS tape, he put it in a leather satchel. They sat down in the living room. Jacques lit a clove. Carlos rolled a blunt. Maxine went through the CDs. She put on Shotgun and Treasure – *Stab NYC.*

"My friend Clifford just joined Tokyo Red Army on synths," said Carlos.

"The hepcat with the braids?"

"Oh, you know him?"

"We met once. In Soho, I think."

"The guy's a genius. Like one of the few around today."

"There's never been more geniuses alive than right now."

Maxine snorted. "That's ridiculous."

"I'll get us on the list for TRA tomorrow night. They're opening for Shotgun. It's a gallery thing," said Carlos.

"That's a good bill. I'll be there." Jacques picked up one of his cameras and shot them separately, together, candid, posing. Maxine had dark brown skin, dreads that hung around three feet long. Purple nails, one-inch gauges in her earlobes, a ring in her septum, a Monroe under her lip. She wore black lipstick, purple eye shadow, and black mascara. She was short with wide hips.

"What time is it?" asked Carlos.

"Nine-thirty."

"We should go soon, no?"

"Didn't we just get here? Can't we take a taxi?" Maxine sat with the music.

"Where are you going?"

"Party in the City, Soho. Fashion people."

"Want to come?"

"No, I have work to do."

"In that case we should go, no?"

Maxine used Jacques' phone and called the car service.

"We have a car in five minutes," said Maxine.

***

The phone rang. "Jacques, it's Maria Grim."

"Yes Maria."

"Is anyone over at your studio right now?"

"No, Maria."

"I'll be there at 10.45 with someone very important. Be ready." He checked his watch, ten thirty. He made a pot of coffee. A Ministry CD got him off the couch and over to his studio. The bell rang. Jacques let in Maria Grim, Virginia Parker and her assistant Madison Toberoff.

"Come on in." He turned his back and walked over to the studio. "Can I get you anything?"

"No, that's fine," said Virginia, looking around.

Jacques lit a clove. He put on a flannel shirt. He arranged canvasses, stretched against the wall, unstretched on the floor. He put out a chair for Maria.

Madison stood still, in the kitchen, uneasy. She'd never been to Brooklyn before. She smoked a Marlboro Light over the sink. Virginia studied each painting, then Jacques' altar.

"Do you see anything you like?"

"I do. Quite a bit." She pointed out three 10×18 canvasses. Baphoment, Set, and a work of Sacred Geometry.

"For you, ninety-three."

"Madison, please write a check for ninety-three k."

"Madison, payable to *MG Gallery LLC*," said Maria.

***

The next night, Carlos rang up with his coke dealer, Manny. He banged his head as he entered the loft and mimed drumsticks. "Bro what is this?" asked Carlos.

"Some punk tape."

"Can I borrow it?"

"Yeah you can take it with you."

"Thanks, Jacques. Cool, cool!"

Manny beelined to the canvass. "This man, fuck. This is cool, Jacques. It's divinity and demonology and the sacred and the profane... Fuck, man!"

Carlos did the rest of his coke. He bought a new quarter ounce from Manny. Carlos and Jacques cut up lines, gave one back to Manny. "I've got rolls, k... For you guys rolls are fifteen k is fifty a lick."

Carlos pulled out eighty bucks. "I'm about to get fucked up, man!"

"You know how to do this? Put it in the microwave for thirty-second intervals. Fifty power, until you get a powder."

"I'm going to use your microwave, man."

Tokyo Red Army went on at nine. It was eight thirty. "Oh shit, it's time to get a taxi. Jacques—" He snapped his fingers. "We need to go."

Jacques put on his wool jacket and fingerless gloves. He put paint markers and some spray caps in his pockets for good measure. He put a black beanie over his bald head. Jacques, Carlos and Manny took a cab to Ludlow St.

They mixed into the crowd outside the club. Revelers fell into the street. Vampires, punks and ravers mixed in the sidewalk. They bummed each other cigarettes and got into taxis. They walked off onto Stanton St. or back to Houston for the train.

HYPE MACHINE called Tokyo Red Army 'Revolutionary Dance Jazz Rock, Situationist Funk.' They were Japanese born guitarist Hiro X and virtuoso bassist Jimmi Jay with a rotating list of musicians behind them. Hiro wore a top hat, brown leather coat with brass buckles, blue jeans and a beard. Jimmi Jay dressed like Jimmy Page and played like Les Claypool. Tonight was Miles Smith on drums and Clifford Mills, the jazz prodigy, debuting on synths. He played shirtless in tight blue jeans, sunglasses and a sweatband. Clifford played like it was '80s Berlin.

Hiro and Jimmi screamed in unison *TURN OUT THE LIGHTS! TURN OUT THE LIGHTS!* TRA launched into their Beefheart inspired *Deli Coffee (24-Hr ATM)*. Hiro's wife, the painter Miyu X stood behind the PA, projecting a collage of images: The Tompkins Riots, The Tet Offensive, Berkowitz, Aleister Crowley, Shoko Asahara, Manson, Susan Atkins, Desert Storm.

Hiro danced on his distortion pedals and cranked out fuzzy, other worldly sounds, a long intro for the band's greatest moment, *Andrija*. An industrial epic, a progressive crescendo of menacing, sinister loops and rhythms. Clifford played disaster movie organs. Jimmi Jay's bass sent waves of anxiety and dread through the room. They crescendoed into a bluesy hard rock and the bar choked on weed. Revelers crawled onto the stage and gawked at Hiro, danced like dervishes, like shakers. Miyu projected L. Ron Hubbard, Jack Parsons, Mao, Zhou Enlai, Ho Chi Minh, Zia-ul-Haq, Carlos the Jackal, Osama Bin Laden, Oliver North, HW Bush, The Sabra and Chatilla Massacres, and the MOVE Bombing. Then Jacques Anzu's screenprints of Kali.

Shotgun hugged Jacques from the side. "Yoo – Shock thatch the shit!" An old French Algerian who documented rock and roll shows took a photo of Jacques and Shotgun. Shotty tilted his head to the side and lifted his chin. Jacques looked into the camera's soul. Shotgun lit a blunt. Jacques sniffed the PCP. Shotgun passed it and Jacques got dusted. Shotgun snapped his finger. "Yoo, why don't you paint during my shet?"

"Dope."

"Good night, New York!" yelled Hiro.

"Thank you, New York!" yelled Jimmi Jay.

"Shotgun is up next," said Hiro. The revelers cheered. "Stick around!" Hiro and Clifford hugged. They took their gear apart. Houselights went up. Revelers took the stage.

Jacques and Shotgun went backstage and found a piece of plywood. The gallery already bought Shotgun a shitload of spray paint, twenty cans were in his rider. Treasure and the sound people helped set up Shotgun's turntables, his board, synths and pedals.

Treasure hit the lights. Shotgun took the mic. "Awww shit! New York Shitty here we are. Lower E Shide where we at? Shock Anzu worldwide legendary is live painting. We're doing music up here!" He pointed to the sound booth. "My brother Treasure from Copenhagen is doing the lights and shound. Lights, camera, action!" Shotgun dropped the needle on a drum and bass record. Treasure dropped the lights, put a spotlight on Jacques.

He sprayed the plywood black. Shotgun improvised on the keyboard. Shotgun recorded his keyboard loop and played it back. He put on a second drum and bass record and recorded new loops. One of Shotgun's friends jumped on stage and started dancing. Maxine Mauve ran out from backstage. Treasure put them under a strobe light. Shotgun passed Maxine a dust blunt. "We're smoking dust! We're smoking weed! We got Angie! We got Maxine all Powerful!" Angie was black Dominican, long dreads, UFOs and a DEATH HURT shirt. Maxine wore a black dress over full body fishnets, vinyl boots. Jacques finished the black background. He switched to a can of yellow and sprayed zig-zag patterns up and down the board. He chose a can of red and repeated the pattern. He randomly sprayed stripes over the red and yellow with silver pant. Jacques lit a clove and looked at the board. He pulled a white can out and pulled a small cap from his pocket. He painted an outline in white: Set's headdress, a beak and ears like antennae. He painted his arched eyebrow. Shotgun chose samples at random, new layers, new loops.

Treasure timed new strobe lights to the music. Jacques left the stage for a few minutes to cool down and blow lines with Clifford and Miles from TRA. He ran back on stage and resumed the painting. Shotgun circulated more dust. The dancing got stranger, more ecstatic.

"Yo, Treasure!" Shotgun shouted into the mic.

"Yo, Shotty!" Treasure answered back over the PA. "Shotty Shot!"

"Itch time to take thish shit into new dimensions, outer shpace." Treasure projected NASA satellite images. Shotgun dropped his and Treasure's *Christlandia to Rotterdam*. The revelers cheered. Pills kicked in. Dust traveled through the dance floor. Treasure mixed in projections from *Shotgun 95*: a subway tunnel, Shotgun in a balaclava, windbreaker, and gray sweats bombing a wall.

Back at Jacques' station he traced Set's outline with blue paint. He painted stripes into his headdress. He filled in Set's face with orange. The profile filled the top half of board. He dropped to his knee with the can of purple. He stared at the black wood. He shook the can and painted a straight line, vertically, down the middle of lower half of the board. He randomly grabbed four cans. Four colors; blue, green, orange and yellow. Four perfect stripes. He picked out the gold and silver cans. He painted two arrows on each of the eight points. Treasure introduced a new round of lights, white strobes and colors that bounced off the painting and back into Jacques' body. He elevated outside the building and through the star gate.

Dozens of percussion tracks looped over each other, samples from street noise, AM radio, sounds so distorted that there was no telling at all. Jacques returned to his body and fell into the crowd to dance. "That's Shock Anzu the infamous the dangerous the powerful Shock! Director, *Shotgun 95!* World famous number one!"

"Jacques, one love!" said Treasure.

***

Back home, Jacques opened a beer, popped Maxine and Carlos' tape in his VCR and sat back on the couch with his feet up.

Maxine Mauve prepares for the ritual. She wears a black silk robe and a red shawl. She draws a circle on the floor with salt. A candle for fire, a bowl of water, paper for the wind, soil for the earth. Carlos undresses. Maxine drops the robe outside the circle and lays down on her back, feet planted on the floor, knees up. Carlos enters the circle, drops to his knees. The Virgin De Guadalupe is tattooed on his left side, the back of his ribs. He has thin arms and legs and a fat belly. Maxine has 1" stainless steel bars through her nipples, a pentagram tattooed on her stomach, sternum to groin. She chants the sutra under her breath while Carlos eats her outs. She cums, she screams, Carlos keeps going. She continues the sutra, they go on until the tape runs out.

Jacques sat up. He put his beer down. He went to the VCR and rewound the tape. He played it again.

Chapter 55

The Lower East Side, 1996

Shotgun put Linda Solomon on the guest list for the next Shotgun and Treasure show on the Bowery. S&T were the headliners, DEATH HURT opened. Linda worked the room, shmoozed, sold out of spliffs. Shotgun took her backstage. Treasure rolled blunts and prepared to perform. Shotgun, upon reentry passed out hugs and pounds. He accepted lines and chatted with a music journalist. An up and coming designer from Brazil started up a conversation about the housing market with Linda. "I will buy this year. I'm waiting for them to clear out the right street for me, then I'll buy."

His date, a photography MFA sat in a corner with cameras on his lap, smoking Marlboro Lights with a model and sex worker named Eloise. She put her hand on Linda's shoulder. "I bet your art is amazing!"

"Oh, wow, thanks?"

Eloise shoveled coke, she grew calmer the more she blew. "I would just *kill* for a smoke right now!"

Linda offered her a Camel.

"*Laura*, you're incredible." Linda let it slide. "Who are you with? You're amazing!"

Someone from the club led Jacques Anzu, Maxine Mauve, and Carlos into the green room. "We're on in five," she said.

"We're ready," said Shotgun.

"Ready," said Treasure.

The designer cut up more blow. The MFA snapped photos of Jacques, Maxine and Carlos. "Stevie is your biggest fan."

"Rudy!"

"No kidding," said Jacques, he put his chin up, spread his legs out and put his arms around Maxine and Carlos. Maxine tilted her head and put a hand on her hip, raised eyebrows. Carlos did crazy eyes and gave the camera the finger. Stevie followed Shotgun, Treasure, Jacques, Maxine and Carlos out the door, snapping photos. Eloise and Rudy wrapped their arms around each other and chatted in Italian.

Linda, Eloise and Rudy took a space in the front row. They got dusted, Linda took off her flannel and wrapped it around her waist.

"New York Shitty how we doing? Bowery! Lower E Shide! No place to hide. I love you!"

Revelers cheered and screamed. "We are Shotgun and Treasure. I'm Treasure, that's my brother Shotgun. We have family here today. That's Maxine, Carlos, Jacques Anzu. They're making tonight magical. Shotgun."

"Wassup, bro?"

"Shotty Shot... Shotgun, hit it!"

Shotgun's synths sounded like a threat. Treasure drummed on an electric kit. Bursts of color, strobes, bright white lights danced over their side of the stage. Spot lights focused on the magicians. They performed in front of a 10×15-foot mirror that reflected the floor back to the crowd. Jacques and Carlos drew a triangle on the stage floor. Maxine drew a circle of salt inside the triangle.

Carlos hooked chains to a rig, he tugged to check it was solid. Jacques slid two hooks into Maxine's back. She hung her head. She muttered a sutra. She didn't flinch. Carlos connected Maxine's hooks to the rig. Jacques pulled the chains, Carlos lifted Maxine up along to distribute the weight better. She swung over the stage, eyes closed. She meditated.

Revelers stopped dancing to watch Maxine fly. They cheered as Jacques and Carlos slowly brought her down. Maxine pierced, hooked, and chained up Carlos. He took his ride in the air. Revelers started dancing again. Linda watched Jacques Anzu take off his shirt and Maxine pierce his back. He hung his head and muttered the sutra, Carlos connected Jacques to the rig. Linda stopped moving. Jacques Anzu flew through the air. Linda didn't blink. She felt Jacques' intensity, she felt his sense of calm. There was no sound or smell, only Jacques suspended. The crowd cheered as Maxine and Carlos brought him down. Treasure was deep in a hypnotic drum loop, Shotgun layered dozens, even hundreds of samples over the percussion. Linda felt the bass in her body as Maxine and Carlos lowered Jacques down.

Shotgun readied a new drop. "Incredible spectacle. My family!"

Smell reasserted, sweat, PCP, crack, White Owls, Dutch Masters, haze, beer, the smoke machine. Linda held her focus on Jacques. She watched Carlos and Jacques press their foreheads together while Maxine removed the hooks. The room shook, revelers gyrated. Linda watched Jacques walk off stage. When he left her view, she closed her eyes and danced.

Chapter 56

Summer 1996

Amanda and Bad Mike got out of bed and over to Tompkins in time for the Choking Victim set. They stood off to the side. Amanda wore Mike's hoodie over her shoulders and leaned into him. Her dreads were thick, wrapped with beads, hex nuts and wires. She wore overalls and a dirty olive t-shirt. Regulars approached Bad Mike and he shook his head, waved them away. Diamond was serving dope over by 10th and B. Amanda hated the crowd. They left the park during the closer to get coffees at Ray's.

Bad Mike and Amanda stood on the corner of 7th and watched half of the 9th Precinct collect a block up, on St. Mark's and A. The uniforms wore riot gear, swung their batons and ground their heels into the street. The plain clothes cops stretched and shadowboxed. When the park emptied, gangs of cops jumped out on punks as they tried to leave through 8th St. They detained whoever they could, ran names, arrested anyone with a warrant. They wrote the rest tickets for dis-con. Half broke off from St. Marks and A and invaded the park. Cops swarmed the benches. They poured out 40s and knifed a box of wine, arrested Gutter Andy, Jerkoff, and Bob Anarcho for dis-con.

"Everyone else to fuck off before we get back. Park is closed!"

Chapter 57

Dolores Farm, April 1984

Katherine St. John Walsh was born on 16 October 1984 in San Diego. As soon as Alice was clear to fly, Walsh chartered a jet to Long Island. The Ram, Bishop Thom welcomed them at the airport. Pierre took their bags. The Ram put Kip on his shoulders. He met Katie for the first time. He kissed her forehead. They loaded into a van. Pierre drove them out of the airstrip and straight to Dolores.

Pierre drove through acres of orchards. "Dolores was my great, great grandma. Grandpa loved her enough to name this place for her. Their ashes are in the soil. Best fruit on the island, has been for a century. You'll have your tastes, right off the trees."

Virginia Parker and Sarah Bremure sat on the front porch of the farm house. Kip let go of Walsh's hand and ran for Virginia. She picked him up and kissed him. "I love you, Kip!"

"I love you, Aunt Virginia!"

Alice walked with the baby over to Sarah, who wept when she held her. "I've never seen anything more perfect! This is her; this is perfection! Thank you, Jehovah."

"We call her Katie."

"Oh, she's perfection! She's an angel on earth!"

Pierre carried the Walsh's luggage into the farmhouse. The Ram prepared the basement for Katie's baptism. Sarah, Virginia, Alice took the baby into the living room by the fireplace. Walsh and Kip played in the backyard. When The Ram was ready, he came upstairs and fixed himself a whiskey.

Walsh and Kip went upstairs and put on their matching three piece suits, red ascots, and black hats with red pompoms. Walsh took his son's hand and led him to the basement, a stone and brick foundation with vaulted ceilings and archways that supported the weight of the house. Pierre set up a row of chairs. Virginia, Sarah, and Pierre sat up front. Alice sat with the baby and waited for the ceremony to begin. The Ram stood in his place before them, wearing a black robe and his 10" steel Celtic Cross around his neck.

"Go sit with Aunt Virginia," Walsh told Kip. He ran over to sit between Virginia and Sarah. Walsh took his place next to his brother. Alice stood up with the baby and stood between them.

The Ram took a bottle from his robe. "This water was drawn from the wells of Jerusalem. We have taken this child to this holy place to free her of sin. We baptize this child in the name of Jehovah so that she may be humanity's chance to win the battle against Satan."

He opened the bottle. "Robert Walsh. Are you the father of this child?"

"Yes, I am."

"Alice Walsh. Are you the mother of this child?"

"Yes, I am."

"Robert Walsh, was this child born in wedlock?"

"Yes, she was."

"Alice Walsh, was this child born for the benefit of sin?"

"No, she was not."

"Will either of you stand in the way of her absolution before Jehovah?"

"No, we will not."

"Alice Walsh, kneel and present this child." The Ram dabbed water on his finger. He touched it to his forehead. He dabbed on more and he touched Katie's face. He drew the swastika. "Katherine St. John Walsh, you are absolved of sin. Robert and Alice Walsh, will you allow this child to deviate from Jehovah?"

"We will not."

"This child is of Jehovah. This child is free of sin."

Chapter 58

Williamsburg, 1996

Jacques Anzu and Eddie Mad Dog sat on Jacques' roof, beers in hand, watching the river. "How long are you in town?"

"Flying back Friday, why?"

"I'm shooting some videos Thursday and I thought you'd look good in the background, hanging out."

"Get the tattoo guy in there?"

"Yeah. Shave your face, get the chin tat out."

"What's the video?"

"It's for *Consumption*. I've got junkies, crack heads, getting high, just rapping for the camera. Telling stories. I buy them a bag of dope, some hits of coke and they're lined up out the door. Remember that party The Werewolves had going on 23rd St., it's all guys from back there."

"Mad Dog's no crackhead, but I'll be in the video… Who's coming over?"

"Paris and Bad Mike."

"Bad Mike from 10th St.?"

"That's the guy."

"That's a hard dude. Yeah, I'll come by."

"Paris is doing the interview. I'm taking Bad Mike's photo for a gallery show I'm doing."

"Paris is fucking crazy."

"Damn right."

"Last time I saw Paris he was like oh shit, Mad Dog? And I was like oh shit what's up Paris and he was like Mad Dog no way!"

"Paris last time I saw him, when we made this appointment he was telling me about these encounters he said were ghosts but they sound Enochian to me. I want more info and I want it on tape." Jacques lit a clove. "If anyone we know is connecting with an angelic force it would be Paris, huh?"

They went downstairs and listened to hardcore tapes, reminisced about the Werewolves, Officer Down, and Civil Diss. "I played bass in Civil Diss from '86–'87 but I went to prison in '87 for Gang Assault. Me and Mitch from Demonikkk's did two years in Fishkill."

"You still hang out with Mitch?"

"When I can. We're on good terms. He'll be like Mad Dog? Demonikkk's, Big Gus, Thin Vince, they're always on me to ride with them. To wear the cut. I've tattooed all of them. I did Mitch's back piece. I did Thin Vince's Demonikkk's tattoo on his chest and his 666 on his hand. That quality Vato-Cholo font, that's all me, I do that better than any other white boy, Hollywood or the Lower East Side I don't give a fuck… All right let's get this stencil going."

Jacques took his shirt off. Mad Dog shaved Jacques' chest and stomach. "What we need to do is go freehand."

"Do it." Jacques lit a clove. Mad Dog drew an eight-pointed star with an arrow at the end of each line. He checked himself out in the mirror. "Looks right."

While Mad Dog set up the power supply, the ink caps and the needles, Jacques set up his tripods and two cameras. One would shoot over Mad Dog's shoulder and one was positioned for a wide shot. They cut up an eight ball and went to work. Mad Dog cleaned Jacques' chest. "Don't hate me 'cuz I'm beautiful." He hit the pedal.

Chapter 59
Soho, 1996

It only took a week for Linda to see Jacques Anzu again. She walked East, early morning. She listened to a Joanne Pardes' Psychic TV mix, chewed Klonopin, drank a sweet deli coffee. Sunglasses gave her confidence. She was headed to Henry St. with $400 in her pocket. Linda saw Jacques outside a place called the Cupping Room on Prince St. He wore a leather jacket and round sunglasses. "Hey! You!" He was set up at an outdoor table. Linda came over. "Here, sit down, I'll order you a coffee." Jacques offered her a Clove.

"I'm Jacques, by the way."

"Yeah, I remember."

"And you're Linda, Linda Solomon."

"Yeah!" She smiled. Jacques smiled back.

He tilted back in his chair, the back pressed against the wall. The waiter came out with a tray of coffee, milk and sugar. Jacques nodded to him, he nodded back and returned inside. Linda poured four raw sugars into her coffee and milk to the brim.

"Whoa this is delicious… What are you reading?"

"Here." He pushed it to her.

Linda felt giddy at the attention, the gift. It was a copy of Maxine Mauve's zine.

"You have to let me know what you think."

"What's your number?"

He opened a Moleskin notebook and wrote down his number. He tore the paper and gave it to Linda. She put it in her jacket. She lingered, nursed the coffee and the clove. Linda caught herself staring. "I should be going."

"Let me know what you think."

She headed east.

Chapter 60

Neptune Hotel, 1996

Jacques Anzu decided to rent a hotel room. He didn't need Paris, 730 or Sincerious casing his loft, plotting out how get back inside. Minimum one out of the three would bite Jacques' hand. Paris came in first. Jacques planned to have all of them arrive at once but didn't wait to get started.

"This is a project I'm doing, it's called *Consumption*. You can shoot dope, I've got rocks, whatever. You just have to let me tape it, take your picture. If you've got anything to say, a story, go for it. I've got a release you need to sign that lets me use the footage but you get high and you can use the room until tomorrow."

"Yeah, yeah, whatever Homie." Paris was skinny, rat-faced, brown dreads, the sides of his head were shaved. He wore wraparound sunglasses, vaguely cybergoth. He spoke in a heavy Long Island accent.

Jacques set up two Super 8 cameras on tripods and shot Paris beaming up at the table.

"So, we've got like six junkies in the house already and fucking Rios, remember Rios?"

"Yeah."

"Rios shows up. He's just gotten thrown out of some apartment in the Village and Rios has this fucking fifty-year-old crackhead from Washington Square! I say to him, yo, you can't do this to me! This ain't my place, this is my girl's place and she's already sore with me. Her friends don't like me anymore, you know? They're all saying 'come with me you don't need him,' so when Rios shows up with a fucking crackhead, oh my god! I said Rios, man, you can't bring a crackhead to my girl's place and he's like he's not a crackhead. He quit, yesterday!" Paris broke out laughing. "He quit yesterday!"

Paris shook his head. "Those were better times... When I had a girl. She was all right too, as far as girls go. There's two kinds and both of them are no good for me. There's the girls who want you to be all proper and work a job and pay their bills. Not happening, man! Fuck that shit. That's out. Do I look like a worker? What is that shit? Come on man, sucky-sucky. Fuck! The other kinda girl, the better kind to be sure, she's cool. She has money, she doesn't get all paranoid about you associating with other women, she's all right. Maybe she's bisexual, I like that. But I like girls who make me money, get me high. This girl was like that and Rios was the kind of guy who'd fuck that up for you. You or me or any motherfucker. Rios didn't give a shit. Rios died last year? 1994? 1995. That motherfucker. He took a guy out. Put him in a coma and the guy died in the hospital. The cops were looking for him. They were going everywhere where's Rios, come on guys, help yourselves out. We said motherfucker we don't know. You know we don't like the guy why are you bothering us? He don't come around here anymore and now he's gone. You think he's coming back?

"They found Rios up in the Bronx dead from an OD… RIP, I guess. He got what was coming. He couldn't get out. He said he was from Puerto Rico but couldn't go back. But you know, he deserved to die because he was out killing people." Paris cooked up three bags of dope. He rolled up a pant leg, scabs, pulsing abscesses. Jacques zoomed in while Paris found a vein. "You got more rocks too, right? I'm doing a big shot I want to stay awake, you get me, homie?"

"Yeah, yeah." Jacques tossed some vials of crack onto the table.

"Good looks though." Paris hit the spot. He sucked his teeth, hissed and exhaled. His eyes fluttered, he swayed, he adjusted his cock. "Ghosts used to come in my room and fuck me and suck on my big ass dick and rim my asshole. You've seen Ghostbusters? That happens. It was like that. They just show up and get busy. I took it in the ass from a ghost once. Wasn't gay of course because it was a ghost. Some living man comes in my room tries to fuck my ass I probably set him aflame? Something like that. Maybe I'd break his knees or something. But a ghost is different. No damage to my asshole." He got the crack pipe ready.

"But it was mostly ghost chicks. You know some of them, they'll look like a chick then they've got a cock. One time I met this chick dressed in Medieval Times, armor and a sword. When I got her naked she had a fucking cock and a pussy! And all this light, man, white light just followed her everywhere. I said let me get some of this pussy! That was probably the best pussy there is. That ghost with both organs but looking like a girl!

Exactly how I like em. When they've got the dick on them you can recognize some of yourself in them. It's how you know these ghosts have got something going for them. Man, I hope when I die I can get another piece of that pussy. I'll suck her dick too. Just let me get a piece of that pussy man for real!"

730 and Sincerious came through a few hours later. Jacques snorted heroin and coke in intervals to avoid falling asleep or getting bored. He had about six more hours of Super 8 left. "Sup!" Sincerious gave Jacques a pound, 730 blew past them and headed to Paris.

"White boy! White boy! Wake up, you said we were gonna party!"

"Don't worry about him, what are you looking for, come here, relax."

"You got clean works?"

"I got works, water, cotton, I've got dope, coke, rocks... I just need you to sign these releases and you can do whatever you want, it just needs to be on camera."

Sincerious grabbed the paper out of Jacques' hand, snatched the pen, and signed his name. He took off his jacket and fixed on dope. Jacques took his picture. "This is proper shit, yo." He hit the nod. Jacques got in close and covered Sincerious.

The smell of dope woke up Paris. "Yo, let's get high!" Jacques photographed the sequence.

Jacques interviewed 730 in front of the Super 8s. "Everybody says they can't take me anywhere since I'm violent... I'm violent. But I'm also the kind of dude the rest of the men need to worry about because they don't fuck their wife's good. When you're not fucking your wife, eating her pussy she doesn't tell you. I just show up. I'll fuck a woman so good, eat her pussy and have her giving me money... You know of some producer, if I got a white Jewish guy to do the business side, you know those guys, right?"

"Yeah, yeah."

"You've gotta introduce us, man. We're leaving money on the table! Because I don't give a fuck!" He packed his stem and beamed up. He held in the smoke and choked it out. Jacques photographed the cloud.

"Man did you hear about what happened to Rios?"

"What happened?"

"He was supposed to be working for this guy and it looked like he was doing good. Rios was getting the shit on consignment and then robbing dudes to get the money to pay the guys and get more. But they got fucked up, man, they lost their shit. But there's I guess enough dudes out there to rob that they could keep up the payments. This is big money, man!"

Sincerious started to freestyle. "Egregious, prestigious, I fucked the high priestess, Sincerious, delirious, Sincerious delirious! Sincerious delirious!"

"Yo, shut up! I'm telling the shit to Jacques, man! Yo, Paris, what's good with that pipe?"

Chapter 61

Dolores Farm, August 1985

Sarah Bremure woke up from a dream on the first day of spring, 1985. She opened her journal and wrote down a recipe Nan gave her, as instructed: grain alcohol, acacia, datura and henbane. She looked out the window. Pinks and purples, she estimated six thirty. She climbed out of bed, put on her robe. She said her morning prayers. She opened the window.

She stuck her head out and yelled, "Pierre! Pierre! I need you. Nan gave me a list! Pierre! Wake up!"

Pierre climbed into the cellar with a flashlight and collected what Nan and Sarah asked for. Their collection took up three ten foot shelves in a corner of the basement. Herbs, tree barks, roots, mushrooms and weeds. Everything was stored in its own gallon sized glass jar. He packed what he needed into a mason jar. He went upstairs, into the farmhouse kitchen and set a pot of water with a steaming basket on the stove to boil. He filled the jar with grain alcohol and carefully placed it the water to accelerate the infusion process. He watched the stove, added water to the pot throughout the day to keep the level steady. At dusk he took the tincture off the flame, dried off the glass and put the jar on a shelf.

Sarah dug up her favorite stationery and her fountain pen. She wrote three letters, to Virginia Parker, Alice and Bob Walsh, and to Maria and Francisco Grim.

YOU ARE CORDIALLY INVITED TO DOLORES FARM THE 3 WAXING DAYS AND 3 WANING OF AUGUST.

Day One

Pierre picked up Virginia Parker and Bob and Alice Walsh from the air strip. "Just wait until all of you see what I've done with the place. Seven days a week, out in the orchards, the gardens, pulling weeds... We have three gardens! Berry bushes and vegetables, all right, herbs and flowers. Sarah has the vision of course, I'm just her hands, but I have my own plot going too – Sarah said I should experiment, use my creativity – wait 'til you see it."

They drove through the orchards. The air was perfumed with fruit and pine. Sarah Bremure and Maria and Francisco Grim drank mate on the porch from gourds. The gardens covered the right third of the house with berry bushes and plum trees. Chard, kale, rhubarb, tomatoes, and carrots grew on plots. Squash, beans and cucumbers climbed up trellises. They kept a flower garden between the vegetable plots and the wrought iron fencing. It perfumed the road all summer. Sarah stood up slowly, she held her hip in place with her left hand. "I love you!"

Pierre carried luggage inside the house then served sun brewed ice tea. Lunch was bacon from down the road, tomatoes from the garden and homemade bread. After lunch, they toured the gardens and orchards. When they felt hot they retired to the shaded patio behind the house. They sat under a canopy of elm and crab apple trees. Sarah fanned herself. Pierre pointed his thumb at the barn behind them. "Later on, I'll show you, we have a cider press in there. The rest is the studio for my woodworking. These chairs, this table, made 'em right over there."

"These are fantastic," said Walsh.

"Pierre made Kip and Katie's cribs. We keep them in the garage now they're too beautiful to give up."

Sarah lit a spliff with raspberry bush, rose petals, and damiana. She breathed in deep.

"Oh! Can I have some?" asked Alice.

"Everything but the grass is from the garden..." Sarah smiled and passed the joint. She closed her eyes and breathed, in and out. "Oh, what a wonderful day! Having all of you here I could get emotional!" She reached for Virginia's hand.

"Alice, Bobby, you traveled all this way. I love you! Maria, Francisco, Virginia, Pierre, I love you! All of you here, I love you the most of anyone I know. Aside from Nan who's – well, we all agree she's here right now, already – but recently, like I said in my letters, we've been talking. In my dreams, it's right under this tree, most nights but sometimes by the barn door, and we talk. Well, recently, it's been happening every night. It's wonderful to see her. She told me to gather all of you, on this day. She told me the process. She told me it will take seven days. On the seventh day we'll rest. The other days will demand a level of spiritual energy that even for us will be a challenge, but this is how it has to be. She wants to know, are we ready?"

"I'm ready," said Virginia.

"I'm ready." Walsh took Alice's hand.

"I'm ready," said Alice.

"We're ready," said Francisco.

"I'm ready." Maria stood up, and they came together. Pierre and Maria locked arms, they gathered around Sarah.

Pierre sang, "Group hug!"

Day Two

Pierre laid down Nan and Sarah's blankets from Nepal on the grass behind the house. Each adept took up a blanket and spent the day in silent meditation. Virginia attuned herself to the ocean, the beach on the other side of the pine forest. She meditated on the aromas from the gardens and the beach winds. She felt the sun's movement across her face, neck and shoulders. She listened to the bird songs, hums from insects, the distant crash of the waves into the beach, the wind in the pines. The sun blazed low. She sat with sunburn, pins and needles, stirs of boredom. She grew thirsty, hungry despite the heat. She meditated on desire.

Sarah broke the silence. "I feel part of this place." She leaned forward, onto her knees. Pierre stood up and helped her to her feet. "Who else feels ready to drink some water? Discuss tomorrow?"

At dusk, Pierre served bowls of wine soaked with cubensis mushrooms from a clay pot. They sat in a circle, sipping the wine from a bowl. Pierre played a drum. Maria sang scales, *amore*. She fell into a laughing fit. The laughter was contagious. They rolled on the grass, held their kidneys, gasping for air.

Sarah, forced out words. "We're under moonlight! We're lit up with moonlight!" She doubled over, she crawled on all fours, laughing.

Walsh splayed out on the grass. He listened to the soil, smelled the moonlight, felt the earth vibrate. Alice fell into him, writhing, hysterical laughing. He saw a halo around her.

Virginia listened to the cracks in her back, the sounds her body made when she stretched. She listened to a language she didn't know; sounds she'd never heard before.

Pierre stood up from the drum, pulled off his clothes and danced naked. He sang Maria's song. *Amore, amore, amore, amore, amore!* They clapped, they sang, they stomped their feet, all to the rhythm. One, two, one, two, three, one, two, one, two, three…

Day Three

Pierre set the table for the seance in the farmhouse kitchen. The kitchen table, his pride and joy, hand made from colonial era wood. He covered it with a lace tablecloth. The kitchen hadn't been touched since the '20s. Pierre only used vintage instruments, nineteenth century cast iron cookware, a WW1 era iron stove, wooden cutting boards and mixing bowls. Pierre decorated with Amish themes, color wheels and needlepoints, an oil seascape of the Montauk Lighthouse.

Sarah's received method for the seance demanded true dark. The sun not only had to be completely set but the moon had to be, regardless of its phase, prominent in the sky. Nan said, "Communion with the dead, toward any meaningful aim, cannot take place when the sun enjoys life."

They gathered at the table at nine thirty, all in white. Pierre laid out Nan's beads in a ceramic bowl Nan hand sculpted and glazed with Nan's bible and one of her journals. They took their seats, they joined hands, they lowered their heads.

"I'm trying to reach Nan St. John. This is Sarah…" Silence. "We're talking to Nan St. John, Nan and only Nan. We have no other tasks in the realms of the dead, but to speak to Nan St. John. Nan, if you're here with us, please, if you're here with us please hear me. I'm here with people who have never forgotten you. They've never wavered in their faith. Nan. I hope you can feel how desperately we all miss you… But you told us to come together and we did just what you said. Now, we just ask for some guidance. What do we do next, how can we talk to you again? How do we know what to ask… Gosh it feels good to talk to you again. It's what I miss most, just chatting…" Sarah collapsed, she let go of Pierre's hand. She dropped her forehead her arm and wept. Pierre patted her on the back, pressed his ear to her heart.

Day Four

Hermes

Nan came to Sarah and they walked through the orchards in the moonlight. When Sarah woke up she knew what to do, everything fell into place. She sent Pierre to the cellar to prepare. He drew a circle on the floor, a pentagram facing south. He placed a candlestick for North, South, East, West, Water, Fire, Air, and Earth. At midnight the group climbed down the basement stairs and took their places. Sarah walked the principles, Alice Walsh and Virginia Parker through the steps. Pierre set the sour wine and mushroom mixture, the sacred meal, in a bowl in the pentagram's center point. Sarah stood on the other side of the circle, facing Alice, Virginia and the witnesses alike, a watering can in her left hand.

Pierre presented the jar to Virginia and Alice. They pulled out tampons, applied the broomstick. Acacia, henbane, datura. They dropped their robes, stepped over the candles, entered the circle naked. They sat facing each other, knees up, backs straight, legs spread apart, eyes locked. Sarah took a chair, Walsh, Francisco, Maria and Pierre sat on the floor beside her.

"What is the word?" asked Alice.
"Hermes," Virginia answered.
"What is the password?"
"Mercury."
Alice drank from the bowl, then Virginia.
"What is the word?"
"Hermes."
"What is the password?"
"Mercury."
They began to float to the ceiling.

Day Five

The Raven
When the moon rose above them, they drank more sour wine. They sat in the grass behind the farmhouse. Sarah heard Nan's voice in the wind. She

listened to the message and grabbed Virginia and Walsh's hands. "Nan! Nan says What the Raven Bringeth, Ye Shall Drink!"

Pierre played out Walsh and Francisco Grim's pulses out on his drum. One, two, one, two, three, one, two, one, two, three...

Virginia and Alice, Walsh and Maria, Francisco and Pierre chant back *What the Raven Bringeth, Ye Shall Drink, What the Raven Bringeth, Ye Shall Drink.* They chant in time with the drumbeat, in time with the heartbeat of every brother in good standing of the Hemlock Circle. Alice transcends language, she howls in time with the incantation. They chant, they wheeze and strain their throats. Pierre's hands go numb. He keeps the beat intact.

Walsh and Francisco stand, they strip and they lock into a wrestling pose. The rest howl the incantation. Francisco falls to his knees, he crawls across the grass, licking his lips. His eyes spiral like a kaleidoscope, pupils trained on Walsh. He drags himself to Walsh's feet, grabs the back of his calves, digs his fingers into Walsh' thighs and looks up. He lifts Walsh's sack and licks and sucks. He takes Walsh's cock in his mouth. He moves his head with the rhythm. Virginia, Alice and Maria stand over the men. *What the Raven Bringeth, Ye Shall Drink!*

Francisco massages the backs of Walsh's calves, slams his forehead into Walsh's stomach. Francisco gags, pulls away. He lies on his back, lifts his knees, spreads his legs. Walsh drops, positions himself and enters. *What the Raven Bringeth, Ye Shall Drink!*

The women clap their hands in time with Pierre's percussion. They chant the incantation. Walsh keeps with the rhythm. He locks eyes with Francisco, who is transported, overwhelmed by what he sees. Electricity runs through his body and into Walsh's. He feels it in the bottom of his spine, the beginnings of an explosion. Walsh reconnects with the mantra, the words chanted above his head. *What the Raven Bringeth, Ye Shall Drink!*

Francisco whales. After the 36th incantation Walsh explodes inside of Francisco. Francisco sprays cum in the air. The women drop to their knees, their bodies spasm, they orgasm and collapse on the grass. The sky breaks, an August storm. Francisco, on his knees, in awe of the thunder and lighting, breaks into tears.

"Thank you, thank you, Jehovah! In the name of Jehovah!"

Day Six

The Ordeal

Nan said they needed to burn white birch. Pierre ventured into the woods with Virginia with an ax. They carried the wood back to the house. Pierre dragged the fire pit to the center of the basement. When night fell, they lit a fire.

Everyone but Sarah received a Celtic Cross brand on their sternum. Walsh was first to accept. Pierre wielded the brand. Sarah stood to his right.

"In the name of Jehovah," she said.

Pierre pulled the red-hot cross from the birch wood fire. The hiss of hot iron on skin echoed through the farmhouse. Sarah doused the burn with a salve.

Alice stood up next, she knelt before Pierre and Sarah, accepted the brand. "In the name of Jehovah." She inhaled while Pierre burned her skin, exhaled as he pulled the brand away, the most agonizing moment of the entire process. She stood up, wiped a tear from her eye and held her husband's hand. She leaned onto his shoulder. This was the next great moment of her life. She knew this feeling. She reassembled the trivia, junk data, cliches, truisms, tautologies into new wisdom. Mysteries unraveled. For the first time in her life, she knew what questions to ask. Sarah doused the burn and Alice began to cry. "Thank you, Jehovah!" She pulled her husband to the floor and they prayed.

Maria and Francisco received their brands next. They came and stood with Alice and Bob and witnessed Virginia accept her brand. She was ecstatic, then serene, then ascended. "Thank you, Jehovah!" Tears streamed down Virginia's face. She felt the floodgates open. Her knees buckled. She smiled wide. From the cellar floor she looked up at the stars, the moon, the gates of heaven. Sarah doused Virginia's burn with the salve and Alice and Walsh pulled her to her feet.

Sarah pressed her hands together, wrapped her fingers, tight. "Praise Jehovah! Thank you, Jehovah!"

Pierre opened the storm doors and left the basement. He led a lamb out of the barn through the backyard and back into the basement. He tied the animal to a hook in the stone wall. He pulled a blade from a sheath on the back of his belt. The adepts formed a circle around him. He raised his knife in the air. "In the name of Jehovah!"

"Thank you, Jehovah!" the circle replied in unison.

"Blessed are the dead who die in Jehovah from henceforth!" exclaimed Sarah.

Pierre dug the blade into the goat's neck. It screamed until it choked. It kicked its feet, tried, to run, then fell to the ground. Pierre cut the torso open with one long slice. He pulled out the liver. He carried it to the fire. "In the name of Jehovah! Thank you, Jehovah!" He dropped the liver into the fire.

Maria cut out the spleen. "In the name of Jehovah!"

Francisco cut out a lung. "Thank you, Jehovah!"

Alice cut out the opposite lung. "In the name of Jehovah!"

Walsh cut out the tongue. "Thank you, Jehovah!"

Virginia cut out the heart. She looked down, held it in her hand. She merged with the cosmos. She mourned for her old self. "Thank you, Jehovah!" She dropped the heart into the fire.

Sarah dipped a birch branch into the lamb's blood. She doused each initiate individually, she doused the adepts as a group, as they cheered in unison: "IN THE NAME OF JEHOVAH!"

Day Seven

Pierre woke up at dawn to burn apple wood for charcoal. He rigged a spit in the backyard and spent the day basting their lamb with a rosemary branch. Walsh and Francisco kept him company throughout the afternoon. Over beers, Walsh and Francisco traded stories of spit roasts in Greece, Pakistan, Morocco, Brazil and Argentina. Francisco wore his shirt open to air out his burn, drank a beer every forty-five minutes, he chain-smoked. Walsh went shirtless. Sarah kept busy treating their brands with salve every hour. The pain, given the trauma inflicted, was minimal. Pierre dragged the rosemary bush through a pan of olive oil, lamb fat and purple garlic from the garden. He basted the skin and inside the cavity. Pierre felt the fire in his burn. He'd never felt so alive.

He left the fire to set the table. He laid down their finest tablecloth. Fine China, silver flatware, water and wine glasses, crystal pitchers, six inch gauged candles. Eight Tiki torches ringed the table. He ventured into the garden to pick herbs and vegetables. Cucumbers and tomatoes for a salad, squash, pole beans and Swiss chard to sauté with garlic.

Pierre timed dinner so that they would have their apple cake and vanilla ice cream at sunset. When everyone cleaned their plates, Pierre uncorked champagne and Sarah gave a toast. "Nan has been spending an eternity in the libraries of Ashurbanipal and Alexandria. She is reading, learning, unlocking the mysteries, she's recovering the lost knowledge. Nan has infinite life, time to pore over the wisdom of our mothers and fathers. She is learning the old rites. She is reading tablets from empires we lost to history, until now.

"Last night, the heavens received our offerings. Jehovah's blessings are already powering us forward." She raised her glass. "I love you all so much. That love got us through. That love got to Nan, she heard it, she felt it. And now, Nan has that direct line she needed. Every time she reads a new scroll, I feel it... And she's come to the conclusion, and I agree with Nan's reasoning here, that we at this table are among the ascended. We are the axis-mundi of earth and the cosmos... the angelic. We are among those chosen to lead the transition; we can guide our nation to the golden age. We've stepped on the path, the hero's journey! Should we complete this task, and do it right, immortality waits for us on the other side. A permanent rebirth in the name of Jehovah!"

Chapter 62

Williamsburg, 1996

Jacques Anzu sat at his altar for hours, eyes shut, deep in meditation. The buzzer rang. "Yeah?"

"Hey man it's Frank... I'm here for the photo shoot."

Jacques massaged his forehead. "You're early." He buzzed him in.

"Jacques thanks for having me over. It's an honor to be part of your work, man. Means a lot to be part of something momentous."

Frank took Ibogaine in a hotel room in Staten Island in 1990 and it kept him off heroin until circumstances changed in 1994, and Frank came home. He took a seat in the living room. Jacques opened trunks of camera equipment and pulled out his VHS camcorder and his Super 8s. He set up the cameras and framed his shots, moved the tripods around for full coverage. Jacques popped a VHS into the camera and got rolling immediately. "Almost ready."

"All right man. I'm down for anything you need because you're all I've got left, man. My only friend left standing, Jacques."

"No way, come on." Jacques set up the Super 8 cameras.

"Everyone else is dead."

"Really? Everyone?"

"Yeah, man. A few guys are upstate. A few guys went Christian on me."

"And they're alive."

"But we're not friends anymore. I'll never see them again. You heard about Mario, right? Millions from the Werewolves?"

"No, what happened?"

"OD'd on benzos and methadone three months ago. I mean it, Jacques. You're it."

"All right, man. All right..."

Jacques grabbed his Leica and loaded a new roll of film. He snapped a wide shot and returned to the kitchen. "All right, I'm ready you can go ahead."

"Thanks, man, I can't begin to say how grateful I am for this opportunity…" Frank had curly, shoulder length black hair. His age was hard to figure, mid-forties. His eyes drooped, his lips were wrinkled from cigarettes, stubble on his face and neck. He took off a chrome studded leather jacket, Johnny Thunders, 4P, and Steve Sinclair buttons. He wore a sleeveless Nihilistics shirt underneath. "Can I, uhh, bum a smoke, man?"

Jacques threw him a camel. *Good improv*, he thought to himself. He shot Frank lighting up. "So, what, *uhh*, what are we getting into?"

"What do you want? We've got dope, coke, rocks, I've got some dust we can smoke."

"Nah dust is too much for me man. I'll shoot some dope and coke, though. That, if you're offering that's what I'd personally like to do."

Jacques emptied a paper bag onto the table. Frank's eyes bugged out. "Jacques, man, that's quite a stash. That's cool!" Jacques shot Frank sort through the drugs with his tongue out. He dropped two bags of dope and a fingernail's worth of coke into a spoon. "Thanks for the clean works, too." He used glass of water Jacques put out and sucked up enough to dissolve the dope. He cooked the solution, dropped his cotton and then sucked the mixture into the syringe. He tied up with a rubber band. "Shooting up with a belt is gay. You're taking your belt off…"

"How do you feel."

"Like a doctor," said Frank. Jacques shot the expressions on Frank's face until he ran out of film.

***

Jacques went to sleep, he swam with mermaids, made them laugh, offered them his body. He won their favor. Later the same night he dreamed he was tied down with rope and leather straps, sacrificed to Inanna. In the morning he drew the goddess in charcoal. He meditated on mermaids, swimming like dolphins, maybe it was time for another round of Oanes paintings.

Shotgun's friend Linda Solomon was scheduled for a photo shoot. The sad eyed chick who sold weed on St. Mark's Place. She was hooked in with Joanne Pardes and Hilaria. He heard she tried to kill herself after Joanne. He drew a mermaid in charcoal until the bell rang. Linda walked up the stairs to Jacques' studio. She was panting when she got up top. She knocked on the door, Jacques opened up. "Linda."

"Hey..." She was nervous, bright red with her shoulders up.

"Come in." He stepped out of her way. She came inside. She looked around. Jacques' loft was bigger than Hilaria and he had it to himself. The kitchen was to her right, by a row of industrial windows, a table and an arm chair, open space. The painting studio was to her left. The living room, two couches, two chairs, a coffee table, and faux-Persian rugs. His bed was up against the wall on the other side of the space, next to his altar in the back left corner.

They took seats in the living room. Jacques sat back in his armchair. He watched her look around, fumble in her jacket for cigarettes. He reached for his Canon and took her picture. She acted natural, Jacques snapped the sequence. She exhaled, found a position where she could keep still.

"This place is great, Jacques." She stood up and toured the studio, stopped at a painting of Hermes. He stood by his guidepost, his pile of stones. A black, nearly starless sky, a desolate plane behind him, a waxing crescent moon. Jacques took her picture. She walked to the wall, a silk-screened canvass, ten trees of life. "Hey, check this out." She took off her jacket and came close, she held out her arm and showed him her Tree of Life.

"Joanne Pardes did this?"

"Yeah..."

He traced the scars with his fingers. "Tunnels of Set." He looked up at her. She stared down at his hand. He felt her body tense. He smelled her sweat. Her scent electrified the base of his spine. Jacques got up, took a mirror from under the coffee table and spooned out a gram of coke and cut up two lines. He gave Linda the rest. She cut up thin lines and blew eight in a row. It did what she needed.

"I've heard things, over the years..." Linda stopped to light a new cigarette.

"What have you heard?"

"I've heard that Joanne taught you magic."

"Joanne *taught me*?"

"That's what she said."

"Joanne taught me one technique. She didn't teach me magick."

"What did she teach you?"

Jacques poured another gram of blow on the mirror. He got up from his chair, went to the kitchen and returned with a container of salt. He walked over to the altar. He drew a circle, arranged his four corners. A candle for fire, a bowl of water, paper for the wind, soil for the earth. Linda watched him work. He went to his armchair by the windows and flipped through his sketchbook. He ripped out his sketches of Inana. Linda blew the gram Jacques laid out for her, stood up and walked over to the altar. Jacques took the clove out of his mouth and gave it to her. She smoked. Linda studied the drawing. Jacques kicked off his shoes. He undid his belt. He stood in front of her naked, hard. Linda stripped. She walked inside the circle. She grabbed Jacques' cock and kissed his lips. Jacques grabbed her back and pulled her toward him, against his chest. He positioned Linda's body to face the South, aligned with the altar. Jacques licked and rubbed until she gasped. He righted himself behind her, fucked her facing the altar, the Goddess. He put his wrists under her armpits. She masturbated with her left hand until she came. She put both hands out and stretched her back, they collided, and Jacques focused.

***

Jacques pulled Perrier's out of the fridge and gave one to Linda.

"Thanks, beb." She stretched out in his armchair by the window, did another line of coke. It felt like a cup of coffee. She took the clove from Jacques' lips and took a drag.

"Stay where you are for a second, like that." He got up and went into the art studio side of the loft and came back with his Leica. He got the photo. She ashed the clove. "Ah do that again."

Linda made new ash, tapped the clove and the it fell to the floor. Jacques caught the sequence. He pulled out more film from the fridge. He pulled out a bag of clean needles from a kitchen drawer.

"I want you to shoot some of this coke while I take your picture."

"OK."

Jacques did a line. He refilled his camera. He set up the VHS camcorder on a tripod in front of the armchair. He arranged a spoon, clean water and his bag of coke in front of her. She tied up her arm, dissolved the blow with water. Jacques killed his roll of film and switched to his Canon. Electricity ran through Linda's body. Her legs extended and her toes curled. Her eyes darted in every direction. She quickly made and released fists. She gasped in ecstasy. Jacques covered each contortion, he stepped back.

Jacques reloaded his camera. Linda put on a black beanie and a pair of sunglasses. She picked up a can of spray paint. Jacques turned the video camera toward his studio. He followed her there. She sprayed a blank canvass leaning against the wall.

KILL 'EM ALL LET SATAN SORT 'EM OUT!

Linda posed with a Camel and the spray can in front of the canvas.

They fucked on his bed until they hurt. Jacques sorted through his lock box for downers: Xanax and hash. They went to sleep. Linda moved in immediately.

Chapter 63

Elmhurst Hospital, 1986

Walsh sat at the head doctor's desk. Not a bad chair for a government hospital. He leaned back, sipped mediocre coffee. More an academic's office than a doctor's, he thought. The furniture was homey and thoughtful. No bars, hard to imagine this floor of the hospital was just an extension of Rikers Island. Walsh brought a pizza and a two liter of Coke for lunch, a carton of Newports. The subject's file said he smoked menthol.

The door opened. A CO came in. "Sir, we'll be outside if you need us."

"Uncuff him and go take a nice long break."

The cops led the patient inside. "This guy says to remove your restraints. He also says it's a mistake to try him." He unlocked the leg shackles. "You got me?"

"Yeah." He smiled, looked in the guard's eyes while he undid the cuffs.

"We'll be right outside if you need us." He turned around and locked eyes with the patient again. He and his partner walked out.

"New Park Pizza from Crossbay."

"No shit. Thanks, Doctor."

"Here, sit down."

"Hey, good to meet you. I'm Jack, Jack Cheskey."

"Bob." They shook hands. Walsh opened the box, Cheskey rubbed his hands. "Beer, unfortunately, isn't allowed on this floor of the hospital, so we'll have to settle for Coca Cola—" He pulled a flask out of his breast pocket. "And a little Chivas."

"Bob, all right! You're my kind of doctor, Bob."

Walsh made himself a drink. "So, how has it been on the island? I'm hearing it's bad these days. Lots of cuttings, that kind of thing."

"Yeah the PR's they're losing that top spot."

"Huh. To blacks?"

"They're getting organized."

"Really?"

Cheskey went for a new slice. "Are you going to eat this?"

"No, I ate. Go ahead. So, what does that mean, day to day?"

"It means that when a Rican asserts himself, the closest black guy half the time is going to 'hey you spic motherfucker go back to your side of the wing.' And then it might go down. Then you got the CO's caught up in this. The guy who brought me in, not the one who you were talking to the one who walked with me, he's with the blacks. The other guy, he's just a black guard, you know."

"Yeah, I understand. You know those gangs they go back to Nam, the bases. They were fighting each other. White GI's, black GI's. Next thing you know you have the AB and the Black Guerrilla Family and what have you. When I was in country I saw it all the time. The shit kickers and the panthers were shooting, bombing each other. 'Hey, the gooks did it, not us.'"

Cheskey looked interested. "When were you in Nam?"

"In and out, '68–'70."

"Wow, that's impressive."

"SEALs."

"Wow!"

"You'd have been too young for Nam, huh."

"I applied for the marine corps in '77."

"What happened?"

"Oh, some bullshit."

"And they didn't let you in the NYPD either, huh?" Cheskey exhaled through his nose, grit his teeth. "Hey, here. Heard you smoked menthols."

Cheskey's eyes bulged. He licked his lips. "Bob! All right." He unwrapped the carton and opened a pack. Walsh lit him up with his gold lighter.

"Look, I don't give a shit. I'm a Navy man and most of the NYPD I've known are whatever the Bronx version of a redneck is. Bunch of half retards, papist weirdos, wife beaters, closet cases."

Cheskey smiled. "That's good, Bob."

Walsh put away his Chivas and coke. "Jack, help me out here. I need to make sure I have the right information."

"What is it you have?"

"Files, the information the DA has… So, you're born to Mikhail and Mary Cheskey, Atsugi, 1960, moved stateside in 1962 and lived in Nevada until 1967 when your father committed suicide. Your mother moved in with her parents in Ozone Park in 1968, that's your current last known address, correct? 92nd Avenue?"

"Yeah, my aunt's house."

"We got a look of the area when we got the pizza. We're only a few minutes away now, really."

"It's true, Bob."

"1968 you enroll in St. Helen in Queens, you graduate high school 1977... all of this is correct?"

"'77? Yeah."

"You're brought in for questioning with a Vincent Ippolito aka Thin Vince, DOB 1955 on an arson in Bushwick but released with no evidence. Arrested ADW in '80, you did ten months in Queens house of corrections."

"Yeah, that's, yeah true." Cheskey went for a new slice, more soda.

"Yeah, they picked me up uh, second weekend of uh January. So, you've got good information."

"How do you like it here, compared to the island?"

"This is better, sure. Most stuff is, you know?"

"Sure, I could see that..." Walsh sat back, legs crossed. He began to tap the table with his knuckles, 4/4 time. He pressed play on a tape recorder on the desk. Black noise. Strange sounds, bizarre rhythms. "Red."

Cheskey sat up straight, looking forward. "Blue."

"Open your mouth."

Cheskey opened his mouth.

"Good, close your mouth, put your hand on your head."

Cheskey closed his mouth, robotically put his hand on his head. Walsh sat with his legs crossed. He stroked his chin and looked at his watch. He counted out thirty second then a minute. Cheskey didn't move.

"Stand up, walk to the window, come back. Sit down. Touch your nose with your right hand, your left palm up."

Cheskey stood up, turned around, touched the window and returned to the chair sat down, touched his nose with his right hand, lifted his left hand. His hand fell back on the arm rest. He stared forward.

"Jack, I'm going to ask you some questions. Are you ready?"

"Yes, sir."

"Tell me your first memory.

"Yes sir. It was my father. I heard an explosion from their bedroom so I came to see. He shot his head off with a rifle. I picked up a little piece of his skull. I squeezed it until my hand bled and I watched my blood mix with dad's brains. I took his blood and smeared it on the walls. I licked his brains off my hand. I sat there, for a while, licking my hand. I found Mom later, in the den of the house. I said, mama look."

"What happened next?" asked Walsh.

"The men came. We took a trip."

"Where did you go?"

"I don't know."

"What happened next?"

"My seventh birthday at Aunt Nancy's. Cake, hot dogs. We sang happy birthday, she helped me blow out my candles, she taught me how."

"Go back, what happened before?"

"We went on a trip."

"Where?"

"I do not know."

"Who took you on a trip?"

"The men who came to my house."

"They said you were going on a trip?"

"Yes sir. They said we're going on a trip."

"What happened next?"

"My seventh birthday with Aunt Nancy, Uncle Sal. Uncle Sal said seven makes me a man I should go and find a job. He gave me a sip of his beer for my birthday. As many hot dogs as I could eat."

"Think, where did the men take you?"

"My seventh birthday with Aunt Nancy."

Walsh caught himself. He took a different tack. "Tell me more about Aunt Nancy and Uncle Sal."

"They're school teachers."

"Where abouts?"

"We live in Ozone Park. Uncle Sal teaches in Howard Beach, at the Catholic school. Aunt Nancy works near the house."

"How are you related? Which side of the family?"

"I do not know."

"Were you adopted?"

"Yes, sir."

"What happened to your mother?"

"She isn't around anymore."

"Is she dead?"

"Yes, sir."

"How did she die?"

"I never asked."

"How did it feel when she died?"

"I don't know."

"You don't remember?"

"No. I'm thinking about it, I don't remember."

"Tell me about when you came to live with Aunt Nancy and Uncle Sal."

"It was my seventh birthday party with Aunt Nancy."

"That was your first day with Aunt Nancy and Uncle Sal?"

"No, sir."

Walsh smiled, sat back, impressed. Three years unaccounted for. "Do you know a Dr. Black?"

"No, sir."

"Do you know a Dr. Brown?"

"No, sir."

"Do you know a Dr. Green?"

"Yes, sir."

"When did you meet Dr. Green?"

"When I was a boy, still a kid."

"How old?"

"I was eleven I'm thinking."

"How did you meet Dr Green?"

"I was locked up in the Bronx."

"What was the charge?"

"Burglary."

"How long had you been in detention before you met Dr. Green?"

"Three months."

"Tell me about the days before you met Dr. Green."

"There was an older kid who the guards relied on to keep things quiet. When I first get there the guards say 'get with the program.' They make a kid responsible for teaching us the program, anybody does anything they're not supposed to, the older guys give the kid a beating. When the guard told me 'get with the program.' I just nodded my head. Later a boy came and punched me in the brain. He said I should have said sir yes sir when the guard told me to get with the program. If I did it again there'd be problems.

This kid, he talked like the guards taught him English, but he wasn't smart enough to use the words right so he sounded like a fucking retard. And he'd get angry, look all crazy… That was supposed to scare me but it didn't work on me.

"I watched him fuck around with the younger kids, blacks got it bad, he would jerk off and make them lick the cum off his hand. If they said no, he'd tell the guards they were out of program and they'd get a whack right in the kidneys. He tried that with me once, I told him if he came any closer I'd knock him out, that my father was a Green Beret and I knew how to kill. I guess he believed me because he punked out. But that's dangerous too. He was going to have to do something before he lost that top spot. The guards let him be the predator on the floor. If he lost control, they'd have to put him somewhere else. I felt like I only had a few days before something was going to happen. I found a wire coat hanger. That night, when he was asleep I snuck up to his bunk and I started whipping his face with the wire. He was sleeping so he didn't wake up until the second hit sir. There was blood in his eyes he was screaming 'mommy, I can't see mommy, help me!' He turned around so I whipped him in the back of the head, the back of the neck, I pulled down his pants, I whipped him in the ass and the back of the thighs and the lower back and he shit the bed. Blood was splashing into my face and I was licking my lips clean and none of the kids stopped me. They gathered around to watch. They were laughing, called the kid a punk bitch. They said he wasn't so tough he couldn't take a beating; he wouldn't be safe anymore. I heard later that a few weeks after I did that some of the boys took that kid into the closet and fucked him so bad they had to lock him up in the fucking nut house. A few years ago, homeless on the street he killed some queer fag with a shiv. He was a tough kid when I met him. I turned him around. I felt high, my prick got hard. I went to the toilet and I had blood on my hands and I beat off my prick and I smeared the wall with blood. That's when the cops came in. One of them hit my kidneys with the stick, He said get with the program! I said sir yes sir!

"Dr. Green showed up a few days later. I was in the box which was fine by me, but the cop that hit me in the latrine that night, he never liked me. When Dr. Green came and picked me out, the cop tried to stop him, give him this PR kid, you want a sick fuck take this kid. Turned out he was too old. Seventeen and a half. He was a fucking adult man, overgrown because of the glands, with a mustache…"

"What did Dr Green say?" Walsh cut in.

"That it was... my lucky day. He asked me if I wanted to leave and I said sir yes sir! He said very good, I didn't need anything back in my cell, he had new clothes for me in the car. We left and the cop who hated me looked pissed off, never got a chance to fuck me up. After we got in the car, we both got in the back seat. He lets me roll down the window, look outside. He gave me a stack of Hershey Bars. He has a cigarillo, the black ones. He says that my guardian signed a paper that I was going to go live with him. If I followed the rules, I would never have to go back to juvie."

"How did that make you feel?"

"I was glad to leave jail. I felt lucky."

"What did you say to Dr. Green?"

"I said, sir, yes, sir. He corrected me, 'yes, doctor.' We got to the hospital and they took me to my room. They brought me these nice soft pajamas and I put them on. They brought me a big dinner and I ate it all. There was meatloaf, mashed potatoes, peas and carrots. I ate it all. They took me to take a bath then they gave me some pills. They took me to my room and I went to sleep. They came back when I woke up, more pills. Went on maybe two days like that, all I did was sleep. They put me in a wheelchair and they gave me more pills. You think it's more of the sleeping pills. At that point you like all the sleep. They put me in a rubber kind of room, not the padded kind like on TV. This was rubber. I felt this explosion inside of me, a bomb went off, I started shitting and pissing, screaming. I wanted to fuck and kill somebody, get in a fight. I was licking the rubber. That went on until I blacked out. I came to in my room, where I'd been sleeping. The nurse gave me a shot and I went back to sleep. When I woke up, the nurse was there to give me more and that went on for a while."

"How many times?" Walsh cut in.

"I don't know..."

"Think."

"Three. Three times. They gave me three shots of sleep, one shot of lightning. You feel the lightning in your veins, this cold sensation then heat, in your blood stream. My guts and my balls and my asshole were pulsing, I was rubbing my asshole against the rubber and clubbing my dick with my fists – shitting and pissing on the walls – screaming."

"What happened next?"

"I passed out eventually. I don't know how long it took; I don't know how long I was in the rubber room. It could have been all day or just a couple hours. But when I'd black out, I'd wake up in the room, in bed. And the nurse gave me a shot. This time I had an IV in my hand. I don't know with what. I went back to sleep. This time I started dreaming about the rubber room."

"How did that make you feel?"

"I... I was just in it, raging in the rubber room. The lightning, it hurt but if you kept moving your veins didn't feel like they'd explode but you had to keep shaking. If you stopped moving it was real, real pain. Real bad. So, you'd keep shaking. Then I'd wake up and the nurse would give me a shot and I'd go back to sleep and I'd be back in the rubber room and then I'd wake up and I'd be in the rubber room, and it's real and I'm shaking and pissing and shitting, I'm fucking screaming. I black out and I'm back in my bed and I'm back asleep. And it starts all over. Over and over again. They'd always clean me up, clean my sheets, new pajamas all the time. I'd tear them up do different things to them when I was in the rubber room. Always a new pair, always clean and always exactly the same as before. And it just kept going on like that, forever..."

"How long did this last for?"

"I don't know."

"When did it stop?"

"One day, they put me in a wheelchair, they strapped me in and took me somewhere new. It was Dr. Green. He had an office just like this one, with a big desk, big chair. They wheel me in and there's a big plate of food. I don't remember the last time I ate."

"How did that make you feel?"

"The food?"

"Yes."

"It scared me, I didn't know where to start. I just sort of looked at it for a while. It was on an orange tray. What I really wanted to do was take it all in my hand and squeeze it together and put it in my mouth and throw the rest at the wall. Dr. Green says I've been a good boy. I can have meatloaf, mashed potatoes, peas and carrots. He unties one of my hands. He takes out a plastic, a spork – the ones they've got at Kentucky Fried Chicken, he shows me how to eat. He says we like to make a perfect bite. He cuts a piece of the meatloaf, scoops up some potatoes and puts the peas and carrots on top. He give me the spork, puts it in my hand, and I eat it. He tells me to chew before I swallow. I chew the food and then swallow it. I do what he shows me, I do it in that order. I wave the food around in my hand until I get it into my mouth. I chew before I swallow. I keep doing that until there's no more food. He says good job. After dinner, we have dessert. He gives me a chocolate cupcake and I eat that. He says what do we say? I say thank you Doctor."

"What happened next?"

"After that I went back to my room. I waited for the nurse to come with my shot but she didn't show up. I got a headache. I called for help; nobody came. I said please, come, help me. I got dizzy; I passed out."

"What happened then?"

"I woke up, the nurse gave me a cup of juice. I drank it, I said thank you nurse. She left. About half an hour later I started to hear things inside the bed, from the sink and the toilet. I inspected them, I started to smell something sour, like vinegar. Then I saw the colors."

"What were the colors?"

"The colors. Red – Blue. Green – Yellow. Orange – Pink. The colors."

Walsh wrote THE COLORS and the sequence Cheskey gave him in his notepad.

Walsh had heard enough; this was a genuine subject. "At ease." He turned off the tape.

Cheskey relaxed. He wiped his face, confused at the tears. "Sometimes, I just realize my face is wet, happens, you know?" He lit a new cigarette. "You were saying?"

"Why don't you have another slice of pizza?"

"Yeah, yeah." Cheskey reached for a slice.

"Mr. Cheskey, I'll be back tomorrow and I'll have secured your release into my custody. Tonight, enjoy the cigarettes, the rest of the pizza."

"That's great, Bob. I guess I did well."

Chapter 64

Ozone Park, March 1997

Jack Cheskey watched a Van Dam movie on TV when the phone rang. Half a pizza was getting cold on the couch next to him, the cardboard box protected the pie from his farts. "Yeah," he said, agitated.

A clicking sound, feedback, black noise, drum beats. "Red."

He sat up straight. "Blue."

"Use the key. Port Authority." The caller hung up.

Cheskey got off the couch. He checked his sweatpants for stains. He ate another slice, put on his New Balances. He put on a Giants cap and aviators. Cheskey had a square head and multiple chins, no neck. He lived in a basement apartment in Ozone Park as part of his compensation as a super for HCT Management. He was two beers in, fine to drive. He railed three lines. A white work van and a 1980 Dodge Aspen were parked outside. He took the station wagon. Cheskey listened to K-Rock. He initially planned to take the tunnel but the traffic was backed up for miles. He took the 59th St. bridge. Moderate traffic. Cheskey honked. "Move, asshole!"

He got off the bridge and hit midtown traffic. Rock Block: *No More Mr. Nice Guy, More than a Feeling, Let it Be*. He looked for parking and stayed in the car for the end of *Paradise by the Dashboard Light*. He checked his jacket pocket for the key. He located locker sixty-six. A manila envelope. He locked back up and headed for the doughnut shop on the ground level. He got a large coffee and a box of donuts for the road. Rush went off about feminists and no smoking areas at restaurants. A new pack of Newports, more traffic. He stopped for a cheeseburger, nuggets and fries. He went to the bar. He'd start tomorrow.

Cheskey drank on Jamaica off Woodhaven, an old fashioned Irish Pub. A smokey, wood paneled room with a long mirror behind the bar. An uptight, paranoid atmosphere. Retired detectives and their psychopath nephews garnish their beers with salt. Thin Vince's old lady Sheryl tends bar.

Cheskey's three beers in. His friend for the night rants about demographic trends in Canarsie like it was a genocide. "When I'm driving to Staten Island, past Starrett City and the Canarsie Pier, I can't help but remember my cousin. He thought he'd die in that house, but he might as well have died when he left that house so one of *them* could move in... We're in a holy war against Voodoo, man. Vlad the Impaler... His ass was at the end of Christendom. That's what you've got to do. You need to impale the fucking..." He choked back tears, trailed off. Cheskey put his hand on his friend's shoulder.

"Yeah, yeah, pal." Cheskey's people were rear guarders, paranoid people.

"Jack, buy me a shot."

"Yeah, yeah, you earned it." Cheskey pointed upwards and made a circle, another round. He puffed on a Newport. There was a motel on Flatlands Avenue he could get a blowjob, since his friend mentioned the Belt.

"Make mine a Jamie," said his friend.

Chapter 65

Williamsburg, April 1997

Lillian from *HYPE MACHINE* set up a tape recorder. She accepted a Perrier from Jacques, lit a Camel Light. "Jacques Anzu... 15 April 1997... Jacques, thanks for having me."

"Of course, sure."

"I've gotten the chance to check out some of your new work, *Consumption*, this is a project you've been working on for several years now. It's disturbing, it's thought provoking, it's a vision of hell. What are you thinking about, what draws you to these subjects?"

"I got sick of just taking pictures of models and rappers, skaters or whatever. Consumption is about looking at something new."

"You're photographing criminals, homeless people, drug users but also Steve Sinclair, Mario Millions, Sincerious, Shotgun and Treasure, Joanne Pardes, and she's kind of the nexus of all of those things, an artist, a drug user, a criminal."

"That was Joanne."

"What happened there? She was so promising and you knew her pretty well, right?"

"After Helene Asher died Joanne had to deal with all of that very publicly, everyone's eyes on her, she was falling apart and no one was going to stop her. But no one else but me was stopping to take her picture. And both of them, Helene and Joanne, and this influenced Claire Labas and Lexie G Hinnon, understood that in fashion, in art, in the scene, dying young and beautiful means you'll live forever. Helene dying, and dying from dope did a lot to make sure her look and her style took off the way it did. The day she died her look took over. Now everywhere I look there's a new Helene. Once one of the junkies OD, the rest of them will buy up the shit that killed their friend because they know it's good. Hilaria was the direct result of Helene Asher's death. Joanne needed a place to go. Claire and Lexie needed authenticity. Their paths, their intentions, everything overlapped. Their fates were intertwined. That's what happened. Sheitan intervened."

"Are you a satanist?"

"Satanists tend to fall into two broad categories: Republicans and nerds. Obviously there's an overlap there. There's a sort of third group, an exception, that's… the lumpen satanist. That's your criminals and bikers and shit, you can't call them nerds and they're too hardcore for the republicans."

"So, if you're not a satanist, not a pagan…"

"I'm an assassin."

"The artists you've collaborated with over the years deal with violent themes, they're confrontational, they're…"

"Art should be terrorism. Any piece of art that's at all useful to anyone can be a weapon, otherwise it's just another piece of junk. Absolutely, Shotgun, Joanne Pardes, these are dangerous people."

"Joanne's work was some of the most violent art I've ever seen."

"When she was at her best she could actually shake people out of their complacency."

Linda Solomon came out from behind the curtain Jacques ran around their bed. Lilian turned her head. Linda beelined to the table. "Ghoul Oriented Behavior is tonight!"

"Who's spinning?"

"DEATH HURT." She lit a Clove and curled into Jacques' lap like a cat. She stared blankly at Lillian. Jacques ran his hand through her hair, her eyes rolled back.

"We'll go."

"You're… so… pretty." Linda smiled at Lillian. She smiled back and pressed on. The sarcasm flew over Linda's head. Lillian took a note: GF IN K HOLE.

"You've shot several music videos this year. We've really seen indie music videos take off. What do you see in the medium?"

"Music videos have a singular focus that appeals to me. It's more potent than other forms of video art because the music focuses the imagery, it sharpens it. A good music video plants images in your mind that are triggered by the music. If you want to talk about art as a weapon, you can go to war with a music video. If you create an effective video, the song in isolation can trigger whatever subliminal messages the artist placed in the video. I want my art to drive the viewer insane. I want to charge the environment, inject madness, rage, I want to shock these assholes out of from that milk drinking, Gap wearing, mediocre PC bullshit…"

Chapter 66

17 April 1998

Cheskey hit the ignition in his white van, two fresh packs of Newports from the freezer in his windbreaker. He missed the last hour of Stern. Rock block. *Can You Hear me Knocking, Hurt So Good, More than a Feeling.* He reached behind the passenger seat to the pouch on the back and pulled out a tape. He turned up the volume. The original Jock Jams. Gary Glitter, *Rock and Roll Pt. 2*. He sang the guitar riff, he belched out the *heys,* he switched the tape to Nugent's Greatest Hits at a red. He hit McDonald's for a super-sized Coke and four cheeseburgers. Key bumps waiting in the drive through line, fucked up traffic in Glendale, excitement in his balls and colon. He stopped at a diner bathroom, smoked four cigarettes, read the Post. He bumped coke off a MultiLock key, Miralax, a new round of shit.

The Stones' *Dirty Work* seemed appropriate. Chains of Newports. Key bumps at reds. He idled behind trucks. Metropolitan Avenue was at a standstill. Cheskey ripped through residential streets, over railroad tracks. He cut through Bushwick, over sixty, roll stops at reds. Puerto Rican flags, projects, burnt out tenements, boarded up storefronts. A stop at a cuchifrito under the train tracks for a morcilla and a fruit punch. The rice absorbs the sludge in his guts. A few blocks from the target, he stops at a gas station to take another shit.

Day three after two days of recon. Friday and Saturday were twelve-hour shifts outside the building, an old abandoned factory. The front door is unlocked. Freaks in old clothes and bad haircuts let themselves in. A fat, dark-skinned man in sweatpants takes out the trash.

Cheskey was parked half a block away. He took big bumps off the MultiLock key. He smoked Newports down to the filter. He put on latex gloves and leather gloves on top. He pulled a .22 out of the glove compartment.

He let himself in, read the mailboxes. #5 ANZU. The fifth and final mailbox. A six-story building with no mailbox for the ground floor. Cheskey climbed to the top floor. He heard loud music from the other side of the wall. *The Master Musicians of Jajuka,* a cacophony of horns and strings, frenzy. He caught his breath. He steadied himself. He knocked five times.

Jacques Anzu opened the door. Jack Cheskey raised his .22 and fired. The bullet bounced through Jacques' skull, he dropped instantly. Cheskey walked in, looked for a house guest hiding under a table. He checked the bathroom. He found the loft empty. He left with the pistol in his pocket. The music covered up the sound. The staircase was empty. He made his escape. He pulled the brim of his Giants cap low. He located his keys with his free hand. He left the building and slowed his pace. Calmly to the van. He drove out of Williamsburg. His mind went elsewhere: four hot dogs with kraut and onions, ketchup and mustard. A large Pina Colada.

Chapter 67

Friday, 30 May 1986

Sarah and Pierre picked up Virginia Parker just outside of her townhouse on 70th off Park. Sarah leaned over from the back and kissed Virginia's shoulder. "Pierre will be your witness."

"I love you, Virginia."

"I love you, Pierre." They kissed both cheeks.

When Virginia witnessed Alice enact the ritual, she saw the transformation. She saw a new woman. Alice glowed; she had the secret. Her posture straightened, she breathed differently. She was sublime. When she witnessed Alice take the rite she knew in her heart that she had followed the right path all along. She rejoiced in Alice's accomplishment. Now it was her turn.

"Let's go," said Sarah. They headed North and took the highway uptown. "Here, love. They're just your size." Sarah handed Virginia a box of leather gloves.

"Thank you, Sarah."

"Try them on!" They took the Triborough to Queens and the highway into Nassau. Pierre played classical music on the radio. He hummed along. When Virginia witnessed Alice's rites, Alice meditated on the way there. Virginia closed her eyes and let the thoughts come and go.

"Not yet, but we're getting close," said Sarah. They neared an exit. "This is the one." Virginia came out of her meditation and centered herself. Pierre turned off the highway and they drove into a quiet neighborhood of two story houses with wide windows and big yards. Two car driveways, regulation hedges and fencing. Some kitchen or living room lights were on. TV's flashed. Too much activity. "Pierre, keep driving."

They found an identical block where every house was dark. "I like it here," said Sarah. Pierre slowed down and looked for a good spot to park.

No house was older than thirty-three years or newer than fifteen. The planning was identical. They sat in silence. They rolled their windows down three inches each for air. Sarah and Pierre smoked cigarettes, ashed inside the car. They sat for around half an hour.

Virginia put her leather gloves to her face.

"Aren't they beautiful?"

"They're beautiful, Sarah. Thank you."

"My pleasure, dear."

Headlights appeared. The car slowly turned into the driveway a few houses over.

"Under the seat, Love." Virginia reached down and picked up a .38 caliber pistol. The car finished parking in the driveway. Virginia got out and walked up. The driver was a woman only a few years older than Virginia, wearing scrubs. Pierre started the car. The nurse turned her head toward the sound of the ignition.

"Blessed are the dead who die in Jehovah from henceforth," said Sarah. Virginia fired twice into the nurse's head and again in her chest. She pressed the gun against her chest and ran into the car. Pierre pulled away as she shut the door behind her.

"I love you, Virginia!" said Sarah. She hung her head and prayed. "In the name of Jehovah, amen!" Pierre kept his eyes on the road. He obeyed the traffic laws. Within a minute they were back on the highway toward the City.

Virginia Parker felt electricity flow through her body. "I understand, Sarah. I" – tears began to fall – "I understand now."

"The secret has been revealed to you!"

"I understand!"

"In the name of Jehovah!" cried Pierre. "Thank you, Jehovah!"

Part 3

Y2K

And when there is no hope,
I smoke some crack, I shoot some dope When there's no enemies, I sit and stare at my TV And in my ignorance, I'll be a slave and sycophant

– Choking Victim, "500 Channels"

Letter from Sarah Bremure to Bob Walsh, Spring 1990

Bobby,
Are Kip and Katie flourishing? I'll send Kip his birthday card next month.

Pierre planted the squash, beans and tomatoes today. Cucumbers tomorrow. Lots to do over here! The herb and flower gardens are blooming, the bees are just marvelous, the music. I wish you all could be here at Dolores with me every day. Waiting for Thanksgiving! At my age, time works differently, it moves quickly but when we yearn for something we hold dear, time just drags.

Does Nan speak to you about the year 2000? Whenever I see Nan these days, she keeps bringing it up, the morning of New Year's Day, the year 2000. Has she said anything to you? Please do tell me. Ask Alice too. Clearly this was already a significant date, Nan thinks this moment in time, this coming twenty-two years will determine the coming century. Isn't this exciting? Why now, of all times? Such a neat, tidy little gift, right in front of us!

Sunday morning, I went for a walk through the grounds and when I was back at home I remembered Nan's reading on 2012. We're hearing chatter, reading references to the completion of the Maya calendar in the year 2012. So, between 2000 and 2012, twelve years (what a number!) we have some kind of epochal shift (AEON/YUGA?). I spent the rest of the day meditating. I thought, you know, maybe we're just too far from the dates to really get a grip on what's happening, that's been the case before.

But I know, intrinsically, Bobby that what we have to do involves these dates. Please tell me your thoughts, please ask Alice.

Love,
Sarah

Chapter 68

November 1998

Linda Solomon tried to read *The Voice* from a bench in Union Square on 15th St., the East side of the park. The paper barely kept her attention, too much was going on. Someone called her name. She looked up and felt her stomach turn.

"Excuse me, oh my god Linda? Linda Solomon is that? Is that you?" Morgan Gold rushed to the bench, sat next to Linda and hugged her. "What has it been like oh my god! I thought you were... I mean, I heard you killed yourself. That's what everybody said, you know? I guess..." She stopped, grimaced, and laughed. "Well, I guess you didn't. That's good!"

"Yeah, no. I'm..."

"But look at us now! Wait, I need to—" She dug into her purse, an oversized Kate Spade. "Look at this camera." She took a seat next to Linda, held the camera out, lens facing them both. "Smile... No wait no we need to do this again. It's digital, there's no film. I can do this as much as I need to – *smile!*"

Linda, lowered her chin, without opening her mouth forced a smile.

"Oh! You're so pretty you should, like, smile more... But like, that was what people were saying, you know?"

"That I killed myself?"

"It actually was two separate rumors, first after like everything happened with Joanne and then again after Jacques got murdered, you know? I'm so sorry about that by the way. You know he was, like, a real friend to me..."

Linda had never hated Morgan more.

"I actually missed everything at Hilaria, when Joanne killed Lexie and Claire. Then Marina and Britney... I was in rehab when it was happening. I didn't even hear about it, everything that happened... we're both so fortunate that way. That we missed all of that..."

"Yeah... Sure."

Morgan changed the subject. "So... what are you? Doing these days?"

"Oh, uh, you know." Linda ground her teeth, dug her heels into the cobble stone. "A bunch of things, really."

"Do you live near here?"

"I'm off B these days with my boyfriend." She bit her lip.

"That's good! B's so hip these days. B you're Bold, right?" Morgan smiled wide, red lipstick, white teeth. Linda massaged her forehead, then her neck. Morgan brought it back. "...I have a boyfriend too. He's a musician. Do you know TRA, Tokyo Red Army?"

"Yeah, sure. *Andrija* right?"

"Yeah! He's, yeah, he's in TRA."

"Hiro?"

"No, no! Clifford. The keyboard player."

"Oh wow, yeah... He's cute."

"Right?"

"How long?"

"Oh, for almost a year now. We were friends before. I met him right when he joined the band."

"You know I have to go soon."

"Oh, me too, do you want to come over to my place," – she leaned in, whispered – "get high?" Linda left her body, watched herself agree. "I'm just over there." Morgan pointed to a white brick apartment building off Irving with a doorman out front.

They took the elevator up. Morgan lived in a small but fancy one-bedroom with a view of the Irving Plaza Marquee. White carpeting and big windows, a leather living room set, huge speakers, a big screen TV, a record player, CD player and tape deck. Hundreds of CDs were stacked on shelves. Linda took a seat in the couch and felt herself sink in. Morgan came from her bedroom with a shoe box full of coke, dope and pills. "You know the director, Phil Salo, he said Jacques Anzu and Joanne Pardes were his biggest influences. I was like no way I knew them both!"

Post Hilaria, Morgan Gold reinvented herself as an indie film and scene personality. She'd grown into herself, shed *most* of Lexie's influences. "My next roll I play a teenage runaway, like all on dope, she's a hooker. It's so raw. And no one cares if I just shoot into my arms, makes the film more authentic…" Morgan was going for young Giulietta Masina. Short hair, long eyelashes, a dark navy blue eye shadow, red lipstick and pearls. She took off her blazer, underneath she wore a navy-blue leotard, suspenders, and wide beige plaid pants. She unbuckled her belt, pulled it off her waste and put it on the table next to her.

"Here." She produced a bundle of heroin and an eight ball of coke. "It's like, you know research, for the film. They just like send this guy over whenever I ask." She gave Linda a clean needle. They shot up together. The coke and heroin shorted the resentment in her biceps, neck, shoulders. She was suddenly serene.

"I never see you smile… so pretty." Morgan's eyes fluttered. She smoked a cigarette and sighed as she exhaled, then she nodded out. A few minutes later, she opened her eyes. "My boyfriend was nominated for a Grammy last year. He's writing an opera right now."

"Oh no way."

"Yeah." She cooked more dope. "It's about The Assassins. Nothing is real, everything is permitted…" She fixed again, fell asleep. Morgan said the dope was free. Linda stole half. She got up and dug Morgan's wallet out from the bottom of her Kate Spade bag hanging on the front door. She pulled a handful of 20s and 50s, creeped silently across the room into the bathroom. She found Adderall, Concerta, Valium, Xanax, Ativan, Klonopin. She built a pile of pills, five or six each into the Camels' cellophane wrapper, sealed with her lighter. The money and the benzos rounded out her edges. She flushed the toilet and ran the faucet. She felt like she'd restored a modicum of justice. She went back into the living room. Morgan snored lightly with her hand in her pants. Linda pulled six barely smoked Camels out of the ashtray and put them in her pack. She looked around for something else to steal. She snatched CDs at random and put a stack in her bag. She put on her sunglasses and popped her TECHNO tape into her Walkman. She chewed on one of the pills, lightly sweet, not at all unpleasant. She let Morgan sleep.

Chapter 69

Spring 1998

Jack Cheskey was a salaried employee of HCT Capital Management, a building super in Ozone Park and the rent collector for South Queens and Eastern Brooklyn. His van and basement apartment on Arnold Avenue in Ozone Park came as part of his salary. He was responsible for over fifty buildings. He was present for evictions, he bounced out squatters. He kept the buildings up to code so HUD and the City were off his ass and the boss didn't pay any fines.

All he needed to do on any given day was answer the pager, call the associated contractor, and cross the job off his list. He kept a big steel loop full of master keys and multi-locks, immediate access to about 1900 apartments city wide. Once a week he stopped by the management office in The Five Towns for an updated list of anyone more than a month behind. He paid those people a visit. He got results.

First stop of the afternoon was in Woodhaven, collections. He let himself into the building and hit the first name on the list. Cheskey knocked like a fed. She opened up. Cheskey put one foot in the door, looked through his tenant and took a look at what he could see from the doorway. "I'm here to collect the rent. You're on your final notice. Do you have a check or money order ready for your full balance due?"

"Not today, mister, I'm working on—"

"I'll be back next week if we haven't received your full balance due. Mail your check or money order to 123 Hemlock Circle Drive…"

"I just need a few more."

He shook his head. "If you haven't paid the full balance due by the tenth of the month HCT Capital Management will take legal action against you. Have a nice day." He dropped a copy of the bill on the floor and walked away. *Pay your bills, you lazy bitch. Section Eight motherfucker. Fucking bitch.* Onto the next door, just a flight of stairs up.

He knocked like a cop. "I'm here to collect the rent. You're on your final notice. Do you have a check or money order ready for your full balance due?"

The Woodhaven canvass yielded one satisfied balance, $800 in cash. The last of the three names paid up. He drew X's next to everyone else, they'd received their warnings. They each got two X's. Three X's meant they'd receive an eviction order. They weren't his problem once they were in court and he wouldn't see them again until it was time to put their personal property on the street.

Cheskey had a dozen more doors to knock on before the end of the day. East New York, Bushwick, Williamsburg. He cuts up three lines on the van dashboard, rolled up a twenty. Two lines in the right nostril, one in the left. Left side needed some rest. He lit a Newport and put on the radio. He turned from Steely Dan on 104.3 to something hard on K-Rock. He turned off Pitkin Avenue onto Pennsylvania, toward Bushwick, driving fast. "If you don't like it," said Cheskey. "Fuck you, bitch. You section 8 motherfucker."

Chapter 70

Summer 1998

The sun rose over the river. Homebums slept against the gate. Pokeweed woke up, looked around. He gathered it was around five thirty based on the light. He barely remembered how he got there. Can't mix beer and dope, gotta stop that shit.

Nora, Flip, Tenderloin Tim, and Gutter Andy slept on the grass. Some teenagers in for the weekend leaned against each other, passed out off Devil's Springs and Steel Reserve. He put together his recollection of the night before. Bane stepped in Hatred's shit and spend the night laughing about it. Chaos, Tom and Laura sang *Carmelita,* Flip and Max played guitar.

A huddle of teenagers shaking themselves awake on the grass helped each other up. One of them lit a Camel Light and passed his pack around. "Hey-man-lemme-get-one!" Pokeweed grumbled.

"Oh, uhh, last one." The lying asshole was blond, blue eyes, thin nose. He looked like an oil painting of a puritan.

"Here, take mine." She was short, black hair, heavy eye shadow. She wore fishnets, a Catholic school skirt cut short and a Choking Victim shirt.

"All right-cool. What's-ya-name-girlie?"

"Verite."

"You're-all right."

The blond boy grabbed Verite by the arm. "Come on, let's go. I want breakfast."

"You-got-any-money-kid?"

"We've got to go!"

"But Nora!" Verite stage whispered.

"Now, come on, let's go!"

Pokeweed laughed. He still had half his teeth. He ripped the filter off Verite's cigarette and saved the Top for later. The smell woke Flip up. He made sure not to wake up Nora. Pokeweed passed the smoke over, re-lit his top. "Flip-you've-got-beers?"

"I have one in my pack."

"Whaddya say?"

They split a warm Cobra. The sun kept climbing over the river, over Brooklyn. "I see that blond boy again I'll change his life," said Pokeweed. "But that black haired girlie's all right."

***

Verite and Kevin met in the basement at The Wetlands. Officer Down headlined. A crust band called Fcuks was in from the Midwest. Steve Piss played an acoustic set and a ska band from Long Island called The Girls Love Me's opened. Verite watched Kevin help the openers carry their drums inside. Kevin was known to carry equipment into shows either just to be seen with the band or better yet to get his hand stamped.

Between Fcuks and Officer Down, Verite approached Kevin while he talked pop punk with the openers' front man. Kevin was sweating, topless, a new Fcuks shirt over his shoulder. She stared at his tattoos, the Black Flag bars on his shoulder and a bar code under the nape of his neck. He was thin with wavy hair that hung below his ears, big nose.

Verite wore a Bratmobile shirt, fishnets, a black miniskirt with buckles and straps randomly sewn into the fabric, denim jacket, red and white Chuck Taylors. Black hair down to her shoulder blades, long bangs, heavy black eyeliner. She ditched Flip and Nora and grabbed onto Kevin. She shook his hand. "I'm Verite."

"Kevilicious."

Officer Down's roadie Jambi hung the backdrop, **187**, sprayed inside a barbed wire circle. The band took the stage. Revelers yelled out song titles: *Mad Bomber, Fear City, Gang Wars, Revolutionary Suicide...* Jambi lit a spliff and blew the smoke into the spotlight. His beard grew down to his chest. He wrapped his dreads into a knit Lion of Judah hat. Revelers cheered. Yonkers born Jambi affected a patois. "Babylon!"

The punks screamed *Fear City! Revolutionary Suicide!* The punks collided and repelled off each other, shaking, swinging. Punks jumped on stage, danced in the spotlight and stage dived back into the crowd. *Larry Davis 86.* "When the fucking pigs come to kill you, fight back! Fucking make them pay!" They launched into the song twice as fast as when they recorded. Next came the beat down hardcore classic *Urban Guerrilla Combat*. They played their hits, *Gang Wars, Bane of Your Existence, Mad Bomber, Family Values Panopticon, Fear City, Self Defense*. They closed with a cover of Nausea's *Cyber God*. The punks went mad. The venue turned up the houselights and blasted *To The Slaughter* by The Werewolves on the PA.

Punks spilled out to street. The Wetlands was a block away from the mouth of the Holland Tunnel. Verite grabbed Kevin's arm just above the wrist and led him out of the venue. They ran around downtown, made out in doorways and alleys. Verite paid for a bottle of wine and they drank by the river. Kevin tore Verite's fishnets ate her out in Battery Park.

Her weekend was over. At four a.m., they took the subway to Penn Station and they waited for the first train back to Jersey. "I need to see you again. It needs to be soon, when can you come back?"

"Babe!" Verite kissed him. "I promise, I'll be back on Friday."

On the train she thought about him, the way his hair fell over his eyes, how eagerly he fucked, the traces of a six pack, the tattoos… She was sick of the train ride, waiting all week to hit Saint Mark's. Now she wondered how long she could go without seeing Kevin again.

She put on headphones and played her emo mix, *Angels Pissing on Society*. Verite was sick of the suburbs. Nora got out July '96 and her life was a party 24/7. When Verite and the rest of the Jersey kids rushed to 34th St. for the last train, Nora and Flip just stayed. Nora dodged cops until her eighteenth birthday and the warrant expired. No one ever reported Flip missing. They met every Friday night at the Cube and hung out on 8th St. all weekend. Verite was sick of going home.

Chapter 71

Christmas, 1998

Cheskey pissed himself off a bottle of Zubrowka. He woke up on the couch. He went looking for his Newports. "You bitch." He had to get up and go to the kitchen for a fresh pack from the freezer. Rotting garbage, the Bison grass aftertaste made him gag. He puked into the trash until he felt better. He took off his jeans and stained underwear and stuffed everything down and tied the bag. He lit a Newport to freshen his mouth. He showered, put on clean clothes.

He took $800 out of his lock box and took the station wagon to Thin Vince's place on Pitkin off Cross Bay. A Christmas Eve party was still going strong. Sheryl's friends, Jamaica Avenue regulars, mixed drinks and blew coke. They talked about bullshit. Thin Vince came to the door with a Collins glass filled with Vodka and Sprite. "Merry Christmas, Jackie." He patted Cheskey's shoulder. He kissed his cheek.

Cheskey came inside. "Sheryl, how's it going? Hey Georgie, Shane, Rodge, Mary, Susan. Merry Christmas!" Thin Vince and Sheryl shared a one bedroom with a big living room and a pass-through kitchen. Everything but the bathroom and kitchen was covered in tall white carpeting. A 60" TV, a CD player, big speakers. A framed Jason Seahorn poster and a souvenir lithograph print from the Sands resort in Atlantic Beach. Sheryl, Thin Vince's old lady, the leaseholder, made Cheskey a Sprite and Vodka. She had freckles and reddish-brown hair, stark white skin. She wore a Christmas sweater and dayglo leggings. "What are your plans?" she asked in a thick Rockaway Irish accent.

"I'm thinking about Chinese food. A Peking Duck."

"You're Jewish, Jack?" The room laughed. Cheskey smiled big. He could take a little ribbing. We like to have fun here.

"Would a Jew come over here spending money? Or would he just kinda hang out on the couch, hey it's Christmas… a Jew's birthday!" Rodge and Cheskey laughed but the joke fell flat.

"Hey, Vinny, Jack's going out for a Peking Duck!"

"Is that so? Very continental!" Thin Vince, *Capo Supreme* of Demonikkk's nodded his head. "Hey come in the back." Thin Vince took Cheskey in the back and got his coke ready. "Jack, you should stay and party, Christmas Eve."

"Vinny, it's Christmas."

"There you go, the main event!"

"What do we have going on?"

"Why don't you do a line, watch some TV, drink your drink… Stay a while, you said it's Christmas. Mitch is coming over with the sausages. We'll have sausages, peppers, onions, going to fucking get everything going, I've got a whole method…" Sheryl joined them in the bedroom.

"Yeah, Vinny, I'll hang out." Cheskey found Sheryl intensely erotic.

"Not getting in the way of your Jewish Christmas?"

"What is this shit?"

"I'm breaking your balls, relax!"

"You're calling me Jewish, back off with that!"

Thin Vince started laughing, put his arm around Cheskey's shoulder. Sheryl packed a stem. She lit up with a butane torch. She held in the smoke and passed the stem to Cheskey. "Let's get really fucking high, bro," said Thin Vince.

Cheskey sat on the bed and beamed up, he tapped his foot, held in the smoke.

"You've heard about this Y2K?"

"Yeah, yeah."

"The computers, you know what I've been telling all these fucking people about the computers. But now they're saying instead of the year 2000 the computers will say happy 1900 and we do the whole bad boy again."

"I'm sure you and I will be just fine…"

"I don't have a computer, this is one of the reasons," said Thin Vince.

"Some kind of disaster my ass. This is all to sell us something… You know what else? The computers, the internet. Something very gay about it," said Cheskey.

"That's what I've been saying!" Sheryl cut in. "Vinnie?"

"One of the reasons we don't have a fucking computer." Thin Vince pointed back at Sheryl and Cheskey. She grabbed onto Cheskey's thigh. He sat back and smoked more coke.

Chapter 72

March 1999

When Maxine Mauve woke up from her dream, each step of the ritual was clear in her mind. The notes flowed. She wrote for two ghosts who seemed to be friends, speaking with one voice. She wrote everything out before she rolled out of bed. She titled her stack of notes SIDURI + CALYPSO. She lit them incense and new candles. She poured Siduri a thimble of beer and drew blood from her finger into the candle for Calypso. "Carlos, sweetheart, we need hay and white body paint!"

Maxine followed Siduri and Calypso's directions. She convened a ritual. The group assembled at West 4th St. where Maxine and Carlos transferred from the D. The circle that night was the painter Miyu X, her husband Hiro X, Jimmi Jay, Clifford Mills – formerly of Tokyo Red Army, and Clifford's girlfriend, the model / actress Morgan Gold. Clifford was twisting his hair into dreads. He wore thrift store polyester pants and a loud silk shirt. Morgan was in a silver dress with spaghetti straps and a Prada bag. Her hair was bleach blond for a role. It was Clifford and Jimmi Jay's first time together since the breakup, which Jimmi blamed on Clifford. Hiro let him believe it and made a clean break. He was in the studio working on a new Trip Hop inspired solo record.

 Maxine and Carlos met their circle on the platform and they transferred to the F together. They traveled to Brooklyn, hopped out at the 7th Avenue station where the train went underground and they climbed into the tunnel. Halfway back to the mouth of the tunnel, they found a door. It was unlocked, they walked into what felt like a basement apartment. Hiro and Jimmi Jay raised camping lanterns to light the way. Maxine clenched a cigar in her teeth. The circle swept the floor. Miyu fixed a Super 8 camera on a tripod and shot the prep work. Maxine drew a twelve-foot-wide circle and a pentagram inside of it, the lowest points facing south. Carlos blocked Morgan and TRA around the circle. Maxine was going to stand at the northern point of the circle, flanked by Carlos and Hiro at either side. Jimmi Jay and Clifford would join hands with Morgan and Hiro, closing the circle. They changed into black robes. Miyu stripped naked, Maxine and Morgan helped her paint her body white. She laid inside the circle, aligned with the pentagram. Maxine covered Miyu with straw. The sound of the trains boomed in the walls. The brakes screamed. The sound ricocheted through the concrete, through their bodies. The circle joined hands, bowed their heads, they closed their eyes. They incanted: SIDURI AND CALYPSO... SIDURI AND CALYPSO... SIDURI AND CALYPSO... They stopped, they listened. They heard their heartbeats sync. They heard laughter. They heard sobbing, they felt hunger, they smelled death. The laughter took over. An old light bulb lit up the room up. Miyu felt her body begin to shake. She sat up and the bulb exploded. Startled, the circle broke open.

"We can stop here, it's OK. It's OK," said Miyu. They helped Miyu get dressed. They struck down the camera equipment and they stuffed the hay back into its bag. They left the pentagram undisturbed. Shadows danced on the concrete. Morgan snapped a photo. They emerged from the tunnel, left the train station and piled into a taxi.

Maxine and Carlos' two bedroom on 170th St. was built around their altar. It spilled into the kitchen and took up the most of the living room. Maxine kept the incense, fats and oils burning night and day. She wrote her poetry and practiced piano next to the altar. She meditated, convened with ghosts, and traveled the astral plane from her altar. When Maxine and Carlos got home they lit new incense, refreshed the thimbles of beer, wine, rum and Florida Water they lost to evaporation. They lit new candles for Saint Anselm. They showered, smoked a quarter ounce and went to sleep. That night Maxine dreamed she was trapped under water, pounded by waves. Each collision broke a new piece of her spine. She could hear cruel, hysterical laughter. She woke up and grounded herself in bed. She touched Carlos' back and he sighed. He worked long hours and slept heavy. When Maxine was back to sleep she dreamed of Jacques Anzu and that girl living in his loft when he was murdered. Maxine heard she'd killed herself. She woke up, went to the altar. She kept a clove cigarette and one of his sigils for his ghost. She lit new candles. She lit a stick of incense and a candle for his girlfriend, what was her name?

She rolled a new Dutch. Fire. She exhaled toward the altar. *Thank you, Siduri! Thank you, Calypso!* Linda Solomon.

Chapter 73

3 April 1999

Amanda OD'd 30 March 1999. Everyone organized a memorial Beer-B-Q by the river. Amanda was well-liked; her mourners made a good show of it. Shaggy, Shaun, Hatred, Chaos, Max and Julian Jewels gathered around the grill, cooking burgers and hot dogs. Dozens of cans of King Cobra and Steel Reserve in a cooler with bags of ice. Bad Mike sat at a picnic table close to the water. He chain-smoked a pack of Marlboros someone gave him. He was smashed on bars and whiskey. The neighborhood lined up one by one to offer condolences.

Linda Solomon sat at the water. Diamond said his kind words and came over to the bench, sat down next to her, put his arm around her. She dropped into him, looked at the water. "I met her a few times, like over the years. She never seemed happy, like ever. I don't think I ever saw her smile or – fuck, she was always miserable…"

"Went out like the best of us, though." Diamond was from Venice. He wore high socks, Vans, long shorts with a wallet chain, iron cross belt buckle, white wife beater. Spider webs on either elbow, a diamond on his throat, an x under his right eye. He combed his hair back with pomade. He was part Mexican, part Oakie Aryan, blond hair blue eyes. Diamond lit a Kool, "Valhalla is glory… Chick went out like a legend. She's happier now than she was alive. She'd be happy to see people gathering in her memory. Better than living a lie…"

Linda thought about it. Diamond was preoccupied with authenticity. Nearly everything in his estimation was bullshit. She looked over at the picnic table to her right. "You can tell Bad Mike's heart is really broken. So. Fucking. Sad."

"Bad Mike's a real motherfucker."

A traveler played the *Duke of Earl* riff on acoustic guitar, sang a song about hopping trains. Bad Mike pounded a two-liter of Coke. Shotgun sat next to Bad Mike and whispered in his ear. Mike put his sunglasses on and pulled his hoodie over his head. Tears streamed down his face. They sat in silence. Shotgun lit a blunt, he shook his head, what a waste.

Diamond's beeper went off. "I've got work to do."
"Yeah, OK, let's go?"
"Let's go."
Diamond smoked a Kool, rode his longboard. Linda kept up while he pushed ahead. Linda dug into her pocket for quarters and they hit a payphone. Diamond fired off a series of calls. They made deliveries at the McDonald's on 1st Ave, an apartment on 7th and A. They stopped to serve customers in Tompkins. Linda made a delivery on 12th and B and then they walked home together. Diamond's apartment was on 3rd and B. They went upstairs. Linda got their shots ready while Diamond took a shower and locked his money in a safe. She put on a CD on the stereo, Chris and Cosey *Sweet Surprise*. Diamond came out of the shower. They fixed together. They fell asleep.

Chapter 74

20 April 1999

Alice, Virginia and Maria organized a Bloody Mary breakfast for Kip Walsh's nineteenth birthday in a private room at The Hemlock Hotel Oyster Bar.

The men broke off. Walsh, The Ram, Kip and a bodyguard drove the Suburban to Broadway south of Houston and parked outside an 1870s Factory Building. Walsh turned a key; they toured the building.

"25k square feet of office space. Freight elevator, look at this natural light. Just fantastic. You can subdivide the floors, just tremendous. Everyone gets natural light. Fellas, let's go up to the roof..."

In the fresh air, The Ram passed around cigars. He lit Kip's with a torch. "Congratulations on your first property." The Ram slapped his nephew's shoulder.

"Happy birthday, son." Walsh kissed Kip's forehead.

Kip sobered up, straightened. "This is mine?"

The Ram handed Kip Walsh a pen and a roll of contracts. "We all started somewhere. And I promise your next investment won't be anywhere as easy."

Kip opened his mouth, ran his free hand through his hair. "Dad! Uncle Thom!" He put his hands over his mouth. Curiosity unlocked, he rushed back downstairs and studied the space all over. Walsh and The Ram stayed on the roof and smoked their cigars.

"What time is the chopper?" asked Walsh.

"Four. I booked us the driving range from one-three, it's only a minute's drive to the helipad."

A bodyguard, the Israeli, piloted the 360 Global Assessment helicopter from the Westside Highway to Long Island, One Hemlock Circle Drive. Walsh sent the bodyguard to the Scribes' House, a paid shift watching ESPN. The Ram assembled a quorum. Walsh, Gavin Lee, and Don Toberoff. "Uncle

Gavin will be by your side until we're finished," said the Ram.

"Kip. Happy birthday." Gavin put his hand on his shoulder and led him to a bedroom upstairs. "All right, go in the shower and wash yourself thoroughly, everything clean. Give me your clothes." Kip stripped, folded his suit and gave it over. He showered with the door open. Gavin read the *Journal*. He stood at attention when Kip shut off the water. "Dry yourself off and turn around." Gavin tied a blindfold around his face. "I'll be your eyes." He put his hand on Kip's shoulder and guided him out of the room.

"Your uncle and your father, are my heroes, Kipling. The most impressive men I've ever met. The boldest, most brilliant thinkers out there. They're the best at what they do. They refuse to fail... You made the right choice following in their footsteps. Until I met your uncle, I lacked direction. The Ram taught me the lessons a father should teach his son. If not for him, I wouldn't be anywhere close to the man I am today. I'd probably be just another asshole, I'd be a drain on society, not one of the proud few holding this whole damned enterprise together. I'd be wasted potential... No greater tragedy because for every one of us there's a million of them, Kip." They stopped. "I'm proud of you, brother."

"Thanks, Uncle Gavin." Gavin pushed the door open. He boomed like a drill sergeant. "CANDIDATE FOR BROTHERHOOD APPROACHES." Don Toberoff draped The Hemlock Circle Bible and their mysteries in black velvet. Their path was lit by candles. The Ram wore his robes and his Celtic Cross, a steel crucifix ringed with a halo. Walsh and Don Toberoff wore their black three-piece suits, red ascots and black hats with red pompoms. Gavin pushed Kip Walsh to his knee.

"Kipling Simpson Walsh, what is your business before us?" asked The Ram.

"To initiate into The Hemlock Circle. 96."

"Do you hold property?"

"Yes, I do."

"Have you read the word of Jehovah?"

"Yes, I have."

"You may speak."

"*Wherefore should the heathen say, Where is their God? Let him be known among the heathen in our sight by the revenging of the blood of thy servants which is shed. Let the sighing of the prisoner come before thee; according to the greatness of thy power preserve thou those that are appointed to die; And render unto our neighbors sevenfold into their bosom their reproach, wherewith they have reproached thee, O Jehovah. So, we thy people and sheep of thy pasture will give thee thanks for ever: we will shew forth thy praise to all generations."*

Gavin pulled Kip's hair back and put a hunting knife to his neck. Kip felt the steel against his artery, he felt the exhilaration in the base of his spine.

"Kipling Simpson Walsh, are you prepared to accept the title of vassal?" asked The Ram.

"Yes, I am."

"Will you drink from the cup of knighthood?

"Yes, I will."

"Will you guard our secrets?"

"Yes, I will."

"Will you enforce our law?"

"Yes, I will."

"What is the penalty for revealing our secrets?"

"Certain death."

"Excelsior."

"96."

Gavin pulled the knife away. He untied the blindfold and cloaked the initiate in a velvet cape. Walsh fought back tears. He brought him a hat, three-piece suit, shirt, socks and underwear. He hugged his son. "96." This felt better than the day Kip was born.

Gavin, Toberoff and the Ram clapped and stomped on the floor. One, two, one, two, three. Don Toberoff pulled the velvet curtains off the bible, the crucifix in its halo and a painting of The Archangels Gabrielle and Michael. Kip put on his suit and hat and The Ram sat him down. "Kip, everything inside your mind is a physical object. When you envision something, close your eyes, what do you see?"

"I see the angels."

"That's right. And because of your vision, they are manifest. Your visions, your thoughts are real. The workings of your mind are the workings of angels, do you understand?"

"I do."

"The only thing that separates you from what you want in this world is preparation and meditation. Your thoughts are real. They have wings, Kipling. Your desire is the will of Jehovah."

Chapter 75

August 1998

Friday night at the Cube. Revelers overflowed into the street. Flip and Nora, Kevilicious and Verite held a spot right under the cube. "Kerouac said the world is mine because I'm poor," said Tenderloin Tim, a skinny sickly-looking runaway with wire rimmed glasses, a dirty white T and torn up jeans.

"Yo, that's cool, son!" said Kevin.

Verite and Nora hung out in the middle of the block, under the structure. Nora had blond hair, streaks of pink, blue, and orange. Blue eyes, a round face, a stainless-steel retainer in her septum, glittery makeup. She painted her nails rainbow colors, black UFOs and the Sonic Youth Washing Machine shirt.

Max and Flip spanged across the street by the Starbucks. "Spare any change, get something to eat? 'Scuse me, ma'am. Spare some change?" They made five dollars. Someone kicked down a bottle of Absolut.

The crew assembled and walked south and west. They picked up snipes off the sidewalk. Nora and Verite spanged off passersby. They turned onto West 3rd and they spanged off drunks. Nora and Verite made fifty dollars. They bought beer and pizza on the corner. They went to Washington Square Park. They bought a dime of piff and thirty dollars' worth of Xanax. They ate the pizza, took the pills and washed them down with 40s.

They hit Perry St. and W4th because Andy knew there'd be cigarette butts outside the AA meeting. Nora stole a 40 in her UFOs off 8th Avenue while Gutter Andy and Tenderloin Tim gathered smokes. Tenderloin Tim put a couple snipes, barely halfway smoked into his lips. He lit up, passed on to Andy. "Fuck yes this great! Hells yeah!"

Andy tried to quiet Tim down. "Come on man, you'll wake everybody up."

"Maybe they should wake up, right? Open your eyes!"

Gutter Andy adjusted his pack. "Come on, let's go." The others congregated across the street, feeling the benzos, passing a 40. Max and Flip swayed. Flip kissed Nora. Verite kissed Kevilicious.

An hour later they were back at the cube. Sincerious was bare chested in a jean jacket, sweats, and Pumas. He freestyled for a pack of tourists. "Delirious, Sincerious, Delirious, Sincerious…" On weekends Sincerious put on an English accent. "Sincerious representing Brixton!"

"Oh, shit, Sincerious!"

"Yo! You all know who this is? Mad Dog, top tattoo artist. Number one on West 4th St.!" Eddie Mad Dog and the Vampire Papa Eugene, promoter of the Psychopaths Ball parties hit the Cube from the West Side. Papa Eugene wore a leather vest and pants, runes and an Ankh around his neck.

Mad Dog wore pomade in his hair, a silk flame shirt and baggy jeans with a wallet chain. "You know that Tommy Lee Mayhem tattoo? That was me. We did that at his place. I was like Tommy how much more coke do we have to do before we get started? He was like another quarter ounce. Method Man, Jacques Anzu, Steve Sinclair, Treasure, you name 'em, I've tattooed 'em."

"Yo Mad Dog!"

"What's up?"

"Remember Rakowitz?"

"David Rakowitz? Because Rakowitz fed everybody in the park stew made with his girlfriend's head. He chopped her up, boiled her, made a stew."

"You were here for that?"

"Yeah, bro."

"No way."

"I was up in Tompkins and Rakowitz came into the park with a shopping cart like he was Food Not Bombs. Everybody had some that day. And when the news came out that Rakowitz killed her and cooked her head the peace punks were throwing up all over the place…"

"That's fucking crazy…"

"The bitch was delicious!" yelled Mad Dog to gasps, nervous laughter, *oh shit, no way!* "I've been everywhere. Everyone knows me, I've seen it all!"

Sincerious, delirious, Sincerious, delirious… Sincerious put his hands up, the crowd answered back.

Cops came around midnight and cleared the cube. Papa Eugene hailed a cab, Mad Dog and Sincerious piled in.

Just as soon as they were back at The Cube they had to find a new place to hang out. Gutter Andy from Duchess County had to deal with Tenderloin Tim from posh Connecticut. He embarrassed everyone, on too much Xanax, a can of beer, tearful "my parents are millionaires. I don't need to be out here, oh man!"

Gutter Andy didn't need this kind of humiliation. Tenderloin Tim was shredding his credibility. Inauthenticity, the hex that drives types like Andy from city to city, outrunning his bourgeois origins.

"Dude, my parents are millionaires they bought me a Sega dude!"

"Maybe we should kidnap you Tim. Get a ransom?"

"Yeah we could do that," he croaked.

"Hey how much money do you think your parents would western Union you if you called them up? Hey Mom, please help!"

"Yeah let's try that, let's find a phone." Nora liked this idea. "Flip this is smart."

Chapter 76

April 1999

Verite drank a coffee from Ray's, six sugars and milk. She chain-smoked Reds. Kevin had been gone fifteen minutes. She missed him, she was getting sick.

Kevin came back with Nico Quick, the faded rock star, permanent snarl, Lou Reed sunglasses, straw colored hair. Gaunt, heroin chic, black leather jacket, brown pinstripe slacks and white Rebocks.

"Hey, that's my girl over there, thanks for helping me out, man." Kevin and Nico bumped fists. Nico broke left, toward Avenue A and the Chess Tables. Verite ran toward him. Kevilicious wore an olive-green t-shirt, dirty, skinny jeans cuffed at the bottom. Vans with no socks. He stunk of BO. He smoked Bugler tobacco. Kevilicious drops names. Steve Sinclair, Chuck Puke, Choking Victim, Blatz, The Slackers, Ben Weasel... He was twenty-five or six, prone to younger company.

"Babe!" Verite collided with Kevin.

"Babe! Let's go." Kevin, too loud. "Let's go to the River!"

Baabe. They left the park at 7th and B, hustled to the water. They fixed behind the track. They made out under a tree. They nodded, let day turn to dusk. When it got dark, they shook themselves up. Avenue D, sweet coffees. Kevin smoked his Bugler. Verite smoked her Reds. Kevin walked like a zombie, his shoulders rocked in and out of their sockets. Verite held an arm and pulled him forward behind her. They stopped to make out on the corner of 8th and B. Kevin's tongue hung to the side.

A punk in her early thirties made a face when she walked by. "What the fuck are you looking at? Fuck you!" Verite gave her the finger and threw the ass of her coffee in her direction. "Fuck you! Suck my dick!"

Kevin nodded against The Christadora. Verite grabbed his arm pulled him into the park. Diamond served dope by the chess tables on 8th and B. Crusties walked hunched over, backs permanently bent from their packs, from the benches off A to the handball court with stacks of singles. Tenderloin Tim traded a fresh bottle of Captain Morgan's for a bag. Two guys both named Gypsie copped whatever was left and shop was closed.

Kevin pointed at them. "Those guys know me."

Chapter 77

Oceanside, New York, 1999

Jack Cheskey put his feet up on a plastic footstool, sunk into the lawn furniture. Mitch from Demonikkk's sat next to him. "Whaddya think? I paid real money for the setup."

"Tremendous."

Thin Vince big dicked it on grill duty: burgers, hot dogs, kielbasa and a steak marinaded in KC Masterpiece. "We got wieners, boys!" Demonikkk's lined up for hot dogs, the first of the burgers.

"I bought twenty fucking tiki torches for this thing," said Mitch, drinking a Fosters. "Hey, here." He gave Cheskey a cigar. "It's from New Orleans, good shit."

"Yeah, all right, Mitch."

"Man, you oughtta join Demonikkk's, Jack."

"I'll always have your backs."

"Exactly, bro. Make it official."

"We got hamburgers, we got cheeseburgers!" called out Thin Vince. The boys lined up with buns slathered in ketchup, BBQ sauce, mayo and mustard. The crew lined up by rank, first in line was Big Gus, Sgt At Arms. Two burgers, no cheese. He came over and sat by Mitch.

Mitch introduced Cheskey to Big Gus. "This is Vinny's friend from the neighborhood."

Big Gus ate his burger, nodded his approval. "You ride a Harley?"

Mitch pointed his thumb at Cheskey. "This guy shows class all day."

Cheskey finished up his Fosters and reached for a new can. "You're running low in the cooler, Mitch."

"Come and get it boys!" Thin Vince turned off the grill. He sat next to Cheskey with a piece of steak and three burgers and a hot dog, no buns. He ate with a knife and fork. He sucked down the last Fosters from the cooler. Thin Vince came of age when the mob closed the books, so he became a biker instead. He was small, short and svelte, sunken eyes. He combed his hair back with gel, he wore swastika and iron cross rings.

Wrench put Skynyrd on the boombox and did an air guitar. Wrench took after Thin Vince. He wore his hair the same way, but went shirtless under his cut. Joel Wolfgang, warlock and owner of Buckles in the City ordered the prospects around. They cleaned up the grill and refreshed the cooler. Wrench and Wolfgang were Demonikkk's resident pimps. Wrench made porn out of a motel in Hempstead.

"Hey Mitch, why don't we show Jack your den," said Thin Vince.

Mitch looked surprised. Cheskey wasn't Demonikkk's. Thin Vince nodded his head.

"Yeah, Vinny, sure thing."

"I'm getting tired, come on." Thin Vince, Mitch, Cheskey and Big Gus walked into the house. Mitch closed the sliding doors behind him.

"Yeah, this way." They walked through the living room, a 60" TV, stereo with a stack of CDs and tapes. Leather furniture, a sectional and two recliners. Framed posters on the wall, USMC, DEMONIKKK'S, a Harley Davidson mirror and the Fear City pamphlet. Cheskey admired the carpeting.

"Anyone need the can?" At the end of the hall, Mitch pulled his key chain out of his pocket. "All right, fellas, make yourselves comfortable."

Thin Vince beelined to a leather couch and set up on the glass table. He lit a Marlboro, pulled an eight ball from his pocket and started cutting up lines. Mitch pulled out four Fosters from his mini fridge. They faced another 60" TV and a stack of tapes. This was Mitch's inner sanctum. He stored his arsenal in a gun locker with a padlock on the handle. Posters for rallies in Daytona Beach, Sturgis and Nugent Live 81. The Stars and Bars and the Rhodesian flag hung next to each other. Big Gus took a seat at a round table by the door with two office chairs and re-lit his cigar. Mitch gave Cheskey a Fosters.

"Jack, you want some?"

"Yeah, yeah. I have mine too." Cheskey took out his blow.

Thin Vince took a three-inch rail. "This guy right here is my oldest fucking friend."

Cheskey cut a straw with his pocket knife. "Since '68." He lit a Newport.

"No kidding!" said Big Gus.

Cheskey blew his lines. "This motherfucker right here, a bad influence since the fucking sixties."

The room had a laugh. "This psycho…" Thin Vince pulled a story from memory. "Seventy-four or five, he's back from doing a little juvie, I take this asshole with me on a torch job in fucking Bushwick."

"That was '74. I did two years."

"Yeah. I say we're lighting this one up, you're lookout. What were you fourteen?"

"Yeah."

"Then he says Vinny let me light the fire it's like fucking right?" Everyone but Cheskey laughed. "I took him to Pitkin Avenue and got him his dick sucked after."

"Even then Vinnie was always looking out for his friends," said Big Gus.

Cheskey dumped some of his coke on the table and cut Thin Vince a line.

"I was still seventeen then. I went to the Corps a few days after eighteen." Thin Vince reminisced. "Those were good fucking times."

"Check this shit out, Gus you'll love this shit." Mitch pulled a VHS in a plain plastic shell from his shelf of tapes, mostly porn, militia videos and slasher flicks. "This shit is fucked up, good shit." Mitch put Joanne Pardes' *I'm not Here for Cuntish Questions* on the big screen. Double feature, next up: *Scarlet Woman 89.*

"What the fuck?" went Thin Vince.

"I would break the blond one in half." Big Gus put the back of his hand on Mitch's chest.

Jacques Anzu came on screen. "Huh?" Cheskey whispered to himself. He reached for his straw and took a line, eyes on the screen. He flashed back to his walk up the stairs, knocking on the door, the two in the head. "Well look at that." He felt electricity run from the soles of his feet up into the backs of his thighs. Energy pulsed from the base of his spine. His pager went off. "Vinny I've got to use the phone."

"Hey Mitch, show him the phone."

Cheskey called the number.

Black noise, feedback, low bass. "Red."

"Blue."

"Port Authority. Use the key."

He hung up the phone, rushed back to the den. Big Gus had his dick in his hand. "Fellas I've got work to do. Have a good night. Vinny, see you soon. Thanks for the invitation. Mitch, thanks for the hospitality. Have me over again."

***

Cheskey took the LIE straight, cleared the tunnel, parked on 7th, a few blocks from the bus station. Railed a quarter gram on the dashboard, picked up cigarettes, a bottle of no-doze and a new cup of coffee on the walk. He always kept the key on him. A black backpack with the files, as always.

He got in the car and lit a Newport. He opened the first envelope.

Kevin White, male, 6'1", approx. 150 lbs. Eye, brown. Hair, brown. Ethn., White. DOB 12/11/1974. Arrested, Garden City, NY, possession of marijuana, September 1987. Arrested, shoplifting, New York City, NY June 1990. Arrested, open bench warrant, January 1995. Enrolled, Fall Semester, New York University, September 1992.

A copy of a New York State learners permit, Suffolk County address, expired. A photo of Kevin in front of CBGB, 1992, in a leather jacket and a CBGB t shirt. A photo from 1997, ABC No Rio, wearing star shaped sunglasses and a Werewolves shirt. He put the papers back, opened the second envelope.

DOLORES IPOLITO. AKA "VERITE" DOB, 10/17/1982. Arrested, shoplifting, Middletown NJ, May 1997. Arrested, loitering, Old Bridge NJ, July 1997. Arrested, Disorderly conduct, New York, NY, December 1997. Arrested, disorderly conduct, New York, NY, January 1998. Last completed 10th grade, Manalaplan Unified School District, New Jersey. No DMV records available.

A recent photo of Verite on St. Marks Pl. Denim jacket, plaid skirt, fishnets, combat boots. She sat apart from a pack of kids in raver clothing, wide pants and colorful t-shirts, bead necklaces and pacifiers. Verite was framed by a t-shirt display. YEAH I BLEW MICK JAGGER. FUCK YOU – YOU FUCKING FUCK. WELCOME TO NEW YORK NOW DUCK MOTHERFUCKER!

INSTITUTE SURVEILLANCE. AWAIT FURTHER INSTRUCTIONS.

He started the car, turned around and went home. The drive back to Queens was all fucked up. Rock Block. *Flirting with the Devil, Black Hole Sun, More than a Feeling.* He got into it. He bumped blow off a Multilock key, shot back cold coffee. Traffic got moving at Woodhaven, he got off the highway.

Back at home the garbage was rotten, flies in the kitchen sink. He opened a window, got some air in. He dropped the backpack on the table by the door, took the trash out. He checked the fridge for beer, three left. He took a can, the files and his pack of Newports to the bathroom. He took a twenty minute shit and studied the photos. Recon on these two would commence immediately.

Cheskey worked at least once a week since '86. Millions in pickups, a thousand broken bones, hundreds of hits. He never wanted for action. He'd done it all: he'd shot, choked, cut to maim or kill. He'd tortured bank account numbers out of dozens of victims before he did them in, hits that looked like home invasions. Arsons in East New York, Canarsie, Flatbush, Bushwick, Brownsville, Floral Park, Flushing, and Ridgewood. He firebombed cars, businesses, and homes. He made up different criminal signatures as obsec. Sometimes, he took the jewelry or the cash with him, sometimes underwear. As often as he walked in, popped two in the skull and walked out, he made cuts post mortem. In the drug world he liked to go sloppy, amateurish. The corporate raider might be made to look like a suicide, the banker would be an overdose or a street mugging. A twenty year old Russian coke dealer in Bensonhurst who snorted more than he sold flew off a balcony, COD unknown. The stickup crew in Canarsie was burnt alive with their families in a house fire. He beat a woman to death for letting a made man's daughter OD in Williamsburg. He threw a rapist off a roof top in The Bronx. A pair of junkies in Carroll Gardens extorting fuck-up teenagers were shot in the throat and eyes. A pimp, a heroin dealer and a cop, blown up together with a car bomb. An Upper West Side lawyer's wife shot in the head outside the stretch of Riverside park she liked to jog in. Some bodies disappeared forever. Some were messages to the wider public. A Jamaican snitch in Crown Heights selling crack for a local detective hung from a light pole outside his building with his pants down. A preppy from Riverdale was found in a trash pile in Washington Heights. A heroin dealer's girlfriend who escaped from witness protection ate a full clip in her cousin's Mazda.

Chapter 78

January 1999

Verite and Kevin met Nora's boyfriend Flip and their friend Max by the Cube. "Hey Kevilicious, we're hitting the K-Mart. Come with us?" Flip offered.

"Babe you should go with them and make some money."

"Yeah cool, a'ight, I'll come along."

They walked into Kmart on Astor Place. Flip cruised the aisles, scanning the shelves. He wore a long black canvass jacket with silver belt buckles. He wore an Anime t-shirt. Mission accomplished. He felt the tail of a security guard. Max and Kevin made the tail on Flip and started grabbing deodorant, shampoo, razors. They walked out the front door without incident. Flip turned around and looked at the security guard. "Man, why are you on my ass? Dickhead."

Verite waited at the Cube. Tight black jeans, Doc Martins, a Motorhead shirt and her leather. She wore her sunglasses and black beanie. She caught up with a friend from Jersey, now at NYU in a dorm room a few blocks away. "So, you like, live here, live here?"

"Yeah, all around."

"Where?"

"That way, past the park..." She saw Kevin and Max leave the K Mart and she said goodbye. "I've gotta split, good luck with school. We should catch up again. I can get whatever you want."

They did well; $200 in shampoo, $75 in razors, $50 in deodorant. Kevin sang Choking Victim. *And I wanna see what's on sale what's for free.* Max laughed, patted his idiot friend on the shoulder. They carried everything to Avenue C and sold it all for $200. They gave Kevin $50. "Yeah man, take it easy."

"What are you guys doing now?"

"We have to go to our friend's house in Brooklyn and he doesn't let us bring anyone else," said Flip. Max shrugged and nodded in agreement.

"Kevin, let's go. Now." Verite fumed. Max and Flip went back to 14th St. for the L train. "We need to get a room, come on."

Chapter 79

February – April 1999

Jack Cheskey hit Wrench outside the motel in Hempstead where he shot porn. Cheskey sat in the van all night until Wrench came out for air. Fifteen seconds across the parking lot, two in the head with a fresh .22. He left Wrench's body on the pavement and was back on the highway in two minutes.

Demonikkk's and their closest associates drank to Wrench's memory. Sheryl, Thin Vince's old lady closed down the bar on Jamaica to the public for the night. Cheskey raised his glass. Thin Vince said the eulogy. "You know what I liked about Wrench is he was the biggest pervert in the country, now it's Big Gus!" Vinny and the crew stopped to laugh. "You know he had me over one time to that motel and he showed me how they did the pornos. They'd shoot in ten-minute intervals because the chicks had to fucking beam up every ten minutes. So, they have this fucking revolving door of chicks, right? From the bathroom where they've got fucking rocks the size of my fist and they're fucking in the bedroom…"

"All that pussy, everybody's smoking coke I love it!" Mitch cut in. "When Wrench showed his movies for the crew, Big Gus here would jerk off in his seat."

Cheskey put away another lager. "He was a one-of-a-kind guy, that Wrench." There were hundreds of guys just like Wrench, leather pants, silver jewelry, thin mustache, sunken eyes… Wrench had lookalikes in Philly, Boston, Chicago, Wrench was an archetype.

"All those that times Wrench got me a blowjob in the porno set…" said Big Gus, his arm around Mitch, crushing his Fosters in his hand while he drank.

Sheryl, Thin Vince, Mitch, and Cheskey blew lines off the bar. Mitch gave his straw to Big Gus. Joel Wolfgang drank from a goblet, gold with rubies and emeralds.

"You all right Joel?" asked Mitch.

"He was like a protégé," said Wolfgang. "The wasted potential makes me angry." He bumped ketamine off his inch long pinkie nail. "For every one of us there's millions of them."

***

Cheskey did Wolfgang next. He busted into his building through the roof, asshole cheaped out on his alarm and it cost him his life. Cheskey wore a ski mask, latex and leather gloves. Wolfgang meditated in his silk kimono, played Death in June loud on his four foot speakers. The volume gave Cheskey room to walk freely without worrying about a creak in the floorboards or a squeaky hinge. Cheskey was in and out within five minutes.

Wolfgang's last words were "no – please!" He barely caught a glimpse of Cheskey before the knife ran across his throat. He pulled Wolfgang's head back and snarled, dug the blade into his jugular. The blood sprayed away from Cheskey. Nothing hit him.

Cheskey watched the life switch off like a light. He turned his face away, let Wolfgang drop. He scanned the apartment for cash and jewelry. He found the drug box, he found the cash – $80k! That was a fantastic score. He took the knife to the sink and washed it off, wiped it down and put it back in its sheath. He got out of there. He kept it cool, walked to Grand St. and got in the van. He lit a Newport, hit the ignition and turned toward the Holland Tunnel, to Atlantic City.

Twelve hours later, Cheskey's pager went wild. He called Thin Vince from his room at Caesar's.

"Vinny, what's up? I got your pages."

"Jack, where are you right now?"

"AC, Vinny. Here until Monday for the long weekend. What's happening, what'd you do?"

"I didn't do nothing. It's Wolfgang, man. I just got the fucking call. Someone did Joel last night."

"Who?"

"I don't fucking know, Jack!"

"Vinnie what's up here?"

"There's a war on. They're fighting me from the shadows. None of us are safe."

"What's going on, man? Where are you?"

"I don't know where to go, man. They could be anywhere. The fucking assassins, man."

"Vinnie, calm down. You're no good to anybody if you don't calm down. It's how they get you."

"No, I'm cool. I've got my fucking whits, Jack. You're one the only guys I trust at this point. It could be an inside job. I don't even know if I can trust my own guys."

"Don't say that."

"What would you do?"

Cheskey broke one of his Newports open into a Bamboo and mixed a couple heavy pinches of coke into the mix. He lit up. "I walk alone, Vinnie."

"Yeah but you're an honorable man. Old school…"

"Say, that guy was into all kinds of freak sex shit, right? How do you know it had anything to do with you?"

"Joel was Demonikkk's. It doesn't matter why."

"Matters why. I get that it's your problem, but it always matters why. What if it was one of the chicks? Or a queer? Queer could have done it."

"When I'd go over there, it's true. He'd have a few chicks to choose from, all fucked up on that k shit…"

"That's who I'd look at."

Chapter 80

April 1999

Spike rolled into town in March and declared Pokeweed was her man. She didn't have any rivals for his affection. Pokeweed smelled like puke and old piss. When they were together they were twice as obnoxious as when they were apart. They fucked out in the open, on the grass in Tompkins.

Spike came back to the Park from the 7th and A side with a 40 to share with her man. Pokeweed dug into the bite on his belly, scratching like mad, getting in there. "Hey, you! You fucking deer tick… Urgh, ooh, ahh." Pokeweed puked, shit and pissed wherever he wanted to. She found him behind a bench sprawled out with his dick out.

"Hey, baby! All right, beer, all right!" He rocked on his ass and sucked the beer down. They made out, slack-jawed.

Spike lit a rollie and scanned the park with a mean look on her face. A star tattoo under her right eye, a gang of teeth knocked. She was leathery, permanently sunburnt. She wore an eight-inch mohawk she maintained with glue.

Linda Solomon took cash for Diamond. She set up on a bench in the 7th and A side of the park. Diamond served ten-dollar' bags of coke and dope. Crusties who spanged their dope money bought two bags. She signaled twenty dope. NYU, Cooper Union, and Parsons kids with family backing copped bundles. She took their money and sent them to Diamond. She signaled one hundred coke, twenty dope. They left through 10th and A.

Punk Rock Manny gave Linda a hug. "Linda, listen to this!" He played her a song from his boombox. "It's like Generation X music, but disco," he explained. "I made you a tape." He gave her a mix.

"Thank you, Manny."

"And here is eight dollars. Next time, I can give you the other two?"

Linda signaled to Diamond for one bag. Manny hugged her and rushed away.

Ernie, Julian Jewels, and Hollywood Tony crewed it up from Jersey. Ernie was the mastermind, the high achiever, the man with the plan. Hollywood Tony was muscle and street cred, namesake for the Werewolves track *Hollywood Tony, Hohocus NJ*. He wore a leather vest, no shirt, tattoos of pentagrams, swastikas, the Hollywood Sign across his chest. He was in Attica 1985–1996, now he got by on his rep. A ring of punks offered him cigarettes and swigs of their beers. He took a bench and waited.

Julian Jewels was younger, late teens early twenties. He wore a leather jacket and combat boots, with torn up jeans and a Werewolves shirt. Pokeweed liked him. He was Pokeweed in ten years. They took up a bench talking GG Allin. Ernie gave Linda $120 for the three of them and Linda sent him to Diamond.

A shouting match broke out in front of Linda between Spike and a raver runaway named Nora. Spike got the first shot. Jabs in the eye, lips, and nose. A left hook to her chin on the way down. Nora hit the floor, nose spraying blood. She tried to curl up but Spike pulled Nora's hair backwards, got on top of her back and slapped her cheek. "What the fuck did you say?"

"I don't know!"

"What? What the fuck did you say?"

"Please, I don't know, I'm sorry!"

"What are you sorry for?" Nora screamed in pain. Diamond pushed his way to the front of the crowd and rubbed his hands together.

"Please I don't know!" Spike pulled Nora's hair back again, another scream. She got off of her, kicked the back of her thigh.

"I told you to stay out of here what the fuck are you doing here? You cunt! You fucking slut!" She kicked Nora again.

"No!" Nora wailed.

"Hey, enough!" went Sweetleaf.

"Get off her, you did your thing," went Red.

One of Nora's friends peeled her off the ground, helped her to her feet and kept her up. She cried on his chest.

"Get your skank girlfriend out of this park, man! Go!" Linda watched Diamond nod his head, salivate. She bit into a Xanax. Spike sat down at the bench directly across from Linda and drank the end of a 40. Diamond turned around and pushed away on his long board. Pokeweed did nothing.

Linda met Hotdog in Bellevue, 96, fucked up on Thorazine, drooling and tearing in a chair by the window. With Thorazine it's tears and drool on hyper drive. Hotdog got her name from throwing a dog in a trashcan fire, yelling, "Hot dog." She wore vinyl shorts and an XXL white T like a toga. Her head was shaved into a mohawk. She cradled a 40 of Steel Reserve in her arm. She waddled between 7th and St. Mark's, the chess tables to the playground. She stopped in front of Linda, looked her up and down. She laughed in her face. "Hey, baby." She smiled. "I know you!"

Billy looked like a twenty-year-old baby, like a pinhead, cross-eyed and bucktoothed. Abscesses on his arms, staff scars, stick and poke tattoos. He bought a bag. His breath smelled like rotten chicken.

Lenny was a Russian Jewish ex-stockbroker. Two Ibogaine trips in Staten Island got him off dope from '97 early '99. His nails were long and filed sharp. Pale, translucent skin, puppy dog brown eyes, dark circles. He was malnourished, dehydrated, swigging a can of Pepsi. "Are you holding, please?" He was clammy, limp.

"What do you need?"

He gave her an old twenty.

"Is this real?"

"Yeah, it's antique."

"Go see Diamond." Linda got up and walked away. She lit a Camel. Lenny and Diamond shot the shit for a minute before Diamond gave Lenny a pound. Linda stretched her legs, wandered toward the grass. She watched Bad Mike pull his pit bull's chain. "Come on, it's time to go. Devil, *psst*." He looked depressed, exhausted. She hurt for him. She wished the Xanax would kick in. Bad Mike left the park, Northeast back to 10th and D.

Chapter 81

Ozone Park, 1999

Cheskey called Thin Vince and Sheryl picked up. "Who is it?"

"Sheryl? That's you? Vinnie's home? Put him on, will ya?"

"Who is this?"

"It's Jack."

"Oh, Jack. Vinnie's in booking, Jack. He's all pissed off. He called me, he's in the jail."

"Is that so?"

"Yeah, Jack."

"Which one? Queens, Brooklyn?"

"Queens, I think."

"He'll be out Monday, it's all right. Look, I'm gonna come over, you can take care of me, right?"

"Yeah, all right." Cheskey hung up and had a beer and a rail before he left the apartment. He lit a fresh Newport outside. He took the van over to Thin Vince's apartment off Crossbay on Linden Blvd. Sheryl opened up. She'd been crying, blowing coke and drinking a bottle of Vodka with Diet Fresca.

"Sheryl, what's the matter? It's all right, it's fine. Vinnie's fine."

"He's all pissed off. He said this was all my fault!"

"It's because he's locked up. Everything will be fine."

Sheryl did a line, rubbed her gums with freeze. "You mean it right?"

"Sheryl, come on. Don't make a mountain out a molehill, don't get hysterical. Now get me, uhh, here's $400."

"Yeah, sure Jack."

Thin Vince had to do three months for a DUI. This was the opening. The low hanging fruit, Wrench and Joel Wolfgang were already eliminated. Cheskey mapped out the hits on Big Gus and Mitch.

Big Gus maintained a four night a week bouncing gig at The Works Gentlemen's Club in Maspeth. He had a call scheduled three times a week with Thin Vince and he came to Rikers twice a month to visit. Mitch kept to Long Island, drinking at home, watching lots of TV. He was bouncing at a bar in Long Beach. If he didn't hit them both in the same night one of them would go to ground and they'd be nearly impossible to kill before Thin Vince got out of jail.

Chapter 82

19 April 1999

Lawrence, Screaming Jesus, towered over seven-feet tall. He wore sandals, blue jeans, a fanny pack and a Christmas-colored long-sleeve shirt, striped red and green. His system arrived to him in a revelation during a stay in King's County. The everlasting light of the daughter meets the everlasting darkness of the son through wedlock. The clergy, in its commandment to be fruitful and multiply, is encouraging the consumption of the light of the daughter by the darkness of the son. He was a prophet. It was his mission to take this to the people. He walked the double yellow line on Avenue A. He strained his voice. "THE EVERLASTING LIGHT OF THE DAUGHTER! MEETS THE DARKNESS OF THE SON!"

Linda realized she'd heard these words before. It was a tape she watched with Joanne Pardes and Claire Labas in the back room at Hilaria. A heavy set older woman with a southern accent dressed in a smock gave a lecture behind a podium. "What is the clergy doing? They're charging the atmosphere. The clergy says be fruitful and multiply!" She smiled wide, raised her eyebrows. The crowd laughed, applauded. "They're saying get to it, y'all! What are they doing? They're encouraging an atmosphere where the eternal, shining, blinding light of the divine feminine, the, *The Daughter*, collides with the void, the everlasting darkness of *The Son*."

She had never seen Claire so fixed on anything. She didn't move, let alone smoke or bump coke, she just leaned forward, watched and listened, let her emotions play out on her face. By the middle of the lecture, Claire was in tears. Linda remembered putting her hand on Claire's knee to comfort her. Claire grabbed Linda's hand and didn't loosen her grip until the end of the tape. When Linda looked over at Joanne, she was deep in thought. She was doing math in her head, she looked inspired.

She lit a Camel, tried to slow her breathing. She got up and started to head

East along the Southern side of the park, the site of the old Bandshell, destroyed in '88. Diamond caught up on his long board.

"Hey what happened?"

"I'm tired and want to get high, let's go home."

"How much cash do you have?"

"I have to count."

"Go in that doorway."

She counted $110. "A hundred."

"All right give it to me." Diamond went into his pants and pulled out the rest of the unsold dope. "Put this in your bag." Diamond put the money in his chain wallet. He wore a SUICIDAL hat, with the brim up against the forehead, a white bandanna covered his eyebrows, low baggy shorts and a fresh white tank.

They hustled down Avenue B, Diamond on his board, Linda keeping pace. A black Chevy and a black van pulled up; five cops jumped out. Giants and Yankees gear, Wrangler jeans, square heads and Long Island accents. Linda watched a fridge shaped detective in a backwards cap, gun in one hand bash the back of Diamonds head open with a Maglight. "Hey Diamond! Fuck you! You're under arrest."

Linda tried to run away but she slammed into his partners. One of them took her by the arm and ran her toward the wall face first. He pinned her cheek against the brick and cuffed her.

"Where are you going?" She couldn't place the voice.

"Do you know what this piece of shit did? Do you know who you're hanging out with?" asked the cop with his knee in her back. "Got anything on you? Any needles? You know what happens if I prick myself?"

He went into her pockets. "She's holding… Now you're under arrest."

He lifted the weight of his body off of Linda, clearing her airways to breathe again. "Diamond!"

"*Shut.* The fuck up… She rides with me. Take that fuck to the precinct."

"This one is clean. But hey, guess what faggot? We've got a warrant with your name on it."

***

Linda spent a night in a cell in the 9th Precinct. She tried to soothe herself but she'd fallen out of the practice without cigarettes, pills, heroin. She chewed on her fingernails, massaged the cuticle in her thumb with her forefinger. She sat on the metal bench, doubled over, clutching her neck, staring at the floor. The narc from her arrest in his Giants jersey, that stupid fucking backwards cap, his badge around his neck now on a chain. He came in first.

"Look, look at me," he said as he sat down in front of her. "Look at me."

She looked up.

"Look at me." He pointed his index and middle fingers at his eyes. "There's a guy who wants to talk to you. Today can be your lucky day. OK. Talk to him, consider what he says. If you go with him at the end, you'll do what he says. If you don't go, sit tight and wait for booking. You understand?"

Linda focused on his eyes. She nodded her head. She felt tightness in her biceps, bugs under her skin, cramps in her legs. She felt her guts dissolve. "I understand," she said to him.

The narc stood up. "All right get up." He cuffed her and led her out of the cages and through a hallway, into an interrogation room. He uncuffed her and put his hand on her shoulder, he guided her body into her chair. Her eyes followed him out, before she turned back to the man in front of her.

Bob Walsh sat across the table. "Linda Solomon…" He looked up from his files. "I know who you are. If anything I propose to you for from here on out is going to work, this is very important, I need you to understand that. We know who you are."

"OK?"

"Here you go." Walsh pushed a fresh pack of Camel Lights and a book of matches to her. She tapped the pack on the table, opened it, lit up. "Thank you."

He looked at her, watched her smoke. He leaned back. He wore a navy blazer, a pocket square and a light blue button down with the three top buttons undone. "Linda Solomon… Linda Solomon… Linda, I'm here today to help you out. We're in a position to make things happen for you. It doesn't even have anything to do with this case you're facing. I just happened to find out that you were here, in the station. This is when well, once you're in booking it's difficult enough but – once you go in front of the judge, really by the second you're losing options. Now, you have a bonus option. You can go with us…"

Linda assumed Walsh for a lawyer. He felt like one. The nicotine soothed her. She focused on her cigarette. She pulled herself away from the edge.

"Linda, Diamond isn't getting bail. He's facing second degree murder, attempted murder, assault with a deadly weapon, armed robbery, kidnapping…"

Linda was stunned.

"He's going away for a long time."

She wept for him.

"But no one out there thinks you had anything to do with that. You're not facing any of those charges. That's the good news. But, Linda, you're facing felony possession of heroin. Intent to distribute. Do you understand what that means? None of that diversion bullshit. No rehab. Heroin dealers, scum of the earth. Heroin dealers they're… selling poison to children. That's Bedford Hills. Sounds like a country club but it should fucking terrify you. It's Clinton for Women."

"What, what do you want me to do?" Linda wrapped the back of her head with her palms and looked at the table.

"Linda, calm down a bit, have another cigarette." Walsh picked up a can of Coke that had been sitting by his feet. "Here." He cracked the can open and gave it to her. The sugar did something. She followed his advice and had another cigarette. She started to hope Walsh would offer her a way out. The cop had mentioned something. She stopped crying. She didn't know when she'd started.

She was getting curious. This was her world now. "What do you want?"

"You're going come work for us. You'll get out tonight, with me, and you'll receive a cash advance once you sign on," said Walsh.

"What are you asking me to do?" Linda started tapping her feet. Her eyes darted.

"Calm down, Linda."

"You want me to suck your dick, is that it?"

Walsh let himself crack and laughed at her. "Linda, come on." He shook his head, smiled wide. He picked up a new soda from his feet and cracked it open. He took a few sips. Walsh took one of the cigarettes and lit up. The ridicule left Linda feeling foolish. The shame cowed her. "We're talking about *work* Linda. Not prostitution, work," said Walsh.

"All right, get me the fuck out of here."

"All right Linda, I was hoping you'd say that. But, now understand something." Walsh looked Linda in the eyes. "Once we walk outside, you owe us your freedom. You're not being booked, but these cops know what you're up to and they can recreate the charges you're avoiding at any time they see fit, until you've completed your task. I don't expect to pay you the first disbursement, and then never see you again. If that happens, you'll be back in here without a chance in hell of seeing freedom for fifteen years. But that doesn't need to happen. We're giving you a chance to change your life. And as long as we get what we want we'd rather make that happen for you."

Wash and Linda left the station together and stopped at the corner. "That's your ride." He pointed to Jack Cheskey's white van. "He'll take you home. He'll give you your instructions."

She got in the van. "Hi, I'm Linda."

"Jack." He smoked a Newport. He adjusted his seat upwards and started the engine. "You're probably hungry, right?"

"I guess, maybe?" They got moving. Linda sat silent, dazed. Cheskey didn't have anything to say. Linda broke the silence. "So, you're a cop?"

"No."

"So, you're what a lawyer?"

"You met my lawyer."

"You're a, uhh, PI?"

"You could say PI."

"How does a lawyer and a PI investigator just like get someone out of jail like you did though?"

"You should try making some friends in the police department."

"Were you a cop?"

"Ask me a different question, jeeze."

"Why did you bail me out?"

"I'm a nice guy."

"No really."

"We need someone like you to do a job for us."

"PI work?"

"Yeah, actually."

"Because I'm not going to suck your cock or fuck you or anything."

"That's not a problem for me. But you shouldn't talk to me like that, you know. We're the ones who paid your bond." They went cruising for a drive through, windows open. "No offense but you need a shower, Linda. Let's get you a uhh, let's get a motel room you can clean up."

"I have my own place."

"That shithole on Avenue B? Your boyfriend's place?"

"Yeah, actually."

They found a drive through Wendy's. Cheskey ordered twenty dollars' worth of burgers and baked potatoes. "Eat up, and I'll take you back to that shithole."

Back on Avenue B Cheskey gave Linda a pager. "You'll hear from us very soon, get yourself together," he said coldly. He shut the door and sped off. Linda went upstairs. The apartment was trashed, thoroughly ransacked. Searched by narcs, the neighbors? Depending on who went through it, she might still have a hit stashed. She went into the bedroom. The bed was destroyed, the mattress was split open with a knife, mangled stuffing and springs exposed. That was a good fucking bed, the bastards. The dresser was taken apart, the shelves were smashed. The closet was emptied, whatever was left was strewn around the floor. In the bathroom the top of the toilet was smashed in the tub. The medicine cabinet and storage under the sink were emptied out.

A fresh sense of violation back in the kitchen, the fridge was tossed. The old Puerto Rican and Chinese food was all over the place, but whoever did toss the kitchen and the pantry didn't check for her stash behind the stove. She pulled it out. Four bags of dope and a vial of crack. "Holy shit thank you." Divine providence. She fixed on the couch. She got high. The pain in her joints and stomach disappeared. She felt the heroin in her sphincter. The headache, the tension in her shoulders went away. Her heartbreak, anxiety, indifference toward death fell by the wayside. When the shot wore off she wept for Diamond. She curled up into a ball, she was alone again.

She packed the crack rock into a stem. She smoked. She remembered she was supposed to clean herself up. She dug the smashed porcelain out of the tub and turned on the shower. She smelled herself, rotten. She scrubbed jail off her skin and out of her hair. She sat for a while in the tub and cried. She stared at the tiles until the hot water ran out. She picked clothes off the floor. She got dressed. The coke wore off, she fell onto her bed and screamed. The shock that saw her through her arrest wore off. She broke down. She shook until she summoned the focus to cook the last of the heroin. It was dark outside. She fell asleep.

***

Cheskey knocked on the door, Linda let him inside. The place was still fucked up. She'd cleaned up most of the broken glass and splintered wood. Trash was piled into corners. "You live like this, Linda?" Cheskey asked.

"It was like this, worse, actually, when I came back," she protested.

"Who did this?" He held the state of the apartment against her.

"I don't know." She was annoyed. Cheskey raised an eyebrow at her, for her tone. "What? Fuck!"

Cheskey looked around for a clean place to sit. "Let's get out of here. Get your things, let's get in the car."

They took a drive to Chinatown. They found a place off Canal Street. Cheskey ordered General Tso's. Linda ordered House Special Lo Mein. Cheskey ranted with food in his mouth. He took a ten-minute shit and Linda sat at the table, smoking cigarettes and waiting for him to pay the bill. She deflected dirty looks, poured sugar packets into her tea cup. Cheskey came out of the bathroom, sweating, wearing sunglasses, counting money. He gave the waiter a twenty, and waved for Linda to get up and go. He lit a Newport, smacked and rubbed his gut. "Good food, amiright?"

"Yeah, thanks."

"Yeah, yeah." He smoked and belched. They got back into the van. Cheskey lit a new Newport, Linda lit a new Camel. "You're going back home?"

"Can we actually go up to Houston and Bowery? I'll get out there."

"Whatever you say." They drove over to the Bowery. Cheskey peeled out fifty dollars. "Here."

"Oh, wow, thanks Jack."

"Yeah, yeah no problems."

Chapter 83

Big Gus and Mitch

Cheskey spent a week figuring out how to approach the hit. The Works, the strip club had a camera, no guarantee Big Gus would brake at a Stop sign at four a.m. No sure things in the vicinity of the club. For all the desolation, dark corners to hide in, there were too many ways out, too many variables. The cops had a garage nearby, just too many variables. He scooped out Big Gus' block, more promise. It was a sleepy side street in Glendale. Lots of two family homes, he didn't make a camera. He drove the distance from the club to the apartment, fifteen minutes.

Night of the hit Cheskey arrived on the block at four. Big Gus' truck pulled in at 4.45. Cheskey rolled his mask down. Latex and leather gloves. He walked fifteen steps, shotgun in hand, his .22 in his pocket ready to go. Big Gus smoked an Al Capone parked in the driveway. Cheskey fired into the passenger side window, hitting Big Gus directly in the chest. Broken glass exploded through the car and sliced Big Gus in the face and neck. Cheskey lowered the shotgun and shot Big Gus in the head with the .22.

Big Gus was Sgt at Arms. Mitch was VP. He had to die before word got out. He hustled back to the van and got out of there. He turned onto Central Avenue, back toward Woodhaven. He cruised through Maspeth, the van blended in with dozens like it. He killed a pack of Newports. It was half an hour to Mitch's house, the Belt then the Sunrise Highway. Cheskey stayed at sixty the whole way. Rock Block. Steeley Dan, Santana, and Steve Miller. The adrenaline from the hit on Gus powered him forward. He railed three lines when he reached Oceanside. He felt the blow in his prostate.

The fucking Panopticon, a street as dense as Ozone. Nevertheless, all of the lights were out in the kitchen and living room windows on the block. He sat for a second, listened. The whole neighborhood slept. He got the pistol and silencer ready. He dragged down a Newport. He put it out in the ashtray, left the van.

BEWARE OF THE DOG? BEWARE OF THE OWNER!

Sure, Mitch. The front lock took Cheskey six seconds to break. From across the street, he looked like he had a key. Ski mask and gloves, stealth embodied, Cheskey walked in. He opened Mitch's bedroom door and unloaded. Murderous Mitch aka White Mitch aka Little Mitchel never woke up. Cheskey had thirty seconds to scan the room. He snatched Mitch's money roll on the dresser and got out of there. No change in the conditions outside. The block slept through it. The same decoy lights, the same quiet. Cheskey hit the ignition, lights out until he left the cul-de-sac. He took off the mask. The coke and the adrenaline drove him home. He pushed back into the city along the LIRR tracks, past JFK and onto Crossbay, back home. He was starving: corned beef hash, eggs over easy, fries, ketchup and rye toast.

Chapter 84

May 1999

Linda took a walk down Bowery to Bleecker St. and rang upstairs. A stranger opened the window. "Who are you?"

"Who are you?" Linda took umbrage.

"Nah, who are you?"

"Linda!"

The big, medieval door to the storefront on the left side of the building was locked. No display in the windows, just heavy curtains. Linda fixated on an old *ZIKES!* stenciled over the storefront door for a while. The door upstairs was on the right side of the building.

Someone came down a few minutes later. They were stoned, smelled like stale sweat in a dirty thermal. "Yeah, Neil said you can come up." Shop was open, the scale was out. Hangers on hung out, smoked Neil's joints. It was loud, chaotic. Sweat, weed, cat piss.

"Linda! Wow, man! Linda! Where have you been?"

Linda hugged Neil with one arm. "It's so good to see you."

"Where, have you been?"

"It's been a bad year."

"Yeah, wow, it's been about a year. We're moving full steam ahead over here. Could have used the help but we're getting along. But now that you're back, that's good. There's work to do." Neil passed his joint to Linda. "There's an anti-Giuliani protest in Tompkins Park that refused to include our platform in their demands. They want our organization's mobilization abilities but they won't, um, get involved full-time. They'll just use us to fill up their demonstration…" He lit a new inch wide joint. "We're convening a counter protest against disunity tomorrow. We'll see you there." He gave her a flier. "I have Jai at Kinko's now making 420 copies. He'll be back soon, take some copies with you."

"Can I get five of the 2's?"

"The 4's?"

"You don't have 2's?"

"You should get the 4's."

Linda kicked some dust. Irving took a seat in his big leather chair and measured out her order while he flipped through a stack of composition notebooks where he kept his phone numbers. He picked up the phone. "Yeah, Philip... you were the one talking about the grail, right? That it was Iboga in the grail..."

Linda's attention turned to the opposite side of the loft, up front. A crew of skinny guys in wire rim glasses and ponytails, eyes glued to their monitors, but carrying on six different arguments. It was hard to hear anything else. Neil got off the phone.

"What's up with those guys?"

"They're getting us up to date on the Y2K. We developed a preparedness, uhh, model that we're following to make sure we're ready when Y2K hits. We'll be a lifeboat..."

"Oh... well, I guess I'll see you later?"

"Oh, uh, Linda, before you go, rub my shoulders?"

Chapter 85

June 1999

Jack Cheskey paged Linda once a week through May and into June. He took her out to lunch and gave her some pocket change. Linda started to look forward to meeting up. Free food, free money.

They sat in Cheskey's van. Cheskey dug through a bag of fried chicken on the dashboard. Linda sat in the passenger seat, eating a thigh. Cheskey gnawed on a drumstick. He wiped his hands off, threw the bones out the window and lit a Newport. He gave Linda Verite's photo. "You're going to take this girl on. She gets high, that's your way in... Make her your problem." He gave her Kevin's photo. "This is her boyfriend, why not him too? Keep him around, he keeps her occupied and he's dumb as a rock. No self-awareness. I think you'll need a few months, so start now."

"What do you want me to do?"

"Be her friend."

Cheskey pulled out a thousand. "Here. You get this every two weeks until the job is done. Don't spend everything in one weekend, all right?"

"Yeah, sure, of course not." Linda felt electricity run from the base of her spine into the top of her skull. "Thanks."

"Yeah."

"So just be this girl's friend?"

"You're my problem, she's yours. I want updates every week."

"So, I'm spying on her?"

"Sure, Linda. Your kind are the best secret agents on earth."

"I guess."

"Every week, I want a day by day. I want to know what you did, what she did. What the boyfriend did. I want to know where you all went, when you weren't together where they went. Everything."

Linda started counting the money. Twenties and fifties, bursting out of the envelope. It made her blood pump. It made her salivate. "Yeah, man.

I'll call you."

"Every week. Monday. We'll set up a place to meet. And if something significant happens, let me know that too, right away."

"All right, cool. If anything big happens, I'll let you know."

"I'll take you back to downtown."

"Take me... to Union Square?"

"OK, Union Square, here we come." He went digging for a new drumstick. He started the engine.

Verite wasn't hard to find. She was on St. Mark's almost every day. Linda immediately recognized her when Cheskey showed her the photos. She found Verite on a bench off 7th and B in Tompkins. Linda took a seat next to her and lit a smoke, she left around two feet between them. "Hey, beb, are you OK?"

Verite would've told her to fuck off, but she'd seen Linda before and with the right people. This was a contact. "Yeah." She wiped her eyes.

"Do you want one?" She gave Verite a Camel. "Are you sick?"

"Yeah," whined Verite. "I'm waiting for my boyfriend."

"Is he copping?"

"Trying to, yeah."

"I can help you cop."

"Really?"

"Where is he coming from?"

"I don't know, probably close."

It took them five minutes to find Kevin on 6th off B. His head hung low; his skin looked green. "Fucking no one is out... Hey can you spare a cigarette?"

"It's sweeps. Today is a Tuesday," said Linda.

"Babe, give her the money." Kevin gave Linda forty bucks in 10s, 5s and 1s.

"You counted right?" Linda asked Verite.

"Yeah, yeah. Totally."

"Come with me." Linda stuffed the money into her purse. They walked past Avenue B, turned left on C toward 10th St. On 9th, she had them wait. "Hang out here."

"Choking Victim lives over here," Kevin told Verite.

Linda went toward Avenue D and hid in a doorway. She had a bundle in her pocket, she broke off four bags. Now she had to go all the way back to Tank on Henry St. so she'd have something for the morning, but this was worth it. She put the dope in a spent pack of cigarettes. She hustled back to 9th St. and served Verite. "Here's my pager number. This was free. Just hook me up next time. Turn on 8th and go back to the park." Linda turned south on C toward Henry St. In her estimation, she'd done well.

Chapter 86

July 1999

"Parenting, marriage, work, prayer. In this day and age very, very few best sellers tackle all four at the same time. She's taught so many of us how to stay positive in the face of so much darkness, so much sin. It's such a pleasure to welcome Alice Walsh, author of the indispensable series, *Managing Modern Life*, whose Part Three was just released in paperback. Alice Walsh, welcome back to *Walk With Nations*."

"Mary, thank you for having me back."

"Alice, when we talked off the air you told me how you've healed from watching this horrific tragedy at Columbine High School in Littleton Colorado. It's so inspiring and I think our listeners need to hear this."

"It was my son's nineteenth birthday on 20 April. I woke up that day overjoyed, but that night I was inconsolable. I was with my best friend, in her living room watching the news and my heart broke and for the next week I cried and I prayed. I asked how we keep failing our sons and daughters. These are our children! But about two weeks ago, I got my answer. The cure for this sickness is simple, not easy, but simple. This kind of violence, the satanic aspects, the trench coats and the heavy metal music. This is what we can absolutely call the Darkness of the Son. What is the solution to this spillover of darkness and sin and nihilism? Of teenage pregnancy and atheism and drug use? It's a collision with the Everlasting Light of the Daughter. There is no greater force in the universe! Let's direct that force at this sickness in our society. I woke up that next morning and I called up my publisher and I said let's donate a thousand copies of each book, right now. Let's get this message in our children's hands."

"Such generosity!"

"The next thing I did was I called up the day camp my children attended, here in San Diego. I called him up and I said I want to come talk to the children. We set up a time that coming Monday. We gathered around, in the classroom. I said 'today we're going to have some fun, and while we do that, we're going to make the world a better place. How does that sound?' The kids all cheered, because that's our impulse, as children, to make the world a better place. Every child got a place mat and then a small tube of toothpaste. I said 'All right everybody! Let's push all the toothpaste onto the paper. Ready, set, go!' Mary it was wonderful, the kids squealed and laughed while they emptied the tubes of toothpaste. When the tubes were empty, I said 'OK! Great job. Now let's take all of this toothpaste and put it back in the tube!' The kids tried all different techniques, they're yelling back at me 'it doesn't work!' The kids were anxious, agitated and I said to them 'maybe that's because you can't do it. You can't put the toothpaste back in the tube. And what if our words were just like the toothpaste? What if once we say something, we can't put it back in our mouths? This is why before we speak we should think first. We should think about what we say before we say it. That way we won't hurt anyone's feelings, or say things we don't mean.' The kids thought about what I said. They really took the lesson to heart. And ever since this day I've felt better, I really have. This is what we need to do. In the face of this violence, we need to teach our children to love each other, to love God."

"Alice Walsh I could cry that's so beautiful. Thank you for taking the time to call into *Walk With Nations* on K-ABN and W-ACL."

Chapter 87

September 1999

Thin Vince watched his inner circle die while he was locked up for DUI. Practically every time he talked to Sheryl or Cheskey, it was bad news.

Cheskey picked Thin Vince up from Rikers after three months inside. He was pissed off, visibly stressed out. Freedom in and of itself, a welcome reprieve for anyone else wasn't enough for Vinny. They drove Hazen St, a straight line from the bridge to Astoria Blvd. Cheskey stopped the car at Jackson Hole. "Let's get some burgers. Good burgers here. You've got to be hungry, right?"

"I can't trust anyone, Jack."

"Hey I just picked you up and I'm buying lunch!"

"They're out there, Jack."

"Not around here. It's all cops and Narcos around here. The Colombians... they're the ones who did Mitch?" Cheskey cut up lines.

"I don't know who they are. When I find them I'm gonna make it slow man. I'm gonna find out everything. The whole conspiracy." Thin Vince railed his blow. "Ah that's the stuff."

"You're feeling better now?"

"I could take a shit, now."

"There you go."

***

Overlapping with Thin Vince's stretch, Bad Mike sat in Rikers Island for three months waiting out a possession case. Out of nowhere, a cop came and told him his charges were dropped and he was getting out once he was processed. He took the bus to Queens Plaza. He found a snipe on the ground outside a doughnut shop and lit up. Spring air, it felt good to be out. He had eighteen dollars in his pocket. He went to McDonald's for three cheeseburgers and a coke. He inhaled the food. He paid the fare for the subway back downtown. He didn't need to try his luck.

He rode the N to Union Square and walked to St. Marks. Linda Solomon sold joints outside Search and Destroy. She gave him a hug and he took a seat next to her. "When did you get out?" she asked.

"Like just now. You're the first person I know who I've seen."

Linda beamed. She took a spliff out of her pocket and gave it to him. "Welcome home." She gave him her lighter and he lit up.

"Aw man, Linda. Thanks. This is – ahh." He made a chef's kiss. He'd grown a beard over the racing stripe on his chin.

The smoke attracted some teenage punks and a goth girl. She sold them six joints for $40. Bad Mike appreciated a good upsell. They strolled St. Marks together. Linda bought them coffees. Bad Mike bummed cigarettes off passersby. They made it into the park. Punks gathered to welcome Bad Mike home. He petted everyone's dogs and took swigs from 40s. Math on 4th St. was looking after Devil, his Pitbull. He'd pick him up that night.

Bad Mike and Linda hung out on the benches off the chess tables and caught up on gossip. Punks in Manic Panic, leathers, miniskirts and fishnets bought joints for five dollars a-piece. After an hour, Bad Mike stood up. "I still haven't been home or nothing yet. Let me go." Linda stood up.

"Come to the river tonight, we'll have a beer-be-q in your honor," said Gutter Andy.

They held hands on the way to 10th St. Bad Mike called up to Luis who lived on the second floor. He popped his head out and danced in place. He dropped a pair of keys into Bad Mike's hands. The Missing Foundations logo, the upside-down martini glass was painted in red on the door. He picked his apartment door open in a few minutes. The place seemed intact. He went into a corner of the apartment and pulled a coffee can out from behind a bookshelf. He opened the can and lit up. He tilted the can so Linda could see the bundles of heroin. He took out two bags and gave them to her. "Thanks for that smoke before."

They got high. Bad Mike shot one bag since he hadn't had any dope for three months. Linda shot her two. They fucked in Bad Mike's bed and fell asleep in each other's arms.

Bad Mike pulled a Black Flag shirt off the floor and scrubbed the cum crusted onto his stomach. He got out of bed, opened the window, found Linda's cigarettes. He took a shit, shot some heroin. He played a mixtape on his Walkman. Crass, Missing Foundations, Officer Down, MDC… He sat at his kitchen table and watched Linda sleep. She moved in immediately.

Chapter 88

Summer 1999

Verite paged Linda two days later. The first call, early in the morning went unanswered. She called again a few hours later.

Linda and Bad Mike watched videos of hardcore shows in bed. "Fuck. I need to go to the park, I'll be back." Linda ran out and rushed to Tompkins. She found Kevin and Verite under a tree in the grass.

"Hey, what's up?"

"I was paging you." Verite was upset, glassy-eyed, chain smoking, pulling grass out from the lawn.

"I'm here now, get up, come with me."

They went back to 10th St. and Linda took them upstairs. Steve Sinclair from The Werewolves had come upstairs to cop since Linda left. He took over the kitchen table. His wallet was embroidered with an iron cross and attached to a three-foot chain. "Check day." They did their business. Sinclair cooked up a speedball. "These guys, Mass Murder, they were better as Right Sector. That was these assholes without that fag singer and that fag drummer."

"Nah, the drummer was in Right Sector."

"No way. That drummer's weak. Otto Paladin was the drummer for Right Sector. Otto was my boy."

"He got murdered, right?"

"Right over there on 13th St.

"But this guy, he was in Right Sector, maybe after Otto died..."

"When we did *Punk Rock Pogrom*, Right Sector opened up for us and the Cro Mags. Hard dudes."

"And the guitarist is in prison, right?"

"Yeah he killed a motherfucker. He's never coming back. Dude's in Clinton."

"That's fucking hardcore," said Bad Mike.

"Al Killer, one of our drummers was upstate with him for five years. Hardcore shit."

Linda came back in with Verite and Kevin.

"Oh hey, Linda. Looking nice, real nice," said Sinclair, nodding his head. Linda was wearing her CBGB shirt and jeans. She hadn't taken a shower in eight days.

"Oh shit! You're Steve Sinclair!" Kevilicious practically jumped.

"That's right bro." Sinclair grabbed Kevin's hand. "And what's your name, sweetheart? All right."

"I'm Verite."

"Nice, nice. Linda, I like your friends."

"Steve, I fucking love Punk Rock Genocide." He put his fist to his hand like a mic. *"Genocide – Genocide – This is Punk Rock Genocide!"*

"Genocide – Genocide – This is Punk Rock Genocide!" Sinclair joined in. "Yeah you know your shit."

Kevin launched into *Atrocity Fucks!* Off The Werewolves *Punk Rock Killing Fields* "*I'll be the killer in your closet / I'll be a fucking one man Phoenix Project/ Wolfman tears you up the original sadist / You'll never be free/ Lyconography—*"

Sinclair jumped in to harmonize. He closed his eyes and pointed his finger at the ceiling. "MOTHERFUCKER!"

Linda bit her lip and put her arms around Bad Mike. She whispered in his ear, "Sorry."

Verite felt Sinclair's eyes, she shot his looks back. Bad Mike served the kids. Sinclair bumped fists with Kevin and gave Verite a final, vulgar once over. "Linda, take her easy. Bad Mike, good shit Brother." He pointed his finger, big silver ring and long dirty nail at Bad Mike.

"I just sang *Punk Rock Genocide* with Steve Sinclair!"

"I'm so proud of you, babe."

"I'll see you guys later," said Linda.

Kevin's voice carried through the building while they left. "We're talking *Methadone Mayhem, Me and Spacely Out By The River, Robbed Cut Up by City-As Chicks!*"

***

Linda slept on Hippie Hill. She wore sunglasses and oversized headphones, an olive tank top and a pair of ocher pants with the legs cuffed. Kevin dug a hole in the grass and read a copy of some zine. Verite flipped through *HYPE MACHINE*. Nora sat inside Flip's spread legs. They leaned against the big tree at the foot of the hill and weaved their fingers together.

Nico Quick sat on a milk crate, played a glam rock medley on acoustic guitar. *Cum on feel the noise* and a jerky rendition of *Diamond Dogs*, in his scratchy snarled voice. Crazy Jay from Avenue A staggered, leaned against the fence. "Keeping America Beautiful!" Swill pissed through the fence into the grass. Pokeweed woke up on the other side of the lawn. "What's with all this shit? Who took a shit on me?" Hatred and Chaos read TAZ and The Manson File. Shawn and Shaggy passed a spliff in the shade. Mystic, Straps, Raven and Gutter Andy shot dope by the fountain and staggered onto the grass. Straps and Mystic puked at the foot of the hill and rolled up menthol Top.

Linda woke up with neck pain. She chewed a Klonopin. "Verite let's get some coffee."

English smoked a Newport dipped in wet by the Chess Tables on 7th and A. Linda and Verite passed him by on their way to Ray's.

"I like your boots!" he called out to Verite.

She turned back. "I don't think they'll fit." She winked at him.

"I'll make em fit!" he yelled back at her. He ground his teeth.

Chapter 89

September – October 1999

Cheskey drove down to the Lower East Side to check on the principles. He watched Linda, Verite and Kevin leave 10th St. and march east to the river. Kevin lugged his pack. Verite kept her Jansport on one shoulder. Linda wore a sleeveless Assuck shirt and her black jeans. Her hair was knotting together into dreads. Cheskey slipped strips of calzone and a chicken roll into his mouth, eyes on the target. When they crossed the street he started the engine and followed them east. Hours later he watched Linda alone return to the squat, turn the key and go back upstairs to Bad Mike.

He drove a block down and parked outside the projects. He walked over the footbridge, over the FDR onto East River Park. He smoked Newports, he scanned for campers. He watched Kevin and Verite cuddle against a fence, facing the water. They shot heroin, fucked on the grass, went to sleep. Cheskey kept watch.

***

A week later, Bad Mike kicked Linda out. "Not doing this bullshit with you anymore." She was on her way out to meet Verite when he dropped it on her. She didn't know how to respond. She stopped in the middle of the room and gawked at him. "Get your shit together, and leave, all right? Give me my keys. Right now, you can't leave with a key."

"What did I do?" Linda started to panic.

"I'm just, like, fucking, sick of you. I just can't be around you anymore. Just like you were there and I was there but... I don't know. This is my place I don't need to explain why you can't just live here anymore. And these fucking kids you keep hanging out with are annoying as fuck. Shit... You're just always so fucking depressing. I have to watch my back out there, you know. I can't be like, worried about your shit all the time. I've got to focus on *numero uno*. You get that."

"What does that mean?"

He found her backpack in the corner of the room and started scanning for pieces of clothing. She had some zines, her CD book. He gave her a bundle of dope. "You can have this for free, but you should cop from someone else... like Rory or Devo or Tank or someone. I just can't deal with it anymore, it's just I got too much to do."

"Did you meet somebody?"

"Even if I did it wouldn't make a difference. Look, you need to go. I need the keys back."

Linda dug into her pocket for the keys. She cried when she handed them back. She lit a Lucky Strike. "I'm sorry I'm such a fucking bummer."

"My girlfriend died and then I had to spend all my time taking care of you. You're always whining and complaining and shit."

"That happened to me too!"

"We were together for fucking five years! Every minute! five years! Every fucking minute for five fucking years. Shut the fuck up, get the fuck out of here with that. How dare you? How dare you?" He looked like he might break. She saw the torture in his face. He turned his back to her, lit a Marlboro. She found a corner to hide in. He sat down on the mattress. Linda saw the hate in his eyes.

"I need my pack," she said.

Bad Mike gave it to her. "Did I miss anything?"

"I don't think so."

"I don't want anything of yours, I'm not trying to forget anything, all right?"

"I think that's it."

"Then get out Linda, leave me alone."

***

Linda paged Cheskey. He called the payphone. "Yeah."

"I..." Linda gasped between sobs. "I... Mike fucking..."

"What happened to you?"

"I just got fucking dumped, OK!"

"Why–what do you want from me?"

"I need some cash."

"For what?"

"For a place to stay."

"Yeah all right, fine. Sure."

She calmed down a little bit. She sucked down smoke. "Thanks."

"Yeah, yeah. You need it today, right?"

"Yeah. Please."

"All right. Get on the subway. Take the A to Rockaway Boulevard and I'll meet you there."

"I'm meeting her soon."

"Do that, then come over here. Just send me a beeper and I'll wait for you at the stop, downstairs. All right?" Cheskey sounded impatient.

"All right."

***

The accumulation of stressors was breaking Linda physically. A tension in her arms, a weight on her shoulders, canker sores, intense pain in the soles of her feet. She felt a knee breaking down. She could imagine a bone snapping in her shin mid step. If she lived long enough, she'd age terribly. She saw her future in the women at the Delancey St. McDonald's hanging out in a booth, trading pills. Four or five ladies per unit, thick layers of makeup, talking at each other. The thought of it triggered the tension in her arms, aches behind her eyes and in her temples. She counted on the premise she'd be dead by then. She couldn't imagine life without her youth. But for now she still feared death. She wasn't ready yet. Her perfect arc, echoing Joanne's, sunset at thirty-five.

Verite let Linda cry on her shoulder on a bench by the handball courts in Tompkins. She patted her shoulder. "It's OK, it's OK, we have each other."

Linda sold Verite four bags out of the bundle Bad Mike gave her and went Delancey Street to catch the F. She paid the fare since she had dope on her and waited on a bench. A mixtape with Shotgun and Treasure, Psychic TV on one side. Suicide and Bowie Berlin stuff on the other.

She took the A into Queens and got off at Rockaway Blvd. Cheskey waited in his station wagon. Linda saw him through the window, a window cracked to let out smoke. She got in the car.

Cheskey handed her a wad of money. "This is $300 and something extra... You saw her?"

"Yeah."

"What happened?"

"She was sweet." Linda massaged her forehead. "I took care of her."

"Aright, good. Did you see Kevin?"

"No."

"Get back in contact with him, bring him in. We need to keep them close the next few weeks. Make sure they don't go anywhere, keep 'em out of jail, out of trouble. Get a room for a night or two, I'll send you a page when I have a place worked out."

Chapter 90

October 1999

Cheskey gave Linda the keys for a studio in Chelsea, the back of a six story walk up on 24th St., fresh paint on the walls, drop cloths on most of the floor. "Bring them here with you. The three of you can stay the week." He gave her $600. "Just don't give me too much of a cleanup."

"I'll clean the place up. Thanks, Jack." They went upstairs. Linda turned the key. The apartment was empty except for a mattress on the floor. "There's nothing in here!"

"There's the mattress right in front of you."

"But like, where do you sit or?"

"I'm going to pretend you're not complaining at me, all right?"

Linda looked down at the $600. She pushed it in her pocket, lit a Camel. "Thanks for this place, Jack."

It occurred to Cheskey he could whip it out and she'd probably drop right there. "I have shit to do." He lit a Newport. "Page me on uhh, Sunday and we'll meet up. Lock up behind me, will ya?" He left the apartment. Linda cracked a window. The fresh paint gave her a headache. She lit a new smoke, sat on the toilet and took in the silence, the privacy. She cleaned herself up. She got high and took a nap on the mattress. She woke up around dusk and hit the street.

Linda took the R to 8th and found Kevin and Verite on Astor Place spanging outside Cooper Union. Kevin flew the sign, Verite smiled and did the talking.

"Linda!" Verite jumped up.

"Guys, get up. I got a spot for us for a few days."

"No way! Babe, fold up the sign." Kevin got himself together.

She brought Kevin and Verite up to 24th St. "We have this for three weeks. Don't bring anyone over, don't fuck anything up, don't let anyone know you're here."

"Yo, if we start getting mail here we'll have squatter's rights."

"No, don't do anything like that, please. Fuck."

"No, we won't. It's cool," Verite assured Linda.

They shared the mattress. Verite in the middle, flanked on either side by Linda and Kevin, who both snored. Sleeping pills made Linda roar. Kevin whistled then wheezed. Verite pretended it didn't bother her or kept her up until she'd snap. She shook Kevin. She whispered in his ear, "Babe, you're snoring." She turned him around, wrapped herself around him.

Linda woke them up at six. "Go to Union Square and get Food Stamps." She wrote them a letter that they each paid her $200 in rent to sleep on the couch.

"Yo, that's a good idea! Like both of us that's like three bills!"

She gave them each a Klonopin. "Go, before there's a line. And don't come back without them." She locked the door behind them. She got high and went back to sleep.

Verite stopped Kevin on the street outside. "Babe, whatever you're doing to annoy Linda you need to stop."

***

Verite and Kevin came home with bags of groceries: bread and Nutella, two liters of soda, three kinds of ice cream. Linda made a sandwich and drank some coke. Linda pushed the mattress against the wall so she had a place to sit up. She put on her headphones, smoked a cigarette and listened to a mixtape. Kevin and Verite fucked in the bathroom. The bathroom door was the only potential barrier between Linda and Verite / Kevin. She would have rather they fucked in the kitchen and let her take a long shit and a shower, even a hot bath. Linda was with them all day, every day for weeks without an interruption. They never shut up. They never stopped making out, groping, jerking off and fingering each other, sucking and fucking by the river or between cars. They stunk of pussy. They were feral. Kevin, forever sixteen. One of the most frustrating, most incredible assholes she'd ever met. Verite still had time to grow out of her worse traits, Kevilicious would die this annoying.

Separating from Kevin and Verite was the same physical sensation as taking off a heavy backpack. She didn't need quiet. She needed those two to shut up. Linda got high; she zoned them out. She listened to one of Jacques' Death in June / Boyd Rice tapes. She turned it off and switched to Marilyn Manson.

Kevin splayed across the mattress, wearing headphones, smoking rollies. He croaked along to Punk Rock Genocide. *Genocide, Genocide, This is Punk Rock Genocide, Time to Die, You're Gonna Die, Die it's Punk Rock Genocide...*

Linda did Verite's makeup in the bathroom. Linda stole the best eyeliner, foundation, lipstick and mascara she could find. Only the best for Verite. She boosted new stockings and a pack of razors. She applied foundation, painted cat eyes, crimson lipstick, black mascara. "Beb, you look fucking gorgeous." She crushed a new Adderall and snorted the pile off the sink.

Verite checked herself out. She affected sinister, maniacal, hateful, then dismissive. She made a pistol with her fingers and posed for the mirror. She fired. She sat Linda down on the toilet and gave her eyeliner and lipstick. "You're so beautiful Linda, you should let me do this more!"

At the door, Verite and Kevin swayed, made out with their mouths open. This again. Linda grunted through her teeth. "Don't... fuck up your lipstick..." In the hallway she gave Verite two Adderall. She crushed one up and snorted half. She extended the back of her hand and Verite blew the rest. They hit the street, they smoked cigarettes, bought coffees on the corner. Revelers packed the sidewalk, the best part of the night, on the street between parties.

They took the train to W4th. Larry lived on Mercer Street, a two bedroom with large windows overlooking Washington Square Park. A condo building from the '50s with a doorman and two elevators. Linda caught a glare from the doorman as he let her up. Larry liked the abject, dirty socks and underwear, sniffing boots and farts. Of all the village's creeps, Larry was probably the most humane. He was waiting at the door when they came up.

"He–hello, mistress, please come in." He unchained the door and opened up. He was wearing a shirt and no pants or underwear. He had a small, crooked dick and shaved pubes. He dropped to his knees.

"This is Mistress Lucy," said Linda, presenting Verite, who looked at Larry like she might kill him.

They walked into the apartment. Linda snapped her fingers twice and led Verite to the living room. "Get us drinks, Camels, and an ashtray. Hurry up." Larry went into the kitchen and made Scotch on the rocks and pulled two fresh packs of Camels from the freezer. He served their drinks. "Thank you, Mistress."

He assumed the position, all fours, back straight. Linda put her feet on his lower back and ashed on the back of his neck. She sat back and smoked and drank. He didn't make a sound. She put on the TV and surfed through commercials and soap operas. "Ugh, I'm bored," she said, dramatically. "This is boring." She kicked Larry over. "Boring!" Verite hackled, pointed, couldn't contain herself. Linda got in his face. "You're boring, you little bitch!" She stood over him, he cowered. She went back to the couch and sat down. She untied her boots and took them off. She peeled off her socks. Three days' worth of walking. "You stay like that. And don't you touch that weird fucking dick of yours. If I see you touch your fucking disgusting dick I'll fuck you up. OK? Do you understand me?"

He made puppy dog eyes and nodded his head. She listened to him wheeze through his nose. Linda and Verite went to the kitchen and pounded glasses of water. When they returned to the living room, Larry was lying on the carpet, the sock out of his mouth and in his hand. A load of cum smeared on his potbelly.

"You disgusting little bitch!" Linda marched over theatrically and pulled him up by the ear. "How dare you?" She smacked him across the face. He smiled and she did it again, harder. Verite pointed and laughed. Linda dog walked him into the bathroom. "Slave, get ready." Larry went to the bathtub, turned on the shower and lay down. Verite took off her underwear and stood over Larry's face.

"Mistress—"

"Shut the fuck up you piece of shit!" She sprayed his face with piss and laughed hysterically. When she finished she spit on his face and slapped her knee. "He's so fucking disgusting oh my god!"

Linda took off her pants and underwear. She stood over Larry's face and pissed in his mouth. "Don't you dare waste a fucking drop."

Larry gave Linda and Verite bathrobes. They washed up. He gave Linda new socks and underwear and bought the old ones for twenty-five dollars a-piece. He paid $400 for their time. They got dressed and left.

Linda and Verite bounced up and down Broadway, Union Square to Houston St. and back again. They stole someone's purse unaccompanied on Waverly outside a bar. They got a CD player, $200 in cash and three credit cards. Standing still was torturous, they kept it moving.

Chapter 91

The Hemlock Hotel and Casino, Atlantic City, NJ, 1999

Virginia Parker, Madison Toberoff and Morgan Gold took third row center seats. Alice locked eyes with Virginia, waved with her notes. She walked on stage to a standing ovation, cheers, whoops and screams. "My gosh! This is, you're all so incredible. Oh my! Give *yourselves* a hand, come on." She stepped back and clapped into the mic.

"Incredible! Incredible! Look what we can do!" The crowd began to sit down. "My goodness. It's so wonderful to be here. Atlantic City! I'm so excited to be here, at the Hemlock! I'm so grateful that my work brings me to places like this. On this tour I've been to, we started in Miami, Boca Raton, Daytona Beach, Atlanta, Virginia Beach, The Capitol, and now here we are! Every event I've met the most wonderful people. They've all shared with me what our work has done for them. I've met people who found the courage to get off drugs, to get their weight under control, to come back to their families!" The crowd hooted, clapped.

"I met a woman who stopped working at Hooters and started investing in real estate. I met a man who learned how to build websites. This was after years of inaction, watching TV, refusing to exercise, eating without a thought as to whether he was even hungry. This is our movement! We're people who have made strides! We said no more mediocrity! We said before we waste our time criticizing others, we're going to work on ourselves! And we're going to compare notes. We're going to study how a woman stuck waiting tables in a bikini became a multimillionaire in real estate. We're going to study how someone uses our techniques to get off the wrong track and go back to school, no matter how late you think you are. Because what do we know?"

"IT'S NEVER TOO LATE!" The crowd called back to her.

"That's right! I know tonight when we sign books I'm going to shake hands with someone who's already found success and I'm going to shake hands with someone who hasn't yet. And both of you are going to have something to teach me. But first, I think I should give you all a bit of what you paid for, right? That's right! I'm going to be reading from Managing Modern Life Part 3, which you've all made the most successful book yet." The revelers wailed.

"I'm going to do a bit of an advanced reading today. I'm going to start with the something from the new book, one of my favorite sections." She took a drink of water. The revelers applauded, cheered. "This is from Chapter 2 of *Managing Modern Life*, Part 3…"

I don't think we should let the past determine our future. That's not how this ought to work. Not if we're doing things right. If we've gotten connected, we're paying attention to the seasons, and we've found our spiritual selves, we don't need to be burdened by the past. What others have done to us, what we have done to others needs to be re-contextualized. It needs to be pre-infite information. It's in your way. It's the stumbling block in the road. We've already promised to never admit defeat!

This of course, is between two people who are hitting all three marks. We're not talking about Negatives or Supressives or anything like that. We have our guard up for anyone who would do us wrong. We know what we're doing by now. We know how to protect ourselves. This is one of the million and one reasons we've formed our community. But if we're among equals, and we had a history before we ascended, we should put it where it belongs. We should change that history. We should look at this history and think about how we'd act toward each other if we were living these moments out now. This means that if we were enemies in the temporary, we may still be best friends in the infinite. What use do we have for all the negativity, the twists and turns when we could look back and remember holding each other up, challenging each other, bringing the best out instead? Let's make our shared history positive rather than negative.

She looked up to a standing ovation.

Chapter 92

November 1999

It first occurred to Linda about a month into the mission that she should seduce Kevilicious. His leer was obvious. She took mental notes on his gaze. She thought about the logistics of getting him alone. She sent Verite to Larry's for a long session. She told Verite lock him in a closet and watch HBO. Linda put on a shade of red lipstick Lexie G Hinnon suggested in '93.

She got Kevin alone. Linda found him sifting through snipes of Dunhills, Exportes, Camels and Marlboro Lights. She took off her leather. She felt his eyes scan her skin. "Want to shoot some coke?"

"Yeah, absolutely!" He ran to the kitchen for a plastic bag of syringes. They shot up next to each other on the mattress. Linda leaned over and kissed Kevin on the mouth. He slipped his tongue into her soft palate, a hand under her shirt. He groped at a breast, kissed with his jaw slacked, a young teenager's tact. She undid her belt and moved her jeans off her hips. She pushed his head down, he pulled her pants off and he went down on her. They fucked on the bed. They slowed down as the cocaine wore off.

Linda took a shower. Kevin rolled and smoked cigarettes, naked except his socks. He pulled a Subhumans shirt from his pack and a pair of jeans cut off at the knees. He played a mixtape, Crass, Choking Victim, Steve Piss, OPMS, Dr. Ack, Anti-Aspirin, Black Flag, and Citizen Fish.

Linda shot three bags out of the shower. She put her dirty clothes back on and opened the bathroom door. "I'm gonna split." She took out a camel and lit up.

"Can I have one of those?"

She tossed Kevin a smoke. "You should wash your dick." "Yeah, I was going to do that before Ver gets back – you're not going to like tell her right?" Linda looked at Kevin like he was crazy. She scoffed. She rolled her eyes. She shook her head and turned around to leave.

"OK cool! Yeah… Nice…"

Chapter 93

November 1999

"When this shit dies down, we hit back at the motherfuckers who slayed our brothers, I'm opening an after-hours place on Metro by the cemetery with Sheryl's uncle – he's got a whole mess of buildings out there. We'll do something nice, high end clientele." Thin Vince's eyeballs darted wall to wall. He lit his stem with a butane torch. When his lungs filled to capacity he passed Sheryl his pipe. She sucked on smoke until she choked. They were holed up in the basement of a house Sheryl inherited earlier that year on 97th and Pitkin, a quiet dead end street in Ozone. "It's twenty-four-hour watch over here, Jack."

Cheskey admired Thin Vince's new Mac 10 he bought for the siege. The rest of his collection, two modified semi auto pistols, an Uzi, and a pair of shotguns were out on the table. Cheskey stood straight and picked up the Mac 10. He smelled the steel. "This is real nice."

"I need to take a shit!" Thin Vince threw Sheryl off and stomped to the bathroom. Sheryl smoked more crack. "Jack, you're the only person Vinny will listen to. We need to get out of here, we need to move to Florida or Malibu or Hawaii, even. There's too much going on here, they're coming at him from every angle, but he'll listen to you. You've got a clear head, you know. Just tell him we need to go…"

Thin Vince came back from the can. He made a new batch of freebase on the hot plate. He made prayer hands around his nose. He leaned his forehead on his forefingers. He wore a silver swastika ring and an iron cross, left and right. "Jack, you're gonna stay for dinner?"

"What's for dinner?"

"We're going to smoke this jar of base and then I'm going to fuck Sheryl in her ass, she'll want a dick in her mouth. No one's been over in weeks." Sheryl nodded her head. She cleaned their crack pipes and packed them with clean steel wool.

"Vinny, I pushed all the stems clean, look what I've got."
"That's good shit, baby. Why don't you keep it?"
"We've got clean stems, new filters."
"Good job, now let me concentrate."

Sheryl pushed what she gathered into the new pipe. She sucked until her lungs overflowed. She gave the pipe to Cheskey. She exhaled, a long thick cloud of smoke. He found it intensely erotic. He sucked on the pipe, played with the butane torch.

Cheskey's erection ran down his thigh. He measured his cock against the Mac 10. In the abstract he supposed that it was too bad about Sheryl. Thin Vince came back over with a massive rock. "Jack I was working with pure shit. Check this out."

Thin Vince handed the rock to Cheskey. Cheskey pulled his .22 out of his pocket, pressed it against Thin Vince's skull and fired. The bullet juiced his brain. Sheryl screamed. Cheskey spun and executed her point blank with two shots. He gloved up. He cleaned his prints off the Mac 10. He took the torch, the rock, the rest of the base. Cheskey pushed everything into his front pocket. He took Thin Vince's roll from his track jacket. He finished his beer, crushed the can and took it with him. Before he left he walked to Sheryl's body and patted it down. He pulled a pill bottle from her fanny pack. Oxy-Contin RX Mildred Felipe.

Chapter 94

15 December 1999

Linda had to walk all the way to Henry and Rutgers to cop. She picked up two bundles and went searching for a place to shoot up when her pager went off. She found a payphone. She called Cheskey.

"Where are you? I'm coming to pick you up."

"I'm near Canal St."

"Stay there."

Cheskey hung up and Linda snuck into the bathroom for a Chinese Restaurant under the bridge. Cheskey's white van pulled up ten minutes later. "Get in."

Cheskey peeled off. "Hey, Jack." Linda was rocked.

"Cold, huh?"

"Yeah, it's cold."

"I don't mind a bit of cold. Four seasons, am I right? But this is too much, too cold. Not comfortable. A little cold, it's brisk. That's refreshing..." He lit a Newport, grinded his jaw and exhaled out of one nostril. Each red light, he dug into his pocket and did a key bump. He lifted his foot off the brake. "Too cold, not refreshing, not brisk. Brisk weather, it's energizing. It puts pep in the step, right? Right?"

"Right."

"Exactly. Brisk weather. Too much to ask?" He honked his horn. "Pick it up!" He changed lanes. "Pick it up, asshole!" He put the radio on, a parody of *Sex and Candy*, Bill Clinton – *Sex is Dandy*. Cheskey was hysterical. "I should write one of these." Cheskey took another key bump. He offered one to Linda. It leveled her off. She dug for more. It felt like coffee.

They parked the van on 29th St. off 1st Avenue, the shadow of Bellevue. Cheskey pulled out his ring of keys. They entered into a small building a few doors off from the corner, up a flight of stairs. It was a shithole one bedroom, '80s furniture, brown carpeting and chessboard linoleum. The bedroom had a window but the living room, kitchenette and bathroom were dank and still. A ceiling fan circulated air and lit the room yellow. "Jack this place is awesome!"

Cheskey gave Linda a set of keys. "Front door over here, this is the front door, hey are you paying attention?"

"Yeah, yeah."

"This is the top lock over here. Make sure you lock the top lock, all right?"

"Yeah, Jack."

"You've got somewhere else to be?"

"No, nothing like that."

"Once you get all of this explained to you. Uhh, slowly enough, then we can hang out for a while. First I need to make sure you understand how the door works. You can't fuck this up, understand?"

"Yeah, this black key is for downstairs and this key is for the bottom lock and this key…"

"All right, yeah, good job… You've got a place to stay separate from the kids, thought you'd like that."

"Yeah Jack it rules, oh my god…"

"Just keep it clean, don't leave me a cleanup like last time."

"Yeah Jack I promise."

Cheskey had a good laugh. Linda Solomon was full of shit; her word was worthless. "You kids can have this place until next week. Then we put you in a hotel." He dumped an eightball on the coffee table. "Let's hang out for a while." They got high. They finished the first eightball in half an hour and they stretched the second out to forty-five minutes. When they ran out of blow, Cheskey ate a Xanax and got up. He felt like going somewhere to get his dick sucked. "I'm about to head downtown."

"OK, cool. I'm going to uhh."

"Are you going to do some heroin?"

"Yeah…"

"All right, do it while I'm here." He sat back down. He lit a new Newport.

"You want some?"

"I just want to see how it works."

Cheskey watched Linda cook her dope, tie up, shoot and sit back. The Xanax slowed his heart rate and the blood returned to his cock. He stood up. He needed to get to Chinatown before his balls hurt. "Lock the door behind me." He pulled Linda up so she could follow him to the door.

"Yeah, cool, thanks Jack."

Chapter 95

The Hemlock Hotel, 27 December 1999 (continued)

The brothers turned the heat up. *Eye of the Tiger* crescendoed. They clapped, they stomped. They were ready. "Brothers of the Hemlock Circle!"

"Excelsior!" they roared back.

"96! Oh, 96. This is among the proudest days of my life! This is it, brothers! I introduce to your next president of the Hemlock Circle. Four years of martial service, 1965–69. Thirty years in the public and private sectors, one of the foremost experts on security and risk assessment in the country and the world. Founder and former CEO of 360 Global Assessment!" The brothers pounded on the tables. *96! 96!* "A man who has drunk from the cup of knighthood! A man who had slain his adversary and wept before Jehovah! Brothers, I present to you Brother in Good Standing, Robert Walsh!"

The spark that lit the room on fire. The tempo increased. *96! 96! 96!* The stomps moved the silverware. Brothers pounded one, two, one, two, three on the tables. Shrieks, *YES! YES!*

Bob Walsh took the stage. His brother kissed both cheeks, tears in his eyes. They raised hands together. The song played out. Walsh yelled into the microphone. "Brothers of the Hemlock Circle!"

The loudest *Excelsior* yet.

"96! Thom, thank you. Brothers, let's hear it for The Ram! No one else could have done it. Let's hear it for the best to ever do it!" *One, two, one, two, three! one, two, one, two, three!* Thom took his bow and walked off stage. He sat back at his table with Gavin, Kip, and Bob's empty seat.

"Brothers. Thank you for your mandate. The vote speaks for itself. 119 for, one, myself, abstained. But it was incredible. So, thank you. And just like Gavin said before, if there's an example for how to guide the Hemlock Circle, how to embody the Hemlock Circle it's my little brother Thom. My brother and I have spent hours together planning this transition. We are not simply continuing the EXIT plan. The EXIT plan was revolutionary but brothers, the revolution is over and we won."

A new round of applause. Walsh motioned; the brothers quieted down. "Now we expand the empire. We won't just diversify our holdings; we'll expand into new markets. We will create our own markets, out of the ether. We will grow The Circle. Hemlock Circle 2.0." Brothers jumped on each other's shoulders and howled. *96! 96! 96!* They stomped and clapped. One, two, one, two, three.

"The Ram, the executive committee and each one of you Brothers have brought the Circle a surplus we have never seen in the history of this organization. My first act as president is to convene a study group to determine how we invest the windfall. How we win the twenty-first century. Brothers, over the next year we will grow our endowment ten percent minimum. Remember that number, because when we blow past it, you'll know that I've taken what my brother has built and I've taken the next step upwards. Brothers. Thank you!"

The sound of the five-note call swelled. Walsh shouted over the rhythm. "I've been a fighter and I've been an entrepreneur. I've seen things that would blow your mind. It's all been leading up to this. We are about to make history. Now let's have some fun tonight!" The brothers went mad. *September* played over the PA. They stomped, they clapped. One, two, one, two, three.

Chapter 96

Christmas Eve, 1999

Jack Cheskey drove Linda Solomon into Williamsburg. They crossed the bridge, she looked through Cheskey's window. Jacques Anzu lived right there, under the shadow of the bridge. Southside was shabby tenements, warehouses, abandoned factories. They parked. "This is a good spot, real good, nice clean place."

A hotel employee buzzed them in. Cheskey made it over to the counter, protected with bulletproof glass. "I'm renting a room for my friend here." He pointed to Linda. He peeled off a $100 and slid it through the slot. A guy with gelled back hair and a rectangular face gave them key 202. They took the stairs to the second floor and found the room. Cheskey unlocked the door. Linda followed. A bed next by the window, a desk, a chair, a radiator.

"Well, here you go... what do you say?"

"Yeah, thanks." It was warm enough to take off her jacket. Linda looked around. She put a knee on the bed and looked out the window, a brick wall five or so feet away, dumpsters below.

"I'll be back tomorrow. Don't go anywhere. You had somewhere you were going to be?"

"No."

"Just stay here."

***

Linda stared at the ceiling, a mix CD, headphones on, one hand in her jeans. Hard knocks on the door. She came to. "Yeah, yeah one minute." She stood up and opened the door.

Cheskey let himself in. He looked around again. "Your laundry, you have any clean clothes? Your clothes, Linda, they're always filthy..." Cheskey pulled out another 20. "Gather up all your clothes and take them to the Chinese and get them cleaned for later today."

"OK, yeah, thanks."

"The one at the corner."

"Yeah."

"Not across the street, they're fucking disgusting those people they live in filth. At the corner."

"OK gotcha."

"Clean yourself up. I'll be back tomorrow." He gave her a bundle of dope in a paper bag. "Do your laundry and then go get the kids and keep them here."

***

Verite and Kevin walked around all day, from the River to Washington Square. From Union Square to Delancey. They put down their packs when they were tired to fly a sign. JUST TRYING TO GET HOME FOR THE HOLIDAYS, ANYTHING HELPS GOD BLESS. Kevin sucked at spanging because no one liked him. Verite could raise $20–50 an hour but hated working. They took breaks from the cold in a McDonald's and a Starbucks. They rode the subway for a few hours. They listened to tapes and read some zines. They were back in the village around seven.

After an hour of walking the neighborhood Linda found Kevin and Verite at Alt Coffee. "Guys, I got us a room."

"Yeah?" asked Verite.

"I'll get your coffee." Kevin surprised himself, he clapped his hands and got up. He went to the counter and bought her a coffee with milk and sugar.

Linda lit a cigarette and chewed a Klonopin. She rinsed her teeth with the coffee and swallowed. She nursed the cup and smoked cigarettes until the cafe closed. Avenue A was freezing. Kevin talked about punk and zines, dropped names. Verite curled herself into Linda's sleeve.

"How much money do you have?" Linda asked Verite.

"Like eighteen dollars."

"All right whatever."

"Here, thanks." Verite gave Linda sixteen dollars.

They cut through the park, marched down B. They went to Henry Street and Linda copped in a tenement building. Down the block, Verite tried to keep warm inside Kevin's jacket. They stood together in a doorway to avoid the wind.

They walked, silently, back to the J train on Delancey. Linda chewed on her cigarette and let it hang on her lips. She dug into her pockets. She walked ten feet ahead. Three bundles of dope in her jacket so she bought a Metrocard for the three of them. Verite flipped through *HYPE MACHINE*. Kevin scratched his chin and stuck a cigarette to his lip. Linda put on headphones, a mixtape she was sick of. She flipped through the Voice. She was itchy, sore, tired. She needed to eat more, and every day, and not just coffee. More than a slice of pizza or cheeseburgers from McDonald's. She always woke up in the middle of the night with Charlie Horse. She needed to start getting better sleep. The way she was sleeping fucked with her neck. It wouldn't ever be possible to clean up if her neck hurt, if she wanted to get her shit together a fucking neck injury…

A man with loose, gray skin, baggy blue sweats and a 3xl bootleg Tasmanian devil T came into the car. He looked scared, paranoid. He grabbed onto a pole and dug his right heel into the floor. "Ladies and gentlemen, I apologize, I do, for the interruption. But I need some help, please, I do. If you don't have money or food, maybe say a prayer for me. I'm dealing with a hex, a pack of witches have it out for me. I wasn't always like this…" Verite sneered. Kevin ignored him. Linda gave him a dollar and he shuffled away.

Back in the cold. The hotel buzzed Linda in. The guy behind the counter didn't look up. The three rushed inside and up the stairs. Verite and Kevin went for the bathrooms.

"202," said Linda.

"202," said Verite.

"Nice place," said Kevin.

Verite collapsed horizontally across the bed. Kevin broke open a few butts and rolled them into a new cigarette. He lit up. He took the liberty and opened the window.

"Babe, it's cold," said Verite.

"Can't let it get too smokey," said Kevin.

Linda gave them each a bag of dope. They fixed, the pressure on Linda lifted. Kevin and Verite nodded together on the bed. Linda nodded on her chair. It seemed right to let them have the bed. Jack told her to show them a good time.

***

Cheskey was back the next morning in a sour mood. "Get ready." He smoked a Newport in the hallway. "Could you do this any slower, Linda?"

"Who is that?" asked Verite.

"That's my connect, I'll be back. Don't go anywhere."

Linda and Cheskey left the hotel and climbed into the van.

Linda attempted small talk. "Cold, huh?"

"Yeah." Cheskey pulled out and got onto the bridge back into the city.

Linda looked out the window and watched the wind hit the water. Cheskey turned off the bridge and then back toward the River. He parked. He went into his pocket and fished around. He gave Linda a vial.

"Be careful with that. Put that in one of your bags of heroin and make sure—"

"I know how to do this." It was the same poison she administered to San Lo.

"Oh, do you? Make sure you keep things organized and that goes in the guy's arm and not the girl's. It's nothing you've never done before, just calm down."

"What, um..."

"Linda, shut the fuck up." Cheskey pointed his finger, suddenly serious. "It's nothing you've never done before. You make sure he takes it. He doesn't even need to take the whole bag for it to work. Just make sure he takes this bag. The girl dies, I kill you myself."

Linda massaged her forehead. Her biceps were tight, her wrists were limp. He knew. "Yeah, Jack."

Cheskey moved to smack Linda in the back of the head. He lit a Newport instead. He exhaled. "You keep taking this attitude with me and I'll fucking break your nose..." He sat silently for a few beats. "You junkie cunt." He massaged his forehead with his fingertips. He took deep breaths, inhaled his smoke. Long exhales.

Linda stuttered. "Yeah, sorry. I'm really sorry. I've got it." She leaned on the window, away from Cheskey.

"All right, good." He offered Linda a Newport. She lit up. "Tonight, really have a good time." He gave her $300. "In the morning, separate the girl from the guy. Give him this and bring the girl to me."

"All right."

"And make sure that they ain't together when he does it."

"Yeah."

"I don't need her all upset and traumatized from watching him."

"Yeah. Yeah, of course."

"And don't get anything mixed up. I need that girl alive."

"I know."

"And make sure you mix it up with the real thing." He let Linda out there. "Marcy Avenue, nine o'clock."

"Nine o'clock."

He drove off. She pushed the money as deep into her pocket as she could. She gritted her teeth. She hid behind a wall under the bridge and lit a Camel. The frigid air slipped under her clothes. Her skin tightened. A tear froze in her eye.

Chapter 97

December 1999

Madison Toberoff wakes up at 5.45, Monday through Friday, a bottle of Evian, twenty minutes of silent meditation in the living room. She sits upright in front of her picture window. She opens her eyes to views of the East River, the 59th St. Bridge, Roosevelt Island and the Tram. The sunrises are spectacular.

Don and Minnie Toberoff bought Madison's condo at Hemlock Upper East halfway into construction as a graduation gift. Madison was among the first tenants. Don Toberoff's people furnished the apartment with one-of-a-kind pieces from design houses in Berlin, Tokyo and Milan. She moved into the 22nd floor in late 1990. It's among the most prestigious locations in the neighborhood. Two VPs on Wall St. plus a dot com millionaire live down the hall.

Madison plays CNBC on a 40" flat screen while she readies her gym bag. At six thirty, she puts on her spandex exercise gear, takes the elevator to the health club. Twenty minutes on the treadmill, twenty on the StairMaster. She showers, does her makeup and puts on her work clothes in the locker room. Most workdays, she wears a pearl-colored blouse and black slacks. Car service from the lobby to Starbucks to the office. Work is eight till six.

Monday at six thirty is a shiatsu massage session. Tuesday is a mani-pedi at the spa connected to Hemlock Upper East. Wednesday is a run around then through Central Park. Thursday is waxing and possibly a colonic, back at the spa. Friday is for happy hour.

On Saturday, she attends the eight o'clock class at the health club. Out at ten, showered and presentable by ten thirty, she meets Morgan Gold, the former model, now actress for brunch at eleven. Morgan drinks Bloody Mary's, blows coke and picks at a grapefruit. Madison drinks a mimosa and a bilini with her egg white omelet and sliced tomatoes. They go shopping with Minnie Toberoff at one on 57th Street. Minnie usually grows tired around three thirty and they get lattes at The Waldorf. Minnie goes back to Westchester at five.

Sundays Madison reconvenes with Virginia Parker and her friend Maria Grim for wine and conversation. Alice Walsh, the bestselling self-help author is in town. Virginia's best friend since college. They go to Elaine's because Alice loves it. They get tipsy and gravitate toward the Met. Alice is recognized, she signs a copy of *Managing Modern Life* and takes a photo with a mother daughter combo up from Florida. Madison loves being seen with celebrities.

Chapter 98

29–30 December 1999

Linda's gut woke her up. The bottom third of her torso felt ready to burst under pressure. She sat up. Her lower back, neck and right shoulder competed for her attention. Verite was wrapped in Kevin's arms, deep sleep. Linda knew the smell of dope would wake them up. She put on her leather jacket. She went to the bathroom. She began to panic in the stall but the shot did her right. She focused; she rolled her head back in either direction. She cracked her neck, the pain disappeared. This was the moment to bail. Verite and Kevin could wake up and never know a thing. But Linda wasn't going to bail, not any more. She was going through with this, her stomach settled.

***

Linda separated Kevin and Verite. She put Kevin at the desk and hit Verite's spot herself at the far corner of the bed. She turned her head to Kevin. The poison worked just as quick as with San Lo. Kevin's eyes opened; something was wrong. He struggled to breathe. Linda looked away. He tapped on the mattress and Verite looked over. He turned blue and collapsed.

"Babe? Babe? Kevin!" She slapped his face. She shook him. "Linda! Linda, look."

"Oh fuck…"

Verite slapped Kevin's face again. "Babe! Wake up, open your eyes!" She pulled an eyelid open, the ball was rolled back, all white and red. "Linda?"

"We, we need to go."

"No!"

"No, we need to go right now, fuck oh my god, come on." Linda took her bag and slung it over her shoulder. Verite pinned herself to Kevin's body.

Linda started to smell shit. Linda's heart pounded. "Verite, get your, we need to go…" She picked up whatever she could and forced it into Verite's pack. "Right now, we need to go." She put their works in a coke bottle and screwed on the cap. She put it in her bag. She lit a Camel. She wiped tears from her eyes. "Verite, we need to go. We can't go to jail, come on!" She pulled Verite away from Kevin's body, Verite went limp. Linda pulled Verite up from under her arms. Verite collapsed into Linda and sobbed.

"Verite put on your fucking jacket right now, we need to go!" Linda shook Verite's leather.

Eyeliner and mascara stained her face. "Linda!" Verite sobbed.

"Come on, we've got to go. Fuck, OK, what now?" She faced the door. She took Verite's hand. They left the room.

Verite squeaked when they hit the hallway. "Oh my god!"

Linda squeezed Verite's arm. They left the hallway through the staircase. Verite collapsed halfway down the stairs. Linda pulled her back up and dragged her out. "Just keep it together while we leave, OK?" Linda was rocked by fear. They rushed out of the lobby and hustled down the sidewalk. Linda left her body. She watched herself drag Verite down the street.

After a block Linda stopped and let Verite cry. She hugged her. They swayed. Verite was incoherent. She tried and failed to form words. Her knees buckled. Linda held her up. She pinned Verite to the wall to keep her steady. Verite's weight dragged Linda down to the sidewalk. She fell onto Linda's lap. Linda let herself cry into Verite's hair. "We need to go."

On Marcy and South 2nd, Linda hid Verite in a doorway until the benzos hit and she stopped crying. Cheskey pulled the van up and got out. Linda led the way into the back. Verite followed her. "This is my connect," she said.

"Roll up your sleeve, sweetheart."

Verite put out her arm. She whimpered. Cheskey hit her with a shot of Thorazine. Verite collapsed into herself. Linda and Cheskey got out and took their seats up front.

"Where are we going?" asked Linda.

"Out on The Island," said Cheskey.

Chapter 99

Dolores Farm, 28–31 December 1999

Bob and Alice Walsh were the first to arrive. Sarah met them in the driveway. "I love you, Alice! I love you, Bobby!"

The three hugged, swayed. "It's freezing out here!" said Alice.

She kissed her on the cheeks. "Too much time in California," Sarah teased.

Walsh tipped the driver and they carried the luggage into the house. "Merry Christmas, happy new year."

Sinatra sang the Christmas classics. Sarah put on the kettle and mixed hot toddies. Walsh built a fire. Alice gave Sarah an envelope of photos. "If there were two more beautiful young men and women then our Kip and Katie. Gosh, I miss them so!" Kip was at Stanford on the business track. Katie was a junior in high school.

"Katie says she's going to volunteer for the IDF, live in Israel full time when she graduates."

"How wonderful."

"The idea of her moving to the other side of the world? I might have to follow her there; we can't be that far apart!"

"You're never far apart from your babies."

Alice leaned into Sarah and wrapped them together in a blanket. Walsh stared into the fire, sipped his whiskey. Sarah continued through the pile of photos. She stopped at a picture of Kip and Katie at the marina in San Diego, sailboats and a brilliant purple twilight sky. Handsome, confident children. Wide smiles, perfect teeth. Kip stood tall, perfect posture. Katie wrapped her arms around her big brother. "Can I keep this?"

"Of course, Sarah."

The next day, a black Suburban dropped off Madison Toberoff and Morgan Gold. The driver helped them exit the car and trek the ten feet through the snow into the house. He carried their bags inside and left with a tip of the hat. *Happy New Year's.* Alice accepted them at the door, hugs and kisses on the cheek.

"I love you, Madison! I love you, Morgan!" Sarah rushed into the hallway. Another group hug. "It's so wonderful that you two are here! I'm so excited. So excited, my goodness!" Just as soon as they finished hugging each other, the sound of another Suburban cut through the silence outside. Sarah rushed to the window and parted the curtain. She clapped her hands. She squealed. "It's Maria! And Virginia!"

Linda and Cheskey drove out to Sag Harbor and waited for the ferry. They covered Verite in blankets. They landed and traveled to the other side of the island. They traversed the orchards. They arrived at an old farmhouse with one stone wall, wood painted dark green, lavender with black trim. "You're going in there."

"OK… You're not going with me?"

"I'm going around back. You're getting out over here." He reached into a different pocket in his jacket and pulled out an envelope. "Here's enough to get you through the weekend and then some. New Years, right?"

"Thanks."

"See you at the party."

Linda got out of the van. Cheskey turned down the path past the house. Linda breathed in the country air before she lit a Lucky Strike. The headache she had since the Belt Parkway disappeared. She could smell the ocean through the pines. She knocked on the door. Sarah and Alice opened up. "Linda Solomon, come on in, we've been expecting you," said Alice.

"I love you, Linda!" said Sarah.

An 1899 interior, elaborate lilac and black lace wallpaper. An oak banister and a staircase carpeted with a flowery tapestry. Frilly lace doilies, kerosene lamps for decoration. Needlepoints and old framed photos on the walls. A picture of this very house, with its stone walls and thatched roof. In front and to its right, where the gardens now grew, was a grand colonial farmhouse. White wood panels, dark wood shudders on each of nine windows. Two floors plus an attic. DOLORES FARM – ANO DOMINI 1886. Black and white Victorian portraits circled the picture, the farm anchored the family.

The hallway smelled like potpourri, earth, old wood, mothballs, the pleasant notes of mildew. The ladies led her into the kitchen. A round table, big old windows over the counter. The oldest gas stove Linda had ever seen, cast iron and bronze pans hung over the wall. Cluttered but clean. Everything in its place, spices and dry goods were stored in ceramic jars of varying sizes and glazes. China, tea sets, and a big collection of mugs displayed in a hutch.

She recognized the woman in ridiculous eyeglasses, and loud black and white checkered pantsuit as a friend and neighbor of Claire Labas, the landlord. She'd been to her loft around the corner with Joanne. She wore a bowl cut, similar to how she wore her hair in '93, now bleached platinum. She smoked a Marlboro Light with a pot of tea, read from a binder on the table.

"Good morning my love. You're Linda, yes?" She smiled.

"Yes?"

"I remember you. A beautiful girl who tagged along with Joanne Pardes. Her favorite."

"You owned the gallery."

"Yes! And now I'm now retired. Thirty years was enough of my life to dedicate to business. Now it's the things that matter."

"What are we doing here, do you know?" She asked Alice, Sarah or Maria.

"We're celebrating the new millennium, my love," said Sarah.

"What am I doing here?"

"You've been on your way to this house for six years now. Really, your entire life."

"Here she is." A voice from the doorway. Linda turned around. She felt as if she would vomit. Acid burned the back of her throat. She trembled. Virginia Parker, Madison Toberoff and Morgan Gold.

Linda's vision blurred, tears welled up and fell down her face. *Morgan, why Morgan?* She had never looked more glamorous. She glowed. She had a perfect bob haircut, a pearl white blouse and violet slacks with a sinch belt. She came toward Linda, lips trembling. She grabbed her, hugged her as tight as she could. She began to weep. "I missed you so much! I love you, Linda!"

Linda didn't understand what Morgan was talking about. She didn't know what past Morgan had constructed where they had a good relationship.

She struggled to breathe inside her embrace. Linda started to panic. Morgan crying tears of joy, Maria Grim, beaming. The strangers, Virginia Parker and Madison Toberoff hugged, tearful. "I'm so proud of you!" Morgan continued.

"This is your moment!" cheered Maria.

"You were humiliated, you endured torturous pain, you survived it all," said Virginia.

"What do you? Mean? Who are you?"

"My name is Virginia. We're about to be sisters." She came to Linda, she hugged her, soothed her. It worked. Linda felt calmer. "I love you so much, Linda. So much." She held Linda's face and looked her in the eyes. She began to well up with tears, beaming with pride. Linda choked. She was so confused. Virginia pulled her in closer. "I know, I know…" Morgan, Madison, and Maria came close, they wrapped their arms around Virginia, around Linda. Alice and Sarah surrounded them. They wept.

"We love you, Linda!"

Sarah led Linda out of the kitchen, up the stairs, through a hallway. A window glowed bronze light at the end of the hall. Sarah took an old key from her pocket. "This is your room here."

They went inside and Sarah gave Linda the key. A dollhouse master bedroom, a bed in the middle, four ceiling high posts on each corner, a big down blanket and mounds of pillows. White and gold detailed wallpaper, a desk with a pad and an inkwell, a wooden chair with wicker armrests. A rocker by the window. The bathroom door was open. She looked inside. White octagon tiles, a clawfoot tub, a toilet with a chain to flush. An oval shaped mirror over the sink, framed with gold filigree.

A down bathrobe was folded on the bed with a ribbon and bow. "It's time to pamper yourself sweetheart. Be sure to use both the salt and the oil in your bath." Sarah gave Linda a paper box. Large, purple tinted grains of salt. They smelled of lavender, chamomile, and bergamot. Linda put the bottle of oil to her nose, grapefruit, pine, ginger. She unfolded the bathrobe. A velvet pouch of dried flower petals: rose, begonia, and poppy was hidden in a pocket. Sarah kissed Linda's hair. "I'll let you get settled. Goodnight my love."

Linda locked the door behind Sarah. She pushed the gifts to the opposite corner of the bed. She dug into Cheskey's envelope. Three bundles of dope, an eight ball of coke and four Xanax. She took off her jacket.

She bathed in candle light, the flower petals, the infused salt, the essential oils. She studied the ceiling, the pulsating light and shadow. The first time Joanne Pardes gave Linda a bump she told her it was like taking a hot bath. She let her eyes flutter. The salts penetrated her skin. The oils burrowed in her nostrils. She closed her eyes. She floated in the water with the petals. When the water turned cold, she wrapped herself in the robe. She got into bed, under the down quilt, the soft cotton duvet. She fell asleep.

***

The next morning to snow fell off a tree branch. It was quiet enough, long enough for a gentle thud to register. The light from the window hit her face. She started to wake up. She fixed in the bathroom. She got dressed, a new pair of black jeans, her CBGB shirt. She smelled of the oils and flower petals. She looked in the mirror, recognized beauty. The sleep put life back in her eyes. She opened the bedroom door and went into the hallway. She heard voices downstairs. She smelled cigarette smoke, bacon, coffee, fresh scones.

***

New Year's Eve, 1999. Maria Grim unrolled a length of crushed velvet. Three daggers with gold, emerald, and ruby handles, sharp on either edge and at the point. She sang an incantation while she worked, *Amore, Amore, Amoreee...* She sharpened the blades on a series of wet stones, even strokes on either side. She examined the edges, then switched to a smaller grind. She pricked her finger to test the end point. She sucked the blood. *Amore...*

Morgan Gold and Madison Toberoff knocked on Linda's door. Linda opened up, she looked at Morgan, then at Madison, full of rage, fear, confusion. "What are you doing here?"

"Hi, Linda." Morgan tilted her head and smiled.

"What the fuck is going on? What am I doing here? What are you?"

"Hey, Linda... Linda this Madison. She's a friend."

Madison took Linda's hand. "I've heard so much about you! I mean, Morgan is like your biggest fan."

Linda felt muscles twitch, her biceps tightened. Heavier than jail or the weeks following Jacques' murder. "What the fuck is going on?" She sat down on the edge of her bed and cradled her head in her hands. Madison sat next to Linda and held her as if they'd always known each other. She shushed her, patted her back.

"Morgan, what's happening?"

"We made it."

"What do you mean?"

"Everything we've been through? It paid off, we're in."

***

Sarah, Maria and Alice prepared lunch. They played Grateful Dead bootlegs. Sarah tasted her famous chicken soup for salt. Influences from around the world, the sum of a lifetime of travel in one dish. Maria did the knife work and any associated lifting. Alice baked the bread. She had dough fermenting in the corner of the kitchen since she arrived on the farm.

Sarah sat at the head of the table, Virginia and Maria at either side. Alice sat next to Virginia and Madison sat next to Maria. Morgan sat at the corner with Linda at the end across from Sarah. They held hands. Sarah led the prayer. "In the name of Jehovah. Thank you, Jehovah for this meal our family is about to receive. All things in your name. Thank you for these three new sisters, three new members of your church whose futures are bright as the white light, rich as the kings, it's all in your glory. Thank you, Jehovah."

"Thank you, Jehovah!"

Linda joined the others. "Thank you, Jehovah!" She picked up her spoon, took her first sip of soup. It was the best thing she had ever tasted. She looked up, Sarah proudly watched Linda eat.

"I'll be coming back here... What a dream... Linda, I can't wait for *you* to come back here in the spring, you'll see the gardens. Most everything in the soup, except a few spices, the chicken itself, is from right outside in the garden. This is a wonderful place. It's a bountiful place. The orchards produce some of the best apples you'll ever taste, the most incredible cider. This farm has been in our family since 1886. I've always loved this place, we all love this place. Maria, Virginia, Alice... and now you can come here whenever you want. When you need reprieve. You can stay as long as you like. You'll find the farm provides everything you could ever need, nothing you don't. We're free here, from the demands of the less worthy, anyone who'd underestimate us or just try and take advantage of our generosity. We can do anything we put our minds to here. Among the most incredible things I've ever seen or *experienced*, Linda, they've happened here. And that's because this place is closer to heaven than almost anywhere else in the world. I've been to those other places, they're wonderful too, but this place is ours. Yours, Linda."

The ladies passed around hunks of bread to clean their bowls. Linda didn't know bread could taste so good. Maria lit a cigarette and poured another glass of cider. Linda and Morgan followed suit.

Virginia stood up and began to gather the bowls from the table. Sarah stood up to help her. "Don't be silly, stay there, you did all of the cooking!" Madison instinctively stood up to help Virginia. "No, no. You relax, Love." Virginia carried the bowls into the kitchen.

The calm quiet was interrupted with the sound of a Chevy Suburban approaching the driveway. Sarah lit up. "It must be Bobby!"

"I'll let them in." Alice stood up and then returned to the table with Bob Walsh and The Ram, Bishop Thom Walsh behind her.

"I love you, Sarah," said Walsh.

Linda was transported. She sucked down the rest of her cigarette, pounded her cider. Madison looked over, registered Linda's panic. "It's Bob, Alice's husband. And Bishop Thom. We're among friends."

"Madison Toberoff, is that you?" The Ram was astounded. "My lord Jehovah!"

Madison got up, she kissed the Ram on either cheek. She moved on to Walsh.

"Bishop Thom, Bobby, meet tomorrow's other initiates. Morgan Gold and Linda Solomon," said Maria.

"Well, hello, ladies."

"Hello, Morgan; hello, Linda." Bob Walsh smiled ear to ear and held out his hand.

***

Stone walls and earthen archways of load baring columns lined the basement. Walsh and Cheskey readied the space. They drilled holes into a wooden table, tied rope and leather straps across them. Eight restraints in total. When they finished their work, Cheskey left through the cellar door and Walsh went upstairs to take a shower.

He shaved around his mustache, sprayed on a cologne he bought custom from Milan. He looked in the mirror. At sixty-six, he hadn't been in such perfect shape since he was thirty. He stood perfectly straight. He was tan, chiseled. A six pack and defined pectorals.

Alice let herself in. She was about to turn forty-five, looked thirty-five. Alice took off her silk pants and blouse, folded them on the bed. She opened her suitcase and dug to the bottom for her robe, black velvet and silk, leather trims, the velvet and leather belt. She hung it up on the door. She took a shower. When she finished she dried off. Walsh spilled a small glass bottle into his hands and began rubbing her skin. It smelled of clove, bergamot, and opium. She turned around and he covered her back in oil. He was thorough, made sure not to miss anything. Alice spread oil across the front of her body, vigilant, single minded. Walsh bent on his knee to cover the backs of her thighs and calves. He covered each foot, the bottoms of her soles. Alice dabbed oil into her hair, ran her hands through it, anointing each strand. She pushed the oil into her scalp.

Walsh got dressed. Silk boxer briefs, a black three piece linen suit, his Hemlock Circle pins and cuff links. A black silk shirt, a blood red ascot. Monographed socks, handmade leather shoes from Turin.

"I love you, Alice."

"I know, Bobby."

***

Madison, Linda and Morgan piled onto Madison's bed around a portable 20" TV with a built in VHS deck. They turned the lights out, shut the curtains. They concentrated of the tape.

CUT TO: An eight-pointed star and the Celtic Cross, a crucifix with a halo around the axis, are spray painted in white onto a black floor.

CUT TO: A figure in a black cape enters the frame. They take off their hood, Francisco Grim, a black stripe painted across his face, over his eyes. Two more figures in robes enter, carrying a hog-tied lamb into the middle of the circle. They remove their hoods, Maria Grim and Virginia Parker. Maria's black hair is streaked with blue. Virginia has red streaks through her dark blond hair. They both have black stripes painted over their eyes. Virginia holds the lamb in place. Maria pours a circle of salt around the three of them. Francisco mutters in Latin. They drop their robes simultaneously. Maria has an eight-pointed star painted on her back. Virginia has the Celtic Cross painted on hers. Maria produces a butcher's knife from out of frame. She hands it to Francisco. Maria and Virginia restrain the lamb while Francisco slits its throat.

Each time the tape finished Madison stood up, rewound, and pressed play. They repeated the process for hours until Sarah knocked. "Come." Sarah stood in the doorway; she used the wall for support. They put on scarves and jackets and walked outside. It was below freezing. As they walked onto the beach Linda felt her face burn.

"Do you feel it?" Sarah opened her arms. She breathed in the ocean. "Ladies, listen to me. This only hurts if we dilly dally around. Take off your boots, roll up your pant legs, knee high. You're going to stand *ankle deep,* no deeper, no more shallow. You'll answer the questions and we'll have begun our process. Understood?"

"Yes, Sarah," said Madison. Linda and Morgan nodded their heads.

"And keep those feet planted! Do you want to do everything all over again?

"No, Sarah."

"All right."

"Are you prone to jealous anger?"

"Nay," they answered in unison.

"Are you humble?"

"Yay."

"Do you fear Jehovah?"

"Yay."

"Come forward to dry land."

They hustled out of the ocean. Shaking. Linda looked down. Her feet were turning blue. Morgan and Madison wrapped each other in towels. Sarah put her arm around Linda's waist. "Come Linda, let's warm by the fire."

***

Linda found herself sipping fine Scotch by the hearth with Sarah, all the Walsh's and Virginia Parker. She gave up on following the conversation, real estate talk and technology she'd never heard of. She focused on The Ram. Linda was in awe. She thought of him often, the night they met, her visit to the Hemlock Hotel. She still didn't know what to make of his brother, Bob Walsh. Everyone else worshiped the ground he walked on. She supposed she owed him her freedom. But whatever her relationship was to these people at that moment, it was going to be different on the other side. Per Morgan, they were about to make it.

Linda watched the Ram listen actively while Virginia Parker explained a new project. He sat next to his brother with a cigar. Linda felt Walsh's eyes on her. The Walsh brothers turned to Linda in unison and smiled back. Walsh could sense when someone even thought about the Ram.

***

Cheskey and Verite slept in the guest house, out back between the barn and the farmhouse. It had been Pierre's home until he died in the bed Verite slept on. He made her a sandwich, a can of tuna dumped onto two slices of white bread. "Hey, hey, are you hungry?"
"No."
"Eat one bite and you can have a shot."
Verite pulled the corner off the top slice of bread and swallowed.
"Deal's a deal." He tied Verite's arm, found a vein. New Year's Eve, Cheskey gave Verite as much heroin as she wanted. He checked on her every three hours. She always wanted more. He kept a bottle of Narcan if he needed it. When it got dark, Cheskey shot Verite with Thorazine.
"Going to sleep, nice right?"
"Yeah," she answered while he tied her up. He gave her a heavy dose and she went limp. He listened to her sleep. He snapped his fingers in her face. He picked up her hand. He shook her. He slapped her face, confirmed she was out. Walsh said to make sure she was knocked out cold, not to overdo it, but to make sure she wouldn't wake up for hours. He picked her

up and slung her over his shoulder. The tuna sandwich rotted by the space heater. The cabin was due for a fly infestation.

Walsh met Cheskey at the back of the farmhouse. He opened the cellar door from the inside and helped carry her down. Cheskey cut off Verite's clothes. Walsh tied her body down to the table. They tied a hood over her face. Cheskey leered at her skin. Walsh studied her tattoos, an inverted crucifix on her sternum. He wondered how anyone could be so stupid. Cheskey lit a Newport, offered one to Walsh. He accepted. He slapped Cheskey on the back. "You really went above and beyond, Jack. Top notch work." They leaned against the table and finished their smokes.

"Hey Jack, come sit over here." He put his tape recorder on the table. Black noise. Ultra-low frequencies, loops upon loops of drum beats. He leaned in and whispered in Cheskey's ear, "Pink."

"Orange." Cheskey's eyes rolled back, he collapsed. Walsh leaned his limp body back in the chair. Walsh closed Cheskey's eyelids.

"Stay there, kid." He left the basement. Cheskey sat motionless, dormant, a pool of piss collected under his seat. Gravity pulled his chin downwards, his tongue hung in the air.

11.55 p.m., 31 December 1999
They walked in procession down the basement stairs. Virginia Parker acted as torchbearer for Madison Toberoff. Maria Grim for Morgan Gold. Alice Walsh led the way for Linda Solomon. The adepts, in black and red stood on the right. The initiates, in white robes stood on the left. Virginia and Madison led the way, down the cellar steps. Maria and Morgan followed, Alice and Linda at the rear. Everyone wore a black stripe over their eyes.

Maria, Virginia and Alice laid their torches inside the fire pit next to the table. The wood, white birch, rosemary and sage ignited. The smoke perfumed the basement. The fire lit the room. Linda looked at Verite, tied to the table, barely breathing. Sarah and The Ram took seats under an archway. Walsh stood by the table. The torchbearers took their initiates' robes off their shoulders.

Walsh tied a blindfold to Madison Toberoff's face. "You may speak."

Madison took a knee, planted a palm on the floor. She looked up. She smiled. *"Wherefore should the heathen say, Where is their God? Let him be known among the heathen in our sight by the revenging of the blood of thy servants which is shed. Let the sighing of the prisoner come before thee;*

according to the greatness of thy power preserve thou those that are appointed to die. And render unto our neighbors sevenfold into their bosom their reproach, wherewith they have reproached thee, Oh Lord Jehovah. So, we thy people and sheep of thy pasture will give thee thanks for ever: we will shew forth thy praise to all generations."

"Toberoff. Gold. Solomon. Are you prepared to ascend?"

"Yes, I am."

"Toberoff. Gold. Solomon. Are you prepared to accept the title of vassal?"

"Yes, I am."

"Toberoff. Gold. Solomon. Will you guard our secrets?"

"Yes, I will."

"Toberoff. Gold. Solomon. Will you enforce our law?"

"Yes, I will."

"Toberoff. Gold. Solomon. Stand, unveil." Madison took off her blindfold, she hugged Morgan and Linda. Linda wanted to smell like her. She wanted hair that perfect. Linda swayed before she let Madison let go.

Sarah and The Ram stood up. Bishop Thom opened his bible, bound with a steel Celtic Cross. *"And I heard a voice from heaven saying unto me, Write, Blessed are the dead which die in the Lord from henceforth: Yea, saith the Spirit, that they may rest from their labors; and their works do follow them. And I looked, and behold a white cloud, and upon the cloud one sat like unto the Son of man, having on his head a golden crown, and in his hand a sharp sickle. And another angel came out of the temple, crying with a loud voice to him that sat on the cloud, Thrust in thy sickle, and reap: for the time is come for thee to reap; for the harvest of the earth is ripe."* He paused. He smiled. "In the name of Jehovah. Amen."

"Thank you, Jehovah!" the room called back. "Amen!" The Ram took his seat with Sarah and Walsh under the archway.

Virginia passed Madison her dagger. They spoke with one voice. "In the name of Jehovah!"

Madison Toberoff drove her dagger into Verite's chest. Alice and Maria gave Linda and Morgan their blades. Linda cut Verite's throat. Morgan opened her torso, neck to crotch. Madison pulled her dagger out between ribs and eviscerated Verite's lungs. Virginia, Alice and Maria put their hands on their initiates' shoulders. They dropped the daggers on the table, next to Verite's body. Linda felt tears run down her face. She felt her arteries throb. She felt lightning run through her.

The Ram heckled from his seat. "Where is your Satan?"

Sarah and Walsh howled, slapped their knees. Bob leaned into his brother and laughed until he wheezed. "96!"

Linda leaned on the table. She steadied her breathing. Morgan Gold's eyes were saucers. Madison Toberoff's tongue hung out of her mouth. The adepts and initiates listened to their hearts beat. Virginia gave Madison a hunting knife. She excised the liver, kidneys, a lung and the remains of the heart. She dropped each organ in a brass platter. She picked the dish up with both hands. She stood next to Virginia. They led the rest around the table. They circled the fire. Virginia and Madison, Morgan and Maria, Alice and Linda each grabbed an organ with their right hand. They looked to either side into each other's eyes, they dropped the offal into the fire.

"In the name of Jehovah!"

"Thank you, Jehovah!"

The smell of meat choked the basement. Jack Cheskey inhaled the smoke. He opened his eyes. He stood up and knocked over his chair. He screamed. He strained his lungs, shredded his throat. The sound shook the basement. "LISTEN TO ME! LISTEN TO ME! LISTEN TO ME!"

THE END